JADE FIRE GOLD

JADE
FIRE
GOLD

JUNE CL TAN

HARPER TEEN
An Imprint of HarperCollinsPublishers

HarperTeen is an imprint of HarperCollins Publishers.

Jade Fire Gold

Copyright © 2021 by June CL Tan

All rights reserved. Printed in Lithuania.

No part of this book may be used or reproduced in any manner whatsoever without written permission except in the case of brief quotations embodied in critical articles and reviews. For information address HarperCollins Children's Books, a division of HarperCollins Publishers, 195 Broadway, New York, NY 10007.

www.epicreads.com

Library of Congress Control Number: 2021942260

ISBN 978-0-06-305637-4

Typography by Catherine Lee

Interior art by Catherine Lee and Shutterstock/wacomka

22 23 24 25 26 SB 10 9 8 7 6 5 4 3 2 1

❖

First paperback edition, 2022

To C & Z

When the Dragon soars and the Phoenix dances, the people will enjoy happiness for years, bringing peace and tranquility to all under Heaven.

—Ancient Shi proverb

BEFORE

The boy clung tightly to his sister's hand when they fled the palace, afraid that if he let go he might lose her forever. Their home was no longer safe—not with their father dead and the stench of betrayal in the air.

Into the night, they followed their mother through the streets of Beishou and toward the western border, hoping to find refuge in the last place anyone would think to look for them.

The desert.

It was no place for a royal family, but Empress Odgerel prayed to her gods that the shifting labyrinth of sand might keep them hidden.

They followed the nomadic trails and slept in a different place each night. Sometimes in tents, sometimes under a blanket of stars. They changed their names, their appearances, the way they spoke.

But eventually, the soldiers came.

And with them, a man clad in a shroud of black smoke and red fury. The man who would not rest until the royal family was dead.

Against all odds, the boy survived.

A passing caravan of nomads found him a few days after a massive sandstorm. Motherless. Sisterless. Dehydrated and feverish, he teetered on the edge of death. Nails torn off completely, dried blood crusted over his fingers.

The nomads asked no questions of this strange boy.

The boy who hated the desert with every fiber of his body yet was forced to remain in its protection. The boy so broken inside that they thought he might never smile again, that his eyes would never see the light. The boy who could not or would not speak. And when he finally did with a voice full of gravel, he uttered only one word. Again and again.

A name he would repeat in his sleep. Sometimes murmuring, often screaming.

Sarangerel.

The name of his beloved twin sister. The sister he had failed to protect.

He scared the nomads in the early days, but they kept him alive. They healed his wounds, fed him, and taught him their language and ways. Despite their kindness, the boy thought it would be his fate to wander the sands forever, lost in nightmares.

But the crafty gods had other plans.

One day, someone came for him. A man loyal to the dead emperor. He shepherded the boy from the desert and across the waters, bringing him to distant lands in the warmer colonies of the south. Slowly, that broken boy began to stitch himself whole again, though the tears would never align perfectly. A cavernous hunger grew in him. Deep and bitter, it would only be sated when wrongs were made right.

It is said that the gods test a man for a purpose; that they would never place on him a burden he could not bear. But the boy held a different view. The gods were cruel, and men were merely puppets in a grand play staged for the amusement of bored immortals.

He vowed to snatch his fate from their hands.

So, he bided his time, waiting for a sign.

One dawn, an unusual call was heard in the misty mountains of Wudin, and some villagers claimed they had seen the elusive fènghuáng circling its rugged peaks. It was a rebirth—the Phoenix had not been seen for over a century.

Something was reawakening, and the boy was ready.

THE ETERNAL DESERT

1
AHN

One silver coin.

The difference between life and death.

Between having a grandmother and being alone in the world.

My heart races and my mouth turns desert-dry when the healer barely glances at my stack of coins. Copper, not silver. He doesn't have to count them. We both know the stack is the wrong height and color. Too short and lacking the most important thing—more precious metal.

Funny how something pulled from the earth can be so deadly. Mined and forged into swords. Fought over in war. The reason some of us can't fill our bellies.

With a dismissive snort, the healer's attention snaps back to the wooden drawers lining a wall of the apothecary. Pulling one open, he extracts a few strands of cordyceps with a thin pair of tweezers. Carefully, he places the brown worm-like fungus on a round metal saucer tied to a slim wooden rod. Beady eyes squinting at the numbers carved onto it, he shifts the counterweight at the other end accordingly to measure the amount. Not once does he look at me.

It's as if I don't exist.

"Please," I implore despite the fire rising in my chest. "I'll pay you the rest of the money in a week—it's just one silver coin. My grandmother's fever hasn't subsided in days. Let me have the medicine first."

He pretends not to hear me. Putting his scale down, he moves to a large glass jar of macerated liquid, russet-colored and filled with crooked floating roots.

My nails bite crescents into my palms as I force down the cauldron of curse words bubbling in my throat. Maybe a few tears would soften this man's shriveled heart.

"*Please.*" My voice wobbles and I blink rapidly as I heave a few breaths. "My grandmother delivered your son, didn't she? It was a difficult birth and she saved your wife's life—"

"And Grandma Jia was paid well for her services! I'm sorry she's still sick, but I have my own family to feed. You think your life is hard? Shout it out in the streets and see if anyone cares. The desert's no place for sentiment."

"But—"

"I've shown you enough kindness, Ahn. Don't forget you owe me for *last* week's medicine. Why don't you ask the innkeeper for an advance? That bastard's the only one making some money in this wretched town."

"I did, but it isn't enough," I lie, a knot twisting in my stomach.

I lost my job two weeks ago at the only place that would hire me. The innkeeper's a stickler for punctuality and I was late for work a few times this month. I kept missing my ride from our village into Shahmo after staying up through the night caring for Ama. It's impossible to sprint the entire distance in the oppressive heat. I've tried, but sometimes, trying isn't enough.

The healer gives me an odd look. "How old are you? Sixteen?"

I nod, self-consciously tugging the two braids that run down to my waist. Girls my age normally keep their hair pinned up and secured by a fāzān—the ceremonial hairpin that shows they are of marriageable age. Ama wanted to get me one; she felt it was an important rite of passage. I don't see the point. Marriage is the last thing on my mind and money is better spent on food or fixing our run-down hut.

The healer averts his eyes, mumbling, "I hear Madam Liu is looking for new girls for her establishment. The bazaar is finally coming back this weekend, and she expects a crowd. Even with that scar on your cheek, a girl like you wouldn't have a problem."

The knot in my stomach tightens. "Are you suggesting that I work at the brothel?"

"There is no shame in what those women do. It's an honest living," he says quickly, a hand raised to smooth the tension between us. "My wife's second cousin works there as a cleaner. She could help arrange a meeting with Madam Liu."

"I'll think about it," I manage.

Something like sympathy crosses the healer's face before he turns back to his herbs, narrow shoulders hunching. I grab my pathetic stack of coins and stumble out of the apothecary, nausea fermenting in my stomach. I know he's right. The old silvery scar on my left cheek is faint, hardly noticeable except under harsh light, and I have youth on my side.

An honest living.

For the desperate. And I *am* desperate.

But I don't know if I'm desperate enough. I brush those thoughts away. I can think about that later. Right now, I can't go home empty-handed.

The dreadful sound of Ama's rib-rattling cough echoes in my mind. She doesn't know I lost my job. I've kept up my act, waking at dawn each day, hitching the same ride into town and back again, spinning tales of my days at the inn during our evening meals. Meals that have gotten increasingly meager as money runs out.

Time to fix this.

I lower the brim of my old straw hat and drape my linen scarf across my chin and nose. Even though most of my time in Shahmo is spent in the inn's kitchen and not many people would recognize me at first glance, it's best to be cautious.

It helps that an Imperial decree went up in the town square a week ago: we are to dress in white robes for the next forty-nine days as a sign of respect for our dead emperor. But new robes cost money and *white* robes are hard to keep clean. Most of us wear the cheaper but well-woven pale linens the desert nomads trade instead. It's against tradition and an imperfect substitute, but the Imperial troops pay little attention to this far-flung outpost of the Shi Empire and its surrounding villages.

As a town that was formerly part of another country, and more important, one that doesn't fill the Imperial coffers, we aren't worth the effort.

I blend easily into the milling crowd of beige, with the occasional dot of creamy white, and skim past the open food carts. My light fingers pick up some yóutiáo and a couple of mántou. By the time I get home, the crullers will be a soggy mess and the fluffy steamed buns as hard as rocks. But they'll have to do. The food disappears into my robes with practiced ease, honed by years of not having enough.

The cart in front of me has some chuàn'r, grilled meat that would be a treat for Ama. But I'm not sure if the sharp points of the skewers would tear my patched-up robes. As I loiter, instinct turns my head.

A hulking man is walking toward me, his forehead scrunched into a deep frown. Did he see me stealing the food? Pulse quickening, I move to the next stall and examine the display of rough-spun cotton handkerchiefs with feigned interest. Dull and poorly embroidered, they are pitiable imitations of the silk handkerchiefs carried by the ladies from the great eastern cities of the Empire.

My shoulders loosen as the man passes me by without incident. Just to be sure, I watch his retreating back. He can't be from around here. Unlike the men in the Shi Empire who keep their hair long because of tradition, his is razored close to his scalp. His coarse, ruddy skin hints of a southern lineage or too much time in the sun. Showing no regard for the official decree, he's dressed in a dark gray cotton hànfú with no embroidery or decoration on his tunic or pants. Civilian clothes of a lower class. A trader from the Nandah nation in the south, maybe.

Or a soldier on leave, I remind myself. Best to stay away. Besides, I need to get the food back to Ama.

"I saw what you did."

I spin around and find a cheeky grin. Li Guo eyes the lumps around my waist.

"What are *you* doing here? Shouldn't you be at work?" I say to the strapping boy in front of me. He has a laugh that makes you think his life is easy. But Li Guo has a leanness we all share here. A leanness that tells you how often we go to bed with empty stomachs.

"I'm done with today's shift and was on my way home when I saw you."

"How's everyone?" I ask as we walk side by side. I was working at the inn for almost a year; Li Guo's been there for two after moving from our village to Shahmo. He's probably my only friend, but the other workers at the inn were at least civil to me.

"Yingma says she misses you. I spoke up, you know, told Old Pang your grandmother was sick." Li Guo's smile vanishes. "But he wouldn't listen."

I didn't expect him to. The innkeeper became the only success-ful businessman in this shanty town from his shrewd attention to profit, not through concern for his workers.

Li Guo presses something into my hand. Copper coins. I shake my head and hand them back. He opens his mouth but closes it once I give him a look. We've been friends long enough for him to understand. I won't take his money. Not when he and his father need it just as much as I do.

He sighs and drops the coins into his trouser pocket before pull-ing out a red apple and offering it to me. *That* I snatch immediately. Apples are my favorite and fresh fruit is hard to come by in the desert. Juice dribbles down my chin as I bite into it, the sweetness rich on my tongue. This would have cost him a fortune, but I know he probably stole it from a passing merchant.

Truth is, when you live in a dry husk of a place with nothing to

"Now that the war has ended, we could leave," says Li Guo. "I know you want to."

"Only if war doesn't return. Besides, where would we go? I can't do anything," I mutter. "Can't even keep a job."

He drapes an arm around my shoulders, his other hand sweeping the horizon. "We could go anywhere—west, south—try our fortune in the eastern cities or even the capital. I've learned some carpentry skills from my father. I could get a job, and you could learn a trade, too. It'll be fun. An adventure, like we always said."

The gnawing at my chest changes from worry to longing. But I can't abandon the woman who saved my life.

It is a blood debt I must pay.

"I can't leave Ama," I say in a small voice.

"We can wait until Grandma Jia gets better." Wild hope shines in Li Guo's eyes, like it did when he was a child. I want to protect it, to keep it from extinguishing. But I tell myself the sooner he accepts the truth, the easier life will be for him.

"I don't want to leave anymore. If you do, then you should. Don't wait—because if you wait, you'll spend your whole life exactly where you are now." I hold Li Guo's gaze, hoping he can't read my lies as well as he used to. Telling myself that the sooner *I* accept the truth, the easier my own life will be.

"But—"

"Not now, Guoguo." It's been a while since I've used his nickname and it brings a grin to his face.

He squeezes my arm lightly. "I'll convince you one day."

I find myself smiling back. His hope is infectious, even if it is naive.

We stop by the communal well and I untie my waterskin from my belt, heart heavy as a stone. I drop the bucket. The wait before it hits the water feels longer than usual. How long before the groundwater runs dry? How long before Shahmo turns entirely into a ghost town? And if Shahmo goes, what will happen to my village? The fraying rope burns my palms as I haul the bucket back up. Maybe the only way to survive is to grow thicker skin.

Something grabs my leg.

I lurch back with a scream, spilling precious water.

A woman stares up at me. Her short, dark hair is matted in knots, and she's lying on the ground, swathed in rags. She lets go of my ankle, her fingers gnarled and shaking. She's missing a leg, and I smell putrid, decaying flesh. She must have been hiding behind the well. I want to look away, but my eyes latch onto the mark on her forehead.

Despite the dirt smeared on her face, the Shi character branded onto her skin remains an obvious, painful scarlet.

Traitor.

I stagger back into Li Guo. "We should go."

The woman makes an awful sound. A distorted, hoarse gurgle. I know she can't speak. None of the traitors can. Not without their tongues.

Instead of leaving, Li Guo crouches down beside her.

"What are you doing?" I whisper, glancing around furtively. There's nobody and nothing but shuttered shophouses. But the fear of the Diyeh priests is so ingrained in my mind that my heart pounds at the mere thought of them.

Li Guo is unafraid.

"Give her your food," he says.

"No! What's wrong with you? We can't help her. What if some-one sees us?" I cringe at how heartless I sound.

Best to be cautious, even if you must be callous, I remind myself. It's a saying the people of Shahmo have.

Li Guo shoots me a look of disdain. "Don't be a coward. She's hungry and she's going to die if we don't help."

But she's going to die anyway, I want to say.

"What if the priests catch us?" My words ring hollow in my ears as the woman makes that frightful sound again and gestures at the bucket. A dim light pleads from those empty eyes.

"If you don't want to help, get out of my way."

Li Guo pushes me aside as he drops the bucket back into the well. He drags it up and stoops, ladling water into his palms. Greed-ily, noisily, the woman drinks, half choking with eager relief. I see now that she's young, barely older than me.

Traitor.

That red character on her forehead seems to yell at me. I won-der who the girl tried to protect. A mother? A brother? Or maybe a friend. Either way, her crime was painfully simple: she harbored the Tiensai, people who are cursed with magic. The priests raid the towns and villages for them, burning them at the stake in a public display while their family members are forced to watch.

Anyone who helps the Tiensai suffers a different fate.

Like this girl, their tongues are cut out, their hair shaved off. They are marked. Branded. A physical punishment you can't hide. Shunned for life because no one dares to help them. Because every-one knows what the repercussions of helping are.

She must've gotten injured and lost her leg because no one was brave or kind enough to aid her. Again and again, Li Guo offers her palmfuls of water. She drinks gratefully.

You think your life is hard? Shout it out in the streets and see if anyone cares.

The mántou is tucked inside my robes, still warm and fresh. My hands fumble. I pull out a bun and press it into the girl's hands. I can't tell if she's smiling at me—her lips are too ruined.

But I know she's crying.

Li Guo looks up at me, eyes flashing with indignation. "Do you know why the priests cut off their tongues instead of killing them?"

I have no answer.

"They do it to take away hope, to create despair. They know the rest of us will ignore these so-called traitors to save our own skins." His fists clench. "And they are right."

I blink away an image seared into my brain. A memory I haven't been able to forget even after ten years. It scares me to this day, and it reminds me to watch myself. I shouldn't have helped the girl; I can't afford to get into trouble.

"She helped the Tiensai," I say. "She should know that magic is banned in the Empire and for good reason. The priests say the Tiensai's magic created this desert and it's causing the drought in the southeastern village where rice can't grow, and—"

"Are you saying she *deserves* this?" Li Guo cuts in coldly.

"No! I'm saying that we shouldn't help her anymore. The priests—"

Li Guo raises an angry hand to silence me. "We've had this

from my day as we eat—all lies, but I've grown so good at telling stories I almost believe them myself.

We go to bed, and after waiting for an hour or so, I get up and tip-toe back into the kitchen. There, I pry open a floorboard as quietly as possible and grab the small leather pouch hidden underneath.

"Ahn?"

I freeze on the spot. "I thought you were asleep, Ama."

"What are you doing?" she asks, shuffling closer.

It's too late to hide what's in my hands. I open my palm and the jade ring gleams in the light of the lamp. My thumb runs over the silver etching of a fènghuáng—the mysterious Phoenix that is said to dwell on the peaks of the Wudin Mountains in the north. The metal is tarnished; the long train of plumage splitting into several curling tendrils has turned dark. And there's a notch on the ring near the bird's feet with a faint mother-of-pearl sheen. A missing piece must have broken off. Still, it's the most beautiful thing that belongs to me.

Ama settles onto the floor, wrapping her blanket around her. "Are you thinking about selling your ring?"

I nod.

"No," she says firmly. "It is an heirloom, the only thing you have from your parents."

"Parents I don't remember," I remind her. Parents who might have abandoned me. Parents who are probably dead. All I have is a hazy memory of them: a voice and a blurred face. My father and my mother.

"My dear child."

Ama's milky gray eyes meet mine. Her smile is so kind and so warm, like a beacon guiding me through the murky depths of an ocean. She pulls me into an embrace, and even though she has become weak and thin, I feel safe. Hers is a love that shields me endlessly.

"Why did you save me? Why didn't you give me up to the Diyeh priests?" I ask, nestling into her arms. "Why weren't you scared when you found out that I have magic?"

"Because every life is precious—"

"And every child deserves a fighting chance," I finish.

Ama strokes my hair. "You were only a child, not a demon or a monster, no matter what the priests say."

"But sometimes, I *feel* it inside me. I don't want magic, it scares me. It . . ." I trail off, shuddering. I've tried to suppress my magic all these years, for fear of getting captured by the priests or getting Ama into trouble for harboring me. It was easier when I was younger. All I had to do was not think about it. To forget it exists. But lately, something feels different and I'm not sure why.

Just the other day, when I was still working at the inn, I accidentally froze the tea in a cup because Old Pang was yelling at me again. I was so angry that I forgot myself. Thank Heavens he didn't notice.

"I don't know anything about magic, but I know the granddaughter I raised. You won't harm anyone." Ama straightens her back with purpose, a look on her face that can only be gained from the pain of experience. "I have lived long enough to remember a time when our world was green—greener than what you may remember. There was life, not this vast nothingness you see around us now. Why would the desert still spread if those false priests keep killing the ones they call the Tiensai?"

Calling the Diyeh *false* priests is an invitation for trouble. But Ama soldiers on without a care. There's a spark in her eyes as she speaks, as if she has wanted to say all of this to me for a long time.

"There was a time when things were different. We don't speak of him now because it is forbidden. But the emperor before Gao Long didn't believe that the Tiensai were monsters or demons. He was a good man. May the Heavens bless his soul."

I've heard of the peacefulness of Ren Long's reign, even though I remember little of it. He died when I was six years old, before Ama adopted me.

She tries to speak again but a coughing fit overwhelms her. It's clear she needs her medicine. The healer's suggestion darts across my mind and I start to feel sick again.

I fetch a cup of water. "Rest, Ama. We can talk tomorrow."

Ama goes to bed, and after she falls asleep, I sit in the dark, remembering the dirty little thing I was, wandering around in Shahmo all those years ago. How my feet had ached, how tightly I clutched this ring in my hand. How everyone ignored me and walked on. Until a midwife chanced upon me on her way back to her village. The snowflake in my palm was a sign that I had magic. Anyone else would have left me alone or hauled me to the Diyeh priests for a reward.

But not her.

I remember the warm crinkle of the woman's eyes as she bent over and asked for my name.

Ahn, I said.

What a pretty name, she replied.

Ama's heart is big, though her money purse is not. Her children and grandchildren died from a devastating plague that spread across nations years before, and she raised me like her own granddaughter. She is all the family I have now. And selling this ring will save her life.

But it also means I will lose the only connection I have with my birth parents.

A warm prickle of tears traces the edges of my eyes. I blink them back fiercely. Li Guo might know of my desire to leave Shahmo, but he will never understand what I owe Ama. I can't leave her, and I won't watch her suffer. I run my thumb over the ring again before stuffing it into the pouch and under my pillow, burying the emotions rising in my chest.

The desert is no place for sentiment. Here, you learn not to shed tears.

2
ALTAN

"Run, Altan!"

Mother's face contorts with effort, one eye swelling shut from where the man hit her. Blood drips from her nose.

I see panic on her face. Terror. But I can't move.

The man pulls her head back by her hair, slowly slicing her cheek open with a knife. She shrieks as red rivulets stream down her face.

He looks at me. He wants me to watch. His lips curl into a twisted smile, and something savage lurks in his eyes.

His face. There is something wrong with it.

It is melting.

The face of a demon.

I know the demon-man is coming for me next. For my sister. I want to run, but my feet are lead.

The demon-man knees Mother so hard in the stomach that she buckles to the ground. He kicks her as she trembles. The soldiers join in with their metal-toed boots, again and again, laughing as she tries to crawl away.

One, two, three . . . each kick is a number involuntarily counted in my mind.

The demon-man is not a soldier. He is clad in a shroud of black *smoke and red fury. He reaches out a hand, cajoling like a father would. But he is not my father. His cruel smile widens and his palm flares open.*

A flame extends from his hand. Curves, like a snake dancing to a vicious tune. The serpent bares its fangs and a tongue of fire and smoke slithers out.

Again, I want to run. But fear has wrapped its tendrils around my legs and rooted me to the ground. It is only when my sister lets out an inhuman howl that I find myself.

Something pulls from within me, vibrating.

Wind rushes from all sides, knocking the soldiers off their feet. Sand shoots up everywhere, guided by an unknown force, blinding the men.

I see Mother's one open eye amidst the fog and flurry of sand. I hear her voice in my head.

Run, Altan.

I grab my sister's hand, pulling her along, running mindlessly into the abyss of hurtling debris and shadow. Her hand slips but I hang on.

There's too much sand. It scratches my face. Gets into my eyes, my nose.

Can't breathe.

A tug.

My sister pulls me back.

No—keep running, *I try to yell. But sand fills my mouth, and nothing comes out.*

Another finger slips. I must not let go.

I must not.

A yank.

Our fingers tear apart, and she is gone.

I bolt awake, drenched in sweat, shaking as a silent scream dies in my throat.

For a moment, I forget where I am. *Who* I am.

Then it all comes charging back.

I'm no longer eight years old, running away from the soldiers, fleeing from the man with the melting face and terrifying raven eyes. I'm no longer dragging my sister along as she kicks and screams, wanting to go back for our mother. I'm no longer blinded by the sand that envelops us. Crushes us.

Buries us.

No longer digging, shouting my sister's name over and over again. Digging until my fingers bleed. Until my nails tear off.

And then it hits me . . . I no longer have a sister.

The inn is quiet, and the shadows in my room play tricks with my mind as I try to center myself. Outside, the night is silent—a silence I know too well. I drop my head into my hands, listening to my ragged breaths, counting them slowly, trying to forget that I'm stuck in a town being eaten alive by the desert.

Sand.

Tiny, trifling motes that make me feel like a scared eight-year-old boy again. Insignificant specks that make me remember what I want to forget. A decade has passed since I escaped, but my fears still stalk me in the shifting sands.

I muffle the sounds of my mother's screams, bury the moment when my sister's fingers slipped away from mine. I promised myself a long time ago I would not shed any more tears for them. A promise I struggle to keep now that I'm back in the land in which my nightmares were born.

I reach for the amulet at my bare chest. Seeking comfort. Seeking the will to do what I must. Even in the desert heat, the jade is cool to the touch.

Eventually, I get up to push the lattice windows open and stare into the night. The moon hangs high in the sky, her ethereal light creating a landscape of strange silhouettes.

"Sarangerel."

I haven't said my sister's name in a while. She would have been eighteen by now, the same age as me. Even as children, we stood apart from everyone else, our skin and hair a rich golden brown like our mother's people from the north instead of the pale faces and black hair of the Shi. And for that, we were thought by some as less royal despite the fact that our father was the emperor.

"Sarangerel," I say again, voice cracking. "I'm so, so sorry."

I forgive you, the wind seems to whisper.

A laugh, too loud and skittish, comes from my throat. These sands may be full of ghosts, but that was a message from my own guilt-ridden imagination looking for absolution.

"Letting your guard down, eh?"

I pivot and flick my wrist. Metal flashes, but it doesn't connect with flesh or bone.

"*Relax*, it's only me." A figure glides out from the darkened corner with my dagger in her hand.

"Ten Hells. What are you doing here?" I breathe out and flex my hand. A small flame flickers to life at the end of my fingertip, and I light the lamp.

Tang Wei's heart-shaped face appears as the room brightens. She flips her hair and stabs my blade into the wooden tabletop with such force that the teacups rattle. With a smirk, she puts a foot on the seat of the chair and leans an elbow on her knee, her own recurved dagger spinning casually in her hand.

"You lost. *Again*."

I groan loudly. Tang Wei will rub this small victory in for a while. We have been sneaking up on each other since we were children. At first, it was because our respective mentors often pitted us against each other to sharpen our pugilistic skills. Then, it became a rivalry of sorts. Mostly friendly. Although she has come very close to putting that blade at my neck and drawing blood.

"How long were you watching me?"

"Long enough." Her expression turns serious. "Another nightmare?"

I pull on my robes and my eye patch. She doesn't flinch at the sight of my scars—not anymore. But that thin piece of cloth has become a part of me.

The tea in the pot has gone cold, but I pour myself a cup and down it anyway, avoiding Tang Wei's eyes as she observes me. I don't want her tattling any tales of my weakness to Shīfù.

He cautioned me, advised me to stay away from the desert. Told me not to seek this path.

It is your choice. But know this: every choice has its consequence, and you must weigh the consequences of your actions.

I hear Master Sun Tie Mu's voice in my head, clear as a ringing bell in the still of the night. I want to prove him wrong, to show that I made the right choice.

"What are you here for?" I ask Tang Wei again.

"Babysitting." She arches an eyebrow. "You."

"On whose instructions? My shīfù or yours?"

The recurve dagger disappears into her sleeve and she sits on a wooden stool, smoothing out her skirt.

"Both, actually. Master Sun and Elder Hong Feng seem to think that your choice was unwise. No one knows for certain if the Phoenix is alive. The rumor of its cry may have been started by a superstitious farmer or some cunning innkeeper who wants business in his pathetic mountain village."

"Did Shīfù send you here to dissuade me? It isn't going to work, and you know that."

The corner of her lips twitch. "We all know you're a stubborn water buffalo. They sent me to keep you safe."

I scoff. "You don't have magic, and I can protect myself."

"And yet, I managed to watch you for a good five minutes before that nightmare woke you." She grins. "Did you know that scowl of yours disappears when you're sleeping? You look much prettier without it. Keep it off your face long enough and maybe some girl will fall in love with you, Golden Boy."

"I thought we decided you're to stop calling me that." She has been calling me Golden Boy for ages because of my hair, but it is too close to my birth name for it to be safe any longer. Not with what I'm planning.

"Force of habit. Fine, *Altan*. For the record, I like your real name better."

"Your opinion means nothing to me."

"Liar."

I don't deny it. Tang Wei and I have been friends since I was eight years old. I met her after Shīfù found me in the desert. Even though she pledges allegiance to the Lotus Sect and my gratitude lies with the Sun Clan who adopted me, we grew up together in the Southern Colonies.

Shīfù is a cultivator and a Tiensai while Tang Wei's mentor, Elder Hong Feng, is also a cultivator and the leader of the secret society of female assassins. Though not a Tiensai herself, Elder Hong Feng is an old friend of Shīfù's and sympathetic to our cause.

Tang Wei always had her sect sisters to rely on, to share her troubles and joys with. But I was mostly alone in Sun Manor. She likes to think of herself as my closest friend. That isn't far from the truth, I suppose. But I'd never admit it to her.

"I guess you don't want to know what I think of your foolish endeavor—" she starts.

"You just called it foolish—"

"I think you're brave."

Her words surprise me so much I can't think of a clever response.

"Foolish," she says without missing a beat. "But brave. Legend has it there are only two Soul Beasts in our world. One in the sea and one in the sky. An encounter with either can drive a person mad. How many even survive meeting the Phoenix? Even if I weren't instructed to accompany you to the Wudin Mountains, I'd still go." She rolls her eyes at me. "Wipe that sappy look off your face. It's only because if you do go mad, I'll be there to say: I told you so."

I chuckle and pour her a cup of that vile cold tea. "Did you arrive here tonight? Shīfù said you were going to the capital a couple of months ago. Did you see Linxi?"

The smile on Tang Wei's face broadens at the mention of her girlfriend's name, and her eyes sparkle. "I got here an hour ago, and yes, I *did* see Linxi."

Linxi isn't part of the Lotus Sect and she isn't a Tiensai, but she is one of us. Magic does not discriminate. It isn't passed through a bloodline, nor does it restrict itself by class; both noble and peasant have fallen because of it.

Many years back, Linxi's father—then a ranked official in the Shi capital—had no choice but to denounce his Tiensai wife and pledge allegiance to Emperor Gao Long to save his daughter from the priests' scrutiny, even though Linxi showed no signs of developing magical abilities. Subsequently, he was removed from the Imperial courts to the colonies, lucky to escape the gallows with his tongue intact. Linxi shares a personal necessity I understand well.

The need for vengeance.

"How is she doing in the palace? Did she have news for us?" I ask.

"Apparently palace life has been less dramatic than she'd thought it would be. The concubines treat her fairly even though she's just a lady-in-waiting. But now that Gao Long is dead, I expect they'll be scheming for survival. Seeing that none of them have given birth to a royal child yet, there's a good chance the empress dowager may cast them all out."

"I don't care about the concubines. Did Zhenxi murder Gao Long?" I ask, doing away with honorifics. Neither my aunt nor uncle deserve their title or status.

"Linxi isn't sure. The royal physicians couldn't figure out what was ailing Gao Long, and the official line is he died from an infection. *But*"—Tang Wei pauses dramatically—"Zhenxi insisted on tending to him in the weeks before his death. Some of the attendants say she sat by his bedside from dawn until dusk and saw to his meals personally even as he deteriorated."

"Can't say I feel sorry for the bastard if she did poison him." The thought of Gao Long dying the same way he murdered Father is delightful.

"I hear the prince has a strong interest in the healing arts. He studies closely with the royal physicians and is known to create medicinal concoctions of his own."

"Are you suggesting it was *him*?" I say, a twinge in my stomach. Despite our past, it is hard to believe Tai Shun would have it in him to poison his own father.

"I'm suggesting that Linxi keeps an eye on Tai Shun. Maybe she'll find a way to get close to him." Tang Wei doesn't look pleased with the prospect of her girlfriend engaging in dangerous spy craft. But she has a bone to pick with the Diyeh priests, too, and the only way to get rid of them is to bring down the false rulers of the Empire.

"How about the one they call the Emperor's Shadow? What do we know of Zhao Yang?"

"What we already know: decorated war hero who rose to power in recent years, the key strategist in Gao Long's wars, no family we know of. Nothing we can use as leverage." She narrows her eyes. "*Yet*. Don't worry, Linxi will get us the information we need."

"Good. Shīfù thinks the truce with Honguodi may be a ruse."

"But the truce has been on for less than two weeks. The people won't be happy about it if there's another skirmish. Wouldn't Zhenxi want to keep the peace?"

A razor-edged memory scrapes at my back as my aunt's face appears in my mind. "She has the priests at her disposal. Why bother to gain the people's love when you can rule with fear?"

"Great. We now have a new sovereign who may have killed her husband for the crown, which makes her just as bad if not worse than him. *And* we have to worry about the Emperor's Shadow in case he's helping her start a new war." Tang Wei pinches the bridge of her nose. "The gods. I've heard the new head priest is even more vicious than the last. That's why the raids on the Tiensai are getting more frequent. They're hell-bent on getting rid of all of you."

"Gao Long was making up for my father's peaceful reign. No surprise that Zhenxi is following his lead," I say bitterly.

The Diyeh priesthood is loyal to the Dragon Throne, bound by a solemn oath to serve it. They were culling the Tiensai for decades before Father stepped in and called a halt to the atrocities. It was a benevolent act that earned him enemies.

Tang Wei sighs. "The palace says it's the cursed ones' fault the rains haven't arrived this year. But you and I know the truth. The dark magic is spreading, isn't it?"

I nod solemnly. I have seen remnants of my great-grandfather's evil on my travels. Forests—some completely bare—with knotted tree trunks an unusually stark white. Stiff and cold, they looked like deformed statues in a graveyard littered with the corpses of leaves. Water bison plows left to rust in the middle of what once were bountiful rice fields. Abandoned farmland, dry and yellow, like nothing could or would grow on it.

Everything looked like death.

It makes it easy to blame the Tiensai because only magic could be responsible for so much damage to the land. And the priests and the palace have done too good a job erasing the true history of the Empire. Pages can be burned; words, erased. Scribes can be persuaded to write new tales, new books. A new past to suit the agenda of those in power.

History is never written by its victims.

My hands squeeze into tight fists. *My* great-grandfather, Yuan Long, was the one who caused such devastation to his own land and the lands he conquered. Such anguish to the people. To families. To children. *My* blood did this. And like Father, I must find a way to atone for the sins of my ancestors.

"Do you have the name of the head priest?" I ask.

"Not yet. He's elusive, doesn't flaunt his power publicly like the previous one."

"Smart. Safer for him to work in the shadows," I say with no hint of admiration. By all accounts, the last head priest was assassinated. No one knows who did it. Maybe it was a power grab.

Tang Wei sniffs at the cold tea and pushes her cup away with a disgusted face. "Since we're catching each other up, any word on the Life Stealer?"

I shake my head solemnly. "Shīfù is using all the resources he has, but we are still far from knowing who exactly this person is."

Frustration rises in my chest. The Life Stealer is *key* to our plans to overthrow the Diyeh and restore the rightful heir to the Dragon Throne. Some think he is legend, but even legends have their truths—the last Life Stealer who was known to exist was my great-grandfather, the man who cursed the land.

And the new Life Stealer is the only one who can stop the desert from spreading.

"Shīfù still thinks he'll be able to convince the Life Stealer to join our side when we find him."

Tang Wei cocks her head. "But you disagree?"

A kernel of doubt rattles in my mind. The last Life Stealer picked a side in a war and it was the wrong one. No doubt it was the winning side, but it was a choice that led to a century of battles that ravaged entire nations and left affliction on the land.

"I know our history."

"What will you do when you or Master Sun find the Life Stealer?"

"What Shīfù wants me to do. Work with him to recover the sword of light."

"Wouldn't that be giving a tiger wings?" muses Tang Wei. "The Life Stealer is already powerful. With the sword, they'd be capable of untold destruction."

"I don't see much of a choice," I say, and she falls quiet. I need the Life Stealer's help to find the White Jade Sword, an ancient Tiensai artifact said to repel the darkest of powers. That is the only thing that will drive away the dark magic in our land, and only the Life Stealer can wield it.

"Is that why you seek the Phoenix? A wish granted by a Soul Beast is said to be unbreakable. Are you going to ask for the Life

Stealer's identity or location?"

"No, I'm going to ask for immunity from the Life Stealer's magic. I'll track him down and I'll need an advantage against him should anything go south."

Tang Wei nods slowly, eyes fixed on my face.

I wonder if she believes me or if she knows I'm lying.

I want that immunity for another reason. I want to kill the Life Stealer.

Sleep doesn't return after Tang Wei leaves. I open the windows, wincing when one of the rusty hinges gives a muted squeak. The narrow ledge looks firm enough. Stepping out completely, I grab the eaves and pull myself up easily, boots gripping the terra-cotta tiles of the hip and gable roof of the inn.

As a child, I used to climb up to the roofs of the Imperial Palace. Out of sight, I could observe the attendants and other palace officials going about their business. It was a steep and hazardous climb for a chance to be left alone.

But it was worth it.

Thinking back, I only managed to get up each time through sheer grit and a naive lack of fear. Children are not born with the fear of falling. It is life that conditions them to be afraid.

I lean against the roof of the inn now, my mind a riot of thoughts. This knife-edged guilt is a frequent visitor of the night. The number of lives my ancestors and uncle have ruined, the number of families torn apart, the dying land . . .

I sigh and stare up into the indigo sky.

Son of Heaven.

That is what we call our emperors. And that is the reason why the troops don't hesitate to follow the emperor into battle or to carry out his whims and desires. To many of my countrymen, the emperor's word is the holy truth, and the Diyeh priests do their best to bolster this myth.

Father sat on the Dragon Throne before his brother, Gao Long, for many years. During that time, Shi was at peace with its neighbors. The Tiensai lived without fear, and the Diyeh priesthood was removed from its pedestal of power. Father never saw it as his divine right to rule over everyone in the world, whatever the old traditions say.

It was a belief that brought him more enemies than admirers.

We were told that an assassin from Honguodi had murdered him in his own bed. Shi pride called for retaliation: the alleged assassin was executed, and Shi troops marched onto the flame-colored soil of Honguodi tinged ruby like blood.

But it was a lie.

There was no assassin from Honguodi—only some poor fool who took the fall. Father's death was merely a convenient excuse to invade those iron-rich cities of the west.

Father died by the hand of his own brother. A brother whom he loved and cherished, and whom he treated as his equal. A brother who put himself on the throne right away, claiming to be a mere seat-warmer ensuring the safety of the nation during the transition.

Another lie.

My uncle was thorough when he took the throne.

The only way a lion can take control of a pride is to get rid of his rival's cubs. Those loyal to Father were either executed or exiled, and my uncle sent killers after us.

Killed by our mother out of grief before she took her own life. *That* was the official word from the palace about the disappearance of my sister and me. Somewhere among those royal tombs lies my empty coffin, sized for a child.

The world thinks I'm dead. And I want to keep it that way.

The last of the waning moon's gentle light caresses my face, and soon, the sun peeks from the far horizon. I stretch my limbs, intending to climb down, but movement from below catches my eye.

Clad in rust-orange robes that glow ominously in the dawn light, a group of people enter the town, striding purposefully down the empty main street.

The Diyeh are here.

3
AHN

At last, there's color and life in this miserable place. Unlike the usual carts selling quick bites, local produce, and sundries from the region, the bazaar brings together merchants and traders from all over the Empire and other nations in an exchange of goods and information. Shahmo used to be a fixed stop on the route, but the war and the desert changed that. It's been a few years since the town has been this busy and filled with excitement.

Despite the early hour, the bazaar is in full swing. Rainbow-hued silks drape beautifully around the clothing and fabric stalls. A melody of different dialects and accents buzzes in the air, mingling with the scent of fragrant spices and food. Merchants jostle each other, peddling their wares as locals and travelers browse and barter. One hand gripping the jade ring in my pocket, I wander around the town square, looking for an opportunity to sell.

There's a vendor with crates of luscious-looking fruits, probably harvested from the north or across the Straits of Nandah in the south where the land is still fertile. Golden apricots, pale yellow pomelos, large spiky fruits I haven't seen before, and little purplish ones, too. Curiously, I pick one up. It's the size of a small orange, with a hard rind and reddish splotches on its skin. The scrawny vendor is busy with another customer. He won't notice if I slip it into my pocket.

But just as I do, a gravelly voice behind me says softly, "I saw that."

I spin around, half expecting to see Li Guo. Instead, I'm met with a boy who looks a couple of years older than me.

He glares with his one eye, dark brown with a tint of gold. A black eye patch rests where his right eye should have been, and a brutal web of scars radiates down to his cheekbone. But it doesn't take away the rugged beauty of his face.

His hànfú is the color of pewter, with swirly silver patterns on the cross-collar lapel, and his outer robe is pitch black with burgundy trimmings—a complete violation of the Imperial mourning decree. Either he is foreign or he doesn't care. Fitted through the arms and wrists, his sleeves are bound by leather cuffs crisscrossed with metal beads and thread the color of blood. Nobility flaunt their wealth with long billowy silks, while common merchants and peasants like me have sleeves of a modest range, made from hemp or cotton.

Only pugilists or cultivators wear their sleeves narrow like this boy.

Sure enough, I spy a pair of dāo crisscrossing his back and a quiver of arrows hanging from his belt. His bow hangs over his shoulder like it's part of his body. I can't guess why he's armed to this extent. Whatever the reason, he feels like trouble. There's a fierce leanness to him. Like a tiger coiled up, ready to pounce. I'm standing in the open street, but I feel cornered like prey.

Don't be silly. Armed or not, he's just a boy. I haven't left the stall yet. I could put the fruit back and walk free. I stare back, defiant.

"Saw what?" Thank gods my voice comes out steady.

Still staring at me, he steps back, a slight crease between his dark brows.

"Well, what exactly did you see?" I say.

Ignoring my question, he reaches for another purple fruit and clears his throat. "Try this one. Look at the color. When a mangosteen is deep purple, it means it's ripe." He speaks Shi with a strange accent, somewhere in between the pleasing lilt of those from the eastern cities and the more rounded vowels of northerners. "Here, feel it."

He places the fruit in my hand, fingertips grazing my palm with a feathered touch. My flinch brings a scowl to his face and he turns abruptly to the fruit vendor.

I skim his profile, taking in the strong cut of his jaw. He's handsome, I guess. Nothing extraordinary. Nothing that should make my chest stir.

The fruit vendor points at me. "You buying that?"

I smile awkwardly. "I don't have any money—"

"Then keep your filthy hands off my goods," snaps the man.

He reaches to snatch the mangosteen back, but the boy catches his forearm. He flips the vendor's hand palm up and drops some coins into it. Just like that the man is appeased. He bows a few times, urging the boy to take more fruit. The boy collects his bag and starts to walk off.

My throat burns with irritation. I don't know why he is being so generous. I don't want to owe him anything.

"Hey!" I call out, jogging after him. "This is yours."

I try to give the mangosteen back to him, but he waves me away. "Keep it."

"You paid for it."

"Ever heard of a gift?"

"But we're strangers."

He shrugs. "There's no law against giving gifts to strangers."

I want to protest, but Ama would enjoy this new fruit, so I say nothing and keep walking. I don't know if I'm following him or he's following me, but somehow, we fall in step.

Now that his scowl is gone, he looks less intimidating. Tall and broad shouldered, he's much better fed than everyone in my village or Shahmo. I think he might be from the Mengu nation. His skin is a warm golden brown, and his hair is worn in that distinctive northern manner: short on the sides and back with the length on the top tied into a curt ponytail with a red ribbon. I wonder how he lost his eye. But it seems rude to be asking a stranger such questions.

He catches me staring. I fiddle with my braid and blurt out the first thing that comes to my mind. "What brings you to Shahmo?"

"Just passing through. It's my first time here. You?"

"The bazaar."

It'd be sensible to stop this conversation and leave to find a buyer for my ring. But I seem to have lost all common sense. My eyes dart back to him when he looks away. The morning sunrays catch his hair, turning it almost gold, flattering his skin tone. When he moves and the light angles, his hair changes back to the brown of roasted chestnuts.

My neck flushes when I realize I'm gawking at him like a fool again. The spot where he touched my palm tingles. I wipe it on my skirt and gesture at the tents around us, desperate for something to say.

"What do you think of this?"

"Quaint."

I suppress a snort. "Quaint? Do you not have bazaars in your town? Where are you from?"

"Everywhere and nowhere."

"That's mysterious."

"I wasn't trying to be," he says with a crooked grin.

I find myself smiling back and our gazes lock for longer than necessary. *Stop staring and focus*, chides a rational voice in my head. I should hurry, there are a few more rows of tents to visit if I'm going to sell this ring today. Ama had another bad night and she needs her medicine fast.

"I guess I should be going," I say, hesitant.

We stop walking, neither moving away from the other. I'm holding the mangosteen so tightly I start to worry I might squish it into a pulp. The boy adjusts his bag of fruits, glancing at me before staring at the ground and nodding to himself.

"Right. I should . . . go."

"Enjoy the bazaar," I say lightly. A trickle of liquid drips through my fingers. I tuck my arm behind me. I don't want him to see that I've ruined his gift.

"I'll try."

Still, he doesn't walk away. He looks like he wants to say more. My feet seem bolted to the ground, my heart racing like I've been sprinting.

"Would you like your fortune told, my dear?"

A delicate voice breaks my trance and relief washes over me. An old lady beckons me from inside a tent where there's a small altar elevated by a red wooden platform. Her hair is a soft white, coiled around her head like a cloud, and there are bright jewels on her hairpins. I wonder if they are real. A figurine surrounded by fresh peaches rests on the altar. It takes me a second to recognize the goddess Xiwangmu, the Queen of the Western Heavenly Kingdom.

"No, thank you, ah pó," I say politely.

She must be a face reader. Some call themselves palm readers or fortune tellers. I don't believe in the hopes they sell, and I don't know how they manage to make a living. I guess there are plenty of fools in this world.

"You are searching for something," she says cryptically. Lucky guess. A safe thing to say to make a stranger think you know something about them. I can't help but smirk. The old lady shakes her head at me. "Not you, xiǎomèi. I was referring to *him*."

The boy tenses, expression unfathomable.

"*You* are a nonbeliever," the face reader says to me. "It is all right. Not everyone has the sight. Not everyone understands."

It feels like she insulted me, so I decide to play along. "Please, ah pó, I *am* curious—tell me what you see."

"As you wish." Her eyes sweep my face and the lines on her forehead deepen. "I see jade, I see fire . . . and *gold*. The three are bound together. Jade does not melt in fire. And gold—*gold* follows you and the red thread of fate binds you together."

I burst out laughing. "Gold follows *me*? I've been dirt poor all my life and that fact doesn't seem to be changing anytime soon."

She purses her lips and turns away from me.

"There you are, I've been looking all over for you. It doesn't take this long to buy fruit," says another voice from behind us.

A curvy girl with a heart-shaped face walks up. I take a step back, intimidated by the thick iron chains wrapped around her waist. Half her hair is up in a bun secured by two wooden chopsticks with noticeably sharp metal tips, the rest of it lush and loose around her shoulders. Narrow sleeves on her purple hànfú. She must be a pugilist, too.

She peers at me coyly from under her thick lashes. "Who's *this*?"

"Nobody. Let's go." The boy's face is cold. He barely looks at me.

Nobody.

It shouldn't affect me, but it does.

The girl smiles and links her arm around the boy's. I keep staring as they weave through the crowd, trying to ignore the sting of his words.

The face reader makes a sympathetic noise. "What is your birth name, xiǎomèi?"

I tear my eyes away from him. "I was adopted. I don't know what my family name is. My grandmother's family name is Jia and my name is Ahn."

"How is *Ahn* written in the ancient script?"

"I didn't know my name had an equivalent in a dead language."

She reaches out and grabs my hand, examining my open palm. "Interesting. You see, my dear, your name transforms into a homonym in the ancient script. Depending on how it is written, it can mean either peace . . . or darkness."

A shiver slinks its way down my spine despite the heat. I yank my hand back and walk briskly to another row of tents, well aware of her gaze following me.

After some exploration, I catch sight of hastily scrawled characters on a wooden board.

BUYERS AND SELLERS OF ANTIQUES AND TRINKETS

The tent is a mess, the merchant distracted by a couple of hagglers. Two burly men are pressing him for a good price, and he looks like he's about to buckle under the pressure.

A good target.

Inching closer to one of the long tables where his wares are displayed, I consider the assortment of merchandise. The thin gold leaf decorating the edges of a mahogany abacus tempts me. As do the bronze ritual vessels of various sizes and delicate white porcelain bowls painted with cobalt-blue flowers. All undoubtedly pillaged from wealthy nobles during the wars.

Easy pickings. But I'm here to sell my jade ring. Not to pilfer trinkets.

My fingers hesitate, unwilling to remove the leather pouch from my pocket. Unwilling to part with the only evidence that my parents existed. That I was someone's daughter once. I breathe in, and the pain in my chest eases. That was before. This is now. I can't keep thinking about the past. Ama needs her medicine, and this is the only way to get the money for it.

But as I turn to the merchant, my eyes pounce on a flash of red.

A jiàn lies at the end of another table. It's a weapon of beauty with a blade slim and long, tapering to a sharp sly point at the end. The soft silvery-blue sheen of the metal makes it unmistakably clear that it was forged from a foreign material not found in this arid, poverty-stricken region. But it's the blood-red ruby cradled in the intricate metalwork of the hilt that has my attention. Vividly saturated, it looks like it would fetch a good price. I could pry it from the hilt. I could sell *that*. I chew the inside of my cheek, thinking hard.

Sell the ring or steal the sword?

There's a clink of metal as the merchant rummages through a large wooden crate before handing one of the burly men another item of interest. Whatever it is, it must be significant. The men swiftly turn their backs to me to examine the new treasure.

The leather pouch goes back into my pocket. I pick up the sword and walk out of the tent, adjusting my outer robe to cover it. My pulse thrums. Just when I think I'll get away, someone shouts.

"Where's my sword?"

The voice doesn't belong to the merchant. *Ten Hells. Did I steal from the burly men instead?*

"Where is it?" repeats the booming voice.

I force my feet to keep their rhythm. Too obvious to run now.

"It was here!" the merchant bleats.

"You—girl with the braids—turn around!"

Freezing in mid-step, my eyes dart around the crowd.

I am the only girl with braided hair.

Adrenaline pumping in my veins, I dash down the line of stalls, weaving between tents across the town square. Curses and shouts follow me as I shove people out of the way. I make it to the other end and spin around a corner. *The gods!* There's a line of camels sitting leisurely across my path. A man tugs the rope tying one beast to the next, but the stubborn animals refuse to budge so I dash off in another direction.

The streets get more desolate as I sprint on. Soon, a stitch forms in my stomach. Desperately hoping, I crane my neck only to see two moving figures behind me in the distance. I cut across the street into an alley blindly, and trip over some wooden barrels. The force of the collision lands me on the ground. My hands take the brunt of my fall, nicked and stinging from the rough stones. I look up and curse.

It's a dead end.

A ten-foot wall at the back of the alley blocks my freedom. I scramble forward and test it with a weather-beaten boot. Too smooth. Even if I manage to scale it, I may break a leg getting down the other side. The gods know I can't afford to, but I have no choice.

Before I can even try, footsteps skid behind me. My stomach flips. The men have caught up, blocking the only clear path out of the alleyway.

Should have sold the damned ring. Sentiment made me weak, and now I'm paying its price.

The taller of the two men draws a broad sword from his waist. He's muscled and looks combat trained. His companion is stout and pig-eyed with a nasty scar running across his forehead and a spear in his hand. They look like southerners with their short hair, and they wear no mourning robes. Traders? The taller man spins his sword round and round expertly with only his fingers on the hilt. Or soldiers? My heart sinks when I glance back at his companion. His spear is untasseled. He bears no military allegiance.

Mercenaries.

Mercenaries only have the heart for coin. Mercenaries don't appreciate being stolen from.

"Just a peasant girl, Banu," laughs the stout man in heavily accented Shi. He adds something in his own language, and Banu chuckles derisively.

There's nowhere to run and I can't beat them. They're bigger, stronger, and skilled with weaponry. I'm just a street rat living off my wits.

My voice is an octave higher as I blubber, "Please, *noble sir*, please forgive me. You're right, I'm just a peasant girl, a foolish girl to even think of stealing from a brave warrior like you." I let out a huge sniff, wondering if I've exaggerated too much. "Please, take the sword and spare my life."

Stout chortles and claps a meaty hand on Banu's back, giving him a knowing smile. Banu's eyes rove up and down my body before he grins back. "I'm thinking we want more than the sword now."

Revulsion fills my throat, but I stop myself from glaring. The sword isn't worth my life or whatever horrifying ideas the men have in mind. I'll have to make a run for it. I'm fast and the winding streets I grew up in are my advantage.

This time, there will be no dead ends.

"Please, esteemed warriors, my grandmother's ill and I need to go home. Take the sword and leave me be." I choke out a sob that surprises myself with its sincerity. Ama's sickly face crosses my mind but I blink it away. I *will* find another way to get her medicine.

Banu leers. "I think not."

As they approach, something inside me shifts. A strange hum starts in my ears. Bright lights swim in my vision. Energy thrums through my veins as my heart batters my rib cage.

Gods, no.

I shunned my magic for my own safety and Ama's. It lay dormant for so long, but now, that strange creature is awake. Rising inside me, forcing its way out.

A thin layer of ice starts to form around the blade of the sword.

Stout curses loudly in his dialect. "*Magic*—she has magic!"

"A gold tael for each Tiensai *girl* caught alive, that's what the priest said," Banu snarls.

He grabs my robes and throws me back. My spine connects with the stone wall. Air knocks out of my lungs. The humming in my ears crescendos like thousands of cicadas after a desert rainstorm.

Everything liquefies. The shock stops my breath.

A burst of sparkling clarity sweeps through my mind like a tsunami washing away all previous understanding. My senses heighten.

The world unfolds in front of my eyes for the first time. Everything is sharper, brighter. The sky is an astonishing shade of blue, so beautiful it hurts to look. The sun shines with an unnatural radiance, capturing my surroundings in an ethereal halo. Gravel crunches in my ears as things scrape the ground. The stench of sweat assaults my nostrils, mixed with an underlying scent of something else I can't place. Energy courses through my blood and exhilaration floods my body. This euphoric sensation of control—I never knew I could feel it.

Never knew that I *wanted* it.

Guttural, wheezing sounds puncture my rapture. My brain doesn't understand what my eyes show me.

The two men are *glowing*.

A strange pale green light emanates from them, moving like

smoke as they convulse. Hands clutching and clawing at their throats. Faces turning purple, eyes bloodshot and bulging. Their skin loosens. Flesh retreats within. Banu gives a loud, strangled shriek as he starts to shrivel. With heavy thumps, both men collapse.

Lifeless.

I breath in and gag. The world shrinks back into mundane focus. Warmth saps out of me, chased by an inexplicable iciness quenching the fire in my body. I feel empty. Hollow. Like someone dug into my being and took the heart of who I am.

My hands shake. I'm cold, so cold. What just happened? That didn't feel like my magic. That didn't feel like *me*. It was something else. Something unknown. Like a claw yanking me down into the dark depths of the ocean where no light can shine through.

The men.

Nothing's left of them but two corpses that look—Did I do that? But . . . *how*? I've never killed anyone before.

There's always a first time. The new voice in my head is silky and dark as a moonless night.

Pain explodes suddenly in my chest. I bend over and vomit violently, emptying my stomach. My knees collide with the hard ground, grit puncturing flesh.

"It wasn't me," I gasp to the empty alley. "It can't be me." Maybe if I chant it like a prayer, the gods will undo what happened.

My trembling increases. The sword in my shaking hand—it is a burden I'm bound to, sullied by the atrocity it witnessed. I drop it. The clang of metal on stone jolts me, and I run for my life.

4
ALTAN

"What did you say?"

"I was asking you to pass me a pear. Something distracting you?" Smirking, Tang Wei takes the bag of fruits from me. "Or should I say, *someone*? She was pretty, wasn't she?"

"Who?" I keep my face perfectly blank, even though the image of the girl lingers in my mind. She was tall but slight of frame, like she needed a good meal or two. Her features were delicate, skin so pale and her hair so black it emphasized her pallor. She looked like a wraith. I didn't think she was that pretty.

"You *know* who I'm talking about, but never mind." Tang Wei takes a bite of her pear and launches into her usual rambling about Linxi.

Barely listening, I nod at what I hope are appropriate times. She's smitten. It's hard to believe this is the same person who used to flirt with anyone and anything in front of her. But after falling in love with Linxi, no one else can vie for her attention.

Half an hour later, we're back at the inn and Tang Wei is *still* talking. I sink my forehead into my palms. Is that what people in love do? Talk incessantly about the lovers they long to see again?

Hang on to every word they say? Make sacrifices that others would deem foolish?

Once, after we fled the palace, my sister and I asked our mother if she missed her home and her family.

"I miss them every day, but home is where your heart is," she replied with a tender smile.

She had left everything behind—her family, friends, her life—for Father. Even if it was to be empress, she was a stranger in a foreign land. There were whispers in the palace corridors, sly glances whenever she did or said something that was uncommon for the Shi.

Mother tried to shield my sister and me from it all. But we knew. Royal or not, we were not of true Shi blood, and people would always have something to say about it.

I try to listen to Tang Wei now, but the noisy crowd in the inn is distracting, and my mind keeps wandering back to the girl who stole the mangosteen. Her eyes pierced me like a shard of glass in sunlight, and in that moment when she turned around, it felt like the anchor to my world shifted. It must have been the desert heat.

You are searching for something.

The old lady's words—typical face reader nonsense. Probably. Yet, there was something about the way she looked at me that was uncomfortable, like she *knew* something about me that I didn't.

The waiter appears with our tea, interrupting my thoughts. The deep woody scent of oolong leaves floats toward me, but there is something off about it. *Steep it for too long and the oolong will turn bitter*, Shīfù would say.

"How was Master Sun when you last saw him?" asks Tang Wei, finally deciding to talk about something else.

"Imprudently prone to adventure as usual. He talks too much," I say as I pour us some tea. "Like you."

"I have to do the talking because you refuse to," she retorts. "Remember how he used to bring us to teahouses when we were children, and how he'd go on and on about leaf and philosophy? We must have drunk enough tea to fill an entire lake."

"The best teahouse is The Green Needle in Beishou, there can be no doubt about it," we recite together.

"You do know he still says that to me, right?"

Tang Wei laughs and gestures at her cup. "Let's see if *this* is any good."

"This is no yíxīng teapot; it's not made out of purple sand," I say, glaring at the offending piece of earthenware. I sip from my cup and make a face. "Tastes like watered-down grass juice. I wouldn't feed it to a cow unless I want to watch the beast suffer."

Tang Wei slaps the table, laughing harder. "Has anyone told you that sometimes you sound exactly like Master Sun?"

"I do not—"

Sudden shouts drown out my retort.

A man dashes into the inn and runs smack into a waiter. Bowls and plates crash onto the ground. The innkeeper tries to calm the man down, but he won't stop shouting, his face contorted with fear.

"The alley! The alley!"

I'm about to step in when Tang Wei gives me a look, tapping her forearm near the crook of her elbow. Two other people have entered the place. *Priests.* They all have a tattoo there: a wavy vertical line, like a snake, with two dots across from each other, each nestled in the curved parts of the line. Their symbol.

The newcomers, a middle-aged man and a young woman, stride toward the innkeeper and the agitated man. They are dressed in rust-orange robes, their hair up in a topknot secured by an ivory cuff with that same Diyeh symbol branded on it.

The man whimpers, but the rest of the room is dead silent. Fear of the priests is a given, whether you are a Tiensai or not. We have all witnessed or heard of their cruel methods of flushing out people with magic.

Tang Wei trembles ever so slightly, but I know it isn't from fear. Her little sister burned at the stake and she was forced to watch. Her fingers grip the edge of the table, her knuckles turning white. Her other hand reaches for the iron chains around her waist. But I know she won't do anything rash. She and I might stand a chance with the priests, but there are too many people in here. The potential for collateral damage is high. And while killing the priests might bring me momentary pleasure, I need to play the long game.

We wait until they leave with the scared man in tow. I can't tell whether it is to investigate the source of his distress or to imprison him. Whatever the case, I feel sorry for the poor soul.

Tang Wei and I exchange a weighted look.

"Time to get out of here," she mutters.

We abandon the sorry excuse for tea and head to our room to pack our bags. Soon, we're on the road, heading north to the Wudin Mountains, knowing that it's best to keep a distance from a town infested with priests.

5
AHN

Somehow, my feet find their way forward one foot after the other. I stick to the narrow side streets, but the bazaar crowd spills over. I don't remember the last time Shahmo was this crowded. Squeezing through throngs of people, I keep my eyes down. My face is a mask of calm, even as a maelstrom whips in my head.

I need to get back to my village. I need to get back to Ama.

But what if they come for you?

I choke back a sob. I can't go home. The constables of Shahmo might come looking for me, and Ama might get dragged into this mess. Worse, the *priests* might come.

I have to leave this place.

Forever?

If that's what it takes to keep Ama safe. I still have my jade ring; I can find passage out of these desert towns once I sell it. Maybe head north or east across the Emerald Sea to the nation of Xinzhu as far away from here as possible. Find a job, move around from town to town, change my name, tell a new tale about where I'm from. *You can do this*, I tell myself. *You must do this to keep Ama safe.*

A horrible thought dawns on me. What if the priests find out that she harbored me? That she brought me up as her own grand-child? I must do more. I need to leave a trail that will lead them away from her. There must be nothing that connects us. A hazy plan starts to emerge in my mind.

First, I need to get word to someone I can trust.

The back area between the inn's kitchen and storeroom is empty when I arrive. I jump when I hear footsteps. To my relief, it's Mali. She's a few years older than me, and though we're not close, we are friendly enough.

"Could you get Li Guo, please?" I say, struggling to smile. My palms are sweaty, and I'm shaking. But she doesn't seem to notice.

She shrugs and disappears into the kitchen.

Li Guo appears a minute later. He knows something's wrong right away. I beckon, and he follows me out to the alley.

"I'm fine," I say before he can ask. It's the biggest lie I've ever told in my life. "I need a favor from you, please."

"How can I help?" he says without a second thought. "Is it Grandma Jia? I get paid today, and my father's gotten some new customers recently. I can—"

"Just take care of her," I say hastily, glancing around us. There's no one else around and I think we're far enough from the kitchen to be out of anyone's earshot. I move closer and lower my voice. "I've got to go away for a while. I don't know when I'll be back, and I need someone to watch over her. Can you do that?"

Li Guo starts peppering me with questions, but I hold up a hand to hush him. "I can't explain, I'm sorry. I have to leave. *Now*. Please, just do it—for me."

At last, he nods. "I'll take care of Grandma Jia, don't worry. Do you have enough money?"

I show him my ring and his eyes widen. "I need to sell this, but something happened at the bazaar today and I can't go back. I . . ." My voice falters. "I'll get to the next town and sell it there."

"Do you have an hour to spare?"

"Maybe—"

He squeezes my hand. "I know someone who might be able to fence your ring for good money quickly. Let me go talk to him."

"But—"

"Keep your ring, keep it safe. Go wait for me at the temple. If I'm not there in an hour, leave."

One hour. It could mean having enough money to get me far away, and one less thing to worry about. I could even give half of it to Li Guo for Ama. I don't know how long I can keep up this veneer of calm, but Li Guo is determined to help me, and I know I can trust him.

Finally, I agree, and we part ways.

The constant drone of hopes and dreams swirls around the large prayer hall. Worshippers take turns kneeling in front of the altar, pleading eyes fixed on the statue above it.

I beg you, O Goddess, my son has not returned from the war front, please protect him and bring him home safe . . .

Please Goddess, let the rains return . . .

Watch over my wife, I pray for her health and that of our unborn child . . .

I keep my head lowered and find a secluded corner to sit in, as if I'm only here to mourn or to pray for my fortune. Dense and cloying, the scent of sandalwood clings to the air. White-robed and seated in the lotus position with a jar of water in one hand and a willow leaf in another, the larger-than-life sculpture of the Goddess Guanyin casts her benign gaze on me.

It's an iron weight pressing down.

I lock my fingers to stop my hands from shaking. But slowly, the shuddering spreads and before long, my breaths turn ragged and the pounding in my chest starts again.

I am a murderer.

I am a *murderer.*

I am a murderer.

Should I pray for forgiveness? Am I cursed with magic I have no control over? I've known about my ability for a long time. But I didn't know it was this . . . whatever it is. I've ignored my magic and pretended it didn't exist. Because it scared me.

It *scares* me.

I shut my eyes, willing away the images of those withered bodies, the pale green glow drifting from them, the terrible choking sounds the men made as they fell dead to the ground. When I open my eyes, I see a woman with a pinched face staring at me from the other side of the prayer hall. I look away.

She's still staring when I muster the courage to check again. She nudges an older woman next to her. Now both of them are paying attention to me. My stomach churns. It hasn't been an hour yet, but I can't stay here. Not with those two women and their suspicious expressions.

I force my feet to walk at a normal pace out into the streets. A whirl of faces confronts me. *Stay calm. Don't draw attention to yourself.* I decide to make a round and come back; maybe the women will be gone by then and Li Guo will show up.

There's a sudden flurry of activity as I turn into the main street. A woman carrying a wash basket retreats hastily into a side path when she sees me. Another man gives me a worried look before scuttling into his shop. He closes the doors, joining in the percussion of other shuttered windows.

Hazy fear cloaks the air, dampening the noon light like a pall, and the hairs on my arms prickle. A mother runs by with a snotty child in her arms. She spares me a frightened glance as she passes and whispers one word in warning.

My body goes taut.

Priests.

A cry rings out. "I don't know who you're talking about!"

Mali. What is she doing here? Why isn't she back at the inn? I should turn and run. I should forget the desperation in that voice, forget who it belongs to.

Then, she starts to scream.

I head toward the sound. That's when I notice smoke rising in the air, the smell of things burning. My mouth goes dry. What have the priests done? The bazaar tents are in disarray. Some scorched, a few in flames, merchandise scattered on the ground. A man and a woman in rust-orange robes stand around a figure hunched over in pain.

"Is there no one here who can tell us about the Tiensai who walks among you? The one who killed two men today—the *demon* that lives in this town, pretending to be one of you good people?" says one of the Diyeh priests, a stocky middle-aged man with a big beard.

What's left of the crowd stays silent. No one steps forward. The female priest backhands Mali and drops of blood fly up in the air and splatter on the cobblestones. Mali flops flat, whimpering. The priest kicks her. Hard.

Anger builds up in me. But I stay in my spot.

The female priest circles Mali. "Good townspeople, are you going to protect one of the cursed and condemn this innocent girl? Has no one seen the Tiensai?"

"She is a girl of about sixteen," says the bearded priest. "We are told that she wears her hair in braids and has a scar on her cheek."

Again, the crowd keeps quiet.

Bright and deadly, fire plumes from his fingertips.

"It's not too late," he says to Mali, bringing the flames next to her face. She shrinks back in terror. "Go on, girl. Tell us."

Use it. A whisper in my ear, like a shiver you get when the night is too quiet. *Use your magic. You know you want to.*

I swallow thickly and ignore it.

Mali chokes up. "I told you, I don't know anything. I—I don't know where she went."

The priest stares down at her. "You leave me no choice. Pity."

I sense no pity in his voice. Only a sick joy. His flames lick Mali's arm and she shrieks.

Give yourself up. Don't be a coward, Ahn.

I don't move.

Best to be cautious, even if you have to be callous.

Those words ring false in my head. Too sharp. Too wrong. I can't leave Mali to a horrific fate like the mutilated girl by the well. Can I?

Someone pushes through the crowd on the other side of the

town square. Li Guo. That look on his face—

I lunge forward, shouting at the top of my lungs. "Let her go, she knows nothing! It's me you're looking for. *I* killed the two men!"

The crowd gasps, moving aside to make an opening for me. I walk right in front of the priests.

"You?" sneers the female priest, giving me a once-over. "*You* are the Tiensai responsible for what happened in the alleyway?"

I don't trust myself to speak, so I nod.

Her eyes glint. "Prove it."

I gulp and look down at my hands. They're shivering like dead leaves in the wind. I don't know what to do. I don't know what *she* wants me to do. Attack her? Does she really think she stands a chance against whatever I did to the two men?

The bearded priest scrutinizes my face. His wicked eyes land on the scar on my cheek and a sly look of satisfaction spreads over his face. "No need for that. She has confessed. We will take her."

The priests bind my hands behind my back. Rough ropes dig into my skin. This is it. This is my end. No time for tearful fare-wells. No time for hasty prayers. I hear the townsfolk whispering. Some of them must know me. The orphan girl who lives in the nearby village. The girl who used to work at the inn. *Will they come and watch me burn?*

I catch Li Guo's eye as the priests drag me away across the town square. The shock on his face is plain. He starts to move, but I shake my head. Thank gods he stays in his spot.

A hood goes over my head and I smell incense and old blood.

I hope Li Guo understands what I've been hiding from him now.

I hope he remembers his promise to take care of my grandmother.

PALACE OF
A THOUSAND SPIES

6
AHN

Somehow, I am still alive.

Though the reason eludes me. None of the priests have said much. They won't tell me where they're taking me or why they're keeping me alive. *If* they are keeping me alive. The Diyeh priesthood exists to eradicate the Tiensai. I can't rely on them to spare me. They lock me in the wagon and keep the hood over my head like I'm some kind of monster. Which to them, is exactly what I am.

And maybe they're right. After all, I *am* a murderer.

We travel on the road for gods know how long. The wagon door opens and closes now and then, and some food is shoved into my mouth. Days and nights blend together, punctuated only by fitful sleep filled with dreams of corpses and demons.

And strangely, the one-eyed boy from the bazaar. He flits in and out, saying things that make no sense. Sometimes, he's holding the ruby sword I stole, gesturing wildly at me. Sometimes, smoky-green light swirls around him and he fades like the dawn mist.

Ama appears, too. In those nightmares, she's standing at the edge of a dark chasm, about to take a step. I'm always running, shouting at her to stop. But each time, I'm too slow. Each time, she takes that step and falls, and I wake up screaming.

The next time I open my eyes, I sense a change in the air. It's cooler, wetter. We must be heading east toward the sea, away from the dry desert heat. The wagon comes to a halt and I hear the door opening. Someone climbs up next to me and removes the hood. Barely holding my head up, I squint at the figure hunched in front of me.

A priest. But one I've never seen before. Did he join us somewhere along the way? He's surprisingly young, but there's a white streak in his black hair. His slate-gray eyes widen with concern when he sees the state I'm in.

"What have they done to you?" he says softly. "Is this too tight?" He starts to loosen the ropes around my ankles.

My throat is so parched it feels like sandpaper, but I manage to rasp, "Too tight? Aren't you afraid I'll run when I get a chance?"

"If you run, I will have to stop you."

It's not a threat. He's merely stating a fact. I stop struggling. He removes the ropes around my ankles completely, but keeps my hands securely fastened behind my back.

He holds a waterskin to my mouth. "Drink."

I start to shake my head, the obstinate fool in me refusing to be pitied. But the desire to live overcomes pride. I drink my fill and let him feed me some mántou, ignoring the way he's studying me.

He seems so gentle. So *normal*. It's hard to believe he's a priest. Hard to believe that someone like him would raid villages. Or cut off a person's tongue.

It must be a ploy. He's trying to lull me into trusting him.

"I didn't think you priests felt sympathy for your enemies," I say, tone biting.

His eyes are like storm clouds, gray and heavy. "You are not my enemy."

"I don't believe you."

"I don't need you to. I just need to do my job, and my job is to keep you alive."

I sit a little straighter, a seed of hope forming. "Why? *Who* wants me alive?"

He stands, hood in hand.

"No, wait," I say, shuddering at the thought of being in shadow again. Of that revolting stench of dried blood. Of the nightmares that will come. "Please don't put that back on me."

"I'm sorry, but I have to." He looks genuinely apologetic as he draws near. Maybe he's a good actor.

I try to wriggle out of his reach, failing miserably. As he raises the hood, I choke back a sob. "Tell me your name."

His gaze softens. But I can't tell if it's a trick of the light.

"Leiye."

And once again, I'm on my own in the dark.

I jolt awake. The horses are neighing loudly. Urgent voices trail into the wagon.

"She's ours." It's the bearded priest.

A voice like jagged stone barks, "And *I* have orders from the premier himself. You know he speaks for the Dragon Throne. Do you dare to defy Imperial orders?" There's a beat of silence. "Didn't think so. We will escort the girl to the palace. Should you wish to tag along, you may."

The priest says something, but I can't make out his words. I hear the wagon door unlocking. The hood over my head comes off. Arms haul me up, but my legs can't support my weight after so many days of disuse. I fall, knees smashing onto the wooden floor. I gasp in pain. My head pounds and nausea rises up my throat.

Breathe, dammit. I swallow a lungful of air. Slowly, my vision focuses. I see a man clad in shiny yellow-and-crimson armor. Shi colors. A soldier. Not just any soldier. Judging from the style of his uniform, a lieutenant at least.

He slashes at the ropes around my hands. I rub my sore wrists. Why would soldiers stop the priests' wagon? What does the palace want with me? A Tiensai. *A murderer.* Maybe I am to stand trial in the capital. Or maybe my punishment is to rot in the palace dungeons.

"Get up," says the lieutenant, not unkindly. He has a blunt nose that looks like it's been broken more than once, and his face is battle-scarred.

He shakes his head when he sees I'm physically incapable of doing much and lifts me up from the wagon floor, setting me down with more care than expected onto the soft grass.

Grass.

I'm surrounded by green, speckled with cheerful yellow. The field stretches all around us, tall trees hemming the far edges. Flowers scent the air, and a breeze lifts strands of hair off my face. For a moment, I think I'm dreaming again. Or that I'm dead. It's too tranquil, too lovely here.

Then I see a retinue of two dozen armed soldiers standing at attention.

It's not a dream. It's a prisoner transfer.

No hood goes over my head this time, and my hands remain free, but the lieutenant escorting me to the carriage keeps his hand on the pommel of his sword, and I know the soldiers will draw their bows on me if I even think of running.

"Get in."

I manage to drag myself into the carriage, collapsing feebly onto the cushioned seat. The lieutenant climbs in opposite me. He shouts a command and the horses start galloping. The field washes past in a blur. I'm surprised at how frantic our pace is.

"Who are you?" I croak. My tone is impolite. I should be according him more respect as a peasant should to a military man. But I'm thirsty and feverish.

To my surprise, he smiles, and I glimpse the young man he once was before the wars hardened him.

"I am Lieutenant Bao." He inclines his head and I nod back. "I have been tasked to escort you to the Imperial Palace. We should arrive in the capital in about two weeks."

"The palace? Why am I going to the palace?"

"My orders are to transport you there safe and sound. What the premier wishes to do with you is none of my concern."

"The premier?"

"Premier Zhao Yang, former Grand General of the Imperial Army and our Minister of War." He hands me a waterskin.

I drink every precious drop and wipe my chin with my sleeve. "What does a war minister want with me?"

Lieutenant Bao eyes me so cunningly that I'm convinced he can't be someone who only follows orders. There's a mind behind that heavy brow and barrel-chest.

"You have magic, don't you?" he says.

There's no point denying it, so I try to dig for information.

"Magic is banned in the Empire, and only the Diyeh priests can practice it. I should be executed. Why would you, a lieutenant, escort me back to the palace?"

"Our emperor is dead. Just because we have a truce with Honguodi, it doesn't mean their spies do not remain in our land. And it doesn't mean Mengu and Nandah aren't watching, waiting for an opportunity to attack."

Maybe if we weren't so war-hungry ourselves, the other nations would leave us alone, I think. But I know better than to say it aloud.

"The Empire needs help," he says in a matter-of-fact way. "We are always on the lookout for talent."

"Talent? Why don't you tell your priests to stop killing all Tiensai? *They* have magic," I say before I can help myself. I shrink back, certain he'll strike me for running my mouth off.

Instead, he laughs. "Be glad that I'm not a priest. Your words would have consequences."

I look down, pretending to be chastised, wondering if maybe Bao isn't fond of the priests either.

"I believe this is yours."

Something cool lands on my palm. My jade ring. He must've taken it from the priests. They took it from me earlier. My fingers curl, clinging to my last piece of home. Tears threaten, but I sniff and keep them in.

"Thank you."

More questions stack up in my head, but the look on Bao's face shuts me up. He's done with our conversation; the stern expression of a soldier returns.

I stare out the window, soaking in the sights of a land full of life. It's so different from the desert villages I'm used to that I can't help but gawk. But underneath the wonder, worry ripples through me. What awaits me at the capital? Bao didn't act like I was going to be punished as a murderer. Does this mean Ama is safe? That no priest will harass her? If I've learned anything it's to trust my instincts, and they tell me something isn't right. But I can't say what.

All I know is that they want me alive, and I must savor that as long as I can.

The days soon blur into one. None of the soldiers come within ten paces of me except for Lieutenant Bao who brings me my meals. However, he remains taciturn and I get no further information from him.

I think about escaping. But we take roads that wind around towns, far away from populated areas, often riding through the night. From the sun, I know we're heading northeast, but I've no idea where we are. All the moth-eaten maps I've seen in Shahmo never gave me a complete picture of the Empire's extensive lands. And it seems unlikely that I can outrun the soldiers' arrows anyway.

Besides, the priests are always watching. The female priest sends sharp glances my way while Leiye observes me more discreetly. Even when I don't see him, I can't help but feel his eyes on my back. I want to ask him questions, but there's a guardedness between the priests and soldiers, and it feels like I shouldn't be talking to anyone.

From my eavesdropping around the campfire, I know we're less than a week from the capital. In a few days, I'll find out what the premier wants from me. No one has said anything about Ama. I decide she must be safe and undetected, and that gives me some comfort.

We ride hard into the night. Soon, the regular jostle of the carriage lulls me to sleep. This time, I dream of the sea, though I've never even seen it before. In my dream, the water is alive, turquoise waves moving to a secret dance choreographed by twinkling sunlight. Something with a long tail, scaled like a fish, swims in the depths. Red eyes with bright yellow centers. A voice, guttural and violent.

I am waiting for you, it says. *I am waiting . . .*

I bolt awake to shouting from outside the carriage. We jerk to a stop and Lieutenant Bao is up at once.

"Stay here. Keep this locked." He disappears outside.

My fingers fumble but I manage to latch the door. It's a lousy defense, but it's better than nothing. The yelling escalates, and I hear the clang of metal right outside.

Something slams into the side of the carriage. A blade sprouts from the window and I drop to the floor. Blood drips from the sword—it isn't mine. I curse under my breath. I've no way out of this wooden box. It might as well be a hearse.

The horses neigh and the carriage rocks, throwing me against the side. I hear screams and the thump of bodies against the door. Before I can think of what to do, the carriage explodes. Planks of splintered wood burst up and crash back down, smashing onto my back as I use my arms to shield my head.

Someone yanks me out of the rubble.

"Are you all right?" yells Lieutenant Bao.

"I think so."

Chaos breathes around me. The scent of earth and smoke taints the air. There's barely any light. But as fire bursts from the hands of the priests, my eyes find blood-streaked, yellow-and-crimson armored bodies strewn on the ground, expressions of surprise frozen on their faces.

Swords in hand, five figures in black circle the priests, taking turns to attack. The priests wield their flames expertly, but the figures in black defend themselves. It's not only a battle of weapons, but of *magic*. Rocks fly through the air, shooting toward their orange-robed targets. Soil lifts from the ground, snuffing out the priests' fire.

I stagger back as wind gusts from one of the black-robed figures. "Who are they?"

"Tiensai." Bao splices a rock with his blade before it can hit me. "Run! Get somewhere safe!"

Without another word, he dashes off into the melee.

For a moment, I'm too shocked to move. A Tiensai springs to my side, his bloodied blade gleaming.

"*Life stealer*," he snarls, raising his sword.

I scream and scramble to my feet. But it's too late. He slashes, dragging his blade down my leg. Flesh on my calf rips. Blood spurts out, soaking my robes. I drop to the ground, the smell of wet earth in my nostrils.

"Life stealer!" he bellows again.

I don't know why he's calling me that or what those words even mean. But it's clear he wants to kill me.

My hands claw, dirt lodging in my fingernails. Hair sticks to the sweat on my face, obscuring my sight. *Crawl, damn you. Crawl.* The sounds of fighting grow distant. My head feels light. I can't go on.

The man picks me up like a rag doll.

"Why are you doing this? I've done nothing to you," I say, pummeling him the best I can with my fists.

Our eyes meet for a brief, terrifying second, and I see nothing but hatred in his.

"Because of what you can do," he says. "Because of what you *will* do."

He shakes me so hard my teeth rattle. I kick at him with all my strength and connect with his knee. He drops me, and my head hits something. Black spots fill my vision. I'm dizzy, faint. I hear his footsteps crunching dried leaves and twigs. He's near.

Nearer.

A flash of orange darts out from nowhere. A priest stands between us, shielding me. The air in front of the Tiensai ripples with energy and a wall of fire erupts. I hear the Tiensai's screams.

And then, I hear no more.

7
ALTAN

Curving windswept dunes surround us, scantly punctuated by tufts of dry grass. There is nothing ahead of us but a stretch of barren brown. Nothing behind us but more sand. Squinting in the torrid sunlight, I trace the outline of a stray cloud in an otherwise empty wash of blue above.

A wry smile splits my chafed lips and I wince. The gods have an awful sense of humor. Once again, I am back in a place I have strived to avoid. But it is one I have to conquer to get what I want.

We have been traveling for almost a week on camelback. As our food supplies get low, tempers run high. I take the smallest sip possible out of my waterskin. Instead of quenching my thirst, the warm water makes me yearn for more. Tang Wei makes a weak gesture and I steer my camel closer to her and pass the waterskin over. She must be regretting her choice to come along. She clearly hates every single moment we spend in the soft, shifting sand. But she will never hate it as much as I do.

This is the place that took everything away from me.

Tang Wei empties the waterskin in a gulp and crushes the soft leather in her hand. "We . . . are going to die . . . in this godsforsaken place."

"Only because you drank everything in *both* our waterskins," I mutter, surveying the land around us. "There aren't going to be any saxaul trees for us to get water from for a while. You could've been more prudent."

"You said we'd run into the nomads *today*. Where are they? Are you sure you remember how to read the sands? Ten years is a long time."

"Quit your whining."

"Should have stabbed you at the inn and dragged you home to Master Sun."

"And upset Linxi?"

I give her a pointed look. Linxi supports my cause through and through. *She* was the one who suggested I look for the Phoenix. Though I suppose she had a different intention for doing so. She doesn't know I plan to rid the world of the Life Stealer.

"Right. Linxi . . . Happy thoughts, happy thoughts," chants Tang Wei. "I can't die here, not without seeing her face again."

I grunt and ride on, almost wishing I had a sweetheart waiting for me somewhere, too. But some of us are meant to be alone.

Just as the sun nears the horizon, we see a caravan and a line of tents in the distance. My heart lightens. Ten years *is* a long time. I can only hope that I will be greeted with open arms.

We ride up to the campsite and get off our camels.

An old but robust-looking man with curly graying hair and a young boy with a sprinkling of freckles on his cheerful face come up to greet us. The man must be the clan leader. Disappointment settles in my chest. I don't recognize him; this isn't the clan that saved me ten years ago. Nonetheless, he looks friendly and welcoming.

"Good travelers, you must be weary. The desert is not always a friend. May I invite you to rest with us for a while before you go on?" he says in halting Shi. "We are happy to provide water for your camels."

The boy offers the beasts a pail of water, and upon seeing Tang Wei, hands her his own waterskin with a shy smile. She beams at him and takes it, drinking greedily.

I respond perfectly in his dialect. "Good evening, wise one. My name is Altan, and this is Tang Wei. We are on our way to the mountains. Thank you for your generosity."

The man's eyebrows shoot up in surprise. He laughs boisterously, clapping me on the back before pulling me close for a hug. The nomads can be rather exuberant whenever they find a stranger who knows their language and customs. Since they never stay in one place for long, to them, it is like finding long-lost family.

"Good, good, you speak my language. I am Shenla," he says. "You and your friend can rest in my own tent. It isn't often that I meet someone from the north—you *are* from the north, correct?"

"Yes," I lie, thankful that it is his immediate assumption.

Mother used to say I look like Father. But both my twin sister and I inherited Mother's coloring, with lighter hair and skin deep enough to pass convincingly as a northerner. And even though I speak Shi like a native, I have honed my northern accent over the years and kept my hair in the tradition of my mother's people. A style I chose to wear when I first left the mainland as a personal protest against my father's ilk. Now, I wear it for my own protection.

"My family lived among your people for a while and they showed us great charity," I explain.

"Ah, excellent! This means *you* are family."

Shenla embraces me again. This time, longer and tighter and with an invitation to stay for a meal. As he leads us to the tents, I translate our conversation for Tang Wei. She flashes him her most charming smile at the mention of food and shelter.

When it is time to eat, we are both too hungry to care about decorum, scarfing everything down with our hands. Rough grain pumiced into a thick gruel, eggs cooked on a flat rock, preserved vegetables, and some creature slowly roasted over a fire. . . . This food brings back memories for me. Tang Wei merely seems happy to have something to eat.

The nomad children cast us curious glances. Some of the adults smile but make no move to talk to us. Many say nomads of this desert are as old as the world itself and are full of wisdom and secrets. They no longer practice magic openly, and since they make no claim on any land, the Diyeh priests have left them well alone.

As night draws in and food is put away, a hum of folk songs and laughter floats around the camp. Even though this isn't the clan that took me in, the familiarity is comforting.

Tang Wei wanders over to a group of nomad women who are weaving colorful threads into intricate necklaces. Soon she's weaving her own necklace and conversing with gestures as if she's lived with these women her entire life. I watch them, a pang of envy in my chest. Sometimes, I wish I had her natural ability to make friends.

I lean back on my hands, careful to keep them on the woven rugs spread out on the sand. The waxing moon is weak tonight, and the sky is a never-ending ombré from lightest gray to deepest black far in the distance.

A woman with luminous eyes and wavy, dark hair comes and sits next to me, introducing herself as Shenni, Shenla's daughter. She stokes the fire, tosses in more twigs.

"You search for the sword," she says suddenly.

My spine pulls straight. "How did you know?"

Her expression is cloaked. "You believe the sword of light will return the world to what it once was?"

I nod, wondering if she has any information or wisdom to spare.

"Nature and men must coexist in harmony, even if men and other men fail to do so. I understand your desire to undo the misdeeds of your ancestors. But *both* the White Jade Sword and the Obsidian Sword answer to the call of the Life Stealer."

There is a warning in her words.

The White Jade Sword, also known as the sword of light because of its purifying properties, has long been lost to myth and legend. No one has seen it in centuries, and none of the historical texts I managed to get hold of give clues to its location.

Its mate, the Obsidian Sword, was the weapon my great-grandfather used to conquer the lands and expand the Empire. *That* sword appears more often through the course of history. Its dark legacy can be traced by the amount of bloodshed and horror it leaves. Rumor has it that it is buried out here in the sands. If the current Life Stealer is not on my side, it would be devastating if he were to get hold of it.

"I understand what you're saying," I tell Shenni. "But the sword of light is the only thing that can undo the dark magic spreading across our land. I have to find the Life Stealer so that he can track it down. It's a risk I'm willing to take."

Shenni gestures for my hand. I give it to her, and she traces the lines on my palm with her fingers. The expression on her face reminds me of the face reader back at Shahmo, like she knows something I don't.

"I see impending chaos, a fight for survival that will span nations. The red thread of fate ties you and the Life Stealer together. But what that fate is . . . it is hard to tell."

"*I* will decide my own fate."

She smiles. "We still talk about him sometimes, you know."

The warmth in her tone surprises me.

"Who?" I ask, confused.

"The boy with the golden eye. The one who could call upon winds so strong that the sands shook beneath his feet and rose up to the Heavens."

My teeth cut my tongue and I taste blood. The pain keeps me focused. Drives away the memory of that boy with the golden eye.

A lost face that once belonged to me.

I start to feign denial, to muster up a mocking laugh. But Shenni's stark gaze tells me she knows exactly who I am. And that it is pointless to lie.

"That boy doesn't exist anymore." My words sink like stones in a river, truth weighing heavy in my stomach.

"We all carry the burdens and joys of our past. Only those who choose to be blind to themselves forget what once existed and what continues to exist *inside*." She taps her chest lightly and smiles. "A word of advice for a person who seeks what you do: always remember, the heart is not a weakness."

I stay silent, watching the dying embers of the fire.

Perhaps, Shenni sees something beyond what is in front of her. Perhaps, she sees my future and the fate that awaits me. Perhaps, under this armor of blades, she still sees that boy who needed to be saved.

8
AHN

Wind lashes my face like a thousand whips as we race into the night, far from the field of corpses. I cling tightly to Leiye as he urges our horse on, trying to douse the memory of the fiery battle and violence I witnessed.

Leiye saved me from the Tiensai who was trying to kill me. Yet, I can't help but feel scared of *him* instead. His fire consumed that man entirely. I remember the Tiensai's frightened eyes, his screams of agony, the smell of his cooked flesh, sweet and nauseating. I turned numb with shock. Leiye had to drag me into the woods where we found one of the horses that had escaped from the mayhem.

I didn't see what happened to Lieutenant Bao or the priests. I don't know if there are any survivors.

My wounded leg feels cold. Blood drips from it. I try to stay upright, but as time goes by, my grip on Leiye's robes weakens. When I start to slump onto him, he eases the horse to a halt and dismounts.

Before I can protest, he lifts me down and lays me on the ground with my back against a tree.

"How are you feeling?"

My body is chilled to the bone. Cold sweat trickles down my

back. The sight of my own blood makes me nauseous.

"Fabulous," I say. "Like I could sprint a mile."

Leiye doesn't laugh at my stupid joke.

"You're losing too much blood." He parts the torn fabric of my skirt and I wince. The serrated edge of the Tiensai's blade left a gross mess of pulpy flesh, and the gash is a cruel, dark smile on my pale leg.

"I have to cauterize it to stop the bleeding," says Leiye.

"You're going to *burn* me?"

"You don't have to be afraid."

"You're a priest, everyone fears you." Even as I say that, the gentle moonlight softens his features. Again, it strikes me that he doesn't seem like the other priests I've encountered. But I remind myself that I saw him burn a man to death with my own eyes. "Why did you save me and leave your comrades behind? Are the priests so disloyal to each other?"

"I think you should be worrying about yourself instead of others right now. And I told you, my job is to keep you alive."

"But Lieutenant—"

"Your blood isn't clotting. There must be something on the Tiensai's sword that's keeping the wound open. The next town is more than an hour's ride away. I don't want to have to restrain you to save your life, but I will if I have to."

The thought of a priest using his magic on me scares me to the Ten Courts of Hell. But I don't want to bleed to death.

I grit my teeth. "Fine. Do it."

Leiye grabs a fallen branch from the ground and breaks off a thin piece. "It's going to hurt, and I'd rather you don't give away our location with your screams. I don't know if any Tiensai followed us."

I take the stick. He unsheathes a dagger and starts to heat the blade. The flames that spring from his fingers dance prettily, orange-red and blue in the center. I stare, fascinated.

Horrified.

A priest is saving my life.

His flames grow bigger and I hiss in fright.

"One must not fear fire to wield it. That is the first thing we are taught."

"I wasn't brought up in your little priest school," I snap. "In my world, your fire destroys, and it takes the lives of people we care about."

A flicker of emotion passes over his face, but he says nothing. When the metal is hot enough, he extinguishes his flames. "Hold still."

I suck in my breath, squeeze my eyes shut, and bite down on the stick.

The first touch draws a loud gasp from me. A sweet charred smell rises in the air. I bite down harder, tears streaming down my cheeks. With quick taps, Leiye places the hot blade onto my leg again and again, until the entire wound is treated.

"It's done."

I open my eyes to see his ashen face. It's like he felt my pain every single time he burned my flesh.

"How is it?" I ask, wiping my eyes with my sleeve. I can't bear to look myself.

"It'll have to do for now. We have to go."

"Where?"

"The capital. But first, we'll find you a physician."

He helps me back on the horse and ties me to him. My light-headedness returns, so I lean against him, not caring how close I am to a monster. After all, he's protected me this far.

We ride at a brutal pace. My leg feels like it's still burning, like it's covered with hot coals, the pain radiating from the wound. As I drift into sleep, I realize that a permanent scar will form from Leiye's actions.

I've been marked. Branded.

By the flames of the Diyeh.

We find a physician in the next town and upon seeing Leiye's substantial money purse, the man offers us two rooms for the night. He cleans my wound with some herbal mixture and wraps a damp bandage around it to keep the heat down. Leiye watches in silence, expression unreadable. When the physician is finally done, sleep grabs me and pulls me in.

It's mid-morning when a knock on the door wakes me. Leiye enters and hands me a small bundle of clean clothes, placing a bamboo rack of steamed shrimp chángfěn drenched in soy sauce, two custard buns, and a bowl of fresh figs on the table.

He has shed his priest robes and changed into an ivory hànfú. The Diyeh cuff around his topknot is gone, replaced by a simple silver band. Half of his long black hair falls behind his shoulders, an emerald ribbon intertwined with that single white streak running down the middle of his back. His face is clean, and in the daylight, I notice how large his wide-set eyes are and how young he actually is—he can't be more than two years older than me.

The sight jars me. He looks too gentle, too soft. Like someone who should be reciting poetry by a lake instead of tearing families apart or burning people alive. It makes me wonder what the Diyeh do to their recruits to turn them into vicious monsters.

"What happened to your priest outfit?" I ask in between greedy bites of the rice rolls. The shrimp inside is fresh and sweet, and with the pain from my leg now a dull throb, my mood has improved.

Leiye sits across from me, rolling a coin over his knuckles, long legs stretched out. "We need to keep a low profile."

I raise an eyebrow, but he doesn't elaborate.

"Thanks for saving my life last night," I say reluctantly. "Do you know if Lieutenant Bao survived? He was nice to me."

"I don't know if there are other survivors. I did not pay attention to them. My only duty is to protect you."

"Why?"

"Orders," comes his terse reply.

"From the Diyeh? But Lieutenant Bao says your war minister wants to see me." I cling on to the hope that Leiye will bring me to the premier and not the priests who will surely put me to death.

Leiye stays silent.

"What does a politician want with me? After last night, I think I deserve some answers," I press.

Ignoring me, he helps himself to the fresh figs. I pop a custard bun into my mouth, crunch the paper wrapping into a ball, and chuck it at him.

Leiye catches it effortlessly without even lifting his head, looking amused by my pathetic attack.

"Don't you think I should know why people are trying to kill me?" I say, voice raised. I don't care if the physician can hear us. For all I know, he has his ears pressed up against the door to this room. My fear has turned into frustration. I will force answers out of this boy-priest. "Why were those men after me? And why did that man call me a life stealer?"

"Because he was a Tiensai, and that is what you are to them. It isn't a term we use."

We? Does he mean the Diyeh?

"I don't understand," I say.

"Have you heard of the blacksmith and the twin swords?"

"The fairy-tale mothers tell their children to warn them about taking things that don't belong to them?"

"It's not a fairy tale."

I laugh, the sound too loud in the quiet room. Leiye steeples his fingers and casts me a cold look. I stop laughing.

"What do you mean?"

"Tell me the story," he says simply. I purse my lips. "Go on, indulge me."

"Fine. Once upon a time there lived a talented blacksmith—"

Leiye scoffs.

"That's how my grandmother tells it, and that's how I'm going to tell it," I say, irritated.

He gestures at me to continue.

"*Once a upon a time,*" I repeat, "there lived a talented blacksmith who had a son. One day, the Jade Emperor of Heaven commanded the blacksmith to create a sword whose beauty no other mortal or godly weapon could surpass. He needed to forge the blade in heavenly jadefire for a thousand days and a thousand nights, so the Jade

Emperor offered the use of the celestial smithy in his palace. On the thousandth day, the blacksmith went to temper the sword with the tears of Xiwangmu's pet—a fènghuáng, because a phoenix's tears contained magical healing properties. But on his way back, the blacksmith stumbled on an orchard of peaches. Intoxicated by the fragrant aroma, he took a bite from one—which frankly, was stupid, because he was in the Garden of Immortality and no mortal was allowed to take anything from it. As punishment, the Jade Emperor struck the blacksmith's only son with a bolt of lightning and killed him."

"And?"

"And that's when you say to a child, see, bad things happen when you take things that don't belong to you."

"There's more to the tale."

"Pray tell." I wish he'd stop being so cryptic.

The coin between his long fingers moves constantly back and forth as he sits silently. I shove another rice roll into my mouth, wondering if I should stab him with my chopstick and make a run for it. But it's unlikely I'll get far.

"This is the part that survives in some ancient records, but as far as I know, it's never told as part of the bedtime story," Leiye says at last. "Distraught by the death of his son, the blacksmith took the sword and cut off the phoenix's head, casting it down into the mortal world. A chain of mountains sprung up where it landed. Then, he cursed the sword he'd forged, giving it the power to destroy even a god. The sword split in two, twin weapons that were the opposite of each other. One sword transformed into a pure white iridescent jade while its mate turned black as night, dark as hell. They go by many names. Most commonly, the White Jade Sword and the Obsidian Sword, or the sword of light and the dark sword. In his haste to escape Heaven, the blacksmith dropped the white sword. No one knows where it is today. And even though he'd eaten the peach of immortality, he didn't become a god. Instead he became a spirit of the soul world, trapped forever in darkness."

I swallow, the chángfěn suddenly tasting like sawdust. "What's so important about this fairy tale?"

"I said, it's not a fairy tale."

It's my turn to scoff. I wonder if his time with the Diyeh priesthood has led him onto the path of madness. He leans back, index fingers tapping each other lightly. He looks so calm and composed it irks me.

"I'm sure you know that Tiensai magic is poisoning our land," he says.

Why would the desert still spread if those false priests keep killing the ones they call the Tiensai?

"That's what the priests claim," I say, remembering Ama's words.

"The Diyeh are not like the Tiensai. We believe the Life Stealer will bring peace to the world. *They* are the ones cursed by the gods, corrupted by darkness. Their magic is impure, and they want to kill you because they don't want you to find the sword of light, because they don't want to get rid of the dark magic consuming our land. That's why you were attacked last night."

I frown. "What on earth are you talking about?"

"It is said that the sword of light is the only thing that can stop the disease in the earth from spreading. Having been touched by the heavenly magic of the peach, the blacksmith became the first Life Stealer, and only a Life Stealer can find the missing artifact that will heal us."

"What does this have to do with me?"

Leiye doesn't respond and it takes moments for everything to connect in my brain. My blood runs cold.

"You think *I'm* the Life Stealer? But it's just a fairy tale."

"My comrades who found you saw those bodies in the alleyway. From their description, it is clear the men died from life-stealing magic." Leiye walks over and lowers himself by me. He grips my wrist with a certainty that disturbs me, his eyes dark and steely. "Your magic is *different*. And that is why the Tiensai want to kill you."

I push down memories of what happened in Shahmo and turn from his piercing gaze, unwilling to accept what he's telling me. He must be lying. I can't be the Life Stealer, whatever that is.

"This is ridiculous," I say, pulling away from him. "I'm not who you think I am."

Abruptly, he stands, signaling the end of our confusing conversation. "Finish your food and get changed. We'll leave in half an hour and you'll have your own horse. We need to get to the capital quickly."

"My own horse? Aren't you afraid I'll escape?"

"You're clever and you want to stay alive. If you try to run, you'll have to deal with the Tiensai, the palace, and the priests by yourself. You won't run from *me*"—he smiles and heads to the door—"because right now, I'm the only one who can keep you safe."

9
AHN

We reach Beishou three days later. Instead of using a secret entrance to the palace or some Diyeh temple, we canter through the streets brazenly. So much for keeping a low profile. But I'm glad for the chance to see the capital. Never in my life did I think I would be here.

Beishou is more colorful and dazzling than I ever imagined. And so, so wealthy. I try not to gawk at the neatly paved flagstone streets, so clean they practically shine. Majestically sculpted fountains and water features appear at every corner, some as large as a shophouse. Gilded temples with auspicious stone animals and various gods perched on the eaves and roofs stand tall here and there, all painted in vibrant colors of lush green and red with accents of sky blue and golden yellow.

Small pockets of carefully cultivated flowers and plants sprout between streets and along the sidewalks. Everything is so opulent here even the wooden windows of the shophouses are carved with a complicated pattern of alternating rounded rectangular shapes and swirls.

And the people! It baffles my mind to see all of them clad in fine silks, more vibrant than any I've seen in my life. There're no signs of poverty. No beggars, no filthy street kids, no hint of disrepair in any of the buildings. Even the waiters at the inns and teahouses we pass are dressed well.

All the wealth of the Empire pumped into this city while so many other villages and towns languish in squalor; it's hard to swallow my resentment.

We dismount at the end of a long tree-lined path and I stare openmouthed at the imposing structure in front of me.

Massive metal doors rise from the ground. Torches line stone walls over fifty feet high that stretch up and out, obscuring any view of what is inside the compound. Two guards stand at either side of the great doors with several more marching up and down the perimeter.

A guard comes up to us. Leiye subtly slips something from his sleeve. I glimpse a seal set in pale green jade. The guard immediately bows low.

"Young Master, how may I assist you today?"

Young Master? Why would the palace guard address a priest so formally like he's a nobleman?

"The premier is expecting this lady. She is his guest. See that everyone is notified." Leiye's tone has taken a genteel note.

The guard clicks his heels, regarding me with a lot more respect and civility, and some curiosity. Then he slides open a slot in the door and mutters a few words to someone behind it.

The great doors open to show nothing but a large and dull cobblestoned courtyard with another set of doors and another great wall at the opposite end. A different guard greets us and leads us to the new set of doors. He repeats the process of the first guard and the doors open. Another guard is there with another courtyard and *another* set of doors.

Eventually, we go through so many doors and courtyards and paths that everything blends in my head into one long corridor and one big courtyard with random plants. There's no way I will be able to find my way out of this maze.

After we cross the fifth or sixth courtyard, the palace begins to show its true colors. Beishou's manicured charm is a smudge compared to the grandeur and splendor of the palace grounds.

My eyes sweep across the vivid scarlet-and-green double-eaved roofs, the rich wine-hued wooden pillars, and the breathtaking carvings in the polygonal coffers of its ceilings, taking in all the shimmering gold used in the decorations. At one point, I spot a seven-story pagoda overlooking a small lake as we pass an open area between buildings. *A lake.* How huge is this place?

Finally, we are told to wait in a grand hall where a few attendants stand discreetly in the corners. They keep their eyes fixed at some distant point in front of them. No one looks at me. I want to ask Leiye questions about the palace and Premier Zhao Yang, but the blank expressions of the attendants don't fool me. I'm certain every one of them would eavesdrop on our conversation. Why wouldn't they? I would.

A petite girl dressed in a white rúqún embroidered with peonies enters from a screened door. Like most Shi, she is fair of complexion. But there's a layer of pearl powder over her face that makes her skin glow in an ethereal manner. Her cheeks are rouged, lips painted a flattering shade of vermilion, and her hair is done up in elaborate braids and loops adorned with colorful silk flowers. This must be the fashion of the capital. I feel like an absolute slob next to her.

The girl inclines her head. "Welcome to the Outer Courts, my lady. My name is Linxi, and I shall be escorting you to your chambers."

"I—I'm not—call me Ahn, please," I say, painfully conscious of how shabby I must look. I'm quite sure I don't smell pleasant either.

Linxi smiles graciously and bows again. "Please, Lady Ahn, follow me."

I turn to Leiye, hoping he will come with me. He's neither a friend nor an ally, but after traveling together for some time, he is a familiar face. But he disappears down the hallway without a word.

Left with no other choice, I follow Linxi to a room three times the size of Ama's hut. The air is perfumed by fresh flowers. Sunlight streams softly through rice-papered windowpanes. Organza curtains in rich colors of viridian, purple, and sapphire drape around the arched wooden frame of the canopy bed with a double moon design. Beautiful paintings of lush scenery hang from the walls, and dainty gold-painted ornaments rest on top of the cabinets and side tables. At one corner, silk robes lie over a folding screen painted with red-crested cranes and verdant bamboo.

It feels like I'm in a dream, except my dreams have never been so extravagant. Tears sting my eyes. If only Ama could see this, if only she could rest her old bones on that opulent bed. *Get a grip*, I chide myself. *You're not staying for long. You're only here because some politician thinks you're useful.*

Two handmaidens appear, ready to assist, but Linxi dismisses them with a wave of her hand. Like her, the two girls are dressed in white robes since the forty-nine-day royal mourning period of Emperor Gao Long isn't over. But the embroidery on theirs is less intricate and their hairstyles and enamel pins are simply designed. Linxi must be a higher ranked lady-in-waiting or favored by someone important in the palace. I wonder if she was born on palace grounds or brought here.

"This place is lovely," I remark.

"I am glad it pleases you, Lady Ah—"

"*Please*, just Ahn."

Linxi hesitates for a moment before flashing a conspiratorial smile that endears her to me. "All right, but only when we're alone." She ushers me into the bathroom, continuing, "You may be a guest of the premier, but he is a military man and lives sparsely. The Empress Dowager Zhenxi specifically assigned these chambers to you. I will let Her Majesty know that you are satisfied."

"The empress herself!" I half screech, flustered by the attention. "I'm more than satisfied, it's an honor. Why would she even do this?"

"We were told you're an *esteemed* guest." Linxi's eyes are big with anticipation. She expects me to tell her who I am.

I open my mouth and then close it immediately. It's better not to say anything about how I was captured by the priests or why I was captured. I don't want to scare Linxi away.

"That gentleman I was with—do you know who he is?" I ask.

"That was Young Master Xima Leiye, the youngest son of the Marquis of Qin Province."

Xima Leiye. So, he *is* a nobleman. And a priest, too?

"He was very kind to have escorted me to the palace. Does he work with the premier?"

"I attend to the concubines in the western wing of the Inner Court. I don't know much about the politicians in the palace, I'm sorry." Turning her head away from me, Linxi scatters some rose petals into the bathwater, and the heady scent fills the air.

I'm disappointed by her answer, but I guess she's only here on Empress Zhenxi's orders. I convince her that I'm more than able to bathe myself, and after she leaves, I sink into the tub of warm water, relishing this rare luxury.

Soon, I'm dressed in white silk robes that caress my skin like clouds. I watch quietly as Linxi transforms my hair into a complicated swirl. Then, she lifts my chin and taps a light dusting of rouge onto my cheeks deftly.

"There." She's pleased with her handiwork.

Heart beating fast, I examine myself in the bronzed mirror. Dressed in these beautiful clothes, the poor girl-thief from the desert is nowhere to be found. I don't recognize myself. Somehow, it feels like I've lost something.

I blanch at the two-inch heel of the shoes Linxi places in front of me.

"I'm afraid I can't wear those. I got hurt on the way here." I show her the bandages around my leg.

"What happened to your leg? Shall I send for the physician?"

"No, it's all right. I'm fine. I fell off the horse," I say, unsure of how much to reveal to her. Even though I *feel* like I can trust her, she's still a stranger. And my fate here has not been decided.

Linxi frowns and looks around the room, a finger tapping her cheek thoughtfully. "Oh!" She pulls out a pair of silk slippers and helps me with them. "This will do."

I breathe a sigh of relief. "Thank you. I've never worn heels before."

She's polite enough to hide her surprise. We leave the room and she leads me through long corridors and across a large garden. Soon, a clearing opens and a serene blue-green lake unfurls. A pavilion unlike any I've ever seen stands near the shore. Its roof is domed, not curved up. And instead of columns for support, the entire structure is wrapped by a ringed wall, made from stone glimmering a muted white in the sun. Through the polygonal latticed openings carved into the stone, I spy a figure inside. My ears pick up another sound amidst the warbling birds.

Music.

The melody is beautiful and melancholic, like an intimate whisper of secrets.

"Who is that—"

"We must not keep the premier waiting," interrupts Linxi, a look of caution on her face as she gestures subtly ahead.

Two guards are marching toward us. Our escort.

We follow the guards to the next building. They click their heels smartly and station themselves at the entrance. Linxi points me to a large parlor room where I am to wait for the premier.

"I must take my leave now, Lady Ahn."

"Will you wait with me, please?" I clasp her hands in mine, suddenly nervous. My fate is to be decided in a few minutes in this room.

"I'm sorry, but there are palace rules. The premier will not want a servant of the empress to be in a private meeting."

Private? I've already spotted three attendants in the corners of this room, doing their best to blend into their surroundings. A thought strikes me. "Before you go, tell me what's the most important rule in the palace?"

"Be careful who you trust." She slips away before I can question her further.

The attendants stay half hidden in the shadows, not meeting my eyes, but the air is heavy with scrutiny. I get the sense I'm not supposed to talk to them, so I sink onto a chair and wait.

Minutes go by and the weariness from my long journey hits like a heavy sack of rice. My lids droop, even as I pinch my arm to stay awake.

Armor clinks and I startle. The two guards have moved into the parlor.

"Bow!" whispers an attendant from behind me.

I jump up.

"Presenting the Grand Premier Zhao Yang!" calls a voice.

Footsteps come closer, but I keep my head lowered.

"You may rise," says a different voice. It's commanding and hard like the blunt side of a hammer.

I straighten and see a man clad in white robes. A silver mask covers half his face while his uncovered side reveals a deep-set raven eye and an aquiline nose. He stares at me, expression transforming from one of curiosity to recognition.

"Ahn-er? It really *is* you."

10
ALTAN

We leave the nomads the next day, traveling northward by the sun, our rucksacks filled with generous gifts of food that improve Tang Wei's mood. The Wudin Mountains loom ahead of us, growing taller by the day.

I am getting closer to my goal, but Shenni's words repeat in my head each night like a cipher I cannot solve. *The heart is not a weakness.* What did she mean? And what does it have to do with finding the sword of light or the Life Stealer?

We stumble upon a village at the base of the mountain range and spend a night at the local inn, stuffing our faces with a simple but hearty dinner. I manage to convince Tang Wei not to accompany me all the way up to Jiyu Spring, pushing back on all her protests. The trek is too dangerous, and besides, the seeker of the Phoenix must endure their journey alone.

Finally, she relents, saying that she will join me for the start of the climb. At dawn, we set off together.

Even in daylight, mist veils the craggy mountain peak, reminding me of the watercolor paintings that used to hang in the palace. I never had an aptitude for art, but my sister was drawing before she could write her first word. She would have been an accomplished painter if she had lived.

We stop at a barren ledge for a short rest.

"It's an awfully long climb up to the top," says Tang Wei, chewing on a piece of jerky.

And a long fall, I think, looking down.

"We should part ways here," I say. "It'll give you enough time to get back down by sunset."

"You didn't sleep well last night, did you? Maybe you should start your ascent tomorrow. This is a good place to set up camp."

"No time to waste." I snatch the jerky from her and tear myself a strip.

"Give it back!"

"You can spare me some. You're going back to that nice little inn with the comfy bed."

Tang Wei makes a face. "And I'm going to sleep for a thousand years." Her expression turns serious. "How long do you think you'll take?"

"I have no idea."

She looks like she wants to say more, but instead, she punches me on the arm with more force than necessary. "Well, don't die."

"I won't," I say with confidence I don't feel. "And if I do you can still say 'I told you so' to my corpse."

"Don't curse yourself." She punches me again for good measure, lighter this time, and with something like affection. Then, with a sweep of her skirts, she leaps down the rocks like a mountain goat.

Alone, I continue my ascent. The slopes seem deserted, though my ears catch the sounds of wildlife. Perched high on tree branches, a family of golden snub-nosed monkeys observe me warily. Higher up, a thrush trills. I smell the sweet scent of blossoms and ripe fruit and remember the palace gardens I used to play in. Picturesque and tranquil, the Wudin Mountains are safe from the remnants of my great-grandfather's dark magic.

For now.

If I do nothing to stop its spread, this paradise of flora and fauna will turn to dust.

The temperature drops the higher I go. I pull my fur-lined cloak snug around my neck, glad for my gloves. They keep my fingers warm and make it easier to channel my magic.

Tiensai magic works on the principle of qì, which is the most basic substance the world is comprised of. All living creatures and nature itself are connected by this constant cycle and flow of energy. And while all humans are born with a primordial qì, only those sensitive enough to the workings of this spiritual force can harness it as a form of energy and release it through meridian points at their fingertips.

Many Tiensai are born with a strong affinity for one of the five natural elements in our world: wind, water, fire, earth, and metal—which is extremely rare. Though I suppose, the life-stealing affinity is an anomaly outside of the five elements and the rarest of them all.

Few Tiensai can manipulate more than one element. Even fewer have true mastery over their core element for it takes years of cultivation. Most Tiensai are too busy running for their lives and hiding from the Diyeh.

I was fortunate to learn cultivation from Master Sun. Years of dogged training has made me accomplished in more than one element. Unsurprisingly, fire is my weakest affinity. It is the hardest element to control, and after all these years, when I think of fire, I think of my mother. I think of the priests.

And the man who murdered her.

I pause my climb, staring at the cloud of fog circling the mountain peak. It will take me at least two days to get all the way up to Jiyu Spring—the Spring of Memories—where the Oracle Bones of the Soul Beast are said to rest.

No one knows for certain if the Phoenix is alive.

Will this be a fool's errand? Am I wasting my time on a myth when I could be hunting for the bastards who murdered my family?

Unbidden, memories of my sister return again. We were twins, but Father used to say she had a will made of iron. He never said that about me. Even as a child, my sister was the fearless one. The one who would single-mindedly pursue every one of her enemies and strike them down without a second thought. She would not doubt herself. She would not waver. She would be disappointed in me for even thinking twice.

Mother often said I was the sun to her moon. But if she were the moon, I was the tide that ebbed and flowed with her pull.

My sister should have been the one to survive the sandstorm ten years ago. Not me. But the gods, as always, have a twisted sense of humor.

I take a deep breath and banish all doubts. My sister isn't here.

I am.

On the third morning, I reach the edge of the misty ring. Early dawn ribbons of radiant red and orange streak the pastel sky, haloing the mountainside. The icicles on the coniferous leaves will melt with the rising sun, but right now, they sparkle in the light, and my breath puffs like small white clouds. An opaque silence cocoons this place. No stirrings of wildlife. No breeze. No scent. It is as if time has stopped.

Something tells me this is the place.

I disarm myself, removing my double sabers, bow, and quiver of arrows. I leave a couple of knives sheathed along my belt. Just in case. Then, I sit cross-legged, palms faceup on my knees with my eye closed. Focusing on my breathing, I settle down for a long wait.

Legend has it that a woman made the arduous trek up the Wudin Mountains in search of the Phoenix. Her only son had been blinded in an accident, and she was desperate to find a way to heal him. For seven days and nights, she meditated. On the seventh night, when she opened her eyes, the mountain revealed a cavern, and in it, the Spring of Memories. She drank from it, and a Soul Beast appeared. A fènghuáng, the guardian of the skies.

Touched by the woman's devotion, the Phoenix granted her a wish, but it was one that needed to be repaid. She agreed, and when she left the cavern, she found that she had lost her sight. Back in her village, her son woke and saw the world bathed in light again.

It sounds absurd, like a fairy tale to remind children of their parents' love. But Shīfù always says that there is truth woven into our stories, passed down from fathers to sons, mothers to daughters. One only needs to believe that a truth does exist.

Gradually, my breathing steadies. The silence grows louder like a constant reminder that I am alone here on the mountaintop surrounded by magic and mist. Time liquefies, and my body feels weightless. A tingle starts at the tips of my fingers and spreads to my toes. I open my eye.

My breath hitches.

I'm sitting in a cavern *in* the mountain. The knives on my belt are gone. So are my cloak and gloves. But it isn't cold here. Jewels glitter above me, some dripping down like stringed stars. Flashes of brilliant light pulsate all around.

I blink. Not jewels, but glowworms.

Their blue-green fluorescence casts an eerie light on the cavern floor ahead of me. Water. Dark and still, the pool reflects the pinpricks of light from the ceiling. *Jiyu Spring.* This must be it. I get up and walk cautiously forward. The ground seems firm enough. There are no rocks, just a smooth surface eroded for centuries.

Something floats on the surface of the water. A shape made of ivory sticks. *Bones.* A bird's skeleton. The wingspan looks over ten feet, bigger than any bird of prey I have heard of.

The Oracle Bones of the Phoenix.

For a few seconds, I don't move. It's too easy. I haven't done anything worthy to be in here. This feels like a trap. Instinct urges me to leave.

Don't be a coward, Altan, my sister's voice drawls in my head.

I can't fail her. I can't fail my family. I can't fail my country.

I scoop some of the water in my hands and bring it to my lips. It tastes of nothing. Not even of water, if water had a real taste. Will it poison me? Will it show me something? The Phoenix, perhaps?

I take another sip. But nothing happens.

The cavern looks exactly as it was: soft glowing bugs masquerading as gemmed necklaces strung across the ceiling. Have I come all the way here for nothing? A frustrated noise rumbles at the back of my throat.

I dry my hands, wondering if I should leave.

Then, I see it.

Tendrils of smoke slither up from the water like sea serpents of lore. They float toward me. Some spiraling, others swaying. Faint and translucent at first, the human-shaped figures of smoke and mist gain density and their faces fill out. Faces I have seen in my dreams and nightmares, but not in reality.

Not for a while.

"Son." The specter of my father looks too real. Beside him, my mother smiles.

"Impossible," I whisper. My parents are both dead. These are illusions. They must be. This is a test. But what does the Soul Beast want from me?

"Altan," wails Mother's ghost, moving closer.

I stumble back. *They're just illusions, Altan. Prove yourself. Pass the test.*

"You're not real," I say loudly. My own ears pick up the tremor in my voice.

"Come with us," says Father's ghost. He reaches out a gauzy hand. "Come and we can be a family again."

I shake my head despite the longing in my heart. If only it were so easy to erase the past. If only it were possible to bring back the dead.

A small figure appears in the corner. I don't want to go near, but my feet move anyway. The boy is sprawled on the ground, one leg bent at an awkward angle. He lifts his head and reaches out a trembling hand. I start to shake when I recognize his tear-streaked face.

"Help, Jin," cries the boy who looks exactly like my cousin. "Help me."

I have not heard my real name for so long that something in me fractures. A memory rises from its grave. I was seven when it happened. Tai Shun was six. I was up on one of the roofs of the eastern wing of the Inner Court that day, grieving over the loss of my father. It was a place I went whenever I wanted to be by myself. A steep, hazardous climb, but I'd done it numerous times before. It rained the night before and the tiles glistened with dew. Slippery for those who were not sure-footed.

Tai Shun came to look for me, features contorted not with effort, but regret.

If my destiny shifted with Father's last breath, it was completely upended by my cousin's words.

I know who killed your father.

I stared in disbelief as he told me how he overheard his own parents talking about Father's murder. How they'd planned to use a slow-acting nerve-targeting poison. But all that stuck in my head was how Tai Shun had known about it *before* my father died. Known about the malicious plan and never said a word.

He was complicit.

I shoved him away and started my climb down. He followed. I remember the moment he put his foot on the wrong step, slipping on a slick tile. I remember the look on his face as he fell. I remember my own screams.

The gods must have been smiling on Tai Shun that day. He

bounced off a secondary eave and fell onto a balcony instead of plummeting to the ground. A fall that would guarantee his death. He lived, breaking both legs. He took ill with fever right after, and that was the last time we saw each other.

His mother, Zhenxi, personally hauled me up at the crack of dawn the next day. She whipped me herself. She wanted to know what happened, why Tai Shun was on the roof, how he fell. If *I* had pushed him. I told her nothing. Certain that Tai Shun's punishment would be infinitely worse than mine, I never revealed that her own son had betrayed her. I might have died that day by her hand, but Mother found us and intervened.

We fled the palace two days later, my wounds still a mess of raw fire.

A phantom pain rakes down my back now, like a hungry ghost demanding offerings. Memories scorched into the recesses of my mind tumble forward. Mother singing me to sleep; Father lifting me on his shoulders; Tai Shun and I playing in the palace gardens, catching koi we weren't supposed to; my aunt, whip in hand.

My cousin, broken.

Another figure appears. The specter of my aunt hovers over my ghostly cousin, that very whip in her hand.

"*You*," she sneers at me, features beautiful and terrifying. "Still alive, are you?"

"Jin." Tai Shun's specter looks up at me with fear. "Jin, be careful."

I raise my hands in defense as my aunt screams. The whip comes down, but it goes through me like smoke.

I'm alone in the cavern again. Did I pass the test? Is this over?

"Brother."

One word. Crisp as fresh fallen snow, clear as the desert sky.

Her voice.

I spin around.

It can't be her. But my eyes tell me otherwise. She materializes, solidifying before me, dressed in the clothes I last saw her in. Powder blue and ecru, her sun-brown hair curling down her shoulders. We should be the same age, but there she stands. Frozen in time, a child of eight. And here I am, almost a man.

"Brother," she repeats. She holds a doll in her hand, a miniature replica of herself.

A trick. This is a trick. But she looks so real—

No.

"It can't be you." I shake my head. "It's not you."

"Why did you leave me, brother?"

Her voice aches with such pain that I move closer. Somewhere, at the back of my mind, reason remains. It reminds me that none of this is real. That I must resist the lure of the illusions. But right now, all I can see is the little girl in front of me.

My sister.

"Brother, do you miss me?"

"Every day," I choke out.

"Then why did you kill me?"

She bares her teeth. Fangs. Dripping with blood. Her arms reach for me like twisted claws, and I flinch with a cry.

In an instant, the innocent child is in front of me again. She smiles that smile I miss, the right side of her lips lifting higher than the left, a single dimple appearing near her chin. Crooked and mischievous. The smile that convinced Tai Shun and me to join in her schemes around the palace grounds; the smile that got us out of trouble after that.

"I am lonely." Her smile fades, and that aching look returns. "So lonely, brother."

I stagger back, falling to my knees. Shivering. I killed her and saved myself. This is my fault. Nothing can bring her back. Nothing can undo my terrible mistake. I am unworthy of this life, unworthy of the throne I covet. If I could go back in time, I would gladly give up my life for hers.

"It's not too late, brother," she whispers as if she read my thoughts. "Join me, and I won't be lonely again." She reaches out for my hand. I feel her touch.

Warm.

A fist wraps itself around my heart, squeezing. I gasp as hot tears roll down my face. This is real. *She is real.* Everything is a hazy cloud of memories and pain.

"Come, brother. Come with me."

She leads me to the spring. The dark bottomless pool is inviting, its waters whispering a promise of redemption.

All I need to do is to go in.

11
AHN

I can't take my eyes off the premier.

Lesions, long healed, run down the side of his neck to the collar of his silk tunic. Even though half of his face is hidden behind the silver mask, it's like I've seen him before. That aquiline nose, those dark, dark eyes—I recognize him. Could he be? No, he can't be.

He can't.

For years, I hoped my parents or a distant relative or anyone would show up. I prayed that my parents left me in Shahmo by mistake. I prayed that as a silly child, I wandered off and got lost, and it was all my fault, not theirs. I even prayed that my parents were ambushed and killed by bandits, and that I was the only one spared. I was desperate to believe they hadn't abandoned me.

But as time went by, no one came. My prayers went unanswered. Hope dwindled and starved. Eventually, I accepted my fate and stopped appealing to the Heavens, for the gods had turned a deaf ear. My grief was spent, and I decided my parents were gone forever. Blood relative or not, Ama was all the family I had.

And she was enough.

But now, now this masked man stands in front of me. Not just any man, but *Zhao Yang*, the esteemed Premier of the Shi Empire.

I thought my father dead. Of all the wild places in the world, I never imagined I'd meet him in the Imperial Palace.

"Ahn-er," says Zhao Yang. "After all these years, I—I've finally found you."

He takes a step closer. I retreat and bump against the rosewood table. The white and cobalt-blue vase on it wobbles and crashes on the floor. Pieces of fine porcelain scatter everywhere.

"I'm so sorry!" I stoop down, gathering the broken fragments, but one of the attendants shoos me away.

"Be careful. Let them handle it." Zhao Yang takes my elbow and guides me out to the garden.

Numbly, I follow, barely aware of the two guards who flank us as we walk. We stop at a secluded spot among tall willow trees near the lake, and he dismisses the guards.

"Please, sit down," he says.

I collapse onto the stone stool. My head feels light, my heartbeat too rapid. Part of me thinks this has all been a dream and that I'm still in my small village, delirious from the heat.

"I apologize. I must have startled you earlier." His manner is less certain than before. My silence must unnerve him. "Do you recognize me?"

I nod. "I—I think so."

He sits across from me, resting his arms on the small round table between us.

"This is all rather surprising, to you and me both. I have been searching for you for so many years, reaching out far and wide. But despite my vast resources, I've failed time and again. Until now—" His eyes land on my jade ring. "This ring! I thought I'd never see it again. I gave it to your mother many years ago before I left for the war. You look so much like her."

Still, I remain silent. Words stay lodged in my throat. What do I say to him? What do I say to this *stranger*? I want to believe he is my father, but everything seems so surreal. Maybe I'm exhausted from my journey here. Maybe my injury is still bothering me. My head starts to hurt. I press my fingers to my temples, trying to recall my childhood. It *feels* like there's something there, but I remember nothing.

He peers at me curiously. "Do you remember what happened to you as a child? Do you remember anything?"

"I'm sorry, I don't," I manage.

"That's all right. Don't worry." He smiles and reaches out to me and I shrink back. The hurt on his face shames me. "This is difficult, I understand. Especially since it seems that you have forgotten what happened. But *I* remember you, Zhao Ahn."

Zhao Ahn. That name echoes in my ears.

For years, I was like my name: *Ahn.* Singular. Cut off and alone. Without something that came before. Without history. Without family. I don't remember what happened during the first six years of my life. There's a void in my mind where only a single memory lives: a voice and a blurred face.

And that voice is speaking to me now. I stare at him, not quite believing he is real.

Not quite believing that *my father* is alive.

I finally nod and take a deep breath.

"Father."

That single utterance from my lips shakes us both. There's

a tightness in my chest and it's hard to breathe. My father sits motionless. Emotion flickers in his eyes. They go to my mother's ring again. His finger grazes it. He flinches like the ring is a hot flame, burning his skin. Then, he looks away with a strange, sad smile.

I listen with bated breath as he starts to speak.

"You were born on the winter solstice sixteen years ago. When you were little, your favorite fruit was red apples and you wanted to eat the pork and chive dumplings that your nanny made at every meal. You loved the color blue so much you insisted on wearing only blue robes and blue shoes and blue ribbons in your hair. You were spoiled. . . . You were *loved*."

His smile takes a regretful turn. I wonder what else he is remembering.

"That scar on your face." My hand goes up to my left cheek, tracing the old mark. "You were five years old, playing by yourself in the courtyard of our house. Back then, I was a general and we lived in the western district of the capital. Your nanny had gone to get something and when she came back, you were crying, and your face was bleeding. You told us that a bird had flown down from the sky and attacked you. I was furious and sent her away. You didn't speak to me for two weeks until I brought her back. You were a stubborn child." He laughs, and then stops abruptly when he looks at my ring again. "You took after your mother in that way."

"What happened to her?" I ask, heart in my throat. "I don't remember her. I was found in Shahmo alone."

"She left." The pain in his voice is clear. "You were showing signs of magic, and even though Emperor Ren Long had lifted the ban on all magic, many opposed him in secret. Your mother feared for your life, and she took matters into her own hands. I managed to track her down to Xinzhu but before I could get there, Ren Long was assassinated and the war against Honguodi began. I had to serve my country once again. Later, I found she'd left Xinzhu soon after, but to where I never knew. I was devastated, but my people needed me."

He pauses and reaches for my hand. This time I don't move away. His eyes are bright with tears when he looks up at me again.

"Family before self, country before family. That is the honorable way to live."

That mother-shaped wound in me deepens. "I wish I knew what happened to her."

"I wish I did, too. I do not believe for a moment that she would have left you alone if she could help it." He sighs heavily. "Ahn-er, she loved you and did what she thought was best for you."

The ache in my chest increases, the wretched feeling of guilt suffocating. I can't hold back my tears.

"It's my fault that Mother is gone. If I wasn't born with magic, none of this would have happened. We'd be a family. She would—"

"Magic can be a *gift*, Ahn. None of this is your fault. The gods work in mysterious ways, and we can only abide by their wishes."

"We were attacked on the way here. There was a man who tried to kill me. He called me a Life Stealer."

"A Tiensai . . ." My father trails off, brow furrowing. "They are unorthodox, and they mean harm to our empire and people. Do not let them taint your views with their nonsensical beliefs. I'm glad you escaped their attack unscathed; we would not have this reunion otherwise."

"Xima Leiye saved me," I reveal. "Do you know him?"

"I was aware the priests had found a girl your age who had extraordinary magic, and I sent Lieutenant Bao to retrieve you, just in case. I hoped it would be you. I owe Leiye a great debt. He is a bright and ambitious young man. Unfortunate that he is the seventh son and illegitimate. He benefits from nothing but his father's name and status."

"I don't understand."

"Some traditions among the gentry are unfair, and in his case, he will have to make his own fortune because his brothers have staked claim on the marquis's vast estate and his army. I was glad he joined the Diyeh priesthood, such talent should not go to waste. But"—my father pats my hand—"we are not here to talk about him."

"I thought Leiye was going to take me to the priests," I say in a small voice. "I thought I was going to be executed."

"I *am* the premier; I can handle the priests."

"But I have *magic*." My heart starts to pound again. Do I tell him that I've murdered two men? Do I tell him how my magic frightens me? Do I tell him about the wicked voice in my head that urges me to use it?

But if I do, my father will surely disown me.

"There are two things you must understand. Firstly, I will never let anyone take you away from me again, and I will never let you suffer any hardship from this day forth. You will live here in the capital with me where I can protect you. Secondly, I am well aware of the nature of your magic. That was what scared your mother—"

"And she was right to be scared!"

"*Ahn*. Listen to me," says my father, voice raised. "Everything is going to be all right. There is no need to worry, you are safe. Perhaps Leiye has told you something about a sword?"

I shudder. "He thinks I can find some fairy-tale sword that will stop the desert from destroying our land."

"I see." He's silent for a few moments. "That is a matter for another day."

He doesn't elaborate any further. Instead, he starts to ask me about the past ten years of my life. I tell him about my village and Shahmo, and about Ama. He listens quietly, holding my hand as if he never wants to let go, patting it whenever my tears threaten to return. An unfamiliar warmth fills my chest. It seems like the gods have answered my prayers after all. But my joy is short-lived because of who I have left behind.

"How about my grandmother? Is there anything you can do for her?"

"What would *you* like to do?"

"Bring her here. She can live with me. She won't be much of a bother to anyone. I'll take care of her," I say wildly.

My father pauses, considering my request.

I clasp his hands in mine. "Please."

"As you wish," he says at last. "I must repay my debt of gratitude to her for raising you all these years."

I'm so relieved by his answer that I almost start crying again. My father shifts to look at something behind me. An attendant is approaching cautiously. My father nods, giving permission for him to come nearer. The man whispers in my father's ear and takes his leave.

My father stands. "I'm afraid something has come up and I am needed in the Inner Court. You must be tired. You should rest."

He offers me his arm and I take it. We go back to the parlor where we first met and an attendant ushers me back to my room.

Once I'm alone, I sprawl onto the canopy bed, and roll around, half giggling at how decadent the room is. Who would have thought I was the daughter of one of the most powerful men in the Shi Empire?

Gold follows you.

I thought the face reader was a con artist, but here I am in the Imperial Palace. What if there were some strange truth to her words? But that would mean whatever she said about my name might be true, too.

Depending on how it is written, it can mean either peace . . . or darkness.

I give myself a shake. It's utter rubbish. A mere coincidence.

A gentle knock on the door interrupts my train of thought.

I sit up. "Come in."

Linxi enters with a lacquered tray in her hands. She places it on the table and inclines her head stiffly. Her friendly manner from before is absent.

"Lady Zhao, I've brought some sweet cakes and tea. Please enjoy and let me know if you need anything else."

She turns to go but I jump up and hold her back.

"Stay with me."

She looks down at the ground. I frown. She called me Lady Zhao;

she must know who I really am now. She must think I'm command-ing her and that she has no choice.

I grab her hands in mine, half pleading. "I just met my father for the first time in many years. I thought I was brought to the cap-ital to be executed. I'm all alone here. If it's all right with you, I'd like some company right now—you don't have to say anything or entertain me. You can sit and do nothing. But if you want to leave, I understand."

She stares at me, stunned. I try for a smile. She stares a little longer, trying to figure me out. Finally, she sighs.

"I thought I told you to be careful of who you trust in the palace. You shouldn't have told me all of that."

"I feel like I can trust you." I'm not sure why, but something about Linxi makes me feel at ease. I can only hope my instincts are not wrong.

Her mouth twists before breaking into a smile. "I can stay. The empress knows I'm here, so she won't be asking for me. Have some tea and cake. Maybe it'll help you feel better."

I grin and pick up the cup. There are tiny golden flowers and strange red things floating in the tea.

"Chilled osmanthus tea with goji berries. I thought you might like something refreshing," Linxi says.

I take a tentative sip before gulping everything down in one shot. Then I take a large bite of the cake, ignoring the crumbs that fall onto my blouse.

"Delicious," I mumble with a mouth full of food. I haven't eaten the whole day. I look up to see Linxi looking at me oddly. "Is some-thing wrong?"

"It is better for a lady of the court to take her time when drinking and eating," she says delicately.

I stop in the middle of wiping my mouth with my sleeve.

"Oh," I say, flushing. "I'll try to remember that."

She must think I'm an uneducated peasant with terrible manners, which isn't far from the truth. The weight of my newfound identity rests heavy on my shoulders. I'm beginning to realize that my father's status—*my* status—means everything is going to change.

That *I* have to change.

"I need your help."

"I will do my best," Linxi replies right away.

"I want you to tell me everything I need to know about life in the palace," I command. "I want you to teach me how to be a lady of the court."

Her mouth opens slightly in surprise. Then she gathers herself and bows.

"Yes, Lady Zhao."

12
AHN

I didn't think life in the Imperial Palace would be this daunting. There are so many rules to learn, both the ones laid down by Imperial law and the unspoken ones Linxi shares with me. And this is only for the Inner Court where I reside.

My father has requested that I stay in the palace until his residence in the capital is properly prepared. I'm to have my own set of rooms there, and Ama will live with me. Excitedly, I pen a letter and ask Linxi to send it to Li Guo.

Days in the palace begin early. I rise at dawn from the most comfortable bed I've ever slept in to spend a tedious hour in front of the mirror waiting for Linxi to paint my face and coil my hair in some complicated manner. Then I dress in pristine white silks so expensive they could feed my entire village for a month.

With Linxi's help, I try to change my manner of speech to sound more high-born. When walking, I take smaller steps, hands poised primly in front of me instead of striding with my arms swinging loose from side to side. At mealtimes, I make sure I hold my chopsticks the genteel way even though I want to shove food in my mouth. My bites are minuscule and dainty, and my bowl is never empty at the end.

The first time I ate with my father and a couple of minor court officials, I had to hold down my anger at the amount of food that was left unfinished. Later, Linxi told me the attendants would sometimes sneak the leftovers back to the servants' quarters, and only then did I feel a little better.

"Let's try again," says Linxi now, patient as ever.

I mentioned offhand to my father that I liked Linxi, and immediately, she was assigned to attend to me. While I can't get used to the idea of having a lady-in-waiting, it's comforting to have a friend.

I huff and try to stand. The new shoes I have on are square-toed with pretty whorls all over the fabric and a stupid two-inch clog heel that rests in the center of the sole. Clumsily, I teeter up and down my room.

"How am I supposed to run if I need to?" I complain. "Or climb a wall?"

"You won't be running in the palace, and you definitely won't be climbing any walls."

"But what if someone tries to murder me again?" I say, half joking.

"Then you can clobber them with your heels," replies Linxi archly. I laugh, grateful that she is here with me. Born to a farmer in a far-off province, she understands the hardships of life outside the capital in a way the gentry does not.

"I guess they do look pretty deadly. I could give someone a concussion." I lift my skirts to glare at the wretched shoes. "How do women get anything done in this contraption?"

Linxi tugs my skirts back down firmly. "With practice."

I sigh and walk around the room again. I made the mistake of eavesdropping on some court ladies on my second day in the palace, only to hear cruel words about my missing formal footwear. At first, I was ashamed and embarrassed, but that turned into a dogged determination to prove my worth.

My father had the ear of Emperor Gao Long, and he will have the ear of the crown prince when the boy takes the Dragon Throne. He is an important man, and I will not bring shame on my family name.

I continue to practice until it's time to go to my father's private study. He has requested for my presence before noon today. Unusual. So far, we have met for either dinner or tea after as he is busy with state affairs in the day. Through our conversations, I piece together bits of my childhood, forming a kind of mottled painting of my early existence. He likes to share news from across our land, too. Every day, there's a report of a farm that lost its crops overnight, a river that dried up . . .

The Tiensai's dark magic is spreading. If nothing is done to stop the land from dying, our people will starve.

Your magic is different. *And that is why the Tiensai want to kill you.*

Leiye's words return to haunt me. Was what he said true? Am I the Life Stealer? Could the sword of light really cure the disease inflicting our land? My father hasn't said a word about this matter or about my magic, and I'm too cowardly to bring it up on my own.

I dismiss Linxi from her duties and venture out alone. The palace is growing familiar to me and I try to keep a mental map of the various parlors and courtyards and rooms I've been in.

Outside the study, I smooth my fingers over my hair to neaten it, glad that Linxi opted for a simpler hairstyle today. Half of my hair is braided and curled into a bun secured by pearl pins and turquoise enamel hair combs while the rest waterfalls down my back to my waist. Once I feel tidy enough, I knock smartly on the door.

Moments later, it opens. It's not my father but someone else dressed in ivory robes with only an emerald ribbon in his hair to identify his Qin lineage.

"What are *you* doing here?" I demand. The scar on my leg itches, reminding me of the mark he left on me.

Leiye shoots me an irritated look. "The premier wanted to talk to me. Come in, he's waiting for you."

I enter, noticing how familiar Leiye is with this private space that I naively thought was special to me and my father. I haven't seen Leiye since the day he brought me to the palace. Only the Heavens know what ghastly things he's been up to.

The study is large and filled with books stacked tightly on shelves and old maps hanging on the walls. An imposing table piled high with parchment sits in the middle of the room. My father looks up from his desk in the corner and I greet him with a bow.

He beckons me over. "I want to discuss an important matter with you today, Ahn. Your magic."

My muscles tense. Somehow, I expected this, but part of me refuses to accept it. I don't want to talk about my magic or even think of it. But from the look on my father's face, I know I can't avoid it.

He touches a knob along the side of a tall cabinet and slides the door open, removing something bound in red silk. Carefully, he unties the ribbons. The book that emerges is old and worn at the edges, bound by faded blue cloth. He stretches the parchment and the manuscript opens horizontally like an accordion.

"Look."

I scan the writing, trying to decipher its meaning. I did learn to read as a child, but in my village, school was a collection of broken tables and chairs and a teacher who spent most of his days snoozing in the shade. These words in the book seem to be in a different language.

"I don't recognize the characters," I finally admit.

"That's because it is written in the ancient script," says Leiye.

"The dead language? No one has used it in centuries."

"Some scholars and historians still study it here in the capital. I have been fortunate to learn from one of them."

Leiye's bragging gets an approving smile from my father. I bristle, annoyed that I've appeared ignorant in comparison.

My father flips to another page and we turn our attention to an illustration of two beautiful swords. One white, the other black. On the opposite page, a map. I recognize the isles of Xinzhu, curved like a fisherman's hook or a crescent moon, and nestled eastward across the Emerald Sea. My father points at a faint ink mark that looks like an accidental splotch at the southern end of the string of islands.

"Dragon's Teeth Pass. Have you heard of it?"

I shake my head. He turns to Leiye who obliges.

"The pass is at the edge of the Dragon's Triangle, which is in the Emerald Sea. It is an area prone to shipwrecks and the ships they do recover are often empty and missing their crew. Anyone found on board has exhibited signs of madness."

"Sounds preposterous," I say, quietly seething. This boy-priest keeps making me look bad in front of my father.

"The pass does exist." My father's raven eyes pin on me. "And that is where the White Jade Sword is rumored to be."

"What are you saying, Father?" I stammer. "Do you believe in the tale of the blacksmith? Do you think *I'll* be able to find the sword if it even exists?"

Taking in my discomfort, he folds the pages of the book neatly and wraps the red silk back around the book. "Let us take a walk."

We leave the study, and my father gives instructions to an attendant outside who scurries away immediately. Then, he leads us out to the northern wing of the palace where traditionally, the Emperors of Shi have resided. I wonder if the crown prince lives here now.

We cross an empty courtyard huge enough to fit a battalion of soldiers, and head to an enormous building sitting on the top of a long flight of stairs so wide it could fit twenty men shoulder to shoulder. A five-clawed dragon dancing among swirls of clouds is carved into stone in the middle of the stairway. The mark of the emperor.

By the time we reach the pair of bronze guardian lion statues at the top, I'm panting, though my father and Leiye seem hardly affected by the physical exertion.

"This is the Dragon Pagoda," my father says. "The seat of the emperor during the inspection of troops. We are only allowed to be here without the crown prince because he has not ascended the throne, and in the absence of an emperor, the military is under my purview."

We head to the stairs inside. My legs ache as we climb, but I do my best to keep up. At the top, I'm rewarded by two things: the sight of teacups and plates of fresh fruits on the table in the balcony, and the magnificent sight of the capital.

My father looks ahead. "Beautiful, is it not?"

I nod enthusiastically.

"What do you see, Ahn?"

His tone catches my attention. He's expecting something from me. I move to the edge of the balcony and look again, straining to see what it is my father wants me to notice.

From this height, the view extends over the front gates and fortress walls and down into the city. Buildings stretch as far as my eye can see, many with gilded roofs glistening. The streets are dotted with green and bustle with color—silks worn by the people. Water from fountains create sprays that shimmer gently, and everything looks idyllic.

I squint in the sunlight. It's a clear day. Empty of clouds, the sky is an unblemished azure. The longer I stare, the more it reminds me of the sky over my village, over Shahmo. It's the same sky that spans over the hundreds of towns south and west of Beishou, where there are no fountains and no clean streets. No rich silks, but plain cotton. No full bellies, but children who go to bed hungry every night.

No hope, but despair.

There's a growing fury in me against the boy who will rule our empire. I'm sure *his* stomach is always full.

My hands grip the edge of the brightly painted railing as I speak. "I see a city that takes from the rest of the nation and doesn't give back. I see a leader who doesn't know the daily reality of his people, someone who is content to stay coddled within these walls. Maybe the crown prince needs to leave his palace before he takes his seat on the throne. Maybe he ought to *earn* that seat."

I step back, wondering if my father will reprimand me for being disrespectful of the crown prince. To my surprise, he laughs.

"You may not know this, but the Empire is in jeopardy." He holds a hand up to halt my questions.

He takes a seat while Leiye and I remain standing. Lines etch into his forehead, and I see white among his black hair. There's a pang in my heart. His silver half-mask hides the pain of his past, but he suddenly looks too old, too weary. A man who has given everything to his country.

"Yes, there is a truce with Honguodi," he continues. "But the transition of power is a time of extreme vulnerability for a nation. The crown prince is young and by all accounts, still grieving deeply. In his fragile state, we cannot hope to have a firm hand at the helm. So we must do what we can to ensure our nation's survival in this difficult period of change."

Next to me, Leiye stiffens. He's looking intently at my father, though my father doesn't notice. My suspicions rise. Does Leiye disagree? Does his loyalty lie with the damned priesthood and not the Dragon Throne?

"You are right, Ahn," my father says. "Our land is diseased; it cannot support our people and our troops. We must think of the future. We need to secure our peace and prosperity, which means we need to find a way to get rid of the desert."

I meet his gaze, understanding the question it holds. He wants to know if I will help him. If I will find the sword of light.

Why would the desert still spread if those false priests keep killing the ones they call the Tiensai?

Maybe Ama has a point, though not the one she intended. The capture and punishment of Tiensai haven't stopped the desert from growing, which means it isn't the solution. Something else must be done. I don't know if the White Jade Sword exists. Maybe it will all be a futile search and nothing can stop the desertification. But shouldn't I at least try?

I think of home, about how the desert invaded my village and destroyed our crops, and how the children there will know nothing but a bleak future. I think of Li Guo, of how his parents grieved when his brothers died in the wars, how I spent days and nights worrying that he might be shipped out to the front and meet the same fate.

A grim determination settles in my bones.

"What do you need me to do?"

"It is said that the sword of light seeks its master. You must learn to control your magic, learn to use it. The sword will call out to you when you are ready."

I lower my head, a promise knotting itself into my chest. "I will try my best."

"Good. Leiye will train you."

"Wouldn't it be better if my teacher were someone more experienced?" I say in as diplomatic a tone as I possibly can.

"This young man's talent surpasses many masters of magic." The fondness in my father's voice riles me. Leiye's expression is unreadable as he listens to my father's praise. "I have watched him grow up before my very eyes. I trust him to take care of my only daughter."

"But—"

"No harm will come to you, Ahn. Do not worry," assures my father. He has made up his mind and there is no changing it.

"Yes, Father," I concede.

"Thank you for believing in me, Your Excellency." Leiye bows low and I catch a small, enigmatic smile just before he straightens again.

I don't trust this priest. My father may sing his praises, but my gut tells me to watch out.

Night falls sooner than expected. There's a soft knock on my door after dinner. Now that my father isn't around, Leiye drops all formalities with me, and we fall back into the testy understanding we had after escaping from the Tiensai ambush.

"Where are we going?" I say.

"Western wing."

"To revel with the concubines?"

He doesn't look amused. "They've been sent to live in the city." He doesn't elaborate and I don't care enough to ask.

Shortly, we arrive and for once, I don't spot any attendants or guards lurking in the shadows. I wonder if Leiye ordered them to leave. We walk to a garden, and I can vaguely make out a small pond in the middle.

"This will do," says Leiye.

"It's too dark. I can't see anything."

He flicks his wrist and I almost jump out of my skin as flames shoot out of his hand. With a few quick movements, he lights the torches strung up around the perimeter. I didn't notice they were there before. The place is lit well enough now, and I can see everything clearly. I was right about the pond. There's a table near it and, curiously, an empty bronze bowl and a bucket of what looks like soil.

"You've made preparations," I remark, eyeing the setup. "Are you sure we should be using magic out in the open like this? Isn't it banned?"

"Not all magic."

"Then why are we doing this in the middle of the night in some secluded place like a couple of criminals?"

"I wanted to impress you with my fire." He tilts his head and smiles charmingly, as if we are on a romantic date. I give him a withering look and he drops his act, his cool and unflappable manner returning. "Only Tiensai magic is disallowed. You knew that, Ahn. What are you trying to get at?"

"I want to know how the priesthood recruits," I say, stalling for time. "Do you need to have fire magic to become one of them?"

"Fire is preferred because it is one of the rarer affinities and difficult to master because it requires you to be in total control of yourself. Having total mastery over your affinity is also rare and hence, a huge advantage." Leiye flutters his fingers and pretty orange flames, like those from candles, dance across his hand. "And there is a test one must pass in order to be accepted into the priesthood."

"What test?"

"I am not allowed to divulge the secrets of the Diyeh."

"What if *I* wanted to be a priest?" I say, more out of morbid curiosity than anything else.

Leiye narrows his eyes. "I don't think your father would like that."

I don't refute him.

He circles me, sizing me up as he goes. "Ideally, you should've started training when you were a child when your magic first manifested—"

"I was too busy trying to stay alive and hiding from you priests."

His lips curl. "Why are you being so defensive, Ahn?"

"I'm not!"

He circles me again, and I try to stay composed. He stops, gaze piercing into me.

"You're scared, aren't you? You are frightened of your own magic. You fear . . . yourself."

"No, I don't," I say too quickly, refusing to admit how close he got to the truth.

"It's all right to be scared. Magic can be dangerous. A little fear will keep you disciplined."

I try not to shiver.

"Martial arts would help with your cultivation. It allows you to understand your own body, how it works, its limits—*your* limits. Only then will you know how far you can push yourself and when to stop."

"Are you going to train me in martial arts?"

"Of course not. It takes years and we don't have time. What you lack in physical strength you will just have to make up with magic."

I cross my arms, teeth cutting into my inner cheek. "What do you propose we do then?"

"First, we test you." He points at the bucket and bronze bowl.

"Earth, water, wind, fire, or metal—the five elements. We already know about your life-stealing magic, but I think it'd be useful to know what other affinities you may have so that we can start by working on those first until you grasp the full extent of your power."

"If my life-stealing magic is the one that will help me find the sword, why don't we start with that first?" I say without thinking.

"Because you might steal the life of everything around you."

I stop breathing for a moment. That's why Leiye brought me here. *That's* why he cleared out the compound. So that if I lose control of my magic, no one else will be harmed—or killed.

No one else but *him*.

My father entrusted me to Leiye, not only because of his belief in Leiye's abilities.

He did so because to him, this boy is expendable.

"But *you* are here," I whisper, suddenly bone cold.

"Sacrifices have to be made, Lady Zhao," says Leiye, utterly serious. "After all, we are trying to save the world."

13
ALTAN

In the desert, when the moonrise meets the sunset, the world is bathed in beauty. Turn your head to one end of the horizon and you will see bands of cool blues and purples from the deepest indigo to the palest lilac. Glance the other way and the sky bleeds warm tangerine to rosy coral. Look up and the two worlds meld seamlessly into each other, clasping their vibrant fingers into a prayer.

I rouse to that very sky above me, groggy and confused. I'm not in the cavern anymore. There is no spring, no water anywhere. Is this a dream? Or a vision sent by the Soul Beast?

I hear my mother's voice, singing a soft refrain from an old lullaby. I see an eight-year-old boy lying on the sand, looking up. One of his eyes is golden and glinting. A little girl with a cheeky grin is next to him. Suddenly, she bursts into giggles.

Shhh, Mother's asleep, says the boy. He points at the first of the twinkling stars. *That one. If we follow it and head northeast, we will find our way home.*

The girl snorts, laughter gone. *We don't have a home anymore, Jin.*

The boy sits up, his expression pained. *We will always have a home, as long as we're together. We'll find our way back—don't give up.*

The girl whispers back fiercely, *I will never give up. We will find Father's murderer. We will take back what's ours. We will go home.* She squeezes the boy's hand. *As long as we're together.*

I blink, and they vanish. I am alone again, a biting pang in my heart.

There are bones on the sand a few paces from me. A bird's skeleton, just like the one in the cavern. They rattle, slowly floating up. Before my eyes, a giant bird morphs to life. It shimmers, translucent against sand and sky. But there is no mistaking its resplendent pheasant head and indigo and emerald peacock tail.

The Phoenix.

It gazes at me, feathery lashes fluttering over large gold-flecked irises. Its beak opens and dulcet tones echo.

I know why you are here.

In my head, the Soul Beast sounds like Mother.

"Then you must know what I want," I say.

The path of vengeance is a dark one. There must be balance in this world, and in a person. You should keep the light in you while it remains. There are other ways to find peace. Your way requires a sacrifice that you may find too great to bear.

"I am not afraid. *This* is the only way."

The Phoenix raises a leg, touching its claw to my forehead. I gasp as pain erupts. Exhumed memories staccato in my mind: a boy with both eyes intact, one a deep amber-gold; the boy with a blade in hand, raising it to his face; an old man with a snowy white beard running into the room, too late to stop what is about to happen . . .

Why did you do that? asks the old man later. The boy lies in bed, face flushed, brow sweaty, the bandages around his head and eye stained with blood.

I don't want to be like him, he replies, face twisted in pain.

The old man sighs. *Even if you have inherited his eyes, even if his blood runs true in your veins, Yuan Long's affinity does not run in you. My boy . . . remember, you are not your great-grandfather. You are not the Life Stealer.*

The boy says nothing. Grinding his teeth, he reaches a shaky hand toward his own face before abruptly drawing it back, not yet able to come to terms with what he had done.

The memory fades.

The Phoenix removes its claw and the pain in my head dissipates. Hunching over, hands on thighs, I force myself to breathe. Force myself to forget again.

How much more can you lose, child? the Phoenix says softly.

"I have lost everything." My head hangs as the truth hits me. "I have nothing more to lose."

A gust of wind pushes me back as the Phoenix flaps its wings. My hands go up, ready to block the sand, but none of it rises from the ground.

You wish to be emperor. But being emperor is like hearing a crash of thunder from a clear sky. Unexpected things will happen, and their explanations will not always be as they seem. Your crown will become a burden. You must make tough decisions when you hold millions of lives in the palm of your hand.

The Phoenix blinks slowly, and I see a world burning in flames in its eyes.

Lives are fragile; your palm can be a refuge or a cage. Are you certain you are ready for this?

I meet its fiery gaze. "Yes."

Very well. But everything comes with a price and your choice will be paid in blood. You will find it difficult to treasure that which is most precious to you.

The Soul Beast blinks again. A single teardrop flows from its eye and bursts, sprinkling dew on my face, the scent of fresh grass and honey in my nostrils. I start to feel faint. My legs go weak, my vision fades. . . .

Altan!

I'm underwater. This time, I am truly awake. My lungs seize. *Can't breathe.* I thrash my way up to the surface, chest expanding with relief when my head bursts out of the water. I'm not far from the edge of the pool, so I swim over and hoist myself onto dry ground.

What happened? I don't remember going into the spring. I thought I'd fallen asleep and dreamt of the Soul Beast. But it seems I did encounter it. And that voice that pulled me out to consciousness . . . I'd thought it was Mother or my sister. But it sounded like someone else. Someone less familiar. The face of the girl from the desert town flits through my head but that image disappears quickly, and all I am left with is that scent of green and honey in the air, the voice of the Soul Beast in my head.

Everything comes with a price and your choice will be paid in blood.

Tang Wei looks up from her dinner and gapes at me like she doesn't believe who she is seeing. "You're alive."

I put my weapons down wearily. "I thought you'd be happy."

"I *am* happy. You were gone for so long. I'm just . . ."

"Disappointed you didn't get to say *I told you so*?"

"Shut up, shut up. I was so worried. I shouldn't have left you there alone." She stands and throws her arms around me.

I hug her back. I didn't think I'd be so glad to see her, but I am. Eventually, she lets go and sits back down, wiping the back of her hand over her eyes.

"Are you crying?" I tease.

Tang Wei turns her face from me, sniffing loudly. "No."

I can't help but laugh at her obvious lie. "Look at me. I'm *fine*."

My stomach rumbles with hunger and that draws a smile from her.

"Shut up and eat. You must be starving," she nags good-naturedly.

I slide onto the wooden bench across from her, pull the dishes on the table toward me, and start stuffing my face with rice and braised pork.

Tang Wei leans close, voice lowered. "Did you find the Phoenix?"

"Mmm," I say, shoving more rice into my mouth.

"Did you get your wish?"

"I think so. I won't know until I meet the Life Stealer and he uses his magic on me, of course. *If* he uses his magic on me."

Her face pales.

"It'll be fine." I check the dining room of this shabby inn. The waiter has retreated into the kitchen and the innkeeper is dozing off at the register up front. The two other patrons—locals, I assume—are red-faced with alcohol and likely to pass out before they can eavesdrop on us. Seems safe enough to talk. I swallow my food, gulp down some hot tea, and fill Tang Wei in on what happened with the Phoenix.

She doesn't say a word. Doesn't even play with her daggers. I nudge her after a few minutes of silence.

"Are you all right?"

"I'm thinking."

"About what?"

"About our next steps," she replies. "Master Sun has arranged a meeting with our southern contact. They're interested in your proposed alliance. We'll meet under the cover of Gao Long's funeral in twelve days. If we leave tomorrow, we should get to Beishou in time."

I nearly drop my chopsticks. The mourning period will be over in twelve days? Have I been up on that mountain for so long? Time must pass differently in Jiyu Spring. I must have been stuck in the cavern longer than I thought.

I feel her eyes lingering on me. "What's wrong? Is there something else?"

"You seem different, that's all." Tang Wei continues cautiously, "What do you think the sacrifice will be?"

I twirl my chopsticks. That same question has been puzzling me since my encounter with the Phoenix.

Your choice will be paid in blood. You will find it difficult to treasure that which is most precious to you.

"I don't know. At first, I thought it might have been my magic, but I tested it, and I still have it."

"*Is* your magic the most precious thing to you?"

"Obviously."

Tang Wei doesn't question me further. I sense that she doesn't agree with me, but what else could it be? Without magic, I can't avenge my family.

No other thing in this world is more important to me.

14
AHN

The last days of summer are relentless. The afternoon sun is so hot and the air so humid that my hair has fallen flat today, plastering itself to my forehead. I wipe my brow with my sleeve and grimace when I see the smear of powder Linxi had so carefully brushed onto my face earlier.

Leiye stands a short distance away, observing my every move. "Again."

Sighing, I breathe deep and focus. The blue-and-white vase of chrysanthemums on the table in front of me has remained the same all day. Bright, cheerful, and alive.

My father says the only way I can find the White Jade Sword is to master my magic. Only then, will I be able to sense the artifact's presence. So far, my training has been futile. Sure, I've learned the basics of cultivation, how to manipulate my breath, how to control my qì. I can even freeze water at will and move small objects a short distance away.

But the only affinity that matters is the one that killed the two men back in Shahmo.

Every time I tap into that different well of magic, every time I *think* of it, I shut down. Dread descends, pulling me into shadow. Images fly like jagged stone, shredding my concentration: the pale green glow coming from the two men, their shriveling bodies, the terrible choking sounds they made.

In death, the two men from Shahmo are more present than ever.

I don't tell Leiye or my father this. Neither do I tell them about the strange dreams and the stranger voice that haunt my sleep.

There's magic inside you. Reach for it. My father's voice is firm and comforting in my head.

I weight my stance and raise my hands. Qì flows from my fingertips, like a gradual release of warming air. Magic. But not the one I need. Leiye doesn't want me to freeze those flowers or draw the water out from the vase.

He wants me to take their life essence.

The pale yellow petals glow in the sun, seeming to exclaim, *Alive! Alive!* And why shouldn't they be? How can an affinity like mine— one that steals *life*—be the only thing that can save the Empire?

Whatever magic I summoned vanishes.

My fingers curl, fighting the urge to throw the vase. I've learned quickly to control my temper. We're in the secluded nook of the western wing, but I'm on guard. The flurry of attendants elsewhere in the palace compound has trained me. They appear and disappear like mayflies, always swarming to help or usher me around. One wrong move from me could end up in either malicious gossip, or worse—I could hurt someone with my magic.

Leiye clears his throat loudly, unperturbed by the heat despite having stood here as long as I have. His white robes are pristine, his hair perfect, that white streak shining softly in the sun. Unlike me, he looks like nobility. He looks like he *belongs* here. I bet he doesn't even sweat.

"Try again," he says, infuriatingly calm.

"Can we take a break?"

He remains stone-faced.

I roll my eyes, masking my fear as petulance. It's easier that way. "Come on, it's so hot and I'm hungry."

"Only if you best me in three moves. No magic."

"That's impossible." Even though he has taught me the basic skills of wielding a sword, I'm no swordswoman.

"Mind over matter. If you think of defeat even before you try, how will you ever win?"

I make a strangled noise, curse words barely held down.

"Fine," I say. I want this ordeal to be over. There's no way I can beat him. But I could feign an injury. Maybe that'll get him into trouble with my father and teach him a lesson. "Three moves."

He tosses me a sword and I manage to catch it. "I'll give you an advantage. I won't draw my weapon."

He beckons me to attack with a carelessness that grates on my bones. Like all the other swords I've tried from the armory, the sword in my hand feels imbalanced and unwieldly. This is a waste of time. But something in Leiye's expression, that look between disdain and boredom, it wakes a seed of anger—of jealousy—in me.

He has proven himself to my father.

I lunge.

He dodges my first two strikes easily. I retreat, sweat rolling down my back. He beckons again, mocking. I want to slap that smirk off him. But strength and skill are useless here. I have to use my brain. A slight breeze picks up, rustling the dead leaves on the ground. My mind cools. I swipe a strand of hair out of my eyes, a vague plan forming in my head.

I feint the way Leiye taught me a few days back. As expected, he sees through it and sidesteps, swatting me off like I'm a gadfly. I pretend to spin away. At the last moment before my foot lands, I pivot. Thrust my sword. Strike his shoulder.

But there's no resistance. Only air.

Off-balance, I trip and fall.

I brace for impact but Leiye catches me before I hit the ground. He steadies me back on my feet, strong hands gripping my waist. He doesn't let go. We're close. Close enough for me to catch the scent of sandalwood incense on his clothes. To see how his dark lashes line those lovely slate-gray eyes. To feel his heat. To wonder how soft his cheek would feel if I touched it.

A smile ghosts his lips like he knows what I'm thinking.

Ten Hells, Ahn. He burned a man alive.

I shove him back and flick my wrist up. Metal meets skin.

"Three moves," I declare, ignoring the flush creeping up my neck.

The sword is heavy, but I keep it under his chin. The sharp point of my blade at his throat doesn't seem to bother him. What will happen if I apply pressure? How will this priest defend himself?

"I counted four," Leiye murmurs. His smile fades and those slate-gray eyes darken. "Unless your fall was part of that charade?"

"Obviously."

"Clever."

He doesn't believe me. But there's no time to argue. Someone is calling my name.

I lower my sword hastily and turn around. It's Linxi. She curtsies and I nod back. I wonder how much she saw.

"Young Master Xima and Lady Ahn, please pardon my intrusion. Her Majesty has requested Lady Ahn's presence."

Irritation flickers on Leiye's face, but he can't disobey orders from the empress dowager herself. "Of course."

I hand my sword over to him. He takes it without a word, cold demeanor returning.

Once we're in the palace halls and out of his earshot, I whisper to Linxi, "Thanks for getting me out of training with that jerk. Smart of you to use the empress's name this time."

Linxi's eyes are wide with urgency. "It's not a ruse, Ahn. She really wants to meet you."

"What? Ten Hel—" I clap a hand over my mouth. "Sorry. Why does she want to see me?"

"I don't know. You look a mess! I can't present you in your current state." She grabs my hand and drags me along. "We have five minutes to get you ready. *Hurry.*"

Lithe and graceful, Empress Dowager Zhenxi doesn't look old enough to have a son the crown prince's age. Swathed in layers of white silk embroidered with gold phoenixes, jewels drip from the heavy necklace around her neck and the rings on her fingers. Her midnight hair sits high upon her head, fastened by gold and purple jewelry and a turquoise fāzān in the shape of a kingfisher.

Surprisingly, her face remains unpainted except for her lips which are blood-red. It isn't as if she needs any embellishment. She's the most beautiful woman I have ever seen.

Shoulders thrown back, I sit straight as an iron rod, my neck pulled taut by an invisible string. When offered, I drink from my ridiculously tiny teacup. There's barely enough tea inside for a real taste.

"How is the tea, my dear?" asks Empress Zhenxi.

"It's . . ." I search desperately for a suitable word. "Fragrant."

Her lady-in-waiting pours more into my cup before stepping back to a corner of the pavilion.

"It is a custom blend that I save for very special guests." The empress smiles. A slender manicured fingernail strokes her cup. "I call it the Oriole's Tears. I do hope you can appreciate the soothing honey-like flavor under that green burst of freshness."

"Yes, it's wonderful." I take another hasty sip.

There's a melodic lilt to her manner of speech. I wonder how long it took her to mimic the way people in Beishou speak. I heard she was born to a lower-class family in one of the Southern Colonies along the Straits of Nandah. For years, there were rumors of how she worked her way up from attendant to concubine to Imperial consort, and finally, empress. Some say it was her beauty that ensnared Gao Long, others say it was her wit.

"How are you liking palace life? Do you miss your friends and family back home?" she asks.

"Everyone has been kind to me. I do miss my adoptive grandmother, but my father has sent for her."

"How thoughtful of him to do so. When will your grandmother arrive? I shall have a chamber prepared for her. Near yours, of course."

I stand and curtsey with my head bowed low. "Thank you, Your Majesty. But my father says that we will live in Zhao Manor once she arrives."

"But I would like to meet her. Surely the both of you can stay in the palace for a little while longer?"

"Of course, Your Majesty," I agree obediently, and sit back down. I don't think I could have refused her request. "However, I'm not sure when she'll arrive in the capital. My father has been rather busy of late."

"He isn't going all the way to your village himself, is he?" she says with a short laugh.

"Oh, no, he's not. I meant . . ." I hesitate. I asked my father a week ago if he'd sent anyone to my village. He said it slipped his mind, but that he would do so immediately.

"If Premier Zhao does not have the time to oversee this matter, come to me," says the empress firmly. "I am more than willing to handle it. One should not be apart from family for so long."

"Your Majesty, you mustn't think that my father—" I almost gasp when the empress reaches across the table and holds my hand. Her skin is smooth and cool.

"My dear, you have no idea what your father has done for the Empire. He has devoted his life to our people. We are indebted to him." She pats my hand. "He has much on his plate, and anything I can do to help, I will."

She smiles warmly at me, and I can't help but smile back with pride. All this time, I thought my parents were ordinary peasants, but things turned out so differently. A pang of guilt gnaws at me. I need to work harder with my training and master my life-stealing affinity. I want to make my father proud.

"I heard you had trouble remembering your early years." The empress places a small glass vial of clear liquid on the stone table. "This is a tincture extracted from a rare plant that grows alongside the crystal lakes of the north. It helps in clearing the memory pathways and may be useful in cases of amnesia. I thought you might like to have it. It must be difficult not to be able to remember your own mother."

I bite my lips to keep them from trembling. The empress's eyes are kind, her smile understanding. She lifts a palm to my cheek and cups it gently.

"I have always wanted a daughter. But a son . . ." Her smile turns cynical, sad even. Her voice lowers. "A *son* means security. In life, we do what we must to survive—more, if we wish to thrive. I am sure you understand that."

I don't know what to say. It feels like she's telling me a secret, even though I'm sure the two ladies-in-waiting near us can hear every word.

"Speaking of sons," she goes on. "There will be a banquet after the funeral of our late Emperor. I did not see your name on the list, but I would like you to attend it. Tai Shun has taken his father's passing extremely hard, and his mood has been dismal. Will you do me a favor and keep him company while you are there? I am sure he will find the banquet more tolerable if there is someone his age to talk to."

"I—yes, Your Majesty. I will be there." I'm not sure how *I* could help cheer the crown prince up. But I will have to try.

"Tell me, my dear, what are some of your favorite dishes? The ones your grandmother used to prepare for you—I can have them brought to your chambers for dinner later."

My mouth hangs for a second before I compose myself. "That's much too kind of you, Your Majesty. I—"

"Must accept my offer," she finishes with another smile.

I nod shyly. "There is one dish: braised duck, with black peppercorns, star anise, and dark sauce."

My mouth almost waters as I remember the first time Ama made that dish for me, back when she was still working and our village hadn't been destroyed by the desert. The longing in my heart grows. *You'll see her soon*, I remind myself. My father will keep his promise.

"Done." The empress nods at one of her ladies-in-waiting and the woman leaves immediately for the kitchens. I bow to the empress, grateful that I've found another kind soul in this grand place.

I'm on a ship. The sea is a vast expanse of sparkling green tinged with blue. Shiny silver fish jump in and out of the water alongside the vessel like escorts. I blink, and everything turns dark.

Nightfall.

A shriek of metal and bone slices the air. The wail reverberates in my ears as the hull splits. I cry out as the ship plunges, dragging me down into the liquid abyss.

There's another presence in the water. Large, looming—hurtling toward me.

"I have been waiting for you."

"Who are you?" Bubbles come out of my mouth. They float up toward the light above. I shudder as the light fades and the chill of the water cuts through me.

I see a tail, scales, burning red eyes with bright yellow centers.

"Wh-what are you?"

"I am . . ."

The dream changes.

I'm a child at a shadow puppet show, sitting on the shoulders of my father. My faceless mother is beside us, laughing and clapping along to the music.

The melody is a funeral dirge, a mourning of souls.

"Do you see the puppets, Ahn-er?"

I nod.

My father turns to me.

And I start to scream.

I gasp awake. I throw off the blankets and sit up, brow wet with cold sweat. Faint moonlight seeps through a window left ajar. Strange. I thought Linxi shut all the windows before she left.

I get up and pull on an outer robe, rubbing my arms. My dream disturbs me. Something about it felt real. I want to ask my father more questions about my childhood and whether my parents had ever brought me to a puppet show. It's late, but he might be awake since he often works into the night.

Remnants of my dream linger in my mind as I shuffle my way to his private study. A shiver runs down my spine and I pull my robe tight. The palace is too quiet and empty, but I'm sure some attendants or guards are stationed throughout the softly lit corridors.

There's a light from my father's study. He must be in there. Before I can approach, it snuffs out. I stay in the shadows, waiting. The door cracks open. Someone dressed in black slips out. I could recognize that build and gait anywhere, even in a crowd, even in darkness.

Leiye.

What's he doing here in the middle of the night? Why is he behaving so furtively? I catch a flash of red in his hand before he tucks something into his robes. Did he steal something from my father?

I start to follow him but stop in mid-step. I'm not ready for a confrontation. Best to check first. I head into the study and light the lamp. Everything looks to be in place. What could he have taken?

Red.

I go to the glass cabinet where several manuscripts wrapped in red silk lie. After feeling around, I find a small lever and press it. Something clicks into place, and I slide the door open.

"One, two, three . . ." I continue to count under my breath. *Five.*

Six manuscripts were in here. Red ribbons and silks scatter on the floor as I unwrap everything. I exhale slowly. Leiye took the book that my father showed me—the one with the drawing of the twin swords and the map of the Emerald Sea.

I should tell my father about this. Since he's not in here, he must be asleep in his bedroom. But what do I say? Maybe this is nothing. Maybe my father told Leiye to take the book. Maybe I'm letting my jealousy and wild imagination get the better of me.

Thinking, I lean against the cabinet. It tips under my weight and

I almost fall. I clap a hand over my mouth to muffle my surprise as a panel of the wall starts to shift.

A dark, narrow room just a few paces wide reveals itself. The palace is ancient; there must be areas that have fallen into disuse and are lost to memory. It smells musty in there and it looks empty. I doubt my father even knows this room exists. I pull the cabinet back into place and the wall panel slides shut.

Quickly, I rewrap the books and place them back where I found them and return to my room. I could tell my father about everything I saw. If he told Leiye to take that book, then all would be fine. But if he did not . . . Maybe I should keep tonight a secret. That way I could find out what Leiye's true motive is.

I remember Linxi's warning from my first day in the palace. *Be careful who you trust.* I don't trust Leiye. And I won't fall for his tricks.

15
ALTAN

I should not be here.

The capital is too dangerous for a fugitive like me—a prince who is supposed to be dead.

Yet, here I am. Unable to resist the temptation of witnessing the spectacle of my enemy's demise.

I should feel elation. Some kind of joy, even if it is a twisted one. I search for it but come up empty. Perhaps I am disappointed it was not my own two hands that put Gao Long in his grave. His untimely passing is a hitch in my plans. But, I can be patient.

When your list of enemies is as long as mine, you learn how to be.

The crowd lines the streets of Beishou as far as the eye can see. Many cling to their silk handkerchiefs, but most eyes are dry. The familiar lilt of Shi accents, the subtle mannerisms and gestures of my people, the gilded roofs of temples and pagodas, the miniature gardens that surprise at every corner . . . They greet me in a hollow embrace like long-lost friends who have moved on. It has been ten years since I was last here. Little has changed, but nothing remains the same.

Mourners stand in wait for the emperor's funeral procession

to pass by. I'm dressed to blend in to this sea of white. Absent are the vibrant garments so well-loved and displayed in the capital and prosperous towns across the Empire. A display that reflects our nation's wealth, so rich even the lower merchant class can afford to dye their fabrics in a spectrum of colors not found in nature. To me, those colorful robes are a constant reminder of what we paid in blood for the spoils of war.

The deep thunder of a gong reverberates and a hush drapes over the crowd. Beside me, Tang Wei tenses. Once again, she came along despite knowing the risk.

The head of the funeral procession appears shortly. A large contingent of Imperial guards clad in crimson-and-gold armor followed by a hierarchy of nobility and ministers of the Inner and Outer Courts walk by with a solemn air. From this distance, most of the ministers are unknown to me. I want to move closer, to find the one they call the Emperor's Shadow. But someone bumps into me and tugs my robes.

"Where's the prince?" whispers a little girl. She stares at me with eyes big and round, a doll clutched in her hand. She looks about eight years old—the same age my sister was when I last saw her.

"I don't know," I whisper back, exchanging a glance with Tang Wei.

The little girl's mother shushes her, but she pulls my robes again. "Is the prince our emperor now?"

"Prince Tai Shun hasn't come of age yet, so Empress Zhenxi will help him rule for now," says the mother. "Stop bothering this dàgē. He isn't from here."

The woman smiles at me briefly, apologizing for her daughter's questions. I smile back, relieved she thinks I'm a foreigner.

I turn my head in time to catch a group of people clad in rust-orange robes walking sternly by. *Priests.* The little girl gives a small cry and clutches my sleeve. Not wanting to frighten her further, I try to relax, dampening the pulsating fire burning in my chest.

Next comes the bevy of royal consorts and concubines, their wails pealing. Are they crying from grief or fear? Zhenxi is likely to send them away after today.

A murmur flutters through the crowd and dead silence takes over. Heads lower and bodies bend. I force myself to bow, to partake in this show of respect.

Carefully, I angle my head up, glimpsing the back of a young man in white silk with a gold coronet around his topknot.

My stomach curdles, pulse racing like the wind.

Him.

"Is that the prince? Can you see him?" whispers the little girl, excitement trilling in her voice. "Mother, lift me up, I want to see him! Mother—"

I grit my teeth, swallowing rage corrosive as acid.

I have seen enough.

The crowd thins after the procession, but I linger for reasons unclear to myself. I was not present at Father's funeral ten years ago. Was it as grand as Gao Long's? Were the tears that fell genuine?

Father's body lies encased in an armor of white jade and gold silk in the Royal Mausoleum north of Beishou. The ancient Spirit Way lining the path to the tombs intrigued me as a child with its sculptures of old gods and creatures from our legends. As did the royal tombs, each varying in size and splendor, some more imposing than others.

The most magnificent remains are that of my great-grandfather, Yuan Long. His empty coffin sits in a vault filled with thousands of terra-cotta soldiers, horses, and servants to serve him in the spirit world. The emperor who, as our history books will have you believe, *united* the Shi Empire. It reminds me that if I fail in my task, future generations of Shi children will never know the truth about the horror of his reign.

As a boy, I used to go to that secluded valley each spring to pay respects on Ancestors' Day. Fate has not allowed me to fulfill my duty to Father.

Soon, that will change. Soon, I will make things right.

"I don't know why you do this to yourself," Tang Wei says as she brushes something off her skirt.

"Do what?"

She shoots me an exasperated look. "Never mind, we need to go to the temple."

We leave the crowds behind and head west across stone bridges arching over narrow waterways, past sculptures of dragon turtles and fountains carved with yuèfú. Some snippets of the classical poems are known to me, others less so.

Somber faces pass us through the streets, though perhaps their sobriety is a show for the authorities. I doubt Gao Long was well-liked, not after he dragged this country into a ten-year conflict right from the start of his reign.

"Linxi came by the safe house last night."

"Why didn't you tell me?" My tone comes out harsher than I intended.

"You were asleep. After that ordeal with the Phoenix and all the traveling we've done, I thought you needed some rest—"

"More like you wanted to spend time alone with her," I retort.

Tang Wei stops, her eyes cold. "Do you want to hear her news or not?"

I pinch the bridge of my nose, exhaling. "Look, I'm sorry, I didn't mean that. I just . . . It would have been nice to see Linxi. That's all."

"You're apologizing?"

"Don't make me take it back."

"Accepted. And I'm sorry, too."

I bring a hand to my mouth, pretending to be shocked.

She elbows me. "I know Linxi is like a sister to you. You're right, I shouldn't have been selfish. I did want to catch up with her by myself." She smiles knowingly. "It won't happen again. But maybe one day, you'll understand how it feels to be in love."

"Can't wait," I say sarcastically. "What's the news?"

Tang Wei lowers her voice. "She's in the palace."

"She?"

"The one you've been waiting for."

"The one I've been waiting for?"

She.

I smack my forehead. "The Life Stealer is a woman? Why did I think it would be a man like my great-grandfather?"

"Because you can't see past your own nose?"

"Who is she and what is she doing in the palace?" I ask, ignoring Tang Wei's jibe.

"She's only been there for a month. She's Zhao Yang's long-lost daughter, apparently."

"Are you sure? I thought he had no family."

"Linxi is positive. She's even seen the girl training with some priest. Seems like they want to hone her life-stealing ability. They haven't succeeded; all she can do is manipulate water. There's more though—the girl has a grandmother living in that desert town we were in."

"The one with the priests?"

Tang Wei nods.

That town was small. It won't be hard for me to return and find her grandmother. A plan forms in my head. I have finally found an advantage against the priests.

I have finally found my leverage.

The shrine of the Goddess of Mercy rises sharply beyond a majestic willow tree by Mu'an Lake. Mother used to visit this place. There is a temple inside the palace compound, but royals can choose to pray in the city as a public show of dedication. It used to cause the Inner Court officials grief that the empress would choose such a humble and out-of-the-way place to pray instead of the grander halls in the city center built specially for the royals.

How can I understand the people's hopes and fears if I do not pray with them? Mother would say with a gentle but firm smile. The officials would cluck their tongues at their foreign empress, but she always got her way. Father saw to that.

I have long eschewed our gods. But I light three joss sticks now, because Mother would want me to. I kneel on one of the red cushions on the floor in front of the main altar, holding the incense in front of me in both hands at chest-level.

Zhenxi

The demon-man with the melting face

The Diyeh priesthood

Tai Shun

My mind runs through the familiar list, merely the beginning of those who must pay for what they did to my family. I hesitate, fingers rubbing the grainy sticks. Should I pray? But I'm not sure what to pray for. The sculpture of the Goddess Guanyin stares down from the altar. Would she bestow blessings upon me for wanting vengeance? Or would she advise mercy instead?

Tang Wei nudges me with a foot. "They're here."

I stick the incense into the huge metal pot on the table and follow her to the empty courtyard at the back of the temple. I stake claim over an incinerator and throw a few sheets of joss paper into the fire for show, just in case any devotees appear. Tang Wei stands guard in the corner.

A throat clears. I turn and bow low to the two men behind me. One, a familiar face I'm glad to see, the other, a stranger. He must be the Nandah ambassador.

"Shīfù." I nod to the older man dressed in pale green before turning to the other. "Ambassador Tian."

His white robes are a contrast to his brown skin. He reaches out a hand weighed down by thick brass rings and heavy jeweled cuffs and tosses in the entire stack of joss paper. The gold leaf on their centers crumples in the heat before catching flame. Our nations may be divided by land and water, but we pray to the same gods.

"Have you considered my proposal?" I ask quietly.

"I see no advantage in agreeing to your proposition," says Ambassador Tian. He speaks Shi so smoothly, there is almost no trace of his southern accent. "Ever since the Shi Empire and Honguodi have called a truce, the trade routes have been reopened. That helps my economy and my people. Nandah has no quarrel with either nation; we have stayed out of your mindless squabble all these years."

"Vengeance for an assassinated emperor is hardly a mindless squabble," I point out.

He tugs at his thick, wiry beard. "A brother using revenge as an excuse to plunder another sovereign's land is unconscionable. Do not underestimate our intelligence resources."

"Then you should understand why I am seeking justice for my father's wrongful death."

"Yes. Honguodi had no reason to assassinate your father all those years ago. However, you are speaking of usurpation now. That is no small matter. The present crown prince will ascend the Dragon Throne in a year, and he has his *priests*." The word comes out from the ambassador's mouth with distaste and contempt. "They hold no allegiance to you, especially since your father opposed them. They will defend the throne as is, protect it as they are doing now—with *magic*. How do you propose to deal with them?"

I exchange a quick glance with Shīfù. He shakes his head imperceptibly. He doesn't want me to mention the Life Stealer.

I smile at the Ambassador. "I have my ways. When the trees fall, the monkeys will scatter."

"But what monkeys will a boy king have left to command?"

"Not monkeys, but tigers and dragons."

He looks amused. "Should I be worried about crouching tigers and hidden dragons in the Empire?"

My smile broadens. "Not if I were emperor."

"Confidence, nay, *arrogance!* It will get you nowhere."

"Forgive my bluntness," I say, patience wearing thin. "I need to know your king's answer *today*. Don't forget, I'm offering the Southern Colonies for your cooperation."

He chortles. "It has been seventy-five years since the Shi took those islands from us, and now you think you can give them back so easily with no repercussions? Perhaps you are more naive than I thought."

I keep my posture carefully relaxed and my tone neutral. "It seems like your king's answer is no."

"Alas." Ambassador Tian sighs. "My king has decided to go against the advice of all his ministers. The nation of Nandah will send you troops when the time comes." He taps my shoulder, a light touch heavy with meaning. "Do not make my liege a fool for believing in you, boy emperor."

"That went rather well," I remark, watching the retreating backs of the ambassador and Shīfù as they exchange parting pleasantries.

Tang Wei gives me a scathing look. "I don't trust that man. He has poor taste in jewelry."

"I don't trust him either, but only because one should never trust a politician," I say. "Shīfù seems to believe him."

"We both know Master Sun likes to think the best of everyone."

I sigh in agreement, wishing I shared Shīfù's optimism and his willingness to believe there is still some good in this world. But the Goddess of Hope is cunning, and I have grown wary of her immaculate lies.

"Where are you going?" asks Tang Wei as I walk toward the back exit of the temple.

"To the lake. I'll be back shortly."

She knows to leave me alone.

Shadows lengthen around me as I pace to Mu'an Lake, its blue-green waters lit by the evening sun. The tops of the palace buildings peek out above the forest across the lake, gold reflecting warmly. But the serenity of this place does nothing to calm the ferocious storm brewing in my mind.

My ears pick up soft strains of music from a flute, carried across the lake from the palace grounds. My heart skips a beat.

He is somewhere near.

Cousin.

It is a term I can no longer call Tai Shun. A term he is unworthy of. We may share the same blood, but he has long ceased to be family. His parents took everything away from me. The people I love, the honor I deserve. They hijacked my fate and stole my destiny. And soon, Tai Shun will inherit that throne. He will change his name and take up the honorific bestowed upon the Shi emperor.

Tai Long. *Long*: descendant of the Dragon. The Son of Heaven.

I slide a dagger from my sleeve, tempted to throw it at something. Will Tai Shun wish me well when I come for what is rightfully mine? Or will he stand and fight? My thumb presses down onto the blade, feeling the sharp edge against my skin. I hope he fights. The face of the boy I once knew appears in my mind. Maybe I won't recognize him now that he has grown up.

But he will always be the boy who became the crown prince I once was.

16
AHN

The pins in my hair stab uncomfortably close to my scalp and there are too many jewels on the dangly fāzān Linxi inserted into the thick bun on the top of my head. The shiny gems are meant to match my heavy earrings and the gold filigree necklace with blue sapphires around my neck, but they only add more weight to my outfit. I smooth the many folds of my cerulean skirt, richly embroidered with gold thread. Draped across my shoulders, my silk outer robe shimmers as I move. My dress is a gift from the empress; I have no choice but to wear it.

"Are you sure about this?" I ask, fiddling with my mother's jade ring. It's the only thing adorning my hands. The only thing that feels like me.

"Absolutely. I specialize in transforming peasant girls into beautiful princesses."

"I'm not a princess," I say sharply. Linxi tuts and helps me into my new shoes, another dreadful contraption of brocade and blisters. "Aren't we in mourning? This seems . . . a bit much."

"Oh, Ahn. Don't be naive. The mourning ended with the funeral. Everyone in Beishou is dying to wear their pretty clothes and throw parties again. There will be a new emperor soon. Someone else for them to fawn over."

"But the funeral—I've never seen so many people wail and cry in public before. Are they all really moving on so quickly? Was it all for show?"

She shrugs. "It is what it is: a cyclical game the wealthy nobles have been playing for centuries."

And it's one you must play if you stay here. Revulsion pushes back against that thought. My empress-imposed duty to entertain the crown prince seems more like a chore than anything else. But I'll do it because she has been kind to me, and because my father is the premier.

"I have to amuse His Royal Highness tonight."

Linxi replies tartly, "So I hear. That's why I'm dolling you up."

"What is he like?"

"Let's see: spends a lot of time with his books and flute, interested in the healing arts, isn't one for military strategy, can't hold a sword to save his life." Linxi stops ticking off her fingers, grinning. "*But* he's awfully good-looking."

"We'll see about that," I mutter to myself.

She adds a touch more powder to my cheeks. "There, all done. I'll walk with you to the hall, if you like."

"It's all right. You have the night off, don't you? Go meet your girlfriend early. I know you're dying to."

She claps her hands. "Thank you, Ahn. I owe you."

"And I owe you for making me presentable. Let's hope I don't make a fool of myself with that *awfully* good-looking prince."

"You'll be just fine." She squeezes my hand lightly before leaving the room.

With time to spare, I meander my way to the great hall near Mu'an Lake, walking near the domed pavilion by the water. My ears prick as melancholic notes float through the air. The flutist must be there again. Captivated, I stand and listen. I don't know anything about music, but this must be how celestial poetry sounds.

The music stops abruptly, and a slender figure strides out from the pavilion with a dízǐ in his hand. Long sleeves fluttering as he approaches me, he's dressed in a simple unadorned hànfú, the white fabric stark against his surroundings.

I see his face as he comes close. My breath catches. It's as if the gods themselves had a personal hand in sculpting the precise cut of his cheekbones and jaw. His eyes are large and intensely dark and his lips feminine in their lushness. But it's the sadness in his expression that draws me to him.

He notices me and tilts his head quizzically. "Good evening."

"Sorry, I—I didn't—I was just, you were, you are—" I give myself a mental kick and try again. "I'm sorry for disturbing you. You play so beautifully, I wanted to hear more." I gesture awkwardly at his slim bamboo transverse flute.

"Thank you." The single red gem set in the center of the thin gilded headband around his forehead flashes as he bows with a flourish. "I could play another song if you like. It isn't often that I find an appreciative audience."

"That's hard to believe when you play so well."

"I assure you it is only because I was playing *inside* that pavilion."

He waves a hand at the structure behind him. "It was built specially to enhance the musical qualities of any instrument; the placement of each slab of stone in the inner wall was carefully calculated for acoustics. Here, let me show you."

He holds the flute horizontally to his lips. It's the same song, but it sounds different. Less rich, less magical. But I can still hear the loneliness in the notes.

"It's just as lovely," I say when he finishes, unable to tear my eyes from his hauntingly beautiful face.

"You are much too kind. Pardon my memory, but I don't believe we have met. I'm Tai Shun. And you are?"

Ten Hells.

I should have recognized him after seeing his portrait hanging on the palace walls. The plain white robes and that sad light in his eyes make sense now. His grief over his father's death would last longer than forty-nine days. A father who carried out terrible deeds, but still, his father. That twinge in my chest whenever I think of my mother returns.

Hastily, I lower my head and curtsey, burning with embarrassment. "I do apologize, Your Highness."

"Please don't stand on ceremony. What is your name?"

"Zhao Ahn."

"The premier's daughter?"

"Yes, I was on my way to the banquet. I heard you'll be attending."

"Right. The banquet." Tai Shun's shoulders seem to sag. "I suppose I must."

I can't help but feel that I've upset him in some way. "I won't hold you up. I'm sure all your friends are waiting for you."

"You assume a prince has friends," he says lightly. Before I can think of a response, he offers his arm to me. "We are headed in the same direction."

I run through all the rules Linxi shared with me. The banquet is a big event for important officials and guests. It marks the end of the mourning period and it's the first time Tai Shun will be seen in public after his father's funeral. It can only mean that everyone will be looking to him as *emperor* and not prince.

The empress may have asked me to keep Tai Shun company at the banquet but *entering* the room with him would be a different thing altogether. If I were to arrive on his arm, would I be signaling something about my relationship with him? Would I be making a target of myself?

Tai Shun drops his arm. I've taken too long to respond.

"I know what you're thinking," he says. "What will people say if it looked like I brought you to the banquet, if it looked like you were my special guest? Would there be gossip? I can assure you there will be. I apologize for putting you in a difficult situation. Let us arrive separately."

"I wasn't thinking any of that," I lie.

"It is all right, I am used to it."

He looks defeated. I don't know why I care, but I don't want him to be sad anymore.

"Your Highness," I say, loud and clear. "I'd be honored to accompany you to the banquet." I grab his arm and link it with mine, ignoring that I've probably broken ten palace rules about decorum.

Caught off guard, Tai Shun laughs. Loudly. He startles, as if he doesn't recognize the sound. He laughs again, and I glimpse a fragment of a boy who could be happy.

All conversation dies the moment Tai Shun and I step through the grand doors of the banquet hall. My eyes drink in everything: crimson silk drapes across beams spanning the ornate ceiling; lanterns hang in every corner; candles float from cast-iron holders shaped like dragons; music streams in from somewhere. I recognize the sounds of a pípá and dízǐ but see no musicians.

"Presenting the Crown Prince Tai Shun, and . . . and—" The announcer fumbles when he sees me, chubby cheeks turning as red as the silk sash around his waist. Someone whispers in his ear, and he looks like he might cry in relief. "And Lady Zhao Ahn!"

We bow and are greeted in return. Some of the nobles look scandalized when they realize their crown prince has shunned any finery and is still wearing mourning robes. Others tug self-consciously at their own ostentatious outfits and jewels. A few of the court ladies stare openly at me, hardly bothering to veil their interest. Or their distaste. A gnarled knot forms at the pit of my stomach.

I don't see my father as we walk through the room, but I catch the eye of the empress dowager who is seated at the back on an elevated platform. She's dressed in Imperial colors now—ivory, gold, and crimson. A thick sash falls down the middle of her belt to her hem, embroidered with a pair of gold phoenixes. Like some of the other ladies here, her bodice is disarmingly low. But if anyone's eyes were to linger too long on her, they might find themselves short an eyeball or two.

She gives me an encouraging nod. I walk with my head high,

trying not to fall flat on my face in these impossible shoes.

"Are you regretting this?" Tai Shun mumbles under his breath. He looks ill with discomfort. "Because I surely am."

"Not at all, we'll have a blast," I say airily, ignoring the palpitations in my chest.

He relaxes a little. "All right then. Make sure you keep my cup full."

We stride through the path the colorful crowd parted for us. I'm tempted to wave, if only to see the look on everyone's faces. But I shouldn't push my luck, and my father is somewhere in here. That knot in my stomach tightens. Will he be upset at me for showing up with Tai Shun, for blatantly marking myself like this? Especially since he's instructed me to keep a low profile while I'm learning to control my magic.

Too late for regrets now. I sigh silently and walk on.

A gong sounds and everyone moves to the long tables that line the hall on either side of the empress's platform. There seems to be a prearranged order of seating that I know nothing of.

An attendant moves swiftly to us, murmuring, "Her Majesty wishes for Lady Zhao to be seated with His Highness."

Tai Shun looks surprised, but he guides me to a table next to the empress's. I bow to her before taking my seat, and she graces me with an approving smile. Another attendant hurries forward to set the table for two. I wait as Tai Shun exchanges a few words with his mother, glancing around to see if I recognize anyone.

Two familiar faces are seated on the third row from my right. Lieutenant Bao and the female priest who captured me back in Shahmo. So they survived the ambush. They are dressed like nobility and are seated at a table headed by an older gentleman clad in fine emerald silk. He must be the Marquis of Qin, and Bao and the priest must be from his clan. I count six other men of descending ages who bear some resemblance to the marquis. His sons.

Leiye is nowhere to be seen.

The female priest notices me and a snakelike smile touches her lips. I look away. The smell from that hood she forced me to wear engulfs me. I exhale slowly and take a sip of my tea.

Tai Shun settles next to me. "Everything all right?"

"Everything's fine." He stares at me a moment longer, worried. I force a bright smile. "Really, I'm fine."

"I find that it helps if you drink," he says, eyes round and earnest. "Time passes faster."

I snort and immediately regret my crude reaction. But it amuses him, and the corners of his eyes crinkle as he tries to hide his laugh.

"Thank you for coming," he says. "Mother mentioned she had invited a special guest and she just told me it was you. I have to admit I was expecting someone else."

I raise my brows.

His smile is enigmatic. "I'm glad I was wrong."

Another gong thunders and the hall quiets. A line of servers appears from the side doors, holding large plates above their heads. They trickle in as the music gets livelier and place an assortment of dishes in front of us.

Double-boiled herbal chicken soup, fish steamed with ginger and soy, luscious-looking vegetables, abalone . . . My mouth waters as the attendant carves a suckling pig right in front of me. The skin is so crispy it crackles under his knife. More dishes come and go, many of which my peasant eyes don't even recognize.

Conversation with Tai Shun is wonderfully easy. He's clever but humble and isn't interested in petty palace gossip like some other nobles I've encountered. Neither does he seem to care much about the power the throne holds. Instead, he tells me about music, about his love for the countryside and nature, about wanting to explore the world beyond the palace confines, and how he plans to travel across the Emerald Sea for leisure. His dream, he shares, is to study medicine and discover cures for illnesses that plague our people.

I assumed he'd be a spoiled royal who thought of no one else but himself. Now, it feels like the Empire might have a chance with him on the throne.

Shortly, some minister I don't recognize ferries him away. I sit alone, stuffing my face with food nervously and avoiding all eye contact, smiling awkwardly whenever someone else nods at me. I spot my father making rounds among the nobles and foreign dignitaries. Sometimes frowning, sometimes laughing. His metallic half-mask reflects the lights, hiding his wartime injury like a shiny badge of honor.

Every time I see that silver, an ember of a memory long snuffed out keeps sparking at the back of my mind. But it fizzles and dies without catching flame.

There's something about that mask—I want to tear it off.

I feel eyes on me. I look up to see a gentleman with brown skin and heavy cuffs and jewels around his wrist staring in my direction. He nods like he recognizes me, but I've never seen him before. I smile politely back, puzzled by his manner. He sips his wine and starts talking to someone else as if our odd exchange never happened.

"I see you've a healthy appetite," says a voice beside me suddenly. Tai Shun is back. He grins at my empty plates. He left my side sober barely an hour ago, but now, his words are slurred.

"I see you didn't need *me* to keep your cup full," I say.

He manages to look contrite, plopping down heavily beside me. He pushes his cup toward me like a child asking for a treat. Sighing, I fill it with rice wine.

"I hate this," he mutters in a voice low enough that only I can hear. "So very . . . *very* much." He downs the wine and gestures for more. "Look at all these simpering sycophants. They're only fawning because I am to be emperor soon. Nobody actually gives a damn about me."

"If you can figure out who the sycophants are now, it would be helpful for when you are emperor, Your Highness," I whisper, pouring more wine.

Tai Shun's gaze sharpens through the haze of alcohol. "Call me Tai Shun. Please." He rolls his wine cup with his fingers thoughtfully. "The premier's daughter—are you aiming to be a politician, too? Do you have an interest in politicking?"

"No, I'm just a peasant girl who got lucky." I pat my stomach. "And I'm only here for the food."

He slaps his thigh, raucous laughter traveling across the hall, drawing attention to us. I see my father looking at us with a tight smile.

The man with the brass cuffs appears by our table. "Your Highness."

Tai Shun stands, a little unsteady. I'm tempted to prop him up, but that would make his inebriated state even more obvious.

"Ambassador Tian, good of you to come so far for the funeral."

"My king wanted me to apologize in person for not being able to make the journey. He has state matters to take care of," says Ambassador Tian. "I am sure *you* understand." His underlying note of sarcasm doesn't go unnoticed by me. "Who is this lovely young lady by your side tonight?"

I swallow my soup hastily, skin prickling under the ambassador's scrutiny.

"This is Zhao Ahn, the premier's daughter," says Tai Shun.

Ambassador Tian strokes his wiry beard. "Interesting. I did not know Zhao Yang had a daughter."

"We were separated by fate for many years."

"Then it must be a fortuitous stroke of fortune that you have found each other. Pray tell, how did that happen?"

"Like you said, Ambassador, it was a fortuitous stroke of fortune," I reply with a smile. Something about this man makes me want to hold my tongue.

"You Shi are always so coy with your words. The Nandah style is direct and honest. Conversations here have been"—he pauses briefly—"interesting."

I shoot Tai Shun a desperate glare. His eyes focus, and he steers the conversation away from me. I mouth a *thank-you* when the ambassador isn't looking.

The last gong signals the end of the meal and gives Tai Shun the excuse to end the conversation. He tries to whisk me away, but we are pursued by nobleman after noblewoman. He fabricates as many smiles as he has to, nodding along to whatever inane praise and platitude he's showered with. He presents me to a minister here, a lord there, and eager young men who want to impress me for some reason.

I find myself affixing a smile, nodding the way Tai Shun does, like I'm paying attention to what they are saying though my mind is somewhere else.

A few court ladies stop us in our tracks, each proceeding to flirt with Tai Shun in some manner. His discomfort is obvious, and his eyes keep darting to the other corner of the hall, as if there's someone there he'd rather be with. I crane my neck to look.

Leiye. He's finally here.

Clad in his house colors of resplendent emerald and silver, his handsome face is clouded with worry. He's talking to my father, their heads bowed close together.

"I beg your pardon, Your Highness, but my father mentioned he had some important news to tell you about the southeastern provinces," I say loudly above the chittering ladies.

Tai Shun claps his hands and they stop talking. "Then we must see the premier at once." Vicious glares shoot my way as he takes my arm.

"I'm afraid I'm making some enemies tonight," I say through my teeth as we walk away.

Tai Shun's brow furrows. "Does that bother you?"

"Not at all."

"Splendid," he says, stumbling over his own feet.

I elbow him upright. "You owe me."

He blinks a few times. "Don't worry, I am not drunk enough to forget how you just spared me from that tedious conversation. Now, where exactly are you taking me?"

"To my father, like I said, and Xima Leiye."

Tai Shun pales and pulls me back. I can't tell if it's fear or something else in his eyes. It passes quickly.

"No."

"I thought you wanted to talk to them."

"You thought wrong. I don't want to see Leiye." Tai Shun's expression is carefully schooled, but I see his fist tightening around the jade amulet hanging from his waistband. "Or the premier."

"Then why did you keep looking at him? Leiye, that is."

"Please, let us go somewhere else." He looks desperate to leave.

I nod.

Somehow, we manage to escape the banquet hall with little fanfare and end up in a garden by the eastern wing near my chambers—and his. Empress Zhenxi housed me right by her son. I didn't know that. Surely even my newfound status doesn't allow for this.

Tai Shun drops to the ground and lies on his back. He starts pulling out blades of grass from the ground, tossing them into the air. They fall back onto him, scattered green on white. I wonder if he's trying to bury himself somehow. To hide from the world.

After a while, he points at the plum blossom tree next to us. Its branches stretch out above our heads. "That was her favorite tree."

"Her?"

"My aunt. She was always so kind to me."

"I'm sorry." I'd heard that after Emperor Ren Long was assassinated, his wife killed her two children—a boy and a girl—and then herself.

"I miss him."

"Him?" I repeat, despite having an inkling as to who he might be referring to.

"My cousin." The moonlight catches a wet glimmer in Tai Shun's eyes. "The prince who should have been emperor." He wrenches more grass from the ground and raises a finger up at the roof of a tall building adjacent to the garden. "It happened right there."

"What happened?"

"I fell."

"You're lucky to be alive," I exclaim, noting how high the roof is.

"Lucky isn't the word I'd use to describe my fate that day. I lost my best friend."

"I'm so sorry." I don't pry any further, certain that the truth hurts him too much. But my silence seems to move him to speak.

"And now, *I* have to be emperor." He laughs humorlessly. "I have to deal with this mess of an Empire. I am trapped, stuck in a life of power I cannot wield. A life where I control the fates of millions but not my own. I shall make decisions based on the will of my court, smile when I'm asked to, cut off heads when I'm told to." His voice softens. "Marry someone I don't love for political gain, have heirs who will fight over a stupid throne."

I remember the way Tai Shun looked at Leiye, how he reacted when I mentioned his name. I thought he was afraid of Leiye. But now, I realize what he feels is a different sort of fear. It's the fear of someone who has fallen so deep that he is no longer sure if he will be able to dig his way out.

"You *like* him," I say with a smile.

Tai Shun covers his face with his hands and groans. "Am I that transparent? We met only a few hours ago and now you know my secrets."

"Maybe I'm just observant."

He lowers his hands and sits up, face slightly pink. "We grew up together. I've known him since I was a child."

"Once you're emperor, you could do anything. You could—"

"No, I couldn't." He shakes his head. "That is not how it works. Besides, it's not like he feels the same. And more importantly, Mother would never approve. The Empire needs an heir."

Not knowing what to do, I sit down cross-legged next to him, folding my skirt over my lap.

"Sorry for rambling. I don't know why I told you all of that. Perhaps it's because you . . . you're not from here. You didn't grow up here, you're not—" He gestures wildly. "You're not one of us. You are not one of *them*. I know Mother thinks I should be emperor—that I would be a good one. But I don't know. I don't." He looks at me helplessly. "I don't want to disappoint her."

"As someone who is not *one of them*, I'm telling you to pull yourself together. You *can* be a good emperor if you want to, and that doesn't start by feeling sorry for yourself."

I jab him in the ribs to make my point.

Tai Shun makes a face and rubs his side. "Have *you* been drinking?"

"No, I am perfectly sober."

"You just raised your voice at the crown prince and I'm pretty sure you assaulted me."

"I'm not a simpering sycophant."

That draws a genuine laugh from him. Unsteadily, he stands and brushes the dirt from his robes.

"Good, good. Excellent." He grabs my hand and I lurch up. "Come with me."

"Wait." I yank back. "Where?"

"I'm sorry, where are my manners," Tai Shun says, abashed. "What I meant to say was, my dear Ahn—if I may call you Ahn—would you like to accompany me to a shadow puppet performance in the city center?"

"Just the two of us? Without an escort?"

He nods vigorously.

"Are you sure it's a wise idea to sneak out?"

His excitement dulls and he bites his lip, looking morosely at the ground.

You assume a prince has friends.

I sigh, unable to ignore the pang of sympathy I feel for this boy. I kick off my heels and grin. "What are we waiting for? Let's go."

17
ALTAN

I lean out the window of the Lotus Sect safe house, feeling the sun's fading rays on my face. From here, I can see the great stone wall that fortifies the palace grounds, but nothing else beyond that. That wall was built to keep people out, though sometimes it feels like it was made to keep its inhabitants in. The palace is layer upon layer of stone with numerous guards in and around the compound, cloistering the royals from the everyday humdrum life beyond the palace.

A special kind of prison.

I remember the first time my sister and I visited the city. The people bowed when our palanquins went through the streets. Sarangerel stuck out her head and waved, grinning from ear to ear. She was so excited to be outside the palace. No one expected to see her. Their surprised expressions and hesitant smiles told me as much. Official decorum states that no ordinary citizen is to look the emperor in the eye. As for his children, they soon realized that waving back was the sensible thing to do.

I used to stare at the kids on the streets, wondering how different life was for them. I felt a semblance of envy. Unshackled by palace doctrines, they looked so free in comparison.

Not for the first time, I wonder if I could have my vengeance without the bonds it entails. I have spent so long away from life in the palace confines—do I want to go back to it? Could I rid the Empire of the priests and oust my aunt and cousin without sitting on the throne myself? But who would take over then?

You are all we have left, Altan, whispers my sister's voice in my head. My knuckles crack. I don't have a choice. The power vacuum and the ensuing struggle would make the Empire vulnerable to its enemies—and by the gods, we have made many enemies.

The snarl of invisible manacles clamps over my ankles. I have led a nomad's life for the past decade. Without a home, with only Shīfù to call family. But there is freedom in that life. And I know in my bones that freedom is priceless.

We will find Father's murderer. We will take back what's ours. We will go home.

I grip my jade amulet, murmuring, "As long as we're together."

The door creaks open.

"Altan! It's been forever." Linxi skips over and gives me a bear hug.

"It's good to see you again," I wheeze.

She releases her hold and takes a step back to examine me. "You've lost weight."

"It's not like I've been living in a lap of luxury."

"I know. Tang Wei told me all about it. I can't believe you had to eat desert lizards to survive."

"Is *that* what Tang Wei told you?"

"What did I tell who?" Tang Wei strolls into the room, immediately draping herself around Linxi.

"Nothing," I say under my breath. If Tang Wei wishes to

embellish her adventures to impress her girlfriend, so be it.

I start to brew some tea as the two settle in the corner, whispering into each other's ears.

Shīfù joins us shortly, and we get down to business.

"I don't have much to update for now," says Linxi, pulling away from Tang Wei. "For better or worse, Ahn has made no progress with her life-stealing magic. But the empress seems to have taken a liking to her."

Ahn. The Life Stealer's name. It's a pretty name. Unfortunate that it belongs to the most dangerous person in the world.

"That's because Zhenxi finds the girl useful," I say. "How about her adoptive grandmother? Is she still in the desert town?"

Three pairs of eyes dart to me, alerted by my tone. Shīfù strokes his beard pensively, and Linxi stops fiddling with the nomad necklace that Tang Wei wove for her.

"What about her grandmother?" asks Linxi, eyeing me.

Family can be interrogated. Tortured. It is one of the methods the Diyeh use to lure the Tiensai out of hiding.

"Family is leverage. A bargaining chip," I say instead.

My words are met with tense silence.

"If the girl really is the Life Stealer and the priests get to her grandmother first, they'd have a prized chess piece in their arsenal," I continue. "Even if she finds the sword of light, she won't use it against the priests if they threaten her grandmother's safety. They could use her to get to the dark sword, wherever that might be." I repeat Shenni's words ominously. "*Both* the White Jade Sword and the Obsidian Sword answer to the call of the Life Stealer."

Tang Wei bolts upright from Linxi's lap. "Are you suggesting that *we* kidnap her grandmother and hold her hostage? Or that we get rid of her?"

"Those are logical options."

She looks scandalized.

"You kill people for a living," I point out helpfully.

"*Bad* people. Terrible people. Scum of the earth type of people. There is a difference, Altan. And I draw the line at grandmothers. *We* are not the Diyeh."

"But our plan will fall apart if the priests have the sword," I argue. "The *world* will fall apart. We have to make sure the Life Stealer doesn't destroy everything—again."

Linxi glares with surprising ferocity. "Ahn won't do that, she's a good person."

"There's no guarantee of anything."

"You don't know her."

"And you do?" I scoff. "*You* were the one who told me I needed to look for the Phoenix."

"That was before I met Ahn! She knows what's right and what's wrong. If we told her what's actually going on, if we told her the truth, she would understand."

I slam the table. "And if she doesn't? If she burns the whole world down? Then what? Whose side are you on?"

I see the hurt on Linxi's face, but I'm too angry to care. Did the Life Stealer cast some spell on *my* friend? Why is she defending such a dangerous stranger?

Linxi opens her mouth to argue but Tang Wei places a hand on her shoulder, and she quiets.

I stomp to the window. Shīfù comes over. His presence calms me, clears my mind.

"I understand your concern," he says, staring out into the darkening sky. "But even in the deepest night, the stars continue to shine. You must protect the Life Stealer. No matter the circumstance, no matter the sacrifice. As long as the priests don't have her, there is hope, and balance can be restored to this world."

My utmost fear forces its way out. "But what if she's no different from Yuan Long? What if she uses the dark sword to force people into submission?"

"Your great-grandfather may have chosen wrongly, but you must not make the mistake of thinking that every Life Stealer is the same. The girl will walk her own path and fulfill her own destiny." He places a hand on my shoulder. "Remember, Altan, you may share the same blood, but *you* are not your great-grandfather. And neither is the girl."

I nod, but that kernel of doubt doesn't stop rattling in my mind.

"However"—he looks back out the window, eyes turning sad— "if the consequences of her choice result in catastrophe, you will have to stop her. You are, after all, the only one who can."

A crowd has gathered by the time we arrive at the large square in the middle of Beishou. As the last vestiges of sunlight wane, the air fills with animated voices from gossiping adults and scampering children excited for the shadow puppet show.

Convinced that I needed some fresh air, Tang Wei and Linxi dragged me here despite my protests. I know they want to keep an eye on me after what Shīfù said. I wanted to be alone, but they insisted.

Now that I'm here, I can't help but sneak envious glances at the various animal-shaped paper lanterns carried by the children, wishing I could be as carefree. Wishing I could enjoy the night without thinking of revenge. Without worrying about what the Life Stealer may or may not do.

Tang Wei catches me staring at a boy's lantern, an intricate piece crafted to look like a dragon. She tugs my arm. "Want one?"

I shake my head, but I'm still looking at the lantern.

"You're never too old to have some fun," says Linxi with an indulgent smile, browsing through the shopkeeper's wares. She picks one up and gives it to me. "We can get this rabbit lantern. You like rabbits, don't you?"

"It's all right." I hang the lantern back onto its hook. "Come on, the show's about to start."

I lead them toward the back of the crowd, away from the couples and families so we can blend into the rowdier group of spectators passing around ceramic jugs of liquor.

Covered by fabric on both sides, the elevated stage is only exposed to the audience from the front. The screen is set up to hide what goes backstage, but the royal puppet master once showed me his craft when I was a boy.

Each puppet is carefully manipulated by the puppet master, using sticks and strings attached to their head and limbs. Because of the setup, these sticks and strings will be invisible to the audience, and in the light, the intricate designs on each puppet, from their facial features and expressions to the minutiae of their clothing, headdresses, and weapons come to life.

Tang Wei and Linxi take their seats as the musicians tinker with their instruments. I stand behind with the intent of leaving early if I get restless.

Within moments, a gong booms. The lamp is lit, and the crowd goes silent.

Percussive sounds set the tone of the first story, and the troupe's singer spins a tale of the Monkey King and his adventures after he was banished from Heaven. The crowd cheers whenever the mischievous Monkey King smites a demon and roars with laughter when he utters a witty line of dialogue. The sad faces and tears from this morning's funeral are nowhere to be seen. The crowd is dressed in color again, too.

It is only the start of autumn, but the troupe announces the performance everyone has been waiting for tonight: the legend of Chang'e, the Moon Goddess. As the harmonic notes of a flute drift into the air, the puppet master brings out his new set of characters and the singer begins her soulful rendition.

When plaintive sounds of èrhú strings soften, the crowd breaks into thunderous applause, some wiping their eyes with handkerchiefs, touched by the tale of love and sacrifice. The troupe comes on stage to take a bow, nudging a hunched old man forward. He must be the puppet master, the one who pulled the strings behind the stage. The troupe disappears to prepare for the second half of the show, and I walk to the food stalls nearby in search of a snack.

A stallholder greets me enthusiastically.

"Come, xiǎodì! Have a drink." He thrusts an umber-colored jar at me. It jostles and liquid spills onto my robes.

"Good thing they're black," I tell him, waving away his apologies. From the scent, I know the alcohol is low grade and unaged.

Probably made from glutinous rice instead of sorghum. Which means it burns your throat and gets you drunk immediately.

The man continues to badger me, offering me a free sip to test his merchandise. I shrug him off and end up bumping into someone behind me.

"Watch it!"

That voice.

I turn to meet the piercing stare of the girl from the bazaar. She looks different—overdressed, like she was at some important banquet instead of a street show. I'm caught off guard by how happy I am to see her.

"The boy from everywhere and nowhere," she says. I'm pleased she remembers me.

"Mangosteen Girl," I quip, gesturing at the two long sticks of candied hawthorn in her hand. "You're not stealing those, are you?"

"I paid for them." She takes a bite from one of the sticky orbs to prove her point. Syrup stains her lips red, leaving a tiny dot on her chin. I fight the urge to wipe it away.

"Seems like your circumstances have changed." I meant it as a casual observation, but it comes out like an insult and I want to kick myself.

A flash of annoyance crosses the girl's face, but she merely nods and hands me a stick of candy. "Here."

"But you paid for them."

The corners of her mouth twitch. "Ever heard of a gift?"

"But we're strangers."

"There's no law against giving gifts to strangers," she says, repeating my words back to me. She laughs, and I remember the first time I heard her laughter. It reminds me of spring when everything comes to life.

"Thanks, but I don't have a sweet tooth." I return the candy to her. Our fingers brush briefly, and I take a step back, skin tingling. I bow in farewell, expecting her to leave but she starts walking with me as I head back toward the square.

"Where are your weapons?" she asks.

"Don't need them."

"You look far less intimidating without them. Are you passing through the capital?"

"In a manner."

She takes another bite of her candy, chewing thoughtfully. "Mysterious as always."

I sense that she wants me to explain myself more fully. To talk about myself, perhaps. But I choose to deflect. "How about you? This is a long way from the desert."

She turns away, tugging a loose lock of silky black hair. "I'm here with . . . a friend. He wanted to see the puppet show."

A friend, my mind repeats. There's a funny feeling in my chest I can't place. I brush it aside. The sound of drums and the èrhú grow louder as we stroll.

"Did you enjoy the shadow puppet performance?" I ask, suddenly wanting very much to hear her speak again.

"I did. It's the first time I've seen one. At least, I think so. It all seems familiar somehow." She looks perplexed.

I shrug. "There're performances like these in every town in the summer and autumn. They're common enough. My favorite is the one about the Moon Goddess, the one the troupe just performed."

She makes a face. "I never liked that legend."

"Why not? It's a tale of selfless sacrifice. Chang'e drank the elixir of life instead of surrendering it to the despotic emperor."

"And what was her reward? She was separated from her husband—she had to live on the moon with a *rabbit*. It's not fair."

"What's wrong with rabbits? Besides, they see each other once a year during the Mid-Autumn Festival," I counter, wondering why I care so much about a legend that probably isn't true.

"You say it like it's a good thing." She jabs the air with her stick of candy. "Chang'e could have smashed it, and the emperor wouldn't get it. That was what everyone was fighting about—the stupid elixir. If it didn't exist, everything would be fine."

"I don't want to argue over some fairy tale."

"Good." She grins. "Because I believe I won the debate. By the way, I don't think you told me your name. Or is that a secret, too?"

It takes me a moment to realize she is teasing. She doesn't actually think that I have an alias.

"Altan. And yours?"

"I'm—" She freezes mid-sentence, mouth opened in surprise. "Why is he—" She starts coughing violently.

"Are you choking on your candy?"

She pounds her chest and swallows hard. "Ten Hells, I'm in so much trouble. Take this." She dumps the candied hawthorn in my hands and dashes off.

I jog after her. "Wait! Are you sure you're all right?"

She stops and crouches down by a figure sprawled facedown on the ground near a rowdy group of drunkards. A young man. His white robes are caked at the hem with dirt and his hair is disheveled over his face.

She shakes him. "Get up. Get up."

"He passed out," drawls one of the drunks, wiping the alcohol dripping from his big beard.

She sticks an accusing finger in the man's face. "Did *you* give him the wine?"

The man leers at her. I'm tempted to hit him.

"I didn't do anything." He places a hand on her shoulder. She smacks it off immediately.

"If you touch me again, I'll make you regret it."

"Make me regret it?" The man guffaws and his friends follow suit. He leans in, takes a sniff at her. "Just how *exactly* will you make me regret it, xiǎomèi?"

Her fingers unfurl. The air shimmers slightly.

Magic.

It isn't coming from me. Which means—I step in front of her before the situation gets out of hand. The drunks give me a once-over warily, noting the scars on my face and my eyepatch. They seem to come to an agreement, muttering some curses as they slink off.

Mangosteen Girl crosses her arms. "Guess you don't need weapons to intimidate."

"Guess not," I agree, deciding to take what she said as a compliment. "Are you a—"

"Do you mind helping my friend, please?" She drapes the arm of the young man over her shoulder and gestures at me.

I nod. I can ask if she's a Tiensai later.

Together, we manage to get her friend to a more secluded street, away from the crowd and the noise of the puppet show. We lay him down, and he turns on his side and flops an arm over his face.

Mangosteen Girl paces in a circle, clearly vexed by the situation. "He said he wanted candy. Said he wouldn't drink another drop. Shouldn't have trusted him."

Her friend giggles and mumbles something incoherent.

"Get up, you swine." She prods him with a foot. The young man grunts. He moves his arm and brushes hair off his face.

Air rushes out of my lungs. I can't believe who I'm looking at.

Older. Different. But the same.

His eyes open, glazed and bloodshot. They widen when he sees me.

"*Cousin?* Is that you?"

The emotion in Tai Shun's voice stirs some complicated feeling in me. But I remind myself that he is neither friend nor family.

I should kill him.

Mangosteen Girl throws a silk handkerchief over his face in a poor attempt to mask his identity. Tai Shun groans and she shushes him.

"I'm sorry. My friend is drunk and talking nonsense. Thanks for helping me, I'm sure he's going to be fine. You can go. Sorry, I'm so sorry," she rambles, hands flying all over the place.

Tai Shun is her friend? Who is *she*?

"Cousin!" He pulls the handkerchief off. "Cousin!"

I stumble back against the wall.

Tai Shun tries to prop himself up, failing miserably. His eyes are unfocused. "I feel terrible. Where is—where's my cousin? What happened to him?"

Mangosteen Girl whispers to me, "His cousin is dead, and he misses him dearly. I'm sorry you had to see this. You can leave now, we'll be fine. I'll find a way to calm him down."

A small sound escapes my throat. A kind of strangled gasp.

She looks at me, puzzled. "Are you all right?"

"I'm just surprised it's the prince," I say stiffly.

Panic floods her face. "You recognize him? Oh my gods! Please don't tell anyone about this. I'm going to be in so much trouble. My father might get into trouble." She looks like she is about to cry.

I try to think of something reassuring to say. But all I want to do is take Tai Shun by the collar and slam him into the brick wall. To punch him in the face, again and again.

Footsteps.

I turn around, and for the third time tonight, Fate decides to show her hand.

"Linxi!" Mangosteen Girl runs up to her. "Oh, thank gods you're here. I need your help." She pulls Linxi over to Tai Shun and wraps an arm around him, ready to hoist him up. "We need to get him back to the palace right away without anyone seeing us."

Linxi and I exchange a weighted glance. How does she know the girl?

"Yes, Lady Ahn." She hurries to help, pretending she doesn't know me.

Ahn.

Her name is Ahn.

She is the Life Stealer.

Horror chills my blood.

"I think I'm going to throw up," moans Tai Shun.

"Me, too," I mumble.

"Did you say something?" Ahn steadies herself against Tai Shun's weight. Linxi darts a worried look at me.

I shake my head.

"Oh," says Ahn. Her cheeks turn pink. "Well, it was nice to see you again."

Linxi frowns at me, questioning. I don't say anything to Ahn, even though it makes me seem rude. Even though something in me is fighting to tell her I'm glad to have met her again. She turns even redder and looks away, her disappointment obvious. They stagger past me, a drunk Tai Shun muttering to himself.

As I watch their backs, anger seeps out of me, replaced by something colder.

Emptier.

The girl from the desert, the girl who stole the mangosteen—the girl who is inexplicably holding the crown prince in her arms—she is the girl I must kill.

18

AHN

I flop onto a chair, exhausted from dragging Tai Shun back to his chambers. Linxi and I used a more discreet entrance near the servants' quarters, but it was hard to hide the fact that the soon-to-be emperor of the mighty Shi Empire was, in every way, drunk as a skunk. At least we managed to keep the vomit off his robes.

I stare at the lump on the bed now, listening to Tai Shun's fitful snores from under the blankets. His shoeless foot sticks out from the side, but I'm too tired to get up from my chair to tuck it back in.

"Will he be all right?" I say.

Linxi straightens her robes with a purposeful tug. "Nothing a tonic from the royal physician won't cure in the morning."

"Does this happen a lot?"

"He likes his drink. But from what I hear, this isn't like him. Come, you look like you need some sleep yourself."

I get up and follow her through the bedroom and outer parlor.

"I trust you to keep this to yourselves," she says to the two attendants and three soldiers standing guard outside. I can't help marveling at her commanding tone.

The five men had kept their expressions scrubbed of any emotion when we carried Tai Shun into his room and left us undisturbed for an hour as we put him to bed. For my own sake, I hope they will truly keep their mouths shut.

"How did your date go?" I ask when we arrive in my room.

"Wonderfully." Linxi beams and shows me the pink-and-purple woven necklace around her neck. "A gift from her."

"It's lovely," I say, admiring the delicate handicraft. It looks familiar, like the kind of work that the nomads who visit Shahmo specialize in.

"Thank you, I'm going to make her a bracelet in return," says Linxi. "But let's not talk about me. Who was that young man with the eye patch?"

"Nobody. Just someone I met a long time ago."

"If he was *nobody*, you wouldn't have that look on your face."

"What look?"

"Your eyes lit up when I mentioned him and you're smiling. It isn't your usual smile."

I open my mouth, but no words—denial or otherwise—come out.

"Ha!" Linxi's tone is triumphant, but I see a faint worry line between her brows. It's gone so soon it might have been my imagination.

My legs are aching, and my head is starting to hurt. All I want is to lie down. "I don't know what you're talking about, you silly goose. Go to bed." I give her a shove and then another when she doesn't budge. "Go on, I can clean myself up. I'm exhausted from babysitting our child emperor. I'll see you in the morning."

She finally leaves, and I crawl into bed without caring about the dirty state of my clothes or hair. My limbs loosen and the tightness in my shoulders dissipates as I stretch. I close my eyes, willing my mind not to think about the boy in black.

Altan.

His name, his voice, his face . . . my mind replays our meeting. Everything he said, every movement he made. *Ugh.* My fists beat the mattress. It isn't as if I'll see him again. There's no point thinking about him.

Besides, when dawn breaks, I'll have bigger problems.

The attendants and guards may not spread salacious rumors about tonight to other people, but I know for a fact that my father will be informed of our unsanctioned excursion. Anything concerning the throne is the premier's business.

I drag the covers over my face, hoping that fate will be kind to me when he finds out that I aided and abetted the crown prince's escape from the palace.

The boy in black appears in my dream. He shoots arrows into the sky and the sun bursts into flames and splits into ten smaller suns, revolving in a circle. Clad in crimson and yellow, his hair lit gold, and he shoots arrow after arrow. But they keep missing their targets. The burning suns dance, flames waving, their heat scorching.

In a flash, the suns transform into ten rabbits, hopping around in a circle to some unknown tune. The rabbits catch fire and I smell burning flesh.

I hear a distant chuckle and the dream changes.

"Do you see the puppets, Ahn-er?"

I'm a child again, sitting atop my father's shoulders. That distinctive melody—the funeral dirge—plays around us. My mother claps along, her face angled away from me.

"Turn around," I say to her. "I want to see your face. I want to know who you are."

She doesn't seem to hear me.

My father points ahead. "Do you see the puppets?" he asks again.

I look at the stage. I see a man and a woman. Or perhaps, a boy and a girl.

Monstrously human. Misshapen things with twisted limbs and unnaturally bent heads. They twirl and sway as a cackle screeches from behind the screen. The music grows louder, lamenting the grotesque dance.

"What do you see, Ahn-er?"

My father lifts me from his shoulders and turns me around to face my mother and him.

My scream pierces the air as flames engulf them.

I squeeze my eyes shut, blocking out their faces. Their melting faces, like candle wax, leaking, dripping, dissolving. I struggle but my father turns me back to the stage and my eyes open. The puppets contort, dancing out of sync with the deathly requiem. I kick and squirm, but he has me in a viselike grip.

The girl puppet tears the boy puppet's head off and my screams return.

The stage light extinguishes. Darkness submerges me.

"Wake up, Ahn. Wake up, we have to go."

My eyes fly open.

It's still night outside my window. I blink, blurry-eyed and muddle-headed, the night before a mix of discordant images of dreams and reality. Shivering, I try not to think about the night-marish puppet show from my dreams. Yet, that voice echoes in my ears. Gentle, loving.

Wake up, Ahn.

Was it my mother's?

I get up, rubbing my temples, a groan wheezing out of my throat. My mouth is dry and mealy, my hair a knotty mess, my skin feels stretched. The racket inside my head is noisier than a tavern full of drunkards, and I didn't even drink. I wonder how Tai Shun will feel in the morning. I need a bath. As I trudge across my room, moon-light reflects off something on the table.

A glass vial.

It must be difficult not to be able to remember your own mother.

The ache in my chest grows, invading my body like the cursed desert, leaving me hollowed out and bare. The clear liquid swishes in the tube as I rotate it. The empress said the tincture might help me remember things. It looks harmless, and there's no reason for her to, I don't know, *poison* me. I almost laugh. The idea is absurd. She's done nothing but her best to make sure that my stay in the palace has been comfortable.

I remove the stopper. The seed of hope I tried so long ago to weed out threatens to take root again. Maybe this time, I will remember.

The tincture is cool as it slides down my throat. Tasteless, almost like water.

Minutes tick by and nothing happens. Foolish of me to even hope.

I light the lamp, draw a bath, and sink into it. Gradually, my eyes grow heavy. Enjoying the warmth of the water, I slip lower and lower. It feels like I'm floating in the open sea.

So much water, I think. Almost too much. Too deep, too heavy. Pressing against my rib cage.

My chest constricts. I choke and splutter. Water splashes everywhere as I fling myself over the edge of the wooden bathtub, eyes wide, a scream clawing its way out of my throat.

Breathe. Gods damn you, breathe.

I inhale. An ember in my mind sparks.

Fire catches.

I am four years old, in a garden. The grass I am sitting on is shriveled. The yellow-crested sunbird in my hand, lifeless.

"Well done, Ahn-er. Clever girl."

I smile up at my father, my heart bursting with pride. His face is smooth, handsome. He does not wear a mask.

My mother comes running, a hand clasped over her mouth, shock bruising her features.

"What are you doing with her?" She gasps when she sees the dead bird in my hand. "What did you make her do?"

A different memory.

I am crying. My mother has me wrapped tightly in her arms. "We can't do that—we have to keep her safe."

"The block you put on her meridians will not last forever. It only makes her magic unstable. Sooner or later, her affinity will break through, and there will be more accidents in the future. She will hurt herself if she can't control it. Give her to me. Let me train her, let me teach her how to wield her magic."

"No. You will not make her a killer."

"The Empire needs her."

"*I don't care about what the Empire needs! She's your daughter—*"

"*Have you forgotten where your loyalty lies?*" *my father says, a dangerous gleam in his eyes.* "*She is the Life Stealer, and there is nothing you can do about it. Give her to me.*"

He steps forward. The air around him shimmers.

"*You can never have her or her powers, you monster!*" *my mother cries. She shields me and whips her arm out.*

My father yells, covering his face as my mother sets everything on fire.

Another memory.

"*Wake up, Ahn. Wake up, we have to go.*"

My mother is rousing me. I stir, blinking tiredly. "*Are we leaving again, Mother?*"

She nods anxiously, and strokes my hair. "*Yes, darling. I'm sorry, I know it's hard.*" *She removes a small vial with amber liquid from her pouch.* "*Here, time for your medicine. Drink up.*"

I make a face but do as I'm told. Mother says this keeps me healthy, that it helps me forget the bad things.

"*Good girl,*" *she says after I return the empty vial to her. She cups my cheeks, eyes brimming with tears.* "*I love you, never forget that.*"

I love you.

Air rushes into my lungs and I blink back to the present.

I remember.

I remember.

My childhood flares and extinguishes. Memories of jumbled-up conversations, images of my parents, the places I used to hide in our family home, me running as a child, away from everyone . . .

What I did to my nanny.

I scramble up, terrified by what I remember—and what I don't.

But one thing is clear: only my father knows what really happened.

I pace around my father's study, waiting for the attendant to wake him. The once wet trails on my cheeks dry as something else takes over my fear and confusion.

Rage.

I remember. Not everything. But enough.

I'm shaking so badly that I lean onto the cabinet with my father's prized scrolls to keep from collapsing. My father has been keeping secrets from me. Secrets about myself, about my childhood. About my mother.

He has been lying to me.

The cabinet creaks, and I remember the secret alcove it hides. *What if?* I push and the wall panel shifts. I thought this narrow room bare before, but maybe I was wrong. I grab a lamp from the table and shine it in the room. The light scatters on something.

A lever.

I push it down and another false wall slides away. Shelves of ancient-looking scrolls line the walls of this new room. A rack stands at the corner, orange robes hanging on it.

I stagger back into the wall.

Diyeh robes.

Why are they here? *Why?*

I stare at them, the bright orange burning my eyes. There's a red sash running through the fabric of these robes. What does it mean?

"Ahn-er? Is something wrong, my dear?" my father calls out as he enters his study.

It's too late to hide my discovery. I walk out of my father's secret room, clutching the Diyeh robes in my hand and fling them at him.

"Are you a priest?" My voice is cold. Stripped of emotion.

His eyes flash dangerously. "Have you been spying on me?"

"Why didn't you tell me?"

"I have my reasons. My safety, for one. The head of the Diyeh priesthood lives in constant fear of assassination."

The head priest. Ten Hells. My father is the head priest of the Diyeh. Just when I thought things couldn't get any worse.

He studies me shrewdly. "Why does it matter if I'm a priest?"

"Why does it matter?" My voice starts to tremble. "You made me do all those things. The *bird*—I was a child!"

Too furious to control myself, I begin to cry. Memories spin out of control in my head. Flashes of all the cruel things I did—that I was made to do. My nanny's shocked face when I showed her the flowers I killed with magic. How I almost killed *her* by accident.

The real reason why my father sent her away.

"You lied to me," I whisper, wiping my tears fiercely. "You lied about everything."

All he can say is, "You remember. How?"

"The empress gave me a tincture."

"*The empress.*"

I don't understand the implication in his tone, but it doesn't matter. "Did you send the priests after Mother and me?"

"I wasn't the head priest then. The order did not come from me."

"What happened to Mother? What did they do to her?"

"You should ask what it is she did to you. She stole your destiny and made you weak." The disdain in his voice is clear. "It was an honor that our daughter was chosen, but your mother, she didn't understand who you are, what you can be."

"She tried to save me from you—"

"She took an oath to serve the Empire, but she betrayed it—your mother was nothing but a *traitor!*" he thunders.

I leap forward and tear off his mask. Half of his face is covered in old burns. Scars ridge down his forehead to his chin, twisting at his lips. Scars left by my mother.

It looks like his face is melting.

I collapse onto the floor. With an anguished cry I hurl the silver mask across the room.

My father picks it up, his laughter chilling me to the bone.

"Now you see me as I truly am. Now you see what your mother did to me. If only you knew who *she* was. Your mother was not an innocent—she betrayed her family for the priesthood. She was *one of us*. How many did she sacrifice? How many did she kill before she stopped?" My father grabs my hand, raven eyes lingering on my mother's jade ring. I see a flash of something complicated before they turn cold again. "And she stopped only because her own child was revealed to be the Life Stealer. Do not imagine her a martyr."

"You're lying again."

"Am I?"

It can't be true. It can't be. The misshapen, monstrously human puppets from my dream dance in my mind, my mother's laughter turning sour in my ears. My father must be lying. He's a liar. He always lies.

I stare up at his ruined face. "You're a monster."

"So are you."

My voice cracks. "No, I'm not. I won't be one."

"You cannot escape your fate, daughter. The gods have chosen you for a reason."

"Why do you want the sword? What are you planning?"

"I told you. To save my country and to get rid of the desert."

"Liar!" I pull myself up. "I'm leaving the palace right now. Get out of my way. Don't make me use my magic on you."

"An empty threat. I know you, Ahn. You've always been soft inside, like your mother. You will not attack me."

I raise my arms. He doesn't budge. "I said, get out of my—"

My father's open palm hits my chest. I fly across the room and smash into the heavy wooden table.

"I'm afraid I can't let you leave. You're our only hope. I must keep you safe," he says, too gently. The look on his face turns my blood cold.

"I won't help you. I will *never* find the sword for you," I say, gasping in pain.

My father walks over, flames hovering above his hands, looming like a lit shroud over me. His mangled lips twist further into a screaming smile.

A smile that tells me I am wrong. That I will not have a choice but to help him.

19
ALTAN

I sprint back to the Lotus Sect safe house, reeling from my chance meeting with Tai Shun. Once there, I climb up to the roof. I need to think. And I'm not in the mood to face Tang Wei and Shīfù and whatever questions they might have for me.

Eventually, the capital quiets below me, dim with an eerie red tint from the lanterns that line the streets. I toss my dagger up in the air. It spins and falls back in my hands neatly. I do it again and again, slowly settling into a calming rhythm.

Will Tai Shun remember who he saw tonight when he wakes? He seemed drunk out of his mind. But it feels like he's the least of my concerns.

The girl holds court in my mind.

Ahn.

I whisper her name into the wind, letting the shape of it rest on my tongue.

Now that I know *she* is the Life Stealer, something feels different. Changed, somehow. But I can't back down or waver. The alliance with the King of Nandah will stand. I will have my crown and revenge, regardless of who the Life Stealer is.

My thoughts circle back to her grandmother. The logical thing to do would be to remove that prized chess piece from the board, even if Shifù disapproves. I must avenge my family, and I can't leave my country in the hands of warmongering traitors or murderers of Tiensai children. But at what point will my actions make me no better than the priests?

Father would protect both Ahn and her grandmother. Then again, Father is dead because of his belief in the inherent goodness of people. And Mother? I try not to think of her, though she haunts my dreams at night like a specter. Sometimes, those dreams are pleasant, my only comfort.

My sister would—

I turn my head. Someone else is here.

A shape in black perches on one of the gables at the far end. He wears a theatrical mask with bold black stripes around the eyes and swirls of white and blue across the forehead and cheeks. A spy? Or a priest.

The masked man raises his hand.

I flick my wrist without a second thought. A terra-cotta tile dislodges itself from the roof and shoots out, but the man stops it in midair. He doesn't use it to attack. Instead, he lays it back on the roof.

Interesting.

My palms burst open. Several more tiles break off and catapult into the air. He stops all of them noiselessly. Lays them down. The Diyeh priests don't behave like that. They strike back. And they don't wear masks. As supposed holy men and the emperor's elite guard, they can operate with barefaced impunity.

"Enough," he says.

I draw my sabers. "Scared?"

"We're not children anymore and I don't have time for your games, *Jin*." He removes his mask to reveal another face from my past.

"It's been a while," I say, surprised by the steadiness of my voice. It doesn't match the frantic beating in my chest. "How did you know I was here?"

"You, of all people, should remember how fast rumor travels in the palace. But don't worry, no one will believe our drunk little prince. You're still as good as dead to everyone."

His expression seems to say, *dead to everyone but me*. His gaze rests on my face—where my eye was. An unasked question hangs in the silence.

"I removed it myself," I tell him. "You know why."

"Impulsive as always."

He grins so fondly it catches me off guard. I don't have full details of what he has been up to these days. But from what I know, I don't think we are on the same side. Yet, I can't bring myself to feel any animosity toward him.

I lower my sabers. "I'll forget you said that."

"On the account of our past?"

I'm not able to hide my smile. "On the account that it's good to see you again. Besides, I'm not here to kill you."

"Oh?" He turns serious. "I can't let you kill her."

I narrow my eyes. "Who said anything about a *her*?"

"Forget about that and hear me out. Many things have happened tonight."

"Tell me about it," I mutter under my breath, thinking of that shocked look on Tai Shun's face. Thinking of Ahn. He raises an eyebrow. "None of your business," I say. "Give me a reason why I should listen to you."

"You want your revenge, you want the priests gone, and you want your throne. Our goals are aligned, my friend."

Friend. That word is loaded with layers of meaning.

"Are we really still friends?" I don't know if I want to know his answer. I don't know what *my* answer would be if he asked me that question.

He looks at me, slate-gray eyes open and frank. "No, but we can be allies. Know that you can rely on me. Don't question my motives, and I won't spill your secrets."

Seconds tick by.

I see the tensed line of his shoulders, how his feet are spread, the turn of his wrists. He thinks I may yet attack him. I always beat him when we were children, but I suspect he was deferring to me because I was royalty. He was a cultivation prodigy and magic came easy to him. I'm not sure who will emerge victorious if we spar now.

"I will listen to what you have to say."

He relaxes visibly.

I let him speak without interruption. When he is finally done, I keep my face impassive and unreadable. If he's searching for a sign, I'm giving him nothing.

"I'll be at our old spot a week from now," he says. "Same time. If you're there, it means you're in."

"If I'm not?"

He doesn't answer. I watch as he puts his mask back on. He strides to the edge of the roof, pausing for a moment. That white streak in his hair that appeared after his magic manifested gleams in the moonlight. He gives me a final, lingering look and plunges down.

A cool breeze flutters my robes as I weigh my decision, the voice of my once best friend, Xima Leiye, repeating in my mind.

Know that you can rely on me.

20
AHN

Sunlight can't find its way into this place.

There isn't a window in this cell. Just stone and iron and a line of torches along the corridor, which are my main source of light. The irony of it doesn't escape me. My control of water or wind can't help me here. Leiye must've kept my father informed about my inability to manipulate fire or metal. And my father already knows I can't use my life-stealing affinity, so the guards he posted here are safe.

At first, I tried to speak with the guards, pleading with them to let me out. Telling them I'm not a criminal or a Tiensai. Asking them to bring my father here. But to no avail. Now, I say nothing at all.

I begin to lose track of the nights and days. Sleep comes and goes. Often, it's filled with snatches of memories from my childhood. Of Ama and of the desert.

Always, the desert.

I start to think I'm back in the priests' wagon again. That I'm being sent to my execution. Then I see the beautiful shoes on my feet, feel the smooth silk of my rúqún—both filthy now, of course—and even though I hardly touch the food I'm given, I can tell that it's been freshly prepared to keep me well nourished.

That's when I remember why I'm here.

My father wants to keep me alive because I hold the key to what he truly desires: the sword of light. I don't know if the sword can put a halt to the desert, but I do know that if someone like my father wants it, it can only mean trouble.

I'm sending some men out west. You should be happy that I'm keeping my word.

Those were his last words to me before he locked me up here. In my naive eagerness to have Ama live with me, I made a mistake in telling him everything about my village. Now, he has leverage to get me to do his bidding.

And he knows exactly who to threaten.

The courageous thing to do would be to kill myself. A quick brutal slam against the stone walls would crack my skull. And maybe the world will be safe from my father's machinations.

But I am a coward.

All I can do is starve myself until I'm too weak to wield any magic, and there's nothing my father can do.

I stir as I hear footsteps approaching. Is it time for yet another meal I'll refuse? Or has my father finally decided to show his face? He hasn't come to see me since he put me here. For some reason, that bothers me more than it should.

It's Leiye.

He's carrying a tray of food. Strange that he's the one bringing me my meal today when it's normally a guard. He makes a gesture at the guards and one of them unlocks the small opening between the gates of my cell and he reaches in to place the tray onto the ground.

"Leave us," Leiye commands.

Without questioning him, the guards click their boots together and file out of the dungeon. Leiye slips his hand through the iron bars and pushes the tray of food closer to me. I hear a soft sigh from him as I remain shadowed in the corner, lying on the cold ground.

"Eat something. You need your strength."

"No. I don't." I keep staring blankly at the cracks in the unfinished ceiling.

"What are you going to do? Starve to death?"

I shrug, just to annoy him. "Maybe."

He grabs a bar, white-knuckled, whispering, "I *need* you to stay alive."

I struggle to sit up and look at him. In the harsh light of the dungeon, his face loses its softness. Hard edges to match steely eyes. Dark circles under them. Is he having trouble sleeping? Murdered too many innocent people? Maybe he has nightmares, too.

I could ask him about the book he stole from my father's study, but I don't care anymore. Not when everything has crumbled around me.

"At least, eat the rice." He adds with deep emphasis, "Please."

"Did my father send you here to ply me with sweet nothings, little priest?"

Leiye winces.

"Did Linxi get into trouble?" I ask. He shakes his head. "How about Tai Shun?"

"Oblivious to everything but himself, as usual."

"How could you say that?" The crown prince hasn't come to see me, which means either he doesn't know I'm here or isn't allowed to come. Or maybe Leiye's right and Tai Shun is too self-absorbed to notice my absence. I brush that possibility aside, longing to believe the best of him.

"You care about him," Leiye observes.

I look away.

"It's his gift. Everyone who meets him wants to protect him, for better or worse."

"Do *you* want to protect him? He cares about you," I say, trying to gauge how Leiye himself feels without divulging Tai Shun's secret.

There's no change in Leiye's expression or demeanor. Even his eyes remain cloaked.

"You need to find the sword of light," is all he says.

"That's your response?" I guess he doesn't give a damn about Tai Shun. "I just told you something important."

"That piece of information is more important to you than it is to me."

"I forgot. You only care about your *duty*." I wield the last word like a knife. I hope he feels its cut.

"You forget that my duty is also to the prince. *Your* duty is to find the sword of light."

I laugh. A hoarse cackle that echoes through the cell.

"The premier only wants the best for our country, and he will do what it takes to save it," says Leiye. "I think you should reconsider your position. Find the sword, save our country."

"He really did send you here to persuade me." I say nothing else, choosing to lie down again. I keep my eyes on the ceiling, signaling the end of our conversation. He doesn't leave. Instead, I hear him nudging the bowl of rice toward me.

"You don't have to give the sword to him." Leiye's voice is so soft that I have to strain to listen. "He hasn't sent anyone out west yet, I managed to stall. There is time. Eat your *rice* and chew slowly."

With a sweep of his robes, Leiye stands and leaves. Moments later, the guards return.

Expression schooled to one of extreme boredom, I pick up the chopsticks and bowl of rice, trying to keep my hands steady.

He hasn't sent anyone out west yet.

Ama is still safe—for now. I eat the rice bit by bit, chewing carefully until I feel a different texture. Something disguised as a grain of rice. I tuck it carefully under my tongue and return to my corner in the shadows, away from the prying eyes of the guards. I fake a cough and remove that grain. It's parchment, sealed with something that prevents it from disintegrating in my saliva. I unfurl it with my fingers. Two words stamped in ink.

Stay awake.

Heart bashing against my rib cage, I crush the paper and stuff it between the cracks of the stone floor. For some reason, Leiye wants to help me. Is he going to rescue me? It makes no sense. He's a priest under my father's command. Opposing the head priest is a death sentence. Opposing the *premier* is a death sentence. What if it's a ploy from my father? He trusts Leiye, and from what I've seen, Leiye defers to him. Why would Leiye be helping me?

Be careful who you trust.

When I think back on Leiye's actions ever since he saved me from the Tiensai who was trying to kill me, I can't help but wonder if I've read him wrong. I thought him a stooge of the priesthood, a loyal lapdog of my father's, but maybe he is something more. But still, I can't figure out why he would betray my father.

You don't have to give the sword to him.

Does Leiye mean that I should give it to someone else? To *him* instead? Or does he mean that I should keep it? Or hide it?

Question after question springs up in my mind, but I tell myself there's no point speculating until I'm out of this prison and free. Reluctantly, I finish all the rice, and then I eat the vegetables and meat, forcing everything down. Whatever Leiye has planned for tonight, I'll need my strength. My stomach starts to feel queasy. Whether it's from the sudden intrusion of food or my nerves, I don't know. When I'm done eating, I retreat to my usual spot so the guards won't suspect anything.

I wait, trying my best not to fall asleep.

Time stretches endlessly.

Stay awake.

For what? For whom? Just when I start to think Leiye is pulling some elaborate joke on me, the fire from the torches flickers and I jerk up. Nothing happens. I lie back down, heart beating so loud the guards must hear it.

More time passes and my eyelids start to droop. I pinch myself, but the pain doesn't seem to keep me awake. The torches flicker again, but I don't think anything of it.

Then—a guard's shout is cut off.

Light vanishes.

I blink rapidly, adjusting to the darkness. I hear muffled sounds of more bodies falling to the ground as I feel my way toward the bars of my cell. A few long seconds drag by in silence.

Something sparks. A flame from a finger appears in front of me beyond the iron bars.

"Leiye? What's happening?" I whisper to the masked figure in black that takes shape.

The mask comes off.

And I find myself staring at the beautiful sharp face of the boy from the desert.

JOURNEY TO THE EAST

21
ALTAN

It doesn't take long to get to the outskirts of the capital. Just before dawn, we switch horses as planned in a small town. The streets are quiet, but I sense the rest of the town waking. Low murmurs, the creak of doors and windows, the shuffle of feet . . .

We should leave. It won't be long before the guards from the palace wake from the sleeping draughts I foisted on them. Once the alarm sounds, both priests and soldiers will be looking for us.

Ahn pokes a hand over the wooden door of the public bath and waves wildly. I reach over, and she snatches fresh clothes from me. A minute later, she appears, wet hair dripping over her shoulders. Out of politeness, I avert my eyes, wishing the water from her hair wasn't turning parts of the pale blue fabric translucent.

She shrugs on her navy outer robes, secures everything with a chiffon sash, and marches right up to me. Keeping a deathly glare on me, she wrings her wet hair and flicks the water from her hands at me like a slap.

"I held back my questions like you told me to." She speaks finally. "Now that we're away from the palace, I want answers. First, who are you?"

"I told you my name," I say, wiping my face.

"Who knows if *Altan* is even your real name?" I don't react. "And how are you related to Leiye? I thought he'd be the one who'd get me out of jail. Are you friends? Are you a priest?"

"No," I say, insulted.

She continues firing questions at me before I can explain. "But you have magic." Her eyes widen. "A Tiensai? Why would you be working with Leiye? *Everywhere and nowhere,* that's what you said. Do you wander around busting people out from jail—oh gods—" She jumps away from me. "Are you a vigilante or an assassin?"

I hold up my hands. "Calm down."

"Calm down?" she yells. Her hair unravels as she flings her dirty old robes in my direction. I dodge neatly. "Do you have any idea what I've gone through in the past few weeks? I . . ."

She takes a deep breath and turns around. Her shoulders heave and I panic a little. I won't know what to do if she cries. But when she faces me again, her eyes are dry.

"Tell me what's supposed to happen next. Does Leiye have a plan?"

"We're going to find the White Jade Sword. My associate has gone ahead with preparations to procure a ship to get us across the Emerald Sea." It isn't Leiye's plan. Not exactly. The fool should have known that I'd never go along with his scheme.

Ahn scrunches up her face in distaste. "Your *associate* . . . *procure* . . . Who talks like that? Never mind. How much did Leiye pay you to get me out of the dungeon and onto that ship?"

I pause for a beat before deciding to play to her assumptions. I quote a random number and she curses. She slips something off her finger and holds it up. A jade ring with silver etchings.

"I'm not going with you. Take this as *my* payment. Leave but don't tell Leiye anything. Pretend we're on our way to the ship or something, send him updates or whatever it is you were supposed to do."

"Where are you going?" I hope I don't have to use force to stop her. I can't have her derailing my plan.

"None of your business. Pawn the ring, take the money, and leave me alone."

"I'm afraid I can't do that."

"Look, I don't have any money—this ring is worth more to me than you'll ever know, but it's all I have now. Take it!" she snaps.

Somehow, the thought that she sees me as nothing more than a mercenary bothers me deeper than it should. I brush it aside.

"It's a long way back to the desert. The priests and the palace will be after you." That twitch of her jaw tells me my hunch was correct. "You have a grandmother back in that town where we met?"

Her jaw twitches again. "Did Leiye tell you?"

I shrug.

"She's in danger, I have to go—"

"Already handled. Someone's gone ahead to make sure your grandmother is safe. It's all part of the plan."

Shīfù left for Shahmo the day after Leiye found me on the roof. The pieces are falling into place. Only thing I need to do now is to keep the Life Stealer by my side. I need her to find the sword of light. But my real reason for getting immunity from her life-stealing magic remains. The world cannot be safe when such a powerful being exists.

Ahn steps closer. I force myself to stay, despite wanting to keep a distance between us.

"Why should I trust you?" she asks.

You can't.

"Simple," I say out loud. "If everything works out, I get my due."

"And if it doesn't?"

"Then we're all doomed."

She looks at me with scorn. "This isn't a joke."

"I'm not joking." She doesn't believe me. Time to play to her expectations of what a mercenary would do. "Look. We can make a small detour. I'll take you to the safe house where we planned to bring your grandmother, but you have to go to the port after that and get on that ship."

"What's in it for you?" She is still suspicious.

I grab the ring from her. "Is this real jade?"

She nods, eyes never leaving it.

"This should be enough for our small detour, plus a little extra left over for me. Getting you on that ship is the only way I'll get full payment from Leiye. Do we have a deal?"

"Where is this safe house?"

I grab a stick and sketch a rough map on the dusty ground. "We have to go south past this canyon to this town." I draw a circle. "That's the safe house. It's a detour from the seaport and we will lose time. But if you insist—"

"I do insist."

"Fine. We'll go to Heshi. Once you see that your grandmother is safe, we head back east to Cuihai Port where a captain and crew will be waiting. Deal?"

She bites her lip. "Deal. Are you coming on the ship, too?"

"Of course."

"How about Leiye?"

Why does she keep asking about him? He gave no indication that they were close or even friends. I hide my irritation and swipe the ground with my foot, erasing the map.

"He has his own plans," I say.

Finally, she nods. I make a show of looking for the town's pawn shop. She doesn't follow me inside. I walk back out with her ring safe inside the pouch in my robes, shaking a money bag so that the coins inside tinkle.

Something flickers across Ahn's face when she sees me. And it makes me wish I never started this ruse.

I set a brutal pace for the next few days, eager to put more distance between us and the capital. We travel mostly in silence, both too tired and too wary of each other to make any real conversation. Sometimes, I catch Ahn staring at me. People often do because of my scars and eye patch, curiosity overcoming courtesy.

But her glances are different. Less uncomfortable, somehow. Perhaps it's because she's used to people staring at her own scar.

She wakes me up three nights in a row, whimpering in her sleep, repeating a question over and over again: *Who are you?* Each time I think about going to her, waking her so she won't be stuck in that bad dream. Each time, I don't move, watching until she falls back asleep.

On the fourth night, I bolt up, dagger in one hand, flames coming out of the other. The lumpy dark shape near me hisses and I touch my fire to the small pile of kindle on the ground.

The light reveals Ahn's frightened face.

"What the—I could have hurt you," I say, upset.

She pulls her shawl tighter around her shoulders and retreats from me. "I was hungry. I didn't want to wake you."

I grab the rucksack of food next to me and toss it to her. An apple rolls out. She lunges for it immediately and I catch a peep of happiness as she rubs it on her sleeve.

"It's only an apple. Why don't you eat the meat if you're that hungry?" I ask.

"Fresh fruit was hard to come by in Shahmo, thanks to the stupid desert. And I wasn't born in the palace. I remember what it's like to have nothing."

She holds the apple like a child hoarding candy, and it tugs at my chest like a distant memory of my younger self. Relishing each juicy bite, she eats the fruit slowly, stripping it methodically to the core.

She no longer wears her hair in braids like the first time I met her, nor in the sophisticated way that I assume she had to abide by when she was living in the palace. Instead, she has tied it up in a simple high ponytail, loose strands at the sides framing her oval-shaped face. In the rosy firelight, the scar on her cheek loses its severity. The raised silver-white mark reminds me of my own scars, though some of mine are more easily hidden. I wonder how she got hers and if the reason is as unpleasant as mine.

I don't intend to be friends with the Life Stealer. No matter what

Linxi says, I don't trust Ahn. But I could afford to appear friendlier and gain her trust.

"Tell me about yourself," I say in what I hope is an encouraging manner.

Her nose wrinkles. "Why?"

I fight the urge to scowl. "We've been traveling together for a week and I know nothing about you. Seems like an appropriate question."

"I like apples." She takes another bite and chews loudly. I wonder if she's trying to annoy me.

"What else do you like?"

"Fruit."

This is more difficult than I thought. Our walls are built high, and I must find the cracks in hers first.

"How about mooncakes?" I say randomly.

"What about them?"

"When we were children, my sister and I convinced our parents to get us several boxes of our favorite mooncakes one Mid-Autumn Festival. Double-yolks with lotus seed paste—the kind with the chewy skin, not the flaky ones. We had an ill-conceived eating competition and stuffed our faces as fast as we could. My sister threw up into the koi pond and I was sick for two days. The fish were fine though."

Ahn lets out a short laugh before knitting her brows. "That's a waste of food."

"We were children, we didn't know any better."

"Then your parents should have stopped you. Have you seen

how my people live outside of the capital? Most of us barely get by."

Your people are mine, too. I break a twig in two and throw it into the fire.

Ahn finishes her apple and pushes the core into the sandy soil. Then, pointing her fingers to the ground, she exhales lightly. A tiny crescent-shaped dip appears and transforms into a circle, widening slowly. It suddenly stops and she makes a small sound of disappointment before trying again. She twirls a finger. The soil floats up into the air, bits of sand mixed in. I thought water was her other affinity. But it makes sense that the Life Stealer can control more than one element.

My muscles tense as the soil and sand form a spiral above her palm. My eyes don't leave the funnel. Inexplicably, she reaches over, showing me her miniature sandstorm.

A fog of images rush through my head as the sand whirls around her fingers. I hear screams. *Their* screams.

"What's wrong?" says Ahn, noticing my discomfort. She drops her hand and the miniature sandstorm collapses onto the ground.

Get a grip, Altan. Breathe. Breathe.

My lungs release.

"Nothing's wrong. I'm fine," I manage.

She doesn't question me further, hugging her knees close. "You wanted me to tell you about myself, but I'm not sure if you're ready for it."

"I already know you're the Life Stealer. Nothing else could be worse."

"The Life Stealer!" she says dramatically, waving her hands with a flourish. "What a horrible name." She makes a funny face and the tension disappears.

The knots in my shoulders relax. "It *is* awful."

"You're not afraid of *me*?" She looks almost shy.

"Terrified," I reply.

She pretends to glower. "I *am* rather terrifying."

"Then I'll have to stay on your good side, I guess."

"I thought you Tiensai want me dead. Maybe *I* should be afraid of *you*."

"Not this Tiensai." I lean back on my hands, trying not to acknowledge how comfortable it is to joke with her.

"Ha! So you *are* a Tiensai."

She looks so proud of herself for getting confirmation out of me that I can't help but smile.

"Why do the Tiensai hate Life Stealers so much?" she says in a very small voice.

"It's a long story."

"I'm a good listener."

I stretch my legs out and shake the dust off my boots. "I'll summarize. Over a century ago, there lived a Life Stealer. His name was Yuan Long—"

"The emperor?" She is shocked.

"Yes. He's the most esteemed emperor in Shi history, but he was nothing but a paranoid and power-hungry tyrant." My harsh words for my great-grandfather mask my own guilt over my family's legacy.

"That's not what I was taught." Ahn frowns. "Didn't he save Shi from the Mengu invaders?"

"The north never attacked, or rather, all they did was to defend their territory," I say, remembering what Mother told me. "The Shi eventually left Mengu alone because, magic or not, it's too difficult for battalions to cross the steep mountain range that borders the two nations."

"Magic was used in the wars?"

"Yuan Long wanted to rule the world, and since he had magic himself, he started to recruit others who had magic, too. He formed an army of magical elite who were loyal to the throne, fashioned them as holy priests, and formed the Diyeh cult. But some who had magic didn't want to fight. They opposed Yuan Long, so he maligned them. Branded them traitors and heathens, dangerous to society. He hunted them down, a hunt that continues today. The Tiensai weren't the ones who cursed the land—it was Yuan Long. I don't know exactly what he did, but the desert that keeps growing and killing everything in sight? It was a Life Stealer who did that."

"A Life Stealer? I thought—Leiye and my father said . . ." She trails off, staring at her hands, eyes wide with horror. "Of course, they lied."

"Because of what happened, it's not surprising that some Tiensai would hate a Life Stealer," I say.

"Only some?"

"Tiensai aren't a monolith. There are some who fear the Life Stealer and others who believe that the Life Stealer represents hope."

"Because of the White Jade Sword?"

"Yes."

"Well, I'm not going to be like Yuan Long." She sounds so earnest that I want to believe her. "How do you know so much about the Shi Empire anyway?"

I hesitate. She still thinks I'm a foreigner. Best to keep up that charade. "I read a lot. You should, too, if you know how to read."

"Of course I do," she bites back.

I groan inwardly, realizing I may have insulted her without meaning to.

"The Shi believe education is a stepping-stone for the Empire's progress," she continues. "Even women are taught sums, but I guess you don't know that since you're from the north."

"What's the point in education if everything you're taught is false?"

"But you can't deny that education is the only way for a woman to find equal footing in this world."

"Education is only *one* way," I correct her. "If women aren't allowed positions of power, it doesn't change anything."

"There's the empress dowager."

I scowl.

Ahn lifts her chin. "What's wrong with a woman with ambition?"

"Ambition is not the quarrel I have here."

"Then what *do* you have a quarrel with?"

"Historians," I say through clenched teeth. "They distorted Yuan Long's legacy, covered up the truth. Why do you think the smear campaign against the Tiensai works? Their magic isn't cursed. It's similar to what the Diyeh have. But war and conflict are good distractions. Who should a farmer blame for his failing crops? His

gods? His emperor? Or an enemy nation and others who are different? It's easy to find scapegoats and to create new ones if you appeal
to the baser aspects of humanity. That is how the emperors of this
nation have ruled."

"You sound like an old sage philosophizing in a teahouse."

"I was raised by one."

"Things could change with the new emperor," she says, after a
beat.

"That drunkard?" I ask, disdainful.

Her eyes flash. "Don't call him that."

"Oh, I do apologize. I forgot the crown prince was your *friend*."

"He was upset that night," she chides. "And it's not his fault that
previous emperors have ruled so badly. I'm sure he wants things to
change."

I stifle my curses and toss more twigs into the fire, angry at
myself for letting this conversation derail. Confused by her defense
of Tai Shun.

She sighs. "Anyway, it doesn't matter. I don't know how to use
my magic—the life-stealing part that is."

Linxi shared this information, but I was hoping she was wrong.
If Ahn can't use her life-stealing magic, will she still be able to
retrieve the White Jade Sword?

"Didn't stop my father from wanting to use me," she says, more
to herself than to me.

"Never trust a politician."

"You know who my father is? You seem to know a lot about me,"
she remarks, eyes narrowing. "What else did Leiye tell you?"

"Enough to do my job."

She looks at me from across the fire, and I hold her gaze. We say nothing. The crackle of burning twigs fills the silence and the wariness between us returns. She turns away and lays down, pulling her shawl over herself.

I'm too riled up to sleep. I'd set out to gain Ahn's favor, but instead, we are back where we started. Two strangers thrown together by fate, each too scared to trust the other.

You must not make the mistake of thinking every Life Stealer the same. The girl will walk her own path and fulfill her own destiny.

But what will that destiny be? I wish I had the answer.

Eventually, I spread my cloak on the ground, blowing the sand on it away before flopping on my back, staring at the distant stars until sleep takes over.

22
AHN

The canyon dwarfs everything in sight. Looking up at its steep curving walls, striped with different layers of minerals, I feel especially insignificant. Cliffs overlook a ground strewn with rough and uneven rocks, and though I can make out a path ahead of us, it meanders around protrusions and boulders of various sizes. The large body of water that carved the canyon has diminished to an inconsequential stream. But it's enough to make me glad to be near a constant source of water.

Altan walks ahead, black robes dusty from sleeping on the ground. Whistling a solemn tune, he leads our horses carefully across the rocky terrain. I strain to listen. *The Ballad of Hou Yi.* According to legend, the archer killed monsters and shot down nine suns to save his people from starvation. His wife was the Moon Goddess, Chang'e.

My incorrigible stomach growls as I trudge on.

"What did you say?" Altan slows to walk in step with me, a curious look on his face. I must have spoken aloud.

"I said Chang'e should eat the rabbit."

"She's an immortal. Why would she need to eat?"

"For the pleasure of it."

He chuckles. The scowl I've grown used to hasn't appeared today.

"Do you believe in gods and immortals? And monsters?" I jest.

He nod-shakes his head in that usual noncommittal way. "I believe monsters can be killed."

I mull over his words as we walk, wondering if there's some hidden meaning. But soon, my attention drifts to the stream again. I stretch out an arm. Energy flows out of me at a steady pace. A tiny spout of water lifts from the surface of the stream. It's almost as natural as breathing. I start to laugh. I feel like I'm more in control of my magic, and the thought of it encourages me.

A wet chill shocks me in mid-giggle.

My clothes are thoroughly soaked. I spin around to find the remnants of a small wave cascading back into the stream. The reins of the horses swing as Altan clutches his side and laughs. A real laugh. Carefree and light.

"I didn't know you had an affinity for water, too," I grumble, letting out a string of creative curses involving his descendants. It only makes him laugh harder.

I flick water and several pebbles at him, but he dodges them cleanly.

"Tiensai reflexes," he chirps, avoiding another fist-sized rock. I wonder what's the reason for his good mood. Maybe his dreams were pleasant.

I walk on, leaving a wet trail behind me as I try to squeeze out as much water as I can from my rúqún.

"If you take your clothes off, I'll dry them for you—I'm pretty nifty with the element of wind," Altan calls out from behind.

He can't be serious. I ignore the heat on my cheeks. "I am not taking my clothes off."

"Suit yourself." I can hear him trying not to laugh. "I promise not to look if you do, if that's what you're concerned about. Not that there's anything I haven't seen before."

"I would slap you for your rudeness, but then I'd have to touch you."

He catches up to me. "You won't be able to get to me in the first place."

"Keep telling yourself that, arrogant fool," I say coldly, wringing a sleeve, "and you'll wake up one day shackled to a tree."

He smirks like the prospect of me manhandling him is enticing.

"Naked," I threaten.

"Mmm."

"In the middle of *winter*."

"I'd like to see you try."

"Oh, believe me—"

I don't get to finish my sentence. Altan shoves me to the ground. I fall hard. He hisses as an arrow cuts through the fabric of his left sleeve. Another arrow whizzes down and he yells at me.

"Find cover!" He lets go of the reins and our horses bolt off.

I dash to a tall rock formation and crouch, eyes veering wildly for the source of the attacks. A man in black stands at the top of a cliff with an arrow notched in his bow, scouting for a target. Before I can warn Altan, four more men spring from an outcrop yelling as they descend upon him with their weapons raised.

Altan's sabers are out, bow tossed onto the ground.

The air comes alive with grunts, blades grating together as they meet. Blood drips from Altan's arm, but he has no trouble parrying the onslaught of blows from the men. Who are they? Priests? But I only see magic coming from Altan. They must be bandits.

He sends a gust of wind at the archer on the cliff. The man slips but manages to hang on to the edge of the cliff.

I want to help Altan, but my mind is too frazzled to focus on my magic. Another arrow swishes over my head and drops in front of me. Its tip is blackened with a substance that gives off an acrid smell. I move to take a closer look, but an arm grabs my waist from behind, forcing air out of my lungs. A meaty hand claps firmly over my mouth. My neck strains as I'm yanked back.

"Guess your friend's too busy to save you," growls a voice in my ear.

I buck and kick out, but my attacker only tightens his grip. Altan turns in our direction when he hears my muffled screams. He starts to sprint over, waving his hand. Boulders soar through the air, ramming into the bandits chasing him. Two escape unscathed and continue their charge, but Altan doesn't seem to notice.

Turn around, I think desperately. *Watch your back*. The fool is going to get himself killed if I do nothing. I draw a deep breath, ignoring the pain in my chest. Slivers of energy start to hum in my veins.

Metal flashes across the sky. A spray of red and a bandit drops dead. The spinning silver curves back out toward an outcrop, seemingly vanishing into thin air. Who threw the dagger? It wasn't Altan. But at least it gets his attention. He pivots, working his double sabers in a slicing motion. Another bandit falls.

My attacker curses and drags me back.

Use it. Use it, whispers the slithery voice.

I stop struggling and focus, reaching deep, searching for an elusive thread of magic. The cicada hum from the alleyway starts in my ears. I breathe in. The burst of clarity returns. As does the feeling of wholeness.

The world around me transforms. The cloudless sky is a luminous azure. The canyon walls flare a stratum of russet, white, and ocher against the brilliant flaxen hue of the sun. The melodic trickling of the stream dances behind me as the gentle breeze whispers in my ear. My breath catches when Altan strides into my field of vision in a blaze of light, hair igniting gold like a celestial halo over his magnificent face.

He is dazzling, brighter than sunshine.

Someone wheezes on my left. My attacker—I didn't realize he'd let go of me. His eyes roll back, bulging face turning red and purple. An ominous green light leaks out of him like an aura. He gives a final, desperate gurgle and crumples to the ground.

Something else happens.

That soft white light around Altan shimmers to a pale green when he nears me. He gasps and doubles over.

You're killing him! my mind shrieks. I can't stop. I don't know *how* to stop.

Altan struggles to stand, finding strength from gods know where. Our eyes meet, and I see his fear.

Something pushes back at me. The light around him turns white again. I start to shake. Pain impales my chest, and I crash onto my knees in agony. My magic vanishes.

Rocks slide from the cliffside. The archer is hauling himself back up to safety. Altan grabs his bow from the ground, shakily notching an arrow.

"Don't look," he says.

I look.

Dangling precariously on the cliff edge with his back to us, the man is oblivious to what is coming. His hands slip from the force of Altan's arrow and he falls, shrieking. I yelp as his body strikes the jagged rocks below, bouncing like a rag doll. He hits the ground with a solid thud, limbs flung out unnaturally. Bloody trails line the rocks above and the ground around him.

Altan lowers his arms and frowns at me. "Told you not to look."

Then, he takes a swaying step and drops to the ground.

23
AHN

The sky dims. The world blurs around the edges. I command myself to breathe, but all I can do is wheeze. Footsteps disturb the pebbles on the ground. Someone's near.

Altan? Is he all right? Is he *alive*? Or is it another bandit? I groan, the pain in my chest flaring. Through half-opened eyes, I see someone standing over me. A scream curdles in my throat.

A demon.

Its face is red, with bold black stripes around its eyes and swirls of white and blue across its forehead and cheeks. I blink. It isn't a demon. *A mask.* It's someone wearing a theatrical mask. I grope the air in front of me. A hand pushes my outstretched arm firmly away.

"Shhh." The voice is soft, gentle.

I smell something sharp and minty. My head starts to clear. The fresh scent tingles through my nostrils and down my throat. When my vision returns, there is no one around.

Did I imagine it? No, that scent—it's still here. My chest still hurts, but I scramble up to check on Altan.

He's unconscious. Sweat pearls on his forehead and his face is ashen. But there is no sign of withering on his face or body. My magic killed my attacker, but it must have missed Altan somehow.

How else could he have survived it? Relief surges through my body, but it's short-lived. His left sleeve is soaked with blood.

I split the cloth where it's torn. Ten Hells. The arrow *grazed* him. But the gash is bleeding and the skin around it swollen. The blackened tip of the arrow must have been laced with poison.

I rip off a chunk of cloth from the hem of my skirt and wrap his arm tightly to staunch the bleeding. Pacing frantically, I try not to look at the motionless bodies or the destruction I've wrought on the landscape. I need to do something. Anything. I grab the waterskin strewn on the ground and plunge it into the stream. Carefully, I lift Altan's head and part his lips, dribbling some water into his mouth.

An eternity passes before his eyes flutter open, glazed for a moment before he focuses on my face. "Ahn? What happened?"

I'm so relieved I grab him in my arms.

"You hit your head when you fell, and I think there was poison on the arrow." *And my magic almost killed you.* I hug him tighter, letting go only when I realize he's trying to speak. "Gods, sorry, what did you say?"

"Pouch . . . Yellow thing."

I unfasten the leather pouch tied to his belt and empty the contents into my hand. Dried flowers. And a ring.

My jade ring.

It doesn't make sense. Didn't he pawn it? No time for questions. I stuff it back into the pouch and gather the flowers into my palm.

"What should I do?" I ask.

"Crush and rub."

I can barely hear him. After setting the flowers aside, I take a look at his arm. The bandage is stained through. Bleeding freely, the skin around it is an ugly deep reddish-brown. It looks bad. I have to hurry. A sweet earthy perfume fills the air as I crush the faded yellow petals and press them as gently as I can onto the gash. My stomach turns queasy as my fingers meet the warmth of his blood.

"By gods . . . rub it in," Altan hisses.

"Fine. Hold still."

I turn my head to avoid looking at the disgusting mess I'm making. He flinches but I don't stop until a paste forms over the cut. I tear off another chunk of my skirt and wrap his wound again, thankful that this time, fresh blood doesn't seep through immediately.

Unwilling to leave him unattended, I sit in silence, desperately wanting to wash the blood off my hands. A shiver goes down my spine as my eyes wander to the bodies littering the ground. I can't see the blood on their black clothes.

But I know it's there.

My attacker lies farther away. The image of him clutching his neck as the life drained from his eyes lurks in my mind. I remember the rush I felt as he died in front of me. That enticing thrill of power.

It felt so right, so natural. But it was wrong.

The man is dead.

You did nothing wrong. He would have killed you, whispers that wily voice in my head. I choke it off before it can say anything else.

Altan makes a pained noise, propping himself on one elbow. Moving his head gingerly, he takes in our surroundings.

"We're in a bit of a mess, aren't we?" he rasps.

I laugh shakily.

"Thanks for saving my life with the língcǎo . . . I guess."

"I guess? I should've left you for dead," I joke half-heartedly before remembering that I almost killed him. "Thanks for saving my life. The arrow would have struck me."

"We should get out of here."

"The horses are gone. We're not going to make it out of the canyon on foot. Not with you like this."

"I'm *fine*."

"If you're fine, I'm a flying carp."

He tries to move his injured arm, only to flop on his back with a loud groan.

"*See*. You're not fine and we're not leaving this canyon until I'm sure you're not going to die on me."

He grimaces at the sky. "I'm not going to die on you."

"I'm holding you to it." My eyes flit to the corpses again and I shudder. "Let's look for shelter for the night. Maybe there're some caves around. Can you walk?"

"No idea."

I sheathe his sabers and grab his bow and our only waterskin before offering him my free hand. His knees buckle as I help him up. He must be weaker than he thinks. Or maybe that lean physique hides heavy bones. I lead us forward, ignoring the pressure of his weight.

"You're so small," he mumbles in a distracted, cloudy sort of way.

"I am not." I struggle against him to rise to my full height. I'm almost as tall as him. "I'll drag you if I have to. Besides, I took care of that bandit, didn't I?"

My skin crawls when I hear my own words. How could I sound so callous? So dismissive?

"That man . . . something happened," Altan mumbles. He tries to look over his shoulder. "Back there. Have to see."

I don't turn us around. I carry on forward, keeping my grip around his waist. "We can come back after you rest," I lie.

I don't want to come back here.

I don't want to remember what I did.

Shortly, we stumble upon a large, empty cave. I settle Altan down on the rough ground and put a trembling hand to his forehead. He's pallid and burning up. I rip off a piece of his unbloodied sleeve and douse it with water, reaching to place it over his forehead.

He grabs my hand forcefully.

"Heavens!" My scream bounces off the cave walls. "What's wrong?"

"Sorry, reflexes. I'm fine," he mumbles. "Making sure you're real."

"Those are not the words of someone who is fine." I place the cool, wet cloth over his forehead. He looks like he wants to say something, so I shake my head. "Shush. Rest."

"Your eyes." He closes his own.

"What?"

Silence.

At the stream, I wash the blood off my hands and scour it from under my fingernails. I know it's Altan's blood, but it doesn't stop me from thinking about the man I killed.

Every life is precious.

What will Ama say now, knowing I killed another man in cold blood? Will she still welcome me if I blaze a path of dead bodies to get to her? I could have used my magic to knock that man out with a rock or something. But I did not.

Maybe I didn't want to.

Silt stirred up by my scrubbing muddies the once clear water, turning it as murky as my thoughts. *You're a monster,* my father's voice whispers in my head. I remember the look in his eyes. The triumph.

I shiver.

Maybe he is right. Last night, when I was creating the miniature sandstorm in my palm, I felt no heightened sensations, no euphoric control. Today was different. This magic was different. But it was the same kind of magic I used on the two men in the alleyway in Shahmo.

Almost the same.

The bandit's death was quicker.

I try not to think about the exhilaration that coursed through my veins as the man choked to death. About how it was stronger this time.

About how I might have enjoyed it.

When I return, Altan is asleep on the cave floor. And to my irrational chagrin, shirtless. He must have undressed and removed his weapons. The rays of the afternoon sun stream into the cave, and metal on the gritty floor gleams. I gape at the arsenal of blades and sharp things surrounding him. He was armed to the teeth.

There's no blood on his bandage. I touch my hand to his forehead. Scorching. I could use my magic to try to freeze some water to ice him down and lower his fever, but the thought of using any magic now makes me sick.

I lean against the rough wall and draw my legs to my chest, thinking. We have no more food. Maybe I could set up some snares to catch a naive hare or two. But I'd have to leave Altan alone again.

I look at him, worry biting my chest. Curious how sleep changes a person. His strong jaw is soft and his brow smooth. There's no trace of his usual focused and irritated expression. His eyelashes are impossibly long and surprisingly darker than his hair. Freckles sprinkle lightly across his straight nose and there's a rosiness in his cheeks I didn't notice before. I follow the scars that web his right cheekbone, once again wondering what terrible thing happened to him in the past.

I remember how he looked earlier when that strange white light shone from him just before my magic attacked him. How paradoxical it was to witness such beauty coming alive while I was in the midst of extinguishing another man's existence. The two intertwine in my mind.

A memory I abhor.

My eyes run down to his chest, noticing an amulet strung onto a thick black string around his neck. An astonishingly detailed five-clawed dragon coiled in a circle is carved into the jade. Unlike the deep green of my own jade ring, his amulet is a luminous semitranslucent white. Mutton fat jade. Precious and rare.

My nose wrinkles in distaste. He must've stolen it or bought it with some ill-gotten money. What bad luck to be stuck with a mercenary. And to think I thought more of him when we first met.

But he didn't pawn my ring, even though he said he did. What was the point of lying? I chew on my lip. I could ask him about it. Or I could steal it back and pretend he lost it in the fight.

I reach out, annoyed that I tied his pouch back to his belt instead of keeping it in the first place. Carefully, I slip my ring out and secure it under the collar of my top.

As I try to refasten the pouch, Altan shifts in his sleep. "Saran . . ."

I freeze and hold my breath.

"Sarangerel . . ."

It's that name, the one I heard him say some nights ago. A Mengu girl's name. There's a new feeling in my chest I can't quite place. Something like a dull ache. Altan's hand lands on my wrist, fingers wrapping around it. His skin is chilled, his grip surprisingly strong.

"Don't let go," he mumbles.

My spine goes stiff. Warmth creeps over my body. I give a tentative tug. He doesn't let go. The crease between his brows deepens when I tug again and he wakes.

"It's you."

Who did you think it was? I want to ask.

"Stay," he whispers, looking at me in a strange way.

I turn my head, unable to hold his gaze. But I stay.

Slowly, his grip relaxes, and he falls asleep again. I slide my hand out of his. I hear him speak again as I'm leaving the cave, in a voice so soft I almost think I'm imagining it.

"Your eyes are so . . . beautiful."

I walk out of the cave into the night, wondering how delirious he must be, wondering who he thinks he is talking to. Wondering why that ache in my chest is turning sharp.

24
ALTAN

I jerk awake.

Everything is hot and cold at once. My head throbs, my arm aches, my body is stiff and sore. Jewels glitter above me. Flashes of brilliant light pulsating. Am I back in the Wudin Mountains again?

I rub my eye and look again. This is a different cave, and the glittering is sunlight reflecting off minerals in the walls.

Bit by bit, it comes back to me. The men in black . . . the fight . . . the silvery glint that looped back and killed one of my attackers. A recurved dagger. I couldn't see where it came from. But one thing is for sure, I owe someone a blood debt, and eventually, such debts come calling.

The image of the man who held Ahn hostage appears next. That strange green light that leaked from him, how he clawed at his throat, how he writhed in pain. . . . How she stood over him, energy radiating out. In that moment, she was frighteningly beautiful.

Like a goddess of death.

I *felt* it. That aberrant magic. Fleeting but terrifying. *Something* was pulled out of me. Something deep, like the essence of who I was. I couldn't breathe. Couldn't fight back. It was like being lost in the suffocating sand all over again.

I inhale and exhale deeply, letting the images fade as I look around the cave. Scattered weapons, shirt, and outer robes in a rumpled heap. I make a flustered grab at my amulet. Still there.

A sound at the cave's entrance. A figure in blue enters. Ahn. A weapon in her hand—*my* knife. My muscles tense. I'm injured. How much danger am I in with the Life Stealer so close to me? But her magic didn't kill me, which means the immunity from the Phoenix worked. Somehow, I don't feel better knowing that.

"You're alive." She smiles and holds up a dead hare. "Look what I found. I'll return your knife after I gut it."

"How long was I out?"

"Only a day. You slept through the night."

I manage a half smirk. "Told you I wouldn't die on you."

Her mouth downturns for some reason. "I'm glad."

I test my arm gingerly, a hiss escaping before I can stop it.

"Are you all right?" Ahn exclaims, dashing over.

"I'm fine."

She looks away. "Good. Put your clothes back on then."

"But I'm hot." I feel my forehead and neck. "I have a fever." I'm not sure if it means the poison is purging or spreading.

"I know." She shifts her weight from one foot to the other, staring at the cave wall behind me as if it is the most interesting thing in the world. The tips of her ears are turning pink. "Just . . . put your clothes on."

I grab my robes, not bothering to argue. I have more important things on my mind. I want to check on the bodies. One body to be specific. I want to see the consequences of her life-stealing affinity.

Pain radiates across my shoulders as I pull on my tunic, but I'm careful not to make a sound. I don't want to look weak or defenseless in front of the Life Stealer. Just in case.

"What are you doing?" she says as I try to stand.

"Going back. I want to survey the area."

She drops the hare and the knife. I swoop down to catch my weapon before it hits the rock-hard ground blade first, grimacing as another shot of pain bursts up my arm.

"Do you remember what I did to you?" she says in a small voice.

"I do, but it wasn't your fault. You were defending yourself against someone else, and I was in the wrong place. Even a cornered rabbit will bite." *Let alone a tiger.* The words roll off my tongue easily, though I'm not sure I believe them.

"I'm not a rabbit," she says crossly. But she looks scared.

My tone softens. "You don't have to come with me."

"I will," she says quickly. "You'll need my help to get there."

I nod, surprised by her concern. Cautious of her true intentions.

My body rages with fire, but I can't rest until I know. Until I *see* what the Life Stealer did. Vultures circle the air some distance ahead of us. We must be getting near.

Expressionless, Ahn looks straight ahead as she walks. Shoulders tensed, she keeps clenching and unclenching her hands. I should say something reassuring to her, but no words come to mind.

"There was someone else with us yesterday," she says suddenly. "Someone in a theatrical mask, like the kind actors wear on stage for an opera. I think they might have thrown the dagger that killed that bandit."

"What colors were painted on the mask?"

Her brows furrow as she shuts her eyes for a moment. "Red, black, some blue? Maybe white?"

Leiye? I glance at the countless nooks and crannies in the canyons around us that he could be hiding in. Dammit. I don't want to owe *him* my life.

"Do you think those men were sent by my father?"

"I don't know. Wouldn't the premier send a whole contingent of soldiers to get his daughter back?"

We didn't encounter any trouble before the canyon. Odd, now that I think of it. We may have deviated from my original plan to head straight to the port town, but Zhao Yang should be trying harder to find Ahn. The *priests* should be trying harder to hunt us down. But no one seems to have picked up our trail. Perhaps Leiye managed to stall them. But if he's here on our tail, it also means he knows I'm no longer following his plan.

Ahn gasps, eyes bulging as her hands go to her mouth.

We are here.

I am standing in a circle of death.

The grass, wildflowers, and insects in the area have shriveled up and died, creating a funeral wreath fit for the corpse they surround.

A corpse that looks like a husk of a man.

His skin is desiccated, as if all liquid has been drained out. As if he died decades ago and was left to decay among the harsh elements. A dreadful, shocked expression remains on his withered, bloodless face. What is left of his lifeless eyes stare up at the Heavens.

This husk of man—it could have been me.

A small cry tears my attention away. Ahn is shaking uncontrollably. I take her by the elbow and guide her away. There is no need for her to relive what she did.

But as we walk, all I can think about is how the world would be a safer place without the Life Stealer.

25
AHN

Back at the cave, I skin the hare as quickly as I can, trying not to think of death—from *my* hands. Altan's reaction to the bandit I killed told me everything: he's afraid of me. He thinks I'm dangerous. A murderer. A monster.

He isn't wrong.

I clean the carcass in the stream and stake it over the flame. Soon, a delicious aroma rises as fat drips down onto the crackling fire, but that hollow feeling of having taken a life, even if it is for sustenance, lingers. My appetite vanishes.

Altan wanders out of the cave, a little unsteady on his feet, his black outer robe hanging over his bare shoulders. He sniffs the air appreciatively and I hand over the skewer. He promptly tears in with gusto. After a few bites, he stops.

"Sorry." He tries to pass the half-eaten hare back, a sheepish grin on his face.

I wave him away. "Not hungry." My stomach rumbles on cue and I squirm.

"Clearly, your stomach disagrees."

"You're injured, you should eat more."

"I'm injured, I can't help you if you faint from hunger." He parades the meat in front of my face until I finally give in and take it back from him.

As I nibble half-heartedly, he stretches and tests his arm, flexing this way and that. Inevitably, his outer robe slides off.

I cough, almost choking on a piece of meat. "Why do you keep wandering around half-dressed?"

He blinks in confusion. "I wasn't—"

"Are you still feverish? My grandmother says you need to sweat a fever out. She used to bundle me up in blankets even in the desert heat. It works. Try it." I'm speaking too fast and my voice sounds too high to my ears.

Altan shrugs and wraps his robes tightly around himself before settling closer to the fire.

"Don't complain if I sweat up a stink."

"You already stink."

"So do you."

I burst out laughing. We do smell bad.

"I thought you said you didn't know how to use your life-stealing magic," he says out of the blue.

I stop laughing. Why did he have to bring that up now?

"I don't know how to use it. It just happened. I panicked; I didn't want you to die." I chuck the hare bones into the fire. "I didn't know what I was doing."

"Leiye says you need your magic to find the sword, is that true?"

That was what my father told me. Our evenings together in his study come back to haunt me. Bitterness seeps into my heart, twisting it. The pain of his betrayal is fresh even as I avoid thoughts of him. Deep down, I know I can't run away from him forever.

"The sword itself is supposed to draw me toward it like a compass," I say.

"Have you felt its . . ." Altan searches for the right word. "Its pull?"

I shake my head. Something flickers across his face. Disappointment? But why would he care? His job is to get me on the ship. I don't want to think about the sword or my dark magic, so I pull my ring out and show it to him.

"Why didn't you sell this?"

Altan pats down his empty pouch. "You knew?"

I nod and slip the ring onto my finger. The familiar sight of the silver-etched phoenix soothes me.

"It seemed important to you." His tone holds a question.

I don't feel like answering. Not when I have questions of my own. "This is more than just a job for you, isn't it?"

Silence.

I try again. "How did you get involved in this mess that is the Shi Empire? Things seem peaceful in Mengu. Is the money you're getting from Leiye worth all this trouble?"

Altan leans his back against a boulder, gazing up at the night sky.

"It's not about the money," he finally admits. "My mother was from the north, but my father was from Shi. He spoke up against the priests, and they hunted us down. Leiye told me if I helped you find the sword of light, you'd be able to take down the priesthood."

Take down the priesthood? Was that Leiye's plan all along? He *does* intend to betray my father. The thought of it gives me both hope and fear. Leiye may be brave enough to stand up to my father. But he is only one man—a mere boy. My father has the weight of the Empire and the priesthood behind him. It feels like a futile fight. And yet, he's trying.

I . . . am less brave.

Don't you want to avenge your mother's death? questions a small voice in my head. I don't know if she's dead, but I do know *who* drove her to desperate means—the priests. If the sword can stop them, then finding the sword should be my goal. But it would mean mastering my life-stealing affinity, and I'm not sure if I can.

I'm not sure if I want to.

I was so happy to be reunited with my father, only to have that dream shattered. There's a part of me that worries what will happen to him if the priesthood falls. I can't help but remember the grief that Tai Shun held for *his* father, a man who did terrible things. My father needs to be stopped and punished for his misdeeds. But how far should that punishment go, and should I, his daughter, be instrumental in that?

I shove that muddled ball of emotions away and dart a nervous glance at Altan. *He* wouldn't know that my father is the leader of the Diyeh, would he? My father takes pains to hide his identity both as the premier *and* the head priest. If Altan knew, surely he would have mentioned it already?

"So, all of this is personal for you," I say quietly.

"Isn't it always?" Altan slips a dagger out and spins it. "And you may think you can stay out of this mess, but as long as you're the Life Stealer, someone's going to want something from you."

"They should stop treating me like a, like a *thing* they can use. I don't want to do anything for anyone. I want to be left alone," I say, tired of it all.

Tired of men who want to use me.

"You don't have the luxury of living a quiet life." He raises an eyebrow, like he's challenging me. "The sword is powerful and with your magic, it can stop the desert from spreading. That alone is worth the moon. You could use it to rule, make nations bow to your will."

I throw my hands up in exasperation. "I told you, I'm not like Yuan Long. I don't care about ruling the world! That's absurd."

"Few can resist such power."

"I . . . I don't want to kill anyone else." We both hear the tremble in my voice.

Altan's expression softens. He looks almost sad. "The first is always the hardest."

I don't know how to respond.

He repeats himself as though his meaning was unclear. "The first time you kill someone, that's always the hardest."

"You sound like you have a lot of experience." I drag a hand down my face. "This is wonderful. I'm stuck in a desolate canyon in the middle of nowhere with a murderous boy who has enough blades to outfit an army."

The expected retort doesn't come. He sits there solemnly, stoking the fire. I try not to think about how many people he may have killed. Or why he'd be killing anyone in the first place. Maybe he needed the money. Maybe he only killed priests who were trying to capture him. I don't know if that makes me feel any better.

I fiddle with the ends of my shawl, plucking at the fraying threads. "You might as well know this. The bandit in the canyon wasn't the first or the second."

"I know. Back in that desert town—"

"No. Even before that," I reveal.

Altan's dagger stops spinning and his posture tightens. I don't want him to fear me, but it feels like he needs to know.

"Something happened when I was a child . . . something bad. I'm not sure how, and I don't remember all of it." Nausea roils in my throat. I look at my hands, running my thumbs across finger pads, feeling the whorls of skin as I continue. "I think I may have hurt someone by accident. I think I hurt them badly, and that scared my mother into hiding me away."

Altan puts his dagger down and looks up at the stars. Seconds later, he seems to come to a decision. He turns to me and leans close.

"Years ago, after my father died, my mother escaped into the desert with my sister and me." The grit in his voice chafes the air. "We thought we were safe, but the priests found us. My mother was killed, and my magic manifested at that instant. At that time, I had no idea how to control it properly. It went wild and I created a huge sandstorm." The full force of his pain pierces me as he holds my gaze. "That was how I escaped from the priests. But that sandstorm killed my sister. *She* was my first kill."

His palpable fear when I made that miniature sandstorm the other night—it makes sense now. I recognize the look on his face. It mirrors my own from moments ago. He's wondering what I think of him. Of what I might say.

I don't comfort or console him. Instead, I lift my chin

imperiously. "I didn't know we were competing for who had the most awful childhood. Obviously, you win."

For a moment, he's confused by what I said. Then, he starts laughing. It isn't even funny. It's a horribly inappropriate joke. But I know he's laughing because he is relieved.

Relieved that I told him I don't think him a monster.

26
ALTAN

We make our way through the canyon for the next two days. Afraid of losing our only source of water, we keep close to the stream, straying only to hunt for food. My arm improves steadily; the poison nullified by the língcǎo and Ahn's quick response.

Gradually, the landscape changes. The farther we are away from the site of the bandit ambush, the lighter my chest feels. Green creeps onto jagged rock as small trees and then larger ones appear. The stream itself widens into a river, waters gushing like a constant percussive song. We decide to spend another night here—our last— and try our luck at hitching a ride the next day when we hit the small settlement that rests at the edge of the canyon.

Dinner appears in the form of a small deer. I take it down easily with my arrows. Ahn chooses to busy herself stacking little rocks and pebbles near the river until the meat is cooked. If sand is my failing, the burden I have to bear, then death must be hers.

Bellies full, we lie on our backs, side by side, each lost in our own maze of thoughts. I scan the scattered stars in the deep indigo sky, searching for the one that points me home. The one that gave my sister and me hope all those years ago. It seems more distant tonight. Less bright. Less real.

"Altan?" whispers Ahn. "Are you still awake?"

"Mmm."

"The fire's out and I'm getting cold."

"What do you want me to do about it?" I mutter. She huffs. A pebble hits my foot. "Fine. You can have my outer robe," I sigh.

"I don't want your stinky clothes. I want you to start a fire."

Even though it's too dark to see anything, I can feel her glare. Groaning, I sit up. With a quick flick of my fingers, I send a small flame in the direction of the kindling. "There. Happy?"

"Thank you."

In the firelight, I catch a glimpse of Ahn's expression.

"You could've started the fire yourself the usual way without magic. I've seen you do it," I say with sudden realization. My jaw clenches. "You wanted to see me create fire with *magic*. Why?"

"Leiye told me fire magic is preferred in the priesthood. I've seen your flames before, and I was curious. It looks the same as his. If all fire magic is the same, and if the Diyeh are people who sided with Yuan Long, and the Tiensai are those who did not, doesn't it mean they're the *same* inside?"

My hackles rise. I was foolish to think her a bystander caught in the middle of a savage political war. She must have a hidden agenda.

"What's your point? What are you planning?" I demand.

Ahn scrunches up her brows. "Why are you getting so worked up for? I'm not planning anything. I was thinking that if the differences between the Tiensai and the Diyeh are superficial and created *intentionally* by Yuan Long a century ago, why can't we clear things up?"

"You're being naive. This isn't a simple dispute that can be solved by talking."

"I'm being hopeful," she insists. She reminds me of Shīfù. Seems like they'd get along with their endless supply of idealism. "Leiye's a priest and he seems to want to do the right thing. Maybe there are others."

"He's different."

"How?"

I'm neither ready to tell her how I know Leiye nor who I really am. She seems enamored by Tai Shun. I don't know what her reaction will be if she knew I was vying for the Dragon Throne.

I avoid her questioning eyes and walk away into the darkness. She knows by now when to leave me alone. I turn around at some point to stare at the blurry figure by the campfire.

Girl. Tool. Weapon.

Someone I can . . . trust?

I don't know why I told Ahn about what happened to my sister the other night. I haven't shared it with anyone else apart from Shīfù. It's been too easy to talk to her, to share things. This needs to stop. *I* need to stop.

I glare up at the night sky, wanting to shake a fist at the Heavens. I remind myself of who Ahn is: the Life Stealer. A means to an end.

Nothing more.

A kind farmer picks us up after we leave the canyon. Despite our disheveled appearances, he never questions us, choosing to tell us about his farm, his dying crops, and the devastating state of the land. We listen to him, occasionally exchanging troubled glances. I don't know what Ahn is thinking, but the farmer's experiences only serve to strengthen my resolve.

It is past midnight when we arrive in Heshi on foot after the farmer drops us off nearby. The shop fronts are shuttered and the town quiet except for a drunk carouser or two. Dimly lit streets guide our way until we reach a large gray-stoned building with a pair of red paper lanterns marked with the symbol of an ax hanging from either side of the awning.

The Three Axes.

I knock lightly on the door.

"Tavern's closed!" yells a gruff voice from inside.

I knock again: three quick raps with my knuckles, two slow thuds with my palm, and then three raps once more.

"If you're patient in a moment of anger," says the gruff voice quietly.

"You'll escape a hundred years of sorrow," I respond.

What was that? Ahn mouths at me.

"Password."

Keys jangle and the door opens. In the light of his lamp, a bearded, heavy-set man squints, giving us a once-over. I see the resemblance to Luo Tong in the man's face, a Tiensai who visited Shīfù often.

"Come in," he orders brusquely.

He bolts the door behind us and sets his lamp on the counter, revealing a large dining room filled with chairs and tables. Axes of various sizes hang on the wall. On my right, an alcove disappears into darkness, and I spot a staircase at the far-left corner.

"Praise the gods—I was about to call it a night. Luo Hai, owner of The Three Axes." His tone is curt, but his eyes are welcoming.

I bow. "Altan. It's good to finally meet you, Master Luo. Your son speaks of you fondly. This is Ahn."

She flashes him a winsome smile.

"I hope we aren't intruding, Master Luo," I say. "My apologies for showing up unannounced."

He waves away my uncertainty. "I've heard a lot about you, Altan. Ah Tong was here a few months ago, kept saying what a good shot you are." He turns to Ahn. "My son says this boy never misses in archery."

Her eyebrows go up and she gives me an appraising, skeptical look.

"We need a room if it's not too much trouble," I say to Master Luo, ignoring Ahn.

He claps me hard on the back as if to test my strength. "Of course. Dispense with the formalities. The gods must favor you." His voice lowers. "The priests were here a few days ago, searching as usual, but they didn't find anyone, thank Heavens. I don't expect them to return any time soon. I assume you're here to meet Master Sun?"

"Yes."

"I expect him to arrive in a day or so. Wait here." He disappears into the alcove.

"Is he a Tiensai?" Ahn whispers.

"No, his son is."

"Does he know who I am?"

I shake my head. She relaxes and slouches against the table. "Who's Master Sun?"

"My mentor."

She's about to say something when Master Luo returns with another large lamp and a pile of fresh clothes.

"I'm not sure if these will fit well, but they will do for now." He runs through the keys hanging from a thick iron ring, pausing at a small knobby one. "There's a big crowd here this weekend for the Qixi Festival, and I wasn't expecting the two of you, only Master Sun and his guest."

Ahn throws me a questioning look. I give her the briefest of nods to indicate that the guest is her grandmother.

Master Luo clears his throat, eyes sneaking to Ahn. "I have, uh, only one room to spare for tonight. Will that be a problem?"

Ten Hells. I tip my head at Ahn. This should be her decision.

"It's fine," she says wearily.

I smile tightly. There better be two beds in that room. I'm tired of sleeping on the ground.

"Two flights up, last door to your right. The two of you look like you need a good night's sleep." Master Luo's nose twitches as he hands me the key. "And a bath."

We creep up the stairs, careful not to make a sound. I open the door and curse right away.

A single bed greets us. A narrow one. The only way two people could ever fit on it is if one of them slept sideways and rested their head on the other's chest. Which . . . isn't going to happen.

"You can have the bed," we both whisper at the same time.

Ahn throws up a hand. "You're injured."

"I've recovered, and I'm the man—"

"Women can sleep on floors, too."

"I didn't say—"

"In case you didn't notice, I've been sleeping on the *dirt* all this time," she whisper-hisses.

"I'm trying to be considerate."

"So am I."

We stare daggers at each other, whisper-fighting like a married couple worried about the neighbors eavesdropping. I'd have laughed at the absurdity of it all if I weren't so tired. Too tired to bicker.

"Fine. I'll take the bed," I say.

"Fine."

Ahn huffs and drops the rucksack on the floor with a loud thud. She doesn't seem pleased with my decision even though it's what she said she wanted. Not my problem. I disarm myself, rip off my top, and head toward the bathroom.

Ahn makes a noise. Something between a muted cry and a sharp intake of air.

I spin around. "Are we really fighting over the bathroom?"

One look at her face and I know the gasp was for the scars on my back, not the bathroom. She must not have seen them when I was ill with the poison.

They aren't hard to miss in this well-lit room. Long thick cicatrices, some a good twelve inches long. The whiplike marks have lost their pink-red hue over the years, taking on the pale waxen look of healed skin stretched taut. They look bad. But they are a far cry from the bloody, ripped flesh that once split down my back when I was a boy.

Ahn doesn't move, doesn't say anything. She isn't horrified or disgusted. Something about her expression makes me . . . I don't have words for that feeling. It reminds me of the moment when she made that ghastly joke after I told her how my sister died. The same look. No pity or fear or revulsion. Something else.

My instincts want to fight it. Fight whatever emotion she rouses inside me. But the truth is, she makes me feel less alone.

We stand face-to-face, silent. Until the quiet between us grows too intimate and I can't bear it anymore. Then, I head into the bathroom and shut the door behind me.

27
ALTAN

The sensation of heat wakes me up. It's almost noon, and surprisingly I have slept well. No dreams, no nightmares. Just a peaceful, blank slumber.

Ahn is curled up on the blanket I left on the floor. When I try to wake her, she waves me off sleepily and burrows her face into the fabric. I want to take a stroll around town to ease my restlessness, and it's better for her to stay out of sight anyway so I let her sleep on and leave a note: a warning to stay in the tavern in case the Imperial guards or priests have caught up.

Downstairs, Master Luo plies me with food. Lots of it. Our conversation is innocuous. He doesn't know our plan or where we are going or any of the extraneous details. We both know it is safer this way. Before heading out, I leave a cyphered letter to Linxi in the care of Master Luo's messenger.

Most of Heshi is built on and around the tributaries of a snaking river. Canals serve as roads, connected by arched stone bridges carved with various flowers and animals. I spot kingfishers, dragons, lions and tigers, and occasionally, a monkey, all sculpted with astonishing lifelikeness.

Willow trees bow their heads like graceful maidens gently

dipping their mantis-green hair into the waters beside white and gray stone buildings with terracotta roofs, sitting along the riverbanks. The streets bustle with activity. Shopkeepers, street musicians, and other performers hawk their wares and talents along the riverwalk and on colorful gondolas skimming the canals.

As with Shi tradition, lanterns with painted words line each building, informing passersby of its name and purpose. Unlike other towns I have seen, the lanterns here are a vibrant vermilion, the words inked a solid black—clear signs that this town is well-kept.

With the mourning period over, the townsfolk go about their daily lives dressed in rich colors of silk, passing me in my cotton hànfú without a single glance. Lighthearted chatter fills the air, blending in with soft strains of music from reed pipes.

Hard to imagine our land is slowly dying and war is on the horizon. Or maybe, when you are so used to being in a perpetual state of conflict, you begin to treat it like something mundane. Especially when it doesn't affect you.

It is no coincidence that the Empire recruits from the poorest villages and towns. Stealing the young and healthy, leaving the old struggling to survive. Wealthy towns like Heshi flood the Imperial coffers with their taxes, paying for their own security and stability while impoverished areas languish.

As I pass a fountain carved like a lotus flower, I see a young boy playing with his spinning top. He unfurls the string inexpertly, and the top wobbles for only a few moments before falling over. His lack of skill tempts me to go over to teach him like Father once taught me in one of the many grand halls of the Imperial Palace.

It's all in the flick of the wrist and the control of the release.

I hear Father's deep, patient voice, and that aching sense of loss returns. Despite his courtly duties, he always had time for me and my sister. His face appears in my mind as clearly as I see the boy. The humor and affection in his eyes whenever he was with us, his easy smile. How his jaw would tighten, and his forehead would crease whenever our childish exuberance resulted in a broken priceless vase or two. How he'd break into a smile right after we apologized.

He'd carry me on his broad shoulders to explore areas that a child could not see or reach. It never mattered to him that he looked ridiculous, clad in all his Imperial finery and jewels, walking and crawling around with a young son whose face was probably smudged with food and dirt.

Shīfù once told me the years of Father's reign were the closest to peace he'd ever experienced. Father was an idealist. *The best—and worst—trait one might hope to have in a leader,* Shīfù said.

Everything would be so different if Father were alive. Peace would prevail. He would have found a way to reverse the effects of Yuan Long's dark magic and I would not be stuck with Ahn.

To distract from my thoughts, I fleece a bunch of street gamblers playing Heaven and Nine. It is a game of chance, but when you control the dice, you control your luck. Easy enough to cheat with a few little puffs of strategically aimed air and some showmanship.

On my way back to the tavern, I pause at a fruit stall. My money bag is feeling heavy from my game of dice, might as well use it.

While I'm paying for a bag of red apples, a couple of girls browsing the shop start asking me questions about Mengu. I oblige, glad that my disguise still works.

"Gēge, is it true that you men from the north hunt with golden eagles?" asks one of the girls.

"Of course," I say smoothly.

"Do cherry blossoms bloom all year round, and are your lakes as clear as crystal, dàgē?" asks another girl with a shy smile.

"Yes, but some sights in Shi rival even the beauty of our land." I flash her a pointed smile and she blushes all the way to the roots of her hair.

"Yes, dàgē, *do* tell us more about the beautiful sights you've seen in Shi."

That voice—I'd recognize it anywhere.

Ahn is standing right behind us, dressed in a man's hànfú, hair done up in a topknot as is the common Shi way. The two girls eye her with some interest.

I put my coins on the table and grab the bag of apples. "Let's go," I say to Ahn.

She doesn't budge.

"We're leaving *now*." I wrap a firm hand around her thin wrist and pull her out of the shop.

"Why? I thought we were making new friends," she says, throwing another smile over her shoulder at the two girls who are still staring at us curiously.

"It was just a random conversation about nothing."

"It looked like flirting to me."

"I am not dignifying that with a response," I mutter under my breath. I don't stop walking, keeping my grip on her wrist.

She side-eyes me. "Oh, please. How would *you* like it if some girl toyed with your heart for no other reason than her own amusement?"

"I don't know. Maybe some girl should try," I snap before realizing what I said.

She looks me over, arching an eyebrow as she leans in much too close to me. I feel an uncomfortable heat rising up my neck.

She grins. "Maybe *some* girl will."

I drop her wrist and step back.

She starts snickering. "It's a joke, Altan. Lighten up."

"You were supposed to stay at the tavern. It's too dangerous for you to be out here," I say coldly.

"I read your note, but I wanted to get something, so I had Master Luo's daughter help me with my outfit. What do you think of my disguise?"

"It's not a very good one."

It's Ahn's turn to scowl. She shoves a festive-looking red box into my hand. "Maybe I shouldn't have bothered."

"What's this?"

"The Mid-Autumn Festival's nearly here. I got you mooncakes in case I don't get another chance. Double yolks with lotus seed paste. Chewy, not flaky."

"You remembered." My voice is strangely hoarse.

She gives me a look. "Why wouldn't I?"

Not knowing what else to do, I show her my bag of apples. "For you."

Her eyes narrow suspiciously. "Is this some kind of competition?"

"Why would you think that?" I say, bewildered.

Before she can respond, shouts of distress ring out from the street ahead.

I jerk my head at Ahn. She edges away from the crowd that is gathering around two soldiers. One grips the shoulder of a young boy no older than twelve, the other is glaring at a middle-aged woman kneeling in front of him.

"What's going on?" I ask an old lady standing nearby.

She replies in hushed tones, "The official decree came from the palace this morning for a new military draft. One male per household starting from the villages nearby, and not just men who are of age. If you can hold a sword, you'll be called up. The boy's father was a farmer who came here often to sell his produce. He has passed on, and this boy is the oldest of his siblings. There's no one to take his place."

But he's a child! I want to yell.

The old lady shakes her head, muttering, "I'm afraid our town will be next."

"Shh, don't curse us, ah pó," scolds a well-dressed man next to her. "The soldiers will get enough recruits from the village and leave us alone."

I shoot him a menacing glare and he scurries away. My grip on the box of mooncakes is so hard it starts to crumple. There is no reason for this recruitment unless the palace is planning something. Shīfù was right. The truce is a farce; war is coming again. But why would Zhenxi pull such a move? Our troops have suffered losses in the last war, and she will need to rally the people's support.

This isn't the way to do it. Did Zhao Yang advise this? What is the endgame?

The mother of the boy prostrates in front of the soldiers. "I beg you, please. Don't take him! My boy is all I have."

The taller of the two soldiers sneers. His face is hard, nostrils flaring like a bull. He points to a parchment pasted on a wall. "It's a command from the Imperial Palace. How dare you show your defiance, peasant!"

"Please, have mercy," wails the boy's mother. Red-faced and puffy-eyed, tears stream down her face. Desperately, she clings on to the bull-faced soldier.

"Get lost!" He shoves her back forcefully, and she falls onto the ground with a cry.

"Ma!"

The boy tries to run to her, but the other soldier holds him back and cuffs him on the head. "Shut it or I'll make sure you know what pain is."

The boy whimpers and the crowd murmurs disapprovingly, but no one steps forward to stop the soldiers. Of course they wouldn't interfere. This woman and her child aren't dressed in silks like the people of Heshi. She isn't one of them; she must have followed the soldiers into town after they snatched up her son.

Anger drums against my chest and the ball of energy at the pit of my stomach begs for release. But I can't use my magic without revealing myself as a Tiensai and Ahn is somewhere around here. I need to keep her safe and her identity secret.

"Please," cries the mother. She tries to rise, but Bull Face kicks her and a collective gasp rises from the crowd.

Bastard. I run out into the street to help the woman up.

"Are you all right?"

The mother shudders and coughs, winded from the soldier's abuse. Her skinned and bleeding hands reach for mine. "My son, please, give me back my son."

I stand and face the soldier. "Only a coward would strike a mother and child."

Bull Face spits, a hand reaching for the pommel of his sword. "This decree comes from the Imperial Palace. You have no say in this, and you have no right to speak to me like that, *foreigner.*"

I set the box of mooncakes down on the ground, ready to teach him a lesson. But as I'm reaching for my sabers someone grabs my arm from behind.

"Use your head," hisses a voice.

Bull Face scoffs. "Listen to your friend, boy. He's the wiser of you two. It will only end badly for you if you challenge me."

I grind my jaw so hard it feels like it's breaking.

"*Altan,*" Ahn warns in a low voice.

It takes all my willpower to sheathe my blades.

"Come on, we've wasted enough time," grouses the soldier holding on to the boy. "Got a schedule to keep and the sun's setting." He pushes the boy forward and struts away.

With a last taunting twist of his lips, Bull Face turns and follows his comrade. The crowd disperses, carrying on with their lives, unaffected by what they witnessed.

Guilt pools in my stomach. I'm ashamed that none of my countrymen stepped in to do the right thing, ashamed that *I* stood by and let it happen. I am no better than them.

I press the box of mooncakes and whatever coins I won earlier into the trembling mother's hands, knowing there is nothing I can do or say to make up for her loss.

"What's going on, Altan? Why are they recruiting children?" Ahn asks. I walk over to the wall where the decrees are pasted.

By order of Premier Zhao Yang.

The words are red and bold like blood.

"Why don't you ask your father?" I demand.

Ahn pales, a hand drawn to her lips as she reads the decree I'm pointing at.

"It takes time to train a proper soldier," I say. "If they're recruiting at such speed and near a wealthy town like this, all they want is numbers. War is coming."

I rip the parchment off the wall and crush it, casting one last look at the mother of the boy the soldiers stole. She is slumped over. Weeping, reaching out for something lying on the ground.

A child's toy.

I am wrong about one thing: war is already here.

28
AHN

My heart is still weary from what we witnessed in the town square when we get back to our room in the tavern, but the sight of a familiar head of wavy, white hair lifts my spirits.

"Ama!" I cry out, running into her open arms, my heart bursting with relief. She looks surprisingly robust for someone who has traveled all the way from Shahmo. "When did you get here?"

"About an hour ago," she says, her voice muffled in my hair. "I wasn't expecting to see you here, Ahn. Master Sun said you were going on a sea voyage."

Reluctantly, I release her.

"We had a change of plans," I say, deciding to keep things vague.

Altan's engrossed in talking to Master Sun. The old gentleman is dressed in a pale green hànfú, white hair in a topknot secured by an ivory chopstick. A collection of three or four small jade animal talismans hang from a red string attached to his malachite-and-gold embellished waistband. He looks nothing like I expected. Unlike the pent-up energy that vibrates off his disciple, there's a calm manner to Sun Tie Mu. He doesn't seem like a mercenary to me. I wonder why he'd be helping Altan and what he stands to gain from Leiye.

I bow to him. "Thank you for bringing my grandmother here safely, Master Sun. I hope it wasn't too much trouble."

"Grandma Jia is a delightful traveling companion. Though it did take a while to convince Li Guo that I did not have any evil intentions."

"How is he?" I ask Master Sun.

Altan frowns at me. "Who's Li Guo?"

"A friend." The lines between his brows go deeper. I go on before he can interrupt again. "How was Li Guo when you saw him, Master Sun?"

"He was supposed to come with us. He insisted, said he made a vow to you, but we were pursued by some priests. Thankfully, we got ahead of them and no one was hurt. Your friend is brave. He volunteered to lay a false trail for the priests, just in case. Last I heard, he was headed northwest, far away from here and the seaport."

Guilt weighs heavy in my chest. I made Li Guo promise to keep Ama safe. A burden I shouldn't have placed on anyone other than myself. I will have to find him and pay my debt.

"I am sure you and your grandmother have much to catch up on. We can talk more later." Master Sun signals Altan to leave the room.

Once the door closes, I bombard Ama with questions about her journey and health.

She rests her hands on my shoulders. "Slow down, Ahn, slow down. Everything is all right. I'm fine—I really am. Li Guo took care of me after you were taken, and Master Sun has been very kind to me."

"I'm so sorry to put you through this. It's all my fault." Slowly at first, and then in an outpouring of guilt and confusion, words rush out of me. But when I'm done confessing my terrible deeds and what happened with my father, I see no fear nor anger, not even disgust in Ama's eyes. She merely strokes my head, sighing.

"I am sorry your father was not who you thought he was. I do not pretend to understand his actions, but perhaps, as a parent—"

"I don't want to make excuses for him. He chose his path."

Ama goes quiet, giving room to my emotions. After some silence, I speak again, wringing my hands as my fears return.

"I am afraid, Ama. This Life Stealer title or whatever it is—it makes it sound like I've been chosen for something important. But I'm not sure what, and I don't understand. I don't know what to do."

"Like you said, your father has decided for himself. You may have been *chosen* in some way, but you can still choose your *own* path."

"I want to help, but I want you to be safe," I say shakily. "I don't want to leave you again, and I don't think a sword with such power should be given to someone like me."

She cups my cheek. "Dear child, it is the wielder who decides what to do with a weapon. You are a good person inside, Ahn. I believe that, I *know* that. There are some things that are out of your control—focus on what you *can* do. It is time to forgive yourself for whatever has happened in the past. Move on and live well."

I want to believe her. I want to move on. But images of the men I killed are seared into my brain. If I'm to find the sword and use it, will I end up hurting more people?

"Altan says we need the sword to stop a war."

Ama studies my face, eyes shrewd. "Do you trust him?"

"Altan?" Good question. I play with my jade ring, thinking. "I haven't known him for long. At first, I thought he was just some mercenary paid to get me out of the palace dungeons, but he doesn't seem like a petty criminal. I get the feeling that there's more to him than he lets on. He's educated, well-spoken, and kind, and he carries himself with this air—" I pause as Ama starts to smile, suddenly embarrassed. "He's also arrogant and full of himself," I finish harshly.

"But that doesn't answer my question. Master Sun says Altan will accompany you on the sea voyage to find the sword, and he has told the boy to protect you."

Altan never mentioned that, and he never said how his shīfù was involved in this entire thing. I'm not sure if I believe it, but it would ease Ama's mind to think that someone is watching out for me, so I don't contradict her.

Someone knocks on the door before I can reply.

"Ah, it must be time for my treatment," says Ama, expectant.

"Treatment?"

"Master Sun is the reason why I recovered and am well now. But my malaise lingers, and I need some help now and then."

I open the door and sure enough Master Sun is outside. He enters and checks Ama's pulse.

"What are you doing?" I ask, alarmed by the two long, thin silver needles he pulls from his sleeve.

"With the correct placement, these needles can control the meridians in a person's body. Your grandmother is much better, but her qì needs to be stabilized to prevent a relapse of her illness," he replies, sticking the needles into the side of Ama's neck with learned decisiveness. She doesn't show any discomfort.

"Does it hurt?" I ask, worried.

"Just a pinch like an ant's bite. Nothing more." Ama chuckles. I can tell she trusts Master Sun implicitly.

He checks Ama's pulse again. "She needs some rest. Perhaps, you will join me in a cup of tea?"

His invitation is warm and I'm more than a little curious about Altan's mentor. Leaving Ama in the room, I follow him down to the dining area of the tavern.

It's late afternoon and the tavern is filling up with patrons, the sound of chatter and gossip growing more boisterous by the minute. I pause, wondering if it's a good idea for me to be out in the open so blatantly. My earlier spontaneity of going into town to get mooncakes for Altan, despite my disguise, feels reckless and foolish in light of everything that is happening and what my father is doing. That anxious feeling in my stomach returns. I can't help but feel that my father is always one step ahead of us somehow, and I can only hope that we can stop whatever he's planning before it's too late.

Master Luo's daughter spots us and quickly ushers us into a smaller room. There is only one table in the middle, a large one that can sit ten. This must be a private dining area.

"This is better," says Luo Ying. *This is safer*, is what I hear. "I'll bring tea and some snacks."

"You're busy, I'll get it," I offer.

She smiles with gratitude and leads me to the kitchen. "Father says Master Sun is particular about his tea. Make sure you steep it right to keep the flavor."

I listen carefully as she instructs me and return to the room with a tray laden with hot water, cups, tea leaves, and some roasted peanuts and sunflower seeds. Master Sun watches as I prepare the tea. It's like I'm taking a test and he's a teacher hovering over my shoulder, waiting for me to write my answer down so he can determine if I pass or fail.

I count the time down to the exact second before lifting the lid of the porcelain gàiwǎn, nervously peeking in to make sure the tea is the correct shade of yellow-green that Luo Ying described. Then, I place the cup in front of Master Sun. He takes a tentative sip. Squirming in my seat, I wait for his assessment.

It doesn't come. I must've failed.

"I used to work at an inn, but the stingy innkeeper instructed us to water everything down to save costs," I say, trying my best not to sound overly defensive. "I'm sorry if the tea was brewed without precision, I've never handled jasmine green tea before."

"Why are you apologizing? I have meted out no criticism," says Master Sun, eyes twinkling.

"Nor praise," I counter.

My cheekiness draws a hearty laugh from him. "The tea is not bad—for a first-timer."

"Maybe you can teach me more about tea if the sword-hunting thing doesn't work out. At least I'll have a new skill and I could work in a teahouse." That makes him laugh more and I decide that I like this old sage. "Are you a Tiensai?"

He nods, helping himself to more sunflower seeds.

"But you're not a mercenary like Altan, right? You don't seem like you need the money."

He takes my bluntness in stride, more amused than anything. "Altan has his own way of handling things when it comes to the matter of the sword—and you. I am merely assisting him."

And me? It's an odd and evasive answer, but I assume he's referring to Altan and Leiye's arrangement.

I lower my head respectfully. "I'm grateful for your help, Master Sun. Thank you again for healing my grandmother. Speaking of Altan, where is he?"

"He took his bow and arrows and went for a walk."

Worry gnaws at me. "Did he tell you about the boy who was taken?"

"Yes, but he will not do anything rash," assures Master Sun, sensing my concern.

I have my doubts, but I don't voice them. "My grandmother said you told Altan to protect me. Why?" I ask instead.

"Because of what you may choose to do."

He regards me, a clever gleam in his eyes. Once again, I feel examined. But I'm not sure what the test is this time.

"I understand you are having some difficulty with your magic. May I?" He shows me an open palm.

I place my hand on his, and he presses two fingers firmly on my wrist.

"As I thought. Your qì fluctuates irregularly. A block must have been placed on one of your meridians at some point, affecting the flow of energy in your body, and hence, your magic."

I withdraw my hand with a start. That memory I had after taking the empress's concoction—it was my mother who put the block.

"Can you undo it?"

"I'm afraid not. It is too dangerous. I would counsel you to let the block undo itself."

"How can it undo itself?"

"Focus on understanding your magic, and the rest will follow."

He's talking about my life-stealing affinity. I shake my head. "I don't—I can't—" I shake my head again and gulp down my tea.

"It is all right to feel fear. There is a duality to nature, a balance. Water gives life, but it can pierce through stone and carve mountains. The wind ushers your sails, but it can destroy the boats in your harbor. Earth is the foundation for growth but when it is corrupted, life cannot find a way. Fire may kill, yet, in destruction, there is a rebirth and a new beginning. You can choose to protect."

"Choose to protect?" I echo. His words remind me of what Ama said. They both think I have a choice, but I'm not sure if I do.

Someone knocks on the door and enters.

Altan. First bowing to Master Sun, he casts me a suspicious look as if I were the mastermind of this clandestine meeting with his mentor.

"You are back." The hint of relief in Master Sun's voice is unmistakable. Maybe he was secretly as worried as I was that Altan might have gone to find those soldiers. "Ahn has offered to be my new tea disciple. Seeing that *you* have no interest, I'm taking up her offer. She has potential."

Master Sun beams at me and I smile back, happy to be praised. But my delight is greeted with Altan's scowl.

"Does she?"

I roll my eyes at him. "Where did you go?"

"Master Luo invited us to have dinner with his family in an

hour," he says, ignoring me. With that he turns on his heel and leaves, sullen as ever.

I call him an unkind name under my breath.

"He gets this way sometimes." Master Sun has an indecipherable look on his face.

"I'll go t-tell my grandmother about dinner," I stammer, mortified that he heard my insult.

I bow once more before I leave and run up the stairs. Mired in my thoughts, I miss Ama's room, ending up at the end of the hallway. Huffing, I start to turn back but stop at the sound of voices coming from the room next to me.

"If we set off tonight, we can get Young Master Li to the next town east in three days," says a man gruffly.

"We'll have to take the long route round and avoid the soldiers' camp," says another man. "Wang tracked it down. It's between Heshi and the village they've been drafting from."

Are these two men helping someone avoid the draft? I press my ear against the door.

"I suspect they'll stay for another day or two and be off—"

"Or they'll start recruiting *here*," cuts in the first man.

"In that case, let's leave right now. Lord Li says his son is packed and ready. If he's not here, the soldiers can't draft him."

Footsteps come close, so I sprint back to Ama's room. Chest full of anger, I think about reporting the men and what I heard. How dare the rich flee and leave others to sacrifice? But my own hands are tied. I can't report Lord Li's wrongdoing to the soldiers without exposing myself. Besides, that would be helping my father and his thirst for war. The anger leaves me, and shame takes its place.

I can't do anything.

And sometimes, doing nothing is the worst thing you can do.

Altan doesn't join us for dinner with Master Luo and his family after all. If Master Sun is troubled by his absence, he doesn't show it. After a huge meal of steaming bowls of rice vermicelli noodles, shrimp dumplings, and roasted pork, I stumble back to the barn with a full belly.

"Altan?" I call out.

There's no response. He isn't here in the barn either. Exhausted, I flop onto the hay, my makeshift bed for the night since we gave up our room to a paying guest. But it's impossible to fall asleep. I'm worried about Altan and I can't forget the distraught look on that woman's face or how young and underfed her son looked.

Unlike Lord Li's son, she and her child have no one to protect them. I could have. I *should* have. Altan tried.

But I stopped him.

I want to slap the coward out of myself. Cast away the girl conditioned by the Empire to keep in line, to think only of herself. But I can't seem to do it.

It's late into the night when the barn door creaks open and an Altan-shaped figure creeps in. He tries to be as quiet as possible, but in the slivers of moonlight that slide through the barn's windows, I see him taking some things from the corner.

His weapons.

I remember that wild look in his eyes when we were heading back to the tavern after the encounter with the soldiers. It was like he was trapped in some nightmare of a memory. He didn't just see a boy being torn from his mother at the marketplace.

He saw himself.

I whisper into the semidarkness. "Where are you going?"

"Go back to sleep." He sounds angry.

"I wasn't asleep. You're going to find the boy, aren't you?" I take his silence as confirmation. "Do you know where to go?"

"Mmm."

He doesn't.

"What are you going to do? Wander aimlessly around in the dark?" I get up and go to him.

"I don't know." The anguish in his voice is raw. He punches the wooden strut and the roof of the barn shakes.

I place a firm hand on his arm. He flinches.

"I'm coming with you," I declare.

"No, you're not," he growls.

"Yes, I am. You're not thinking straight, you need me around."

"Since when did you become the sensible one?"

"I've always been the sensible one, *and* I eavesdropped on a conversation earlier."

"So?"

He tries to shrug me off, but I keep my hand on him, my mind made up.

"I know where the soldiers' camp is, and I'm not telling you unless you let me come with you." I grin, heart beating fast. "We're going to get that boy back to his mother."

29
ALTAN

The wind howls in my ears as we ride toward the camp. This is reckless, but I can't stop myself. I can't get the image of the soldier kicking the boy's mother out of my head. Can't rid my mind of memories of my own mother bleeding out on the sand.

We tie our horses a cautious distance away and go on foot. A couple of campfires are lit, but by the looks of it, no one is tending to the dying flames.

Ahn peeks through the bushes at the cluster of tents in the field. "Where are the recruits?"

I point at two tents with soldiers at their entrances. "In one of those."

There are always runners on the first night, men or boys who get scared. And who can blame them? War tests the mettle of men and even the steeliest spine can be broken on the battlefield.

"What do we do?" asks Ahn, a little too eager for my liking.

"You? Nothing. You're staying right here." I shouldn't have let her come.

She starts to argue, but I put my finger on her lips to quiet her. Her eyes widen.

"If you lose control, you're going to kill everyone," I say, vaguely aware of how warm and soft her lips are. "You can be backup. If I don't return in an hour, leave."

She smacks my hand away. "That's not what backups do."

"Come save me if I scream then." I don't wait for her response. There is no time to waste, and she talks too much.

With the moon behind clouds, I melt into the shadows in my black robes. Swiftly, I move closer to the tents. The camp is silent. Everyone else besides the sentries must have turned in for the night. Shi troops are known for their discipline. No drunken revelry here.

One of the guarded tents is dark, the other has a faint light shining from within. One for the men and boys drafted, the other for the garrison commander. On a hunch, I make a loop and approach the darkened tent from the back. I slice the fabric with a blade, pull the flaps apart and peek in.

Empty.

A soldier walks out of a different tent and approaches the sentries in front. I drop flat on the ground, the tall grass acting as my cover.

"Go back to your barracks," the soldier tells one of the sentries.

"I was wondering when you'd come to get us," the guard gripes. "Ten Hells. We were standing outside the tent for over an hour for no reason."

"They marched the recruits out early. Everybody left," chimes in the other. "What a waste of time. I could've gone to bed."

"Shut up. Do you want *him* to hear you?" warns the first soldier as the three of them saunter off.

I curse to myself. I'm too late. The boy is gone.

Light flickers near the other guarded tent. The sentries bow low to a figure walking out from it. I should leave before anyone sees me, but the sentries step back to reveal a man clad in robes of deep rust. The sight of a *priest* in a military camp stops me in my tracks. As far as I know, the two entities operate separately. There is no reason for a priest to be here. But there he is, orange robes, with a red sash running through them.

Not just any priest. It's the head priest. What is *he* doing here?

He strides forward and raises his hands. A jet of fire shoots out at one of the waning campfires. In that moment, the light reveals his face.

Waxen scars ripple down one side, giving the illusion that his face is melting. I see a hawk nose. And even from a distance I know his eyes will be dark and terrifying.

My mother's murderer.

I have dreamt of this moment countless times. The moment when I confront him, when I rip him apart limb from limb. But I am paralyzed. Silence blankets my mind. Sand fills my mouth; grit chafes my tongue. My feet are lead. My heart like ice. I'm eight years old again. Fighting to get away. Failing to protect my family. I came here to rescue someone who reminded me of the boy I once was, only to find that I am *still* that boy.

Lost. Helpless. Broken.

"Did you find him?" whispers a voice behind me.

The spell lifts.

"You were supposed to stay put," I hiss, pushing Ahn behind

the trees. "The recruits have left."

"But they were supposed to stay the night." She peeks out and flips back against the tree immediately, her breaths suddenly ragged.

The priest with the melting face is still standing there in the open. He must have scared her. Adrenaline builds in my veins. I may never get another chance to kill the bastard.

Ahn pulls me back. "Where are you going?"

"I'm going to kill a monster."

"A what?"

"That priest standing there, he's the leader of the Diyeh. He's the man who killed my mother."

"That's *him*? He killed your mother?" she gasps. "Are you . . . are you sure?"

"It's not a face I'd forget."

She gets in front of me, blocking my way. "No. It's—It's too risky. There's a whole camp of soldiers and who knows if there're more priests around. What if something happens to you?"

I push her aside. "I don't care. He murdered my mother."

"Wait—" Ahn grabs my wrist. I freeze as she wraps her arms around me tight. "I know you want your revenge, but you said you wouldn't die on me. Keep that promise. I . . . I can't do it. I can't find the sword by myself." She looks up, stricken, a strange kind of panic written all over her face. "We'll look for the sword and you can have your revenge after. I need you with me. Please. I need *you*."

I don't know how to feel. She leans into me, repeating the word, *please*.

"What exactly are you saying?" I ask softly, trying to make sense of her words and the sudden tightness in my chest.

"I—"

"Shh." There's movement ahead. Whatever she wants to say, it has to wait. I nudge her back into the shadows. "Something's happening."

"A messenger," Altan murmurs.

I inch my head out from behind the trees. Sure enough, a figure clad in orange appears on horseback. The priest dismounts and goes to my father who seems to be expecting him.

My father.

My chest squeezes. Sooner or later, I will have to face him. But not tonight. I shiver, a black bolt of guilt twisting my gut. I did the only thing I could think of to stop Altan from attacking my father earlier: pretend I was concerned about him. What will Altan do if he ever finds out that I lied to protect his mother's murderer?

It won't end well, sounds a warning in my head. After tonight's revelation, nothing between us can.

"Can you hear what they're saying?" I whisper, unease prickling down my spine as I watch the priest hand my father a rolled-up parchment.

Altan holds a finger up, *stay.* Minutes later, he returns, face blanched.

"We need to get back to The Three Axes. Now."

The smell of smoke hits my nostrils once we enter the western quarter of Heshi. Flames rise in the direction of the tavern, a bright, vicious orange in the night. People flee from the commotion, blocking our path. We clamber down from our horses and sprint.

My heart plunges when we get close. Fire engulfs the top story of the tavern. The heat is unbearable, and I start coughing from the smoke. Up front, a priest vaults onto a horse, a limp, white-haired figure in his arms.

"Ama!" I scream and lurch forward.

The horse neighs and gallops off at full speed, disappearing into the night. An anguished sound rips from my throat as I start to run after them. Altan pulls me back. I turn on him, hands thrashing, almost scratching his face with my nails.

"Why are you stopping me? Let me go!"

"You can't catch up—the priests are looking for *you*—"

"They've got my grandmother," I snarl.

Energy hums in my blood. I raise my hands and he staggers back.

Debris explodes into the air and blows me off my feet. Altan catches me as I fall and tucks me behind a stone wall.

Altan's lips are moving, but I'm dizzy, my ears ringing. I don't know what he's saying. He presses me back, yelling something.

"—here! Don't move."

I'm too disoriented to do anything, so I nod and rub my ears, hoping the ringing will go away.

Master Sun leaps out from a window of the ruined tavern, a sword in hand. His robes are burnt, his topknot loose. Daggers shoot out as three priests leap out in pursuit. He dodges the blades, twisting in the air to avoid the fire shooting from the priests' hands. With a swing of his arms, he sends a spray of stone into a priest. The man falls to the ground, but my relief is short-lived as more orange robes appear.

Altan is up, one hand grasping a saber, the other poised to strike with magic. He's about to go into the fray when he suddenly freezes. He looks at me, his face a struggle of emotions. Then he sheathes his weapons and grabs my hand.

"Let's go!"

I should say no. I should stay to help Master Sun. But Altan's expression stops me. There is a blank numbness that tells me he has chosen to save me instead of his shīfù.

I want to tell him he doesn't have to, that my life is worth nothing. I want to yell, *Turn back! Turn back!*

But the words stick in my throat and I flee like the coward I am.

31
ALTAN

The scent of burnt wood and smoke lingers in the air, and the streets are empty when we return in the early glow of dawn. It feels unnatural to see so much destruction in the gentle morning light. Doors and windows of the shophouses remain shut, the townsfolk too frightened to venture out. I don't know if the priests have left or if they will return.

It doesn't matter at this point.

The tavern is torn apart, the remaining half of its facade charred. The ruined building bears a skeletal resemblance to a shack. Mounds of crumbled stone, fractured wood, and dirt. No familiar faces among the bodies on the ground. Hope glimmers inside me, alluring like a mirage.

There is a gasp next to me.

Ahn points. I follow her finger, my gaze finding a fragment of green fabric in the wreckage of somber gray.

Scrambling recklessly, I wade into the rubble, moving aside broken earthen pots and bowls, what was once a bed frame, a one-legged chair—

I am not prepared for the pain when it stabs me in the gut.

My heart wants to believe Shīfù is fine, but my head knows

otherwise. I don't see a wound, but that makes it infinitely worse. His face is almost drained of life, his lips bloodless. His barely opened eyes find me, and his hand grips mine.

A grip so weak it crushes my entire being.

"I'm . . . sorry, my boy." Shīfù's voice is a fragile whisper.

I shake my head. Unable to speak. Unable to breathe.

"You must find a way to *live*. . . . Find your peace." He swallows thickly. "I know you will."

I want to say something. But there is too much to say. Too little to say.

The pressure on my hand increases for a moment.

And then, it is too late, and I feel nothing.

I was six years old when I first met Sun Tie Mu.

I'd snuck into the throne room, safely concealed among the rafters. It wasn't like I was interested in Father's daily dealings with the endless stream of ministers, I didn't understand their discussions about political affairs.

I was hiding from my sister.

We were playing a game of hide-and-seek. But the rules were different. To make things more interesting, the perimeter was in the northern wing where the emperor's quarters were instead of the eastern wing where we lived. To make the stakes higher, my sister decided the loser had to give up their most precious possession to the other.

And the possession had to be something living.

We'd been given a pair of lion-dog pups a few months before by the monks. Intelligent little creatures traditionally gifted as pets to princes only, but my sister was not one to be denied. Knowing that my pup was my prized possession, she offered up her own lion-dog as a wager for our little game. There was no outward declaration about what the fate of the loser's pup would be. But already in my young mind, I understood what the tacit consequences of losing could be.

Already, I understood how my twin sister's mind worked.

An old man dressed in a pale green hànfú was speaking to Father. His hair was white, twisted into a topknot and secured with an ivory chopstick, but he stood straight and tall. Although I didn't recognize him, he spoke to Father with the air of a familiar friend. Their voices remained low and I could not hear their conversation. But even from up in the rafters, I sensed the affection Father had for him.

Midway through their conversation, the old man glanced up. It was cursory but at once, I knew I was exposed. I didn't dare to move for fear of alerting Father as we were not allowed in the throne room when he had guests. My sister burst in recklessly, tired of searching for me after a few hours. Father rose from his throne immediately to admonish her, but the old man only seemed amused. And when my sister was finally escorted away by her nanny, the old man looked up at me again and winked.

When the throne room was empty, I climbed back down. I'd won the game of hide-and-seek, but I refused to take my sister's lion-dog from her. Refused to mete out the punishment she would have done to my own pup had she won. We had a screaming match in a garden. She called me weak. Said it was a lesson I had to learn. That our fate as royals meant we needed to understand how to survive—to only and always show strength.

The old man found me afterward sitting by the koi pond, holding the knife my sister had given me earlier. He'd heard everything.

"Just because you have the power to take a life, it does not mean you should," he said, taking the dagger away from me. "Forgiveness is not weakness. It requires more strength than you think, my boy. You may not be able to change the past, but with each action, you can change the future."

The next time I saw that old man, I was in the desert. He was my lifeline, and he became the only family I had.

You may not be able to change the past, but with each action, you can change the future.

Shīfù's first words to me echo in my ears. Vaguely aware of Ahn trailing behind me, I shamble on, his body in my arms. I don't know where I'm headed, but my legs seem to know the way.

I walk for what feels like an entire day. At last, the expanse of sand greets me, a familiar sight I want to forget. It seems apt that this will be the last place I see Shīfù.

I dig at the earth, gritting my teeth as coarse grains rub against my skin. I tell myself to breathe when that feeling of being buried alive returns. I push away my dark memories, my nightmares. Push away the desert that has taken so much from me.

All I focus on is Shīfù and his last words. Even his dying breath was spent worrying about me. I must honor him. I could use my magic to dig his grave, but it is only fitting I use my own hands. It is only right that I should suffer.

It is the only penance I can offer.

Reason tells me I could not have saved him without risking my life or Ahn's. But it sickens me that I didn't even try. Shīfù wanted me to protect the Life Stealer. *No matter the sacrifice*, he'd said. I could tell myself that I was abiding by his wishes. But I know I made a choice.

I chose *her*.

I chose my revenge, my throne, my ambition over a man who loved me like a son. A kind man. A *good* man.

Your choice will be paid in blood.

Is this what the Phoenix meant? Was Shīfù's life the sacrifice for my immunity? Hot tears slide down my cheeks. It isn't worth it. *It isn't.* I'd rather have Shīfù by my side than anything else in this world.

But it is too late for regrets.

I slit my finger with a knife and press on the wound. I can't offer Shīfù a proper burial. No grand tombstone befitting his stature to mark this grave. No crowds honoring his service to the country lining the streets. I scrawl on a slab of stone an old nomad saying: *Life is but a dream, and death is returning home.* The roughness of the stone tears the cut wider and my finger bleeds freely, but the pain brings a twisted solace.

When I'm done, I push the slab deep into the sand, fortifying it with rocks. I stand, spreading open Shīfù's favorite fan. The silk is ripped and blood stains parts of it. I touch the small character seal printed in red on one of the thin bamboo slats that hold the semicircle-shaped fabric together.

Sun.

I gifted the fan to him a few years ago for his birthday, and he has never been without it. I stuff it into my robes, watching the blood dripping from my hand.

"I can't change the past, but I will change my future," I whisper to myself.

My shoulders tense at the sound of footsteps. Ahn. Something flares inside me. Hot, blistering like an untamed flame. This is the girl I have to put my faith in. This is the girl who will help me get my throne back. *This* is the girl who will either be my salvation or the damnation of the entire world.

"I'm sorry," she says. "I'm so, *so* sorry."

She reaches out, her touch gentle. Her arms go around me.

And slowly, the fire in me subsides.

32
AHN

We ride east through the night, fleeing from the wreckage of the tavern. I did not see Master Luo or his family among the dead. I tell myself they must've fled in time, and that they are safe somewhere. I can only hope that this is true.

We find shelter at sunrise in an abandoned monastery half hidden behind a copse of trees. As soon as we arrive, Altan crumples into a heap in a corner of the courtyard, blank and unresponsive. Grief takes form in many ways. He has shed the tears he needs to, and now, there is only silence.

His presence hurts too much, so I wander around, unable to rest despite my exhaustion. The monks must have left this place long ago. Overgrown with tree roots and creepers, it feels like nature is reclaiming this holy site. Leafy climbers spread across the walls and whorl around the reddish-brown timber of the pillars. Anything worth something has either been removed by the monks or stolen by looters. Even the gold leaf that once decorated parts of the altar has been scraped off.

Murals, faded and discolored, peek from beneath the dust and soot. Smudgy images of temples, pagodas, and magnificent palaces; scenes of battles with hordes of armored soldiers on horses and great beasts that look like lions with wings; images of celestial beings, clad in what must have once been glorious colors of red, gold, and ivory, now faint. A phoenix, its tail flaring out, circles the sky. Swimming in the sea below the villages and towns, a blurry painting of snakelike creatures with horns or antlers appears. Lóng—dragons. Creatures of lore that are said to have lived in our lakes and seas.

Protectors of our land. That's what Ama used to call them whenever she told me fairy tales to get me to go to sleep.

Ama.

The thought of her makes me faint with worry. I collapse against the wall and rest my head in my hands. A surge of terror threatens to drown me, but I push back, forcing myself to think.

I could go back to the capital to rescue Ama from my father's clutches. That is, if that's where the priests took her. But even if I did find her, where would we go? Where can we hide? What can I do against the might of both the palace and the priesthood?

I wish things were different. I wish I wasn't born with magic. I *wish.*

My hands start to shake uncontrollably. Neither elegant nor shapely, calloused from work at the inn, they look like the hands of a peasant. Hands that know labor.

Hands that *steal lives.*

You cannot escape your fate. The gods have chosen you for a reason.

My father's laughter echoes in my head. He lied. Magic isn't a gift. It is a curse, and I can find no blessing from it.

I lean back, staring at the mural on the wall. Sunlight streams in, and the faded images of the gods glow. Slowly, my resolve deepens. My father may want my magic for his own purposes, and he may claim to speak for the throne, but it isn't Tai Shun's voice he is echoing.

My father is neither emperor nor god. I will not be his pawn.

Wishing is pointless. Praying is for fools. *I* am the only one who can control my fate.

I go back out to the courtyard.

Altan is still slumped in his corner, staring into the distance. I crouch down and take his hand and squeeze.

"Altan." He doesn't react.

His expression is frighteningly empty. Like he isn't here right beside me. Like he's somewhere too far away for me to reach.

I don't want to lose him.

I grab the lapels of his outer robes, the trimmings now a dull burgundy, faded from our trials, and pull him forward, willing him to sit upright. To come back to me.

"Altan." I give him another shake.

He startles. Finally, he seems to see me. "It's my fault. . . . It's always my fault."

To see him so broken, it's hard to hold myself together. He wears the same look as he did when he was digging Master Sun's grave. Of a grief deeper than time. As if a part of him is dying with each breath he takes.

"It's nobody's fault," I say firmly. "And if you want to blame anyone, blame the priests."

He shakes his head, dazed. "You don't understand. I made a choice. I made the wrong choice."

His words are a knife to my gut. He must mean me. *I* was the wrong choice. The priests were after me and Ama, and Master Sun gave his life for us. I must honor his sacrifice. I have to set things right.

"Altan, I need you with me," I say, meaning every word this time. "Help me, please. Take me to the ship."

"Why should I?"

My heart twists. There's no hope in his eyes. But I soldier on. "You have to help me because we both want the same thing."

"Do we?"

"We do. You're right. I can't stay out of this mess. Not while I'm alive and not while this magic runs in my veins. I want to find the sword of light, I want to heal the land, I want to rescue my grandmother—and I want to get rid of the priesthood. Will you help me?"

He stays so quiet for so long that I start to think I've lost him for good.

"Everyone I love is dead." There's no emotion in his voice. "I'll help you. . . . I have nothing more to lose."

I squeeze his hand again, fighting the urge to tell him he is wrong.

There is always something else to lose.

33
AHN

We meet up with Tang Wei in the next town and head toward the seaport. Deciding that the best way is to hide in plain sight, I keep my disguise as a boy, playing the younger brother to Tang Wei's wealthy landowner's daughter.

Tang Wei seems to relish her part, and as her personal bodyguard, Altan bears the brunt of her bossiness. He doesn't seem to mind, even his complaints are good-humored. Her presence lifts his mood, and the usual scowl on his face doesn't appear as often. I'm glad that she's taking his mind off the loss of Master Sun.

Two weeks pass in a whirlwind of traveling and eating, and we are finally a day's ride from Cuihai Port. We stop for a final meal to brace ourselves for the last leg of the journey.

A typhoon, I decide as I observe Tang Wei flirting with our waiter.

That's what she is. A violent, glorious roar of wind and water that turns everything upside down and leaves you standing in awe of its raw beauty.

She convinces the man to sneak us an extra plate of steamed shrimp rice rolls for free. I wish I had half of her unflappable confidence and wit. I could do with another rack of dumplings.

"Men are simple," she tells me in a conspiratorial tone after the waiter leaves with a self-satisfied smile on his face. "Make a man feel like he's your hero and he'll do whatever you want."

"Hmm," I say, staring hard at Altan.

He looks up from his beef soup. Flat noodles slither from his chopsticks back into his bowl with a plop, and some liquid splashes out.

"Why are you looking at me like that?"

"You're a man."

"And your powers of observation are astounding."

"It's hard to tell sometimes because you're so pretty," I coo. He cracks a smile. I brandish my chopsticks at Tang Wei. "Is what she said true? About men?"

He fidgets in his seat. "It'll work on some, I suppose."

"Does it work on you?" Tang Wei elbows him. "Does anyone make you feel particularly heroic, Golden Boy?"

Altan shoots her a warning look. "Stop calling me that."

She shrugs and turns to me, eyes sparkling. "Girls, on the other hand, girls are a challenge and far more interesting." She plays with a lock of my hair. My cheeks flush. I can feel my ears turning hot as she pats my arm. "Oh, Ahn, settle down—I didn't mean you."

Altan chokes on his noodles. He clutches his side, laughing as if Tang Wei made the funniest joke ever.

"I *can* be interesting!" I protest.

"I'm sure someone out there agrees. In the meantime, play your part, *brother*." Tang Wei shakes her head slowly, eyes twinkling impishly as she gives me a once-over.

My mouth opens and closes, but no sound comes out. I know

she's only teasing, but surely this isn't the way one would look at one's sibling.

She side-eyes a sniggering Altan. "Stop laughing. *You* are exceedingly dull and predictable yourself, just so you know."

In retaliation, he scarfs down two of her rice rolls.

"Petty boy," she scolds.

He grins and eats another.

The waiter returns with our tea, and the mood at the table instantly sobers. Whenever we get a chance, we order a pot of Master Sun's favorite jasmine green tea, and either Altan or Tang Wei will say a few words of remembrance. This has become our ritual, a tribute of sorts to Master Sun.

You can choose to protect.

I hold his words close to my heart. Even though I hardly knew him, my debt to him is immense. The only way I can repay it is to find the sword of light and turn the tide on the Diyeh priesthood.

"Impossible," I insist.

Altan snaps the twig in his hand and tosses it carelessly. "Just because you haven't seen me do it, doesn't mean I can't. I took out that bandit in the canyon, remember?"

"It could have been a lucky shot—"

"It wasn't—"

"But—"

A rock flies in our direction and we both jump back.

"For Heavens' sake, shut up!" Tang Wei's face is puffy with sleep. We settled in a thick bamboo forest an hour ago to rest, and she decided to nap. "You're like two vultures fighting over a carcass.

If I knew there'd be this much squabbling, I'd have thought twice about coming along."

Altan shrugs. "You're free to leave."

Another rock, a larger one this time, shoots toward him.

"We're not squabbling. We're having a civilized discussion about whether he can *curve* an arrow," I chime in.

"Semantics," mutters Tang Wei, looking murderous. She stretches and flashes a playful grin. "Maybe I'll get some peace when the two of you finally decide to stop going after each other's throats and start focusing on each other's lips instead."

My cheeks burn. What in the world is she talking about? I steal a look at Altan. He's examining the bamboo plant in front of him like it's the most interesting thing he has ever seen in his life.

"You can impress her with your brilliant archery after we leave this forest, Golden Boy," Tang Wei says to him. "That'll shut her up."

"I don't have to prove anything to her."

"You're saying that because you can't do it," I sing, sticking a tongue out at Altan.

"Why don't you go hunt? Bring us back a rabbit or two or something," Tang Wei interjects before Altan can retort.

Surprisingly, he obliges without argument, casting me a strange furtive look before he trudges off.

"Why do you keep calling him Golden Boy?" I ask.

"His hair. It does that thing in the sun," she says airily. Her teasing manner returns. "Pretty, isn't it?"

"I've never noticed," I say too quickly, remembering all the little glances I've thrown at his hair, intrigued by how the color changes from deep chestnut to a golden hue in the light.

She adjusts the metal-tipped chopsticks in the bun at the top of her head. "Funny. I could've sworn you spend an awful lot of time staring at him when he's not paying attention."

"I do not!" I say vehemently. Before Tang Wei can embarrass me further, I turn the conversation to her. "Why did you decide to come along with us anyway? Did Leiye recruit you, too?"

Tang Wei hasn't shared much about herself, apart from the fact that she was from the Lotus Sect. I can't help feeling there's more to her story than that of an assassin who hides behind witty remarks.

Her expression hardens.

"No, I don't know Leiye. I'm here because I want the Diyeh priests gone and you're the only one who can get it done. They fear you." A dagger shoots from her sleeve, slicing a bamboo pole in front of us before arcing back into her hand. "And if *you* are not on their side, it means you're on mine. They took my sister once her affinity started to show and my lily-livered father did nothing because he wanted to protect his status." She spits forcefully. "I hate him."

I think about *my* father, wondering if I hate him. Wondering if he's still looking for me. Does he regret locking me up in the dungeon? Or does he justify his actions in the name of serving his country?

"Is that why you joined the Lotus Sect?" I ask.

"As it turned out, I didn't have magic. But I ran away when I was fourteen anyway. I'd heard of the Lotus Sect, and how Elder Hong Feng took in girls who had nowhere else to go. If I'd stayed, my father would've married me off to some conniving official for political gain. A marriage of convenience to a man I didn't choose and would never love. I couldn't live with that." Tang Wei winks at me, lips quirking. "Besides, why darn with a needle when I can have a life with a sword?"

"The crown prince doesn't have a choice either," I say, remembering Tai Shun's words, the look on his face whenever he saw Leiye. I wonder how he is. I wonder how *Linxi* is. My heart aches, hoping my friend is safe.

"That boy could abdicate," says Tang Wei in a matter-of-fact way.

"And who would reign?" *My father?* I shudder at the thought.

She doesn't meet my eyes. "Someone worthier."

"But does such a person exist? The true heir is dead, and the royal family line ends with Tai Shun. The Shi would never put someone without royal blood on the throne."

She waves a dismissive hand and yawns. "We'll worry about crossing that bridge when we come to it. You tired? I'm going back to sleep."

I shake my head, still thinking about Tai Shun.

She yawns again. "When all this is over, I'm going to sleep for a thousand years—I'm so tired and the dark circles under my eyes are dreadful."

"What are you talking about? You look wonderful." I see no circles under Tang Wei's eyes. Despite our travels, she looks as pretty and put together as the first time I saw her back in Shahmo.

She beams at me. "You're sweet. Maybe he'll stop being a fool for once."

"Who?"

She makes a face. "Guess he's not the only fool. Anyway, I'm taking a nap." She lays down and promptly drops her straw hat over her face.

Moments later, I hear a gentle snore that makes me laugh. Tang Wei stirs and I clap my hand over my mouth and move away as silently as I can. I should get some sleep, but Altan's absence makes me feel out of sorts. I've grown so used to him being around all the time that something feels missing. Probably best for me to turn my restless energy to something useful, like practicing my magic. I still haven't felt that pull my father spoke about. The sword of light doesn't speak to me. I don't know if it means I won't be able to find it, or if I just need to get closer to it to feel it.

Or if it's because I haven't been able to use my life-stealing magic. Maybe the block my mother put on me out of desperation is too strong, and it cannot undo itself.

I head toward the edge of the forest, following the gradually cooling air, sure that there'll be a lake or body of water. Soon, the bamboo forest thins, and a stream appears.

There are fish in there.

No one's around and we're far enough from the nearest town. Feels safe to use my magic. Just for a while.

Breathing rhythmically, I focus on my qì, gathering a ball of energy at the pit of my stomach. I stretch out a hand toward the stream and flex my fingers.

A small spout of water rises, curving toward me. Slowly, I move it around, curling it into a sphere and back again. The water sparkles and shimmers prettily against the sunlight, and it makes me smile.

Something chitters behind me and I spin around in surprise,

spraying water everywhere. A flurry of reddish-brown and white fur bounds away into the bamboo. A curious red bear-cat must've snuck up on me. I turn my attention back to the stream, wondering if I should leave or do what I came here to do.

Again, that feeling of nausea returns. I shove it down. The only way to fix everything is to find the White Jade Sword.

And the only way I can find it is to master my life-stealing magic.

Cowards don't make their own destiny, I tell myself. No matter what my father says, I'm the one in control of my life.

I point my fingers at the small silvery fish darting this way and that. *Do it,* whispers that sly voice in my head.

I take a deep breath.

Something rustles. It must be the bear-cat again.

"Catching some lunch?"

I leap back in fright. Yet, I can't deny the sense of relief I feel. Deep down inside, I know I don't have it in me to kill those fish with my dark magic.

But that relief vanishes when I see who it is.

Leiye.

The uneasy feeling that comes with his presence curdles in my stomach. He's dressed in black, a slim green ribbon woven through his dark hair. No priest robes. Does this mean he's here as Xima Leiye, the son of the Marquis of Qin, and not my father's hench-man? Or is he here as himself, whoever that is? There are too many sides to him for me to fathom.

"Nice disguise." He gestures at my tunic and pants. I can't tell if he's being sarcastic.

"How did you find me?"

Wordlessly, he slips a hand into his robes and pulls out a red mask.

My heart beats faster. "You were at the canyon—you threw that dagger. Have you been following us?"

"Not all the way."

"Why?"

"I said I would keep you alive."

I don't bother to thank him. "What do you want? Are you here to join us? I thought I'd see you on the ship."

"No, and that's what I came to tell you. Don't get on it."

I frown, confused. "Why not? Didn't *you* hire Altan to get me onboard?"

Leiye chuckles mirthlessly. "Is that what *Altan* said?"

"Why are you saying his name like that?"

"Because I know him by another name," replies Leiye, stone-faced. "Our agreement was that he'd get you out and keep you hidden. No sea voyage, no sword. Not until I figure things out. Imagine my surprise when no one showed up at the assigned meeting place after your jailbreak. I had to restrategize, stall for time with the Diyeh and your father to give you a head start. I wasn't given any warning and I had to cover my own tracks."

"How resourceful," I remark.

"When you're the bastard child of a marquis, you learn to be," he says dryly.

"None of this makes sense. If Altan wasn't getting paid by you, why would he go to the trouble of getting the ship?"

"Why indeed," Leiye muses, tracing the lines on his mask with a slender finger.

I'm almost certain he was sent here by my father; this must be some complicated scheme of his. I refuse to believe that Altan lied to me. But Leiye did help me escape the dungeon, so I owe him a chance to explain.

"Back in the dungeon, you said I needed to find the sword of light. Getting on that ship is my only chance to do so. Why the change of mind?"

For the first time since I've known him, Leiye's confidence wavers. "I've been studying the archives and historical records in the Forbidden Library—something doesn't add up. There's missing information. Pages that were duplicated, pages that seem forged."

"Is this about the book you stole from my father's study?"

"Yes and no." He takes a step closer; I take a step back. "Have you felt the pull? Has the sword called out to you?"

"No," I admit. "What doesn't add up? What have you found?"

"I'm not sure yet. Just . . . trust me."

"Trust you?" I say, scornful. "How do I know you're not here on my father's orders pretending to be concerned? How do I know you're not lying to me?"

"Think about it, Ahn," he says with exceeding calm. But from the set of his jaw, I can tell he's getting irritated by my stubbornness. "Your father *wants* you to find the sword of light. I'm telling you *not* to."

"Do you know what my father's planning to do?"

He shoots me a perplexed look. "Why else would I be trying to stop him?"

"Maybe you—"

"Is that you, Ahn? Who are you talking to?"

Altan appears from the copse of bamboo, dead pheasant in one hand, dagger in the other. A dagger he seems to want to throw at Leiye when he catches sight of him.

"What are *you* doing here?"

Leiye's slate-gray eyes flash dangerously. "Spoiling your plans, Jin."

The dagger flies. Leiye catches it, almost lazily. Altan drops the pheasant and unsheathes his sabers.

"Wait!" I shout at Altan. "Stop!"

He hesitates.

"You—stay where you are and don't move a muscle," I say to Leiye who does as he's told. I turn back to Altan.

"Why did he call you *Jin*?"

He doesn't look at me. Doesn't say a word.

I falter. "Altan?"

"Yes, *Altan*. Why don't you tell her what your real name is?" Leiye lets the dagger loose.

I yelp but Altan doesn't even flinch. The blade misses his ear by an inch. Leiye grabs him by the collar and shakes him hard, not caring that Altan has his sabers out.

"Doesn't feel good to be betrayed, does it? We had an agreement. Like I said, stick to the plan and I won't spill your secrets." He lets go of Altan and pivots to me. "Why don't you ask him who he really is? Ask him what he wants from you, Life Stealer?"

Be careful who you trust.

A caustic taste burns my tongue. My stomach flips. It feels like I'm falling into a deep, dark hole.

"By the way," Leiye continues. "Tai Shun was terribly upset when he finally recovered from his hangover. He was so sure he'd seen his dead cousin in the flesh, so certain his beloved Jin was still alive." He grins, eyes cold, voice full of poison. "I didn't have the heart to tell him he was *right*."

Altan ices over with rage. "You bastard—"

"I thought the true heir to the Dragon Throne was dead, that's why Tai Shun is next in line." I stare at Altan, uncertain. "Who exactly *are* you?"

The look on his face tells me everything I need to know.

"You!" I slam my palms into his chest, and he stumbles back. "After everything we've been through. You *lied* to me."

"There was never a good time to tell you."

"Liar!" I scream into his face. Something clicks in my head. "You are using me to get your throne back, aren't you? That's why you haven't told me the truth."

"Ahn."

He approaches, looking distraught. I'm too furious to care. On the verge of tears, I shove him away.

"I trusted you—" I choke out.

"Ahn!" Tang Wei bursts through the foliage. "Get on a horse and go!"

The rest of us are too stunned to react. Daggers ready, she stands her ground.

Magic is in the air.

The bamboo forest splits. Pole by pole, the world falls apart.

Clad in robes of rust orange, four figures wave their hands in unison, walking steadily through the green. How did the priests find us? Did Leiye betray me? I look around.

He has vanished.

The female priest draws her sword and rushes at Altan, kicking up a storm of dead leaves behind her. They spring up in the air, each bending a bamboo pole with their feet for support, continuing their fight high above us.

Everything that can be used as a missile flies through the air: blades, bamboo, rocks, dirt. Grunts, punches, and the clanging of metal on metal ring in my ears.

Run, run, run.

My feet finally react, bursting into a sprint back to where we left the horses. But a ripple of flames explodes in my path, cutting my way off, forcing me back into the frenzy.

Tang Wei slices the air with her daggers. The priests discard them with a casual flick of their hands. One of them gets close. She dodges his blows, whips a hand to her hair, and strikes.

Clutching his neck, the priest staggers backward, blood dripping down to his orange robes. To my horror, he pulls the chopstick out as he falls to his knees. More blood spurts out. He slumps over and I retch, turning away from his body.

A silver chain spirals out and wraps around the other priest, pinning his arms to his torso. Tang Wei hangs on to her metal whip, lips curling as she hauls him in. Just when I think things are going our way, a jet of fire shoots up into the bamboo thicket where Altan and the female priest are.

I run ahead, screaming his name. Someone rams me to the ground.

Metal enters flesh.

A knife sticks out of Tang Wei's rib cage—a knife meant for me.

"No . . . the gods . . . *no!* Why did you—" The blade is embedded deep. I can't pull it out, so I press my hands on the wound to stem the flow of blood.

Tang Wei cries out in pain. "Gods, Ahn—why you still here? Leave!"

I keep my hands on her. "I'm not leaving you—you're hurt."

She grabs me, smearing my sleeve red. "I shall die for a worthy cause. Now go!"

A throttled sound between a laugh and a sob escapes my throat. "Don't be dramatic. You're not going to die."

Not if I can help it.

I place her hands over her wound. Then I stand and face the two priests. They hesitate, sensing something different about me. Pleading, searching, I call out to the aberrant magic in me and say a silent prayer to deaf gods. *I accept you,* I tell whatever beast is inside me.

I release you.

The cicada hum starts. My senses heighten.

Power erupts in me.

I fix my gaze on the female priest battling Altan in a vortex of blades and leaves. She jerks in my direction. Her sword falls. Her eyes roll back, whites showing. Pale green light leaks from her as she plummets to the ground. Her life force seeps into me, a thrilling deluge of energy.

Altan lands on the ground in a crouch. The look on his face—I can't tell if it's horror or wonder. Or both. Our eyes lock, and everything fades into the background. That strange halo surrounds him again. Bright and white.

Pure, my mind whispers.

Take it, commands another, stronger voice.

He approaches, his glow dazzling. I reach out with my dark magic. Feeling for his thread. His life force. I tug. But Altan doesn't gasp or choke like he did in the canyon. His light remains white with no hint of green. It's repelling my magic. Pushing me back. It—

"It's the Life Stealer!"

I snap out of my reverie. A priest is pointing at me. The reverence in his tone pleases and repulses me.

He interrupted you, whispers that voice. *He must pay for his insolence.*

The man's neck snaps back. His hands go to his throat. With a whimper he crumples to the ground, pale green light leaking out of him. In a blink of an eye, all that's left is a husk of a man.

The last priest remains where he is. Whether it's panic or awe that stops him from fleeing, I don't know. And I don't care. He knows who I am—I can't let him go. There's a brief struggle on the man's face before he succumbs.

Enough, I cry out to the monster inside me. *Stop.*

I fall to my knees, shivering, head in my hands.

Stop.

But something dark and terrible snakes it hands around my mind.

More. You want more, whispers that other voice from the depths of my soul. *Take it. Take everything.*

My eyes find Tang Wei. Her blood has soaked the soil black. Her qì is so weak, her breaths so shallow. It would be easy to drain her life force.

Easy as breathing.

I reach out a hand.

"Ahn!"

I freeze. What was I doing? *What was I about to do?* I hear myself crying out as a sharp wedge of pain drives through my heart.

And everything goes dark.

34
ALTAN

Ahn collapses with a cry. When I get to her, she's unconscious but breathing. Next to her, Tang Wei is white as a ghost, *barely* breathing. The blade missed her heart by inches, but it's lodged deep. I can't pull it out without the risk of her bleeding to death.

Her eyes flicker open and find mine. In that moment, we have an understanding. She knows I'm thinking of leaving her behind. That her wound is bad enough for me to consider it.

"Go. Take Ahn and leave. They'll send more priests. I'll only slow you down."

"And lose the chance of rubbing this in your face for the rest of your life? I think not," I grin like a maniac, trying not to panic. She has lost too much blood. "If you survive this, you owe me big-time."

"O Immortals, let me die now." Her smile is more of a grimace.

"Shut up."

The flames are still spreading, so I dump some earth on the fires before they reach us. I shake Ahn.

"Stop! No, stop!" She returns to consciousness, struggling and hitting me. I wrap my arms around her tight to stop her from moving or hurting herself.

"Everything's fine. We're all alive—Tang Wei is alive," I repeat as she shudders, trembling against me. "Breathe. It's all right. Just breathe."

Her body softens, hard edges melting into me. I try not to think of anything else, focusing only on the need to keep her calm. When her breaths steady, I release her.

"We need to get Tang Wei to a physician. Can you ride by yourself?"

Ahn gulps, a feral, cornered look in her eyes. "Yes, I'm fine. Take care of her."

I get her to her feet and on a horse. Then, I lift Tang Wei in my arms.

She grits her blood-smeared teeth. "Don't drop me."

"I'm not that weak."

"Be careful . . . I have a *knife* sticking out of me."

"I can see that. Stop talking."

She starts to laugh but I see real fear in her eyes. For a moment, I feel my own terror. I can't lose her, too. I keep my arm around her after we saddle up, careful not to get near the site of the injury.

"This is less romantic than I thought it'd be."

"Trust me, I'd rather be holding someone else," I shoot back.

Somehow, she summons the strength to give me a sly smile. "I know."

"*Shut up.* Concentrate on staying alive."

"Safe house in port town . . . The Scarlet Butterfly," she whispers, turning paler by the moment.

"I'll get us there. No more talking."

She nods and closes her eyes. I set a blistering pace, counting on Ahn to keep up.

35
AHN

Am I losing my mind?

I've asked myself that question a hundred times since we fled from death and destruction and came to The Scarlet Butterfly.

It began with that voice, cunning and smooth like silk in the shape of a leash, ready to wrap itself around my throat. Ready to take control of me. It speaks to me now, even as I sit quietly in the corner of the room watching over Tang Wei as she rests.

The shadows came later.

At first, I thought I was delirious. Then, I thought I was going insane.

Soon, I realized what the shadows were. *Who* they were.

My kills. The souls I have stolen.

I started putting faces to the dark, disembodied shapes that flit around me. The bandit from the canyon, the two men from the alley in Shahmo, the three priests . . . I don't see them exactly. They remain murky and amorphous. But I can *feel* them. I don't know why they are suddenly here or why they are haunting me. Maybe they were around before, but I just didn't notice them.

Maybe I have killed too many people, and this is my punishment.

I don't tell Altan and Tang Wei about the shadows or the voice.

I don't want to scare them. Don't want them to think there's something wrong with me or that I'm incapable of going on a sea voyage.
Even though Leiye told me not to, I'm getting on that ship. And I'm
going to find the sword.

"Ahn?" comes a muffled whisper from the bed.

I bolt up and go to Tang Wei. "I'm here. What do you need?"

"Just water."

She grimaces as she sits, a hand going to her chest. But she's
looking better than she did for the past few days. The healers of the
Lotus Sect are skilled, and they promised me she'd recover fully in
a few weeks. That did little to assuage my guilt. It was my fault that
she got hurt. And even though she forgave me when I confessed
that I'd almost set my life-stealing magic on her, I have not forgiven
myself.

I hand her a cup of water, and she sips from it slowly.

"How are you feeling?"

"Like a mess." Her lips curve up, and the spark returns to her
eyes. "Bet I look like one, too."

I can't help but laugh. She points her chin at the wooden comb
on the table. I pick it up and crawl onto the bed beside her. Taking
a lock of her dark hair, I start to comb, getting rid of the little knots
here and there.

"Ahn." Her tone catches my attention. "Is everything all right?
Have you been eating?"

My lack of sleep and loss of appetite must be starting to show. I
make a funny face. "Have you ever seen me turn food away?"

Tang Wei looks unconvinced, but she doesn't press me. "When
does the ship depart?"

"Three days."

"You're still bent on going despite what that dodgy priest said?"

I stop combing. "I have to. I can feel it now, I know it's out there."

Her shoulders go taut. "The sword?"

I nod.

"Is it in the sea?"

"I think so. I started feeling the pull after we left the bamboo forest." *After I let go of my fear. After I embraced my dark magic.* I don't say those words to her, but she knows.

"What does it feel like?" she asks.

She's curious, but I'm not sure how to explain it to her. My father said it'd be like the needle of a compass, leading me. But it's not the same.

"It's like a tug. Comes from here." I place a hand on my chest. "Like there's a rope tied to me and it's pulling."

Her eyes widen with concern. "Does it hurt?"

"No. It's strange, that's all." I start to comb her hair again.

"I'm going on that ship with you," she announces.

"You're staying here where it's safe," I say with a sigh. I knew she would bring this up eventually.

"Neither you nor Altan get to decide—my life, my choice."

"Finding the sword is my responsibility, not yours. I'm the only one who should get on that ship." I haven't spoken to Altan—or whatever his real name is—since we arrived here.

Tang Wei waves me off. "You're not my mother, Ahn. And my mother couldn't stop me from doing what I wanted anyway."

"It's too dangerous. And you're hurt."

"I'm not letting you do this alone. I'll be fine. I can rest on the ship. Don't try to change my mind because you won't be able to. Besides, I know the captain. I can get him to stow me away no matter what you do." Tang Wei smiles and squeezes my hand. "Now, please, make me look presentable."

I muster a smile back, wondering if she knows that deep down inside, I *do* want her to come with me. It's a selfish desire, I know. But I've no idea what the sea voyage will bring, and her presence is comforting.

"Have you spoken to Altan?" she asks.

I pretend not to hear her. She sticks her face right in mine so I can't ignore her.

"Still angry at him?"

I shrug.

"He had his reasons."

"I knew you'd defend him." I drop the comb and get one leg off the bed before Tang Wei pulls me back.

"I'm not defending him. I just think you should try to understand what he's been going through. Wait, hear me out—"

She blocks my repeated attempts to escape. Even when wounded, she's determined. I make an exasperated noise and sit back down.

"I do think he was wrong to hide his identity from you. But if it helps, he isn't pretending to be someone else when he's with you. I've seen how he behaves. His lets his guard down around you. The Altan you know—it's *him*."

"Oh, so that annoying, obnoxious, and self-important *liar* is the real Altan? Good to know."

"It's been hard for him to trust anyone," says Tang Wei, calmly ignoring my childish outburst. "I don't pretend to understand how he feels, but you *are* the Life Stealer and the last one was his great-grandfather, the man who did all those terrible things."

Her unvarnished honesty isn't something I want to hear. But it makes me think of what happened in the bamboo forest. How that ethereal light shimmered around Altan. Bright and dazzling. How it drew me to it.

How I tried to *take* it.

It was obvious he couldn't see that light. Not in the forest, and not earlier in the canyon when my magic first attacked him. The heat of shame scorches my throat. *He* was the one who stopped me from hurting Tang Wei. He knows what I'm capable of.

Maybe he was right to fear me. Maybe he was right to distrust me.

I school my expression, looking at Tang Wei coolly. "We're done talking about this."

She sighs. "Fine. I'm sorry I brought it up. Will you at least let him get on that ship with you? I know he wants to, and it's not because of the sword."

Not because of the sword? I refuse to take the bait and ask for an explanation. Refuse to read into what she meant. I get off the bed. This time, Tang Wei doesn't stop me.

"You must be hungry," I say, keeping my tone light. "I'll go get some food from the kitchen for you."

I leave the room only to walk straight into a skulking Altan in the narrow corridor outside. He's holding a tray with a bowl of hot soup. He must've come here to give it to Tang Wei.

I've managed to avoid him for the past few days. But now I'm trapped with nowhere to run except back into Tang Wei's room. If I do that, she'll be certain to corner us both and force us to speak to each other through sheer willpower. I could squeeze past. But that would mean having to touch him.

"We need to talk."

His voice is gravel, the hurt in it plain. His usual cloak of confidence is nowhere in sight. That haughty swagger gone. Just a boy who cares about what I think of him. My resolve wavers, but I keep my gaze cold and my mouth shut.

"I'm sorry," he tries again.

I stay silent, fiddling with the hem of my sleeve.

"Don't shut me out," he pleads. "Tell me what you're thinking."

The look on his face pushes me to speak. "I'm thinking about how satisfying it would feel to throw that hot soup in your face."

His shoulders sag. "Go ahead. I deserve it. I'm surprised you haven't already."

I reach out to do just that, but my rage is gone. In its place, a deeper, crueler pain remains. I wish it were anger I felt. Anger I can deal with. Anger, I understand. But this caustic taste of betrayal is hard to stomach.

All the things he shared—that *we* shared. All those late nights on the road, lying awake, talking about nothing and everything until one of us fell asleep. I thought they meant something.

I was wrong.

My hand falls to my side. "Get out of my way."

"Wait." He puts a hand on the wall, blocking my path. "Hear me out. You don't have to forgive me or talk to me. I just want you to know that I'm going with you on that ship, whether you like it or not. I promised Shīfù I would protect you. I have to do this."

I look him in the eye. "Was keeping that promise worth it?"

Regret fills me when he pales, features contorted with pain. I found the cut left in his heart from Master Sun's death and tore it open again, thinking it would give me pleasure. Hoping it would satisfy my spite.

But it only makes me feel worse.

I'm sorry, I didn't mean it, I want to say. But the words don't come out.

Altan lets his arm drop. I push him aside and barrel down the corridor, turning my head so he can't see my tears.

THE DRAGON'S
TRIANGLE

36
ALTAN

Tall tales and rumors surround the Dragon's Triangle. I remember hearing them as a boy: crewless ships found drifting aimlessly back to shore; sudden whirlpools sucking helpless boats into unknown depths; strange weather patterns occurring on a fair day.

I keep looking out at the perfect aqua of the Emerald Sea, waiting for something to happen. So far, the waters have been calm for the last two weeks. The gods seem to favor our passage, but as always, I question their intentions.

The boards behind me creak. Tang Wei appears, rotating her arm gingerly before bringing a hand to her ribs. The healers of the Lotus Sect are renowned, and she is healing well. Still, I questioned why she took a knife for the Life Stealer in the first place. Her answer was simple: she took the hit for *Ahn*, not the Life Stealer.

"How are you feeling?"

She leans her head on my shoulder. "Better."

"Ahn?"

"Asleep. It was a quiet night."

"That's good," I say, but we both know sleep is hardly a safe refuge for Ahn. We hear her screams from the nightmares that plague her. They seem to be getting worse. She makes the crew uneasy, but no questions are asked of us. Captain Yan keeps his men in check.

We watch the brightening horizon in silence, listening to the waves lapping against the ship.

"You should talk to her, you know," Tang Wei says abruptly.

Ahn and I haven't spoken since that brief encounter in The Scarlet Butterfly. She didn't say anything when I showed up on board the ship. I suppose she tolerates my presence. She won't talk to me. If her silence is a form of punishment, it is working. The distance eats into me. I hate that I care what she thinks of me. Hate that I care more than she knows. More than I realized.

"She doesn't want to talk to me."

"Trust me, she does. You haven't tried hard enough." Tang Wei elbows me. "I suggest an apology, preferably one offered on your knees."

I scoff, and then sigh when I find myself contemplating doing exactly that.

"Stubborn water buffalo." Her brow furrows. "Do you think Ahn will be ready when the time comes? The closer she gets to the sword, the more it seems to drain her."

I keep my doubts close. "Have some faith."

"*I'm* not the one who lacks faith." Tang Wei's abrasive tone catches me by surprise. "I know why you didn't tell Ahn about yourself. But if you want her to trust you again, you should trust her. Remember who she's not. You don't see me holding *you* responsible for Yuan Long's misdeeds, and you share the same blood. This is a mess, a mess your great-grandfather started. He made the priests who they are, he ruined everything."

Taken aback by her sudden outburst, I don't control my tongue.

"You think I don't know that? I think about it every single day. I have to *live* with that, with the knowledge that the same blood that runs through my veins is the cause of all our troubles."

She places a hand on my arm, a kinder light in her eyes. "Then stop being a self-righteous, self-absorbed, selfish brat and think about Ahn for once. How do you think it *feels* to be the Life Stealer? To know that the person you love thinks that you're a monster?"

The person she—Did Tang Wei just say . . . ? No. I must have heard wrong.

The corners of her mouth twist. An odd smile, almost wistful. "Yes, I said it."

I scowl at her.

"I did say you were predictable." She shakes her head. "You two."

I refuse to speak or even look at her. A beat later, she tugs at my sleeve, teasing.

"Oh, come on, Altan, you don't fool me. Neither of you do. All your sad little yearning looks, those tortured silences, you're both pining for each other. But you're both too stubborn and foolish to say anything."

"I am not pining—or *tortured*," I burst out like a sullen child.

"Deny it all you want, I'm not blind, and neither is Ahn."

The memory of Ahn standing over Tang Wei back in the forest flickers in my mind.

"Trust has to be earned," I say quietly.

"Trust has to be granted. What do you expect her to do to earn your trust if you don't open your mind first?"

I don't answer. Eventually, she huffs loudly and leaves. Minutes later, the boards creak again with heavier footsteps. I can't help but notice Captain Yan's impressive stature when we exchange bows in greeting. The man looks to be in his forties, broad-chested with a scruff of beard and a quick smile. He bellows a command at his first mate, Ming, who's as reedy as he is tall.

"I checked in with Ahn last night. She says we're still on course."

"Good," I say. The tug of the sword seems to have grown stronger since we entered the Emerald Sea, acting like a compass needle, pointing Ahn toward its location.

Captain Yan strokes his beard, keen eyes fixed on the water. "We are heading into the Dragon's Triangle. I expect to arrive at sunset in two days, which is the only time you want to arrive at those waters."

"Why is that?"

"Because it is the only time a ship can glide safely through and bring us to Dragon's Teeth Pass. Too early and we will miss the guiding current. The winds will change, and the ship will veer off course."

"What happens if we're late?"

His graying eyebrows meet in a forbidding line. "Then, my boy, you will have to pray for our souls."

"The gods have little regard for human life," I say, remembering all the times I'd asked the Heavens for help as a boy and received no respite. "I doubt prayers will save us or our souls, Captain. Please, tell me, what happens if we enter after sundown?"

"We will be trapped in between our world and the soul realm, in between life and the Courts of Hell, and we will have no choice but to navigate the Waters of the Undead."

I start to dismiss this ridiculous notion, but his expression sobers me. He is unsettled, a far cry from the confident man who has been helming our ship. "Are you familiar with the Waters of the Undead?"

"I am, though this fact gives me little joy. You see, I may be the only one who has made it through alive."

I incline my head respectfully. "If it doesn't trouble you, Captain, I'd be honored if you could share your tale with me."

"It isn't one I like repeating, but perhaps it is best you know." A look crosses his face, sorrow mixed with something darker. "I wanted to explore the world after the early wars, and the sea called to me. I'd heard of the old legends about the Dragon's Triangle as a boy, and, eventually, I found a crew as reckless as myself. The plan was to enter at sundown to search for the mystical current that would carry us across safely. But the winds shifted at the last moment, and we were too late."

The man shrinks back, a shadow passing his face. "When the spirits came, and the madness descended, it felt . . . it felt like *death*. Like death was running *through* us—consuming us one by one. Some of the crew removed the ropes that tied them to safety. Others screamed and wailed until they lost their voices. One man broke his own wrists and chewed at the knots so that he could get out of his bindings."

A shiver goes down my spine. "And yourself?"

"The spirits tempt you in many ways, with your deepest fears or your heart's desires. Greed, vengeance, love, anything you can think of. They dredge up the sins of your past and show you who you truly are. I was a military man who fought for over a decade in the wars when I was a young lad. I've seen bloodshed and countless deaths, men tearing at each other's throats with bare hands for survival." He looks at me with eyes that have seen too much. Eyes that remind me of Shīfù's. "But I have made peace with myself, and I did not succumb."

His description reminds me of the spirits that accosted me in the cavern in the Wudin Mountains. Could it be that another supernatural portal lies in the deep sea? Would there be another Soul Beast guarding it?

"I hope you and your crew have been paid enough to warrant this escort." My tone is unnaturally light as I try to shake off the pall hanging over our conversation.

Captain Yan chuckles. "It isn't gold that drives us to embark on this journey, my boy. I'm doing this for my country. Ming was my comrade in the military." He gestures to another stocky man at the stern. "Lishi was in the Imperial Navy. All of us here fought in one way or another. We understand the cost of war. We know what is riding on this mission—we know our people are suffering as the desert takes over our land." He places a firm hand on my shoulder. "There is power in your father's legacy, Jin Long. He was a good man, and he left this world too soon."

I nod slowly as his words sink in. He knows who I am, and so does his crew. But although I have carried my secret as little more than a whisper for so long, having it exposed so clearly doesn't feel dangerous anymore. Perhaps, it is time to let go of that lost boy from the desert.

"Was it Tang Wei or Elder Hong Feng who told you?" I ask, curious.

"When you have traveled as far and as wide as I have, you hear things. Threads of conversations, pieces of truth in rumors. You begin to stitch your own tapestry of the world—your own truth." Captain Yan's laugh lines crinkle as his smile widens. "Maybe someday, if I'm blessed to live a long life, I'll get to tell a new tale of how I once spoke so freely and informally to our emperor."

He bows low and I return his respect. The gravity of his implication weighs me down. I know my vengeance bears a greater significance than a personal vendetta. I know it carries expectations. Responsibilities. Duty. I dampen the spark of doubt building in my chest. Now isn't the time for second thoughts.

"I don't know what you are planning," he says thoughtfully. "But I do know the Life Stealer must be part of it. I have my own concerns . . ."

His unspoken question hangs in the air. *Wouldn't that be giving a tiger wings?* Tang Wei questioned my course of action at the start, but now she seems to be on board. She believes in Ahn. Maybe I should, too.

"I trust Ahn, and I'm honored to have your support, Captain."

He looks back out to sea. "What a burden it is for one so young and unprepared."

"She's stronger than she looks," I say quickly, anxious to reassure the captain. Or perhaps, to convince myself.

"She will have to be if she is to avoid the same fate as Yuan Long."

"What do you mean?"

"Why do you think she's having all these nightmares?"

I hesitate. "I'm not sure."

"The Life Stealer treads the path that separates our world and the soul realm," Captain Yan explains. "Every life she steals is a soul that remains in the realm of the undead, much like the waters of the Dragon's Triangle. These lost souls are unable to go to Heaven or Hell; they exist in limbo. They will follow her, and they won't let her go."

Dread unfurls its talons in my chest. I'm uncertain if I want to know, but I ask anyway. "Yuan Long's body and the dark sword were never found. But some soldiers claimed he killed himself in the middle of a battlefield. Is it true?"

The captain lays a hand on my shoulder, his voice heavy. "I'm afraid so. There were rumors that your great-grandfather was driven to madness in the end. The spirits and the darkness, he must have succumbed to them."

I enter the cabin in the evening. Spinning my dagger, I sit by the bed. Ahn is fast asleep, long hair spilling over her shoulders, dark against the blue blouse of her rúqún. If she was pale before, she is even more wraithlike now. Dark circles ring her eyes and her cheeks are sunken. She looks breakable.

A whisper of a girl.

There is a garden Mother loved in the eastern wing of the palace where a plum blossom tree grows. Often, she would point out that tree to me, marveling at how its pink and white flowers would bloom in the depths of winter in defiance of nature itself. Ahn reminds me of that tree, its fragile blossoms so stubborn they insist on coming to life when there is no life to be found.

She murmurs and shifts under the covers, a crease forming between her brows. I wonder if she is having another nightmare.

Soon, the gentle lull of the ship draws me into slumber. It's only when my foot slips that I stir.

Ahn is awake, staring at me coolly, posture guarded. "What do you want?"

"To see you," I mumble, still groggy. Not what I was planning to say.

"Were you watching me sleep? It's disturbing."

"Seems like you were the one watching me."

She ignores my retort and stretches. I take the tray of food from the table and hand it to her. She picks at the dishes, hardly eating a morsel before putting her chopsticks down and leaning against the wall, staring into space.

"Have you looked at yourself lately? You need to eat," I say.

"Stop nagging me, and stop being mad at me."

"Aren't you the one mad at me?"

"I have other things that bother me more now."

"Is that your way of saying you forgive me?"

Her lips curl slightly.

"Are you sure you want to go through with this?" Her expression changes and I regret my question.

"Worried about your crown?" Her tone bites. Fingers like claws, she places a hand on her chest. "The sword still calls out to me, there's no need to be concerned. I'll find it and you can have your damned throne."

Her words strike me like a slap. She is right. Perhaps it wasn't duty to my country or a sense of honor that pushed me to this point, but selfishness. All I ever think about is revenge. About myself.

Or at least, I did.

Part of me wants to turn the ship around, to take Ahn back to land, to hide her somewhere safe, away from the priests, away from her nightmares, away from everything.

"I wasn't thinking about my crown or the throne," I say softly. "I was worried . . . about you."

Her eyes flicker with surprise. She draws her knees close, making herself as small as possible. "You get nightmares, too, right?"

"Yes."

"How do you deal with them?"

"I tell myself they aren't real, and if they aren't real, they can't hurt me. Not unless I let them." I pull a vial from my pocket and show it to her. She shrinks back. "It's a sleeping draught. The Lotus Sect healers gave it to me."

She shakes her head. "I'm not afraid of falling asleep. I'm . . . I'm afraid of not being able to wake up."

I nod and tuck the vial away.

"Why do you want the throne?" Her question reverberates in my mind. She is hopeful, eyes searching my face, trying to find the good in me. "It can't be for power."

"Don't I seem power-hungry to you?"

"I think you want it for redemption. I think you feel guilty for your great-grandfather's actions, and you want to fix things."

I look away. "I want to kill the people who murdered my parents."

Her lips thin. "I'm not sure if it will bring you the peace you seek."

"Why not?"

"Because I know what ghosts feel like," she says simply. "I've been thinking about things. Maybe you should forgive yourself for whatever has happened in the past and move on."

You must find a way to live—find your peace.

Shīfù's presence hovers over me, comforting yet pressing. I lean against the wall, his words and Ahn's swirling in my mind. Do I have a choice to let this all go? To live a simple life?

I can't.

I can't let go. Can't turn back now. I can't abandon my family and my duty. Too many people have died senselessly.

Ahn rests her head on her knees, hair spilling over, covering half her face. I want to brush it away. I want to see her. All of her. Not this barricade of walls passing as a person. I take in how fragile she looks. How tired. But underneath that, I see the girl from the desert, strong and fierce.

Ahn remains silent for so long that I take it as my cue to leave and walk to the door.

"Stay."

A whisper. One word.

She slides down under the covers and points at the spot next to her. I stare at it until she smiles and dips her chin in the briefest of nods. That fetter of caution tugs at me, but I yank free and join her above the covers, leaving a careful distance between us. But she simply nestles her head on my chest and rests an arm over me like she is protecting me.

Instinctively, I draw her close. She lets me. And somehow, it feels right. If she can hear the rapid pounding of my heart, she doesn't let on. Slowly, I brush her hair from her face. Then, when she doesn't react, I run my fingers through her hair, twirling the soft locks.

We lay like this until the lamp goes out, leaving a comforting darkness.

"I still hate you," Ahn murmurs.

I sigh. "I know."

"I haven't forgiven you yet."

"I know."

I feel a jab at my ribs before I hear her voice again. "You're only here as Tang Wei's substitute."

"Don't tell her that or she'll get mad."

Ahn laughs. "Your real name is Jin?"

"Yes. Jin." I haven't said it for so long it feels almost like a stranger's name. *Altan* cloaked me for a while, but *Jin* belongs to another boy. A boy with a different mantle of secrets. "My mother used to call me Altan. It's a name I've grown up with, it's just as real. It means the same thing in her language as my birth name—gold."

Ahn groans. "That's why Tang Wei keeps calling you by that nickname, Golden Boy. *Jin*." She drags out the syllable, as if tasting my name on her tongue. "I like it, but I'm going to stick with Altan."

"I don't care what you call me."

"Good, arrogant fool." My laughter earns me another poke at my side. "Tell me about Jin."

Trust has to be granted.

"What do you want to know?" I say.

"The happy things."

I hear the smile in her voice, and my chest feels whole again.

So I tell her about Jin. I tell her about a boy who loved his family and thought the world of his father. A boy who hid a toad in his tutor's shoe because his cousin dared him to, and who burned down half the royal stables by accident with his best friend. A boy who used to fake sword fights with his twin sister, and who cried every time he lost. I tell her about a boy who climbed high onto the palace rooftops, wishing he were a bird, so he could spread his wings and explore the world.

Eventually, I run out of happy memories. The night cocoons us in a familiar solace, the beating of our hearts syncing in rhythm. Ahn's breathing slows, but I stay awake, thoughts spinning. I don't know if she asked me to stay out of desperation or out of hope. I don't know if I'm here because I'm her friend or because I want something more. Perhaps, all we are doing is keeping each other safe from the ghosts of our pasts.

Sometime later, when I'm half asleep, I feel her hand on my cheek, a gossamer touch that warms me.

A dream, perhaps. But if it were a dream, even the gods cannot drag me out of it.

37
AHN

My nightmares are starting to lose their shape. All I feel is an endless drowning. Living in the gray corridor between sleep and wakefulness, unable to claw my way out.

And that voice, that wily voice, sleek as the night. . . . It whispers from the darkness. Badgering me, urging me toward the sword. Pushing me to use my life-stealing affinity. Ama said that magic doesn't change who I am inside. But what if she's wrong? What if *something else* lives inside me?

Magic has ruined me. Betrayed me. It was never a gift from the gods.

I have taken too many lives. I have tasted power, felt the sick pleasure of another person's life force feeding mine. Was this how Yuan Long felt after he used his magic? Was it why he carried out his crimes and inflicted such damage on his people and his land?

Because he couldn't stop himself. Because he wanted *more*.

I shiver and pull the covers up. Altan stirs but doesn't wake. I asked him to stay on impulse. I'm not sure why. Maybe I was lonely and needed to be held. Maybe I wanted to see his stupid face.

My arm tightens over him. I must keep him safe. I *will* keep everyone safe. Safe from whatever lurks inside me. I stay awake, feeling his warmth, listening to the steady beat of his heart.

For a few more hours, nothing haunts me.

No nightmares, no voices.

I'm still awake when he rises late in the morning, but I pretend to be asleep, hoping he will stay longer. Carefully, he gets off the bed, resting a hand lightly on my cheek for a moment before leaving the room.

An emptiness returns. And with it, that shadow pulling me down into its depths.

He can't be by your side forever.

I bury my head under the pillow, heart hammering in my chest, hands over my ears, trying to block out that dark, dark voice.

38
AHN

Shouts from above deck jolt me awake. It takes me a few seconds to remember where I am. Altan left some time ago and I fell back asleep. The bed is cold and empty without him. The ship's lulling sway is now a rocky pitch and roll that turns my stomach. Something's wrong. I scramble out of bed and head up.

The wind howls in my ears like an alpha wolf readying its pack for a hunt, determined and ferocious. The sky above is a slash of ominous gray. Not to be outdone, the sea churns, white froth convulsing as aqueous crescents crash back onto themselves. The pitter-patter of rain tapping the deck rapidly transforms into a deluge, as if a dam in the Heavens has broken, its waters gushing forth.

Lightning zigzags, spreading its jagged feelers across the sky. In the rhythmic spurts of light, I catch sight of Captain Yan planted firmly on the slippery deck as his crew struggles to man their posts.

"Ahn! What are you doing up here?" a drenched Tang Wei calls out as she struggles to the stairs. "Get back down!"

"I'll join you soon," I yell back, fighting my way forward. "Where's Altan?"

She gestures at the bow, then disappears below.

"This isn't an ordinary storm," Captain Yan shouts above the wind, squinting as rain beats down his face.

"Typhoon?" I close my mouth quickly as raindrops splatter on my tongue.

"From the gods themselves!" His eyes darken. "We're in the Dragon's Triangle."

"How? I thought we were a day away—"

The ship rolls violently again and I stumble. Barrels of fresh water fly across the deck, some tumbling overboard. I spot Altan helping to secure the sails, but it's too difficult to get to him. I start to turn back when the wind drops with a shout and the sea goes flat.

An uncanny silence follows. The sun is a sliver of fading orange on the horizon. A blink and it's gone. This can't be right. The storm can't have lasted the whole day. It feels like only a few minutes since I've been on deck. A shiver creeps down my spine. The captain's right: something else is at work.

"Get below deck or secure yourselves!" someone roars.

There's a mad scramble of boots, but it's too late.

Smoke curls up from the water, drifting toward us. No one moves, either from surprise or some spell. Ming lurches forward, his hands seizing the empty air in front of him, face desperate and forlorn.

Captain Yan dashes over and drags him away from a wisp of smoke. Altan seizes another man clawing at himself. Blood dribbles from the scratches on his cheeks. The man struggles, and Altan knocks him out cold.

"Better that than to have him rip his own face to shreds," he says.

The captain acknowledges and cuffs another of his crew at the back of his head before turning to me. "Ahn, you should get back down."

"I will. Altan, are you—"

Someone rams into me and I fall onto the deck.

A hand on my bruised ribs, I struggle up. My mouth drops open at the sight of an empty deck. The air is still. But the vessel drifts, propelled by some unseen force, unfurled sails catching a phantom breeze like a ghost ship. Goose bumps erupt over my arms. Where is everyone? Where is Altan?

Something light and cold touches my cheek. A faint lick, like something tasting me. I rub my cheek with a sleeve, fighting the urge to scream.

A spiral of smoke rises in front of me. Then another. And another. Faces, solidifying before me. Li Guo, Mali, the mutilated girl by the well, the men from the alleyway, the priests I killed in the bamboo forest. . . .

They can't be real. I must be hallucinating.

They converge on me. I stagger back, looking for a way to escape.

"You're not real." I squeeze my eyes shut. "You're not real."

The shriek of metal and bone pierces the air and the wail echoes in my ears. The ship vibrates as the hull splits.

Wait.

This is familiar. I've dreamt it. Am I awake? Or is this a nightmare? I bend down to touch the floorboards, then I pinch myself so hard I yelp. *Wake up, Ahn. Wake up.* I pinch myself again.

The ship plunges and I fall with it.

I hit the water hard, sinking to the seafloor like an iron anchor. How long will the air in my lungs last? I try to push myself up toward the surface, but something holds me down. Desperation floods me, followed by shock when I realize I'm breathing normally, as if I'm back on land or I have gills like a fish. I stop struggling. Air fills my lungs and clears my head.

This *must* be a dream. That's the only explanation. And if it's a dream, it means I'm sleeping in the cabin on the ship. I've nothing to fear.

Do I?

Something swims toward me. Something big. Silvery scales. Burning red eyes with bright yellow centers. It moves so fast I can't tell what it is until it unwinds in front of me and rears up.

A pair of large antlers rises from its majestic head, which is shaped like something reptilian. Its snakelike body extends into a tail spreading far beyond what my eyes can see. Four limbs, each ending in massive eagle-like claws, sprout from its body. The creature moves its magnificent head, whiskers swaying gently in the water.

Lóng.

Ah, the Thief of Souls is back again. The Dragon's voice is guttural in my head, barely enunciated.

"Who are you?" I squeak.

You never remember me. I am the Soul Beast, keeper of this realm.

"What realm is this?"

The Soul Beast roars with laughter. *I would have thought you familiar with this place, Thief of Souls.*

"Why do you call me that?"

Is that not who you are?

"I thought I was the Life Stealer." I falter, eyes fixed on its scaly body. How big is this creature?

Thief of Souls, Life Stealer, Phoenix Slayer . . . You have many names, and you are many things to different beings. The Soul Beast exhales through its maw, and I jump back as a jet of bubbles bursts through the water. *What do you want, Life Stealer?*

I take a deep breath. "The sword."

The creature lifts its great head, beastly but intelligent eyes regarding me. *That is what they all wanted.*

"Who are *they*?"

The Soul Beast ignores my question. *What will you do with the sword?*

"I'll use it to get rid of dark magic, to free the Shi Empire from the Diyeh priests and to rescue my grandmother." A wild thought runs through my mind. "I'll use it to give the people an emperor they deserve."

The creature snaps its tail. There's a huge rock behind it on the seafloor, glowing with luminescence.

A tug at my chest.

The sword. It must be there.

I try to get a better look, but the creature blocks me with its massive body.

The previous Life Stealer thought he was the emperor the people deserved, it growls.

"I am not him. I don't want to be emperor."

I do not care about what you want or do not want. And I do not care about what you do with the sword. It fell into my realm, but I am not its guardian. Before you take it, there is something you should know.

The Soul Beast presses its claw on my forehead. I gasp, squeezing my eyes shut. A phantom scene unfolds in my mind.

Soldiers in battle with their weapons raised, some on horses, most on foot. Shi colors of crimson and gold stand out among a sea of steel-gray armor. A man steps up. His face is vaguely familiar. Standing tall among the other soldiers, he commands a presence like a god. He raises his hand. I see a sword. It glows with the same green-tinged smoke that leaked from the people I killed.

The man speaks.

I can't hear him, but the Shi soldiers fall back. A swelling mass of dust rises behind him. I gasp as the dust takes form. Human shapes, shrouded in shadows, some clad in armor, others in ordinary clothing. Men, women, *children*. They gush forward in a cascade of smoke and howls, assailing the enemy troops.

The scene changes.

The man is alone. Kneeling, his eyes are pinned to the sword in his hand. He's older, hair turning white, beard long and unkempt, loss weighing heavily upon each line on his face. His armor has seen better days, and there's a time-wrought weariness in his shoulders. He lifts his head, and I see his face clearly.

His eyes: one black as night, the other yellow as the sun.

He looks up at the Heavens, whispering. He smiles. And in a single fluid motion, he plunges the sword into his own chest.

The images vanish, but wild screams of fear linger in my ears. My heart is beating so fast I'm afraid it may burst. A thought dances around the back of my mind, telling me what it is I've seen, but I can't catch it.

"What did you show me?" I ask. "Did that really happen?"

The Dragon ignores my questions. *Remember my words, Life Stealer: the sword will not be controlled.*

It flicks its tail and curves its languid body away from the rock. I see a hilt. My heart leaps.

The White Jade Sword.

Remember my words, Life Stealer. Remember—

I wrap my hands around the weapon. Blinding light bursts from the rock. I shield my eyes, keeping one hand on the hilt. The blade slides up smoothly with little effort on my part. But once the sword leaves the rock, the Soul Beast disappears and water rushes at me. This time, I'm truly underwater. My lungs burn, and my head feels tight.

A faint light shimmers above. The surface. I start to swim up. But in droves, they come for me. Disembodied voices, cold fingers, the slithering brush of hair—of bodies that were once human.

Thief of Souls, they whisper.

Life Stealer, they shriek.

Free us, they weep.

I push back at the amorphous shapes. *I can't help you*, I try to say. *Go away!*

But still, they cling to me.

My legs go weak as the fire in my lungs rages. A fog spreads in my mind. My vision dims. I'm succumbing to this nightmare.

The light above flickers, and like a spark it comes to life. It's bright. Brighter than sunshine. A light that tethers me to the world beyond this darkness. It halos around a figure.

The figure reaches down into the water.

No, I scream. *Not here! Don't come into the water. It's not safe.*

Fear seizes me—fear for *him* and what he's about to do. And somehow, it gives me strength even as the shadows try to pull me back down.

I whisper his name, and there is a flash.

When I open my eyes, I'm back on the ship. Breathing the air around me, thoughts sluggish. Was it all a dream? But my clothes are waterlogged, and my ribs hurt. The sun beats down on my back as I kneel on the deck, locked tightly in the arms of someone whose wet hair shines a muted gold.

It wasn't a dream, I think dully.

Altan releases me, fingers twined in my hair. He traces the scar on my cheek, his touch gentle, careful. Wonder lights his features. It's as if he can't believe I exist.

"I thought I lost you," he says.

His expression shallows my breath. A fluttering births in my chest, like a hummingbird beating its wings in search of precious nectar. As the beat of wings grows faster and stronger, my heart soars. He draws me near, tipping my face up to his. I see vulnerability, fragile petals of hope blossoming.

No walls. No secrets.

We lean closer, a breath apart.

Something cold slips off my lap and falls onto the floorboards like metal on wood. Altan doesn't notice, but I look down.

The fluttering in my chest dies. My heart plummets.

No. This is not a dream. This is a nightmare.

A sword lies between us.

Black as night, dark as hell.

39
ALTAN

Somewhere along the way, something went wrong.

I believed my heart to be a reliable organ. Believed my will to be resolute and immutable. Then, a girl from the desert walked into my life. A girl whose smile proved my heart weaker than I imagined. A girl whose strange gaze drowns me in starlight even as it offers me a lifeline.

A girl I sought to use, to wield as a weapon, but who became something else.

My faith in her was blind.

In the end, she is both my salvation and damnation.

That kernel of doubt in my mind splits open, a fruition of darkness and doubt. I was wrong. Or perhaps, I was right all along.

She has summoned the dark sword. It lies between us, like a calamitous scar.

"I don't understand, I don't understand . . . How?" Ahn repeats. She pushes me away and reaches for the sword.

"Get away from it."

She shrinks back. Hurt and confused. There is a new chill in my voice that was never there before. Her eyes are fearful, but I see desire in them.

She wants the sword, but I can't let her have it. I pick it up myself, watching her carefully.

Her gaze hardens. Hungry and vicious. Her jaw sets.

A flicker of loathing crosses her face.

And there is nothing I can do about it.

40
AHN

I scream myself awake.

Cold sweat drips down my temples. I run a hand over my forehead and get out of bed, wrapping my cloak around me to preserve whatever warmth my body has. The top bunk is empty. My screams must have roused Tang Wei and sent her out of the cabin.

Almost two weeks have passed, and the ship is well on its way back to Cuihai Port with its crew a little worse for wear. Sails can be mended; bone and flesh will heal. But the invisible cuts and scars—those will linger. Even Captain Yan and Altan seem shaken. Only Tang Wei emerged completely unscathed, knocked out cold below deck when the ship was lurching. She gloated briefly, but I've a hunch she's secretly disappointed she missed out on the action.

My nightmares have been distracting me from Ama's fate. Now, in the quiet of the night, my worry returns. How long before we land at shore? How long before I can get to her? Is Ama even alive? She must be. My father will keep her alive for leverage.

You cannot escape your fate. The gods have chosen you for a reason.

I shiver. Have I been misled? Did my father know that it was the dark sword that was under the sea all this time? Should I have listened to Leiye and his warnings?

There's no turning back time. I can't undo what happened. The sword I have summoned is not the right sword. It isn't a white iridescent jade. I don't know if the legends and lore are wrong or maybe I'm unworthy, unfit to wield the promise of hope.

Even now, the dark sword calls out to me. I hear it. A soft *thump-thump*, like a living creature with a beating heart.

I remember the look on Altan's face when he saw the Obsidian Sword at my feet. How cold he sounded. But I felt something, too.

An immanent desire.

The sword is mine.

That voice was feral, coming from the dark abyss of my own heart. The sword is now locked up in Captain Yan's quarters, and the key hangs on a thick chain around his neck. I don't know why they bother. It isn't as if that would stop me if I truly wanted it.

And I want it.

A sob rises in my throat as that desire eats into me, eroding my defenses with each passing moment. My nails stab my palms, tearing into skin. But it doesn't hurt as much as that hunger. That *want*. I grab a pillow to muffle my scream, the Dragon's guttural roar echoing in my ears.

The sword will not be controlled.

41
ALTAN

A lonely figure leans against the gunwale, her billowing robes a pale turquoise like the ocean. Ahn goes rigid as I step next to her.

"What do you want?" Her voice is frostier than the wind.

You.

I match her coldness with my own. "I couldn't sleep."

A smile ghosts across her face. "Sometimes, I can't decide if you're a good liar or a terrible one."

I don't defend myself.

"I know you never trusted me," she says. "I guess you were right not to, seeing that I've found the wrong sword."

Will it be a lie or the truth if I counter her statement? Helplessly, I stare at her like a fool, remembering all the other times I stared at her like a fool, thinking that if all I did for the rest of my life was to stare at her like a fool, it wouldn't be so bad.

"I understand." She spreads her palms open, flexing her fingers, something conflicted in her gaze. "I'm not some peasant girl from the desert trying to rescue her grandmother. I'm the Life Stealer. You shouldn't trust me. Not with the power I have."

I trust you.

Three simple words that refuse to leave my lips. Ahn straightens, a strange look on her face. A look that tells me she has made a decision, and that I'm not going to like it.

"I need to tell you something. Back in the bamboo forest, I tried to take your life force with my magic."

A numbness spreads over my body. "You tried . . . to kill me?"

"I don't know if I was trying to kill you. There was a light around you. It called to me and tempted me, but you repelled my life-stealing magic. You felt a touch of it in the canyon, didn't you? But it didn't kill you or harm you the way it should have. To put it simply, my life-stealing affinity doesn't work on you. I think you're immune. I don't know why or how exactly, maybe it's because you're related to Yuan Long." She draws a shaky breath. "It was *you* who saved me from the Waters of the Undead, from the spirits pulling me down. I know it. There must be something connecting us somehow."

The numbness turns sharp. *Tell her what you did. Tell her about the Phoenix. Tell her about what you planned to do. Tell her you've changed your mind. Tell her you'll find another way. Tell her everything.*

But once again, I stay silent.

"It doesn't matter how or why," she says, biting her lip. "I need you to do something."

She stares at me with such stark honesty that my heart twists. I don't want to know, don't want to hear what she has to say, but she grabs my hand before I can leave. Her touch releases a dam of emotions and I pull her close, wrapping my arms around her like she is the most precious thing I have.

"Don't say it," I say in a choked whisper. *"Don't."*

I feel her melting in my arms, her warm breath against my neck.

Abruptly, she pulls away and rests a hand lightly on my cheek. I lean into her touch, and she smiles, voice tender even as her words leave wounds in my chest.

"You're the only one I can trust to do what needs to be done, Altan. If something terrible happens, if I fall into the shadows like your great-grandfather, *you* are the only one who can stop me." She lifts my face gently. "Promise me that you will."

"I . . . I can't," I say. "There must be another way."

Her smile turns sad. "I'm afraid not. Promise me, please."

Everything comes with a price and your choice will be paid in blood. You will find it difficult to treasure that which is most precious to you.

The Phoenix said this would happen. And yet . . . *yet*, I went ahead.

"Promise me," Ahn repeats.

My head hangs. "I promise."

42
AHN

I promise.

Altan's words float away with the wind. He brushes my hair off my face, and the feeling I had that night in his arms fills my heart. That *rightness*. My body is warm despite the chilly air. I want to keep my distance, but my heart thunders, drowning out all rational thought. As if pulled by some unseen thread, we lean closer.

A starburst of crimson sparks lights up the night sky, the red hue illuminating us. I turn to the sea. Three warships. Murky but imposing, silhouetted in the moonlight. The flare of their fires shows a hint of gold and blue on their sails.

"Imperial ships?" I gasp.

"No—Nandah," says Altan.

Captain Yan appears, shouting orders. The crew scrambles on deck.

Tang Wei comes running. "We're so close to port. Why are Nandah warships here? What do they want?"

"To sink us," says Captain Yan as another red flare goes up.

"The ambassador?" Tang Wei looks at Altan, eyes wide.

"Has lied to us," comes his grim reply.

Captain Yan pivots on his heel and barks out new commands before coming back to us. "They're well-armed and too fast for us to outrun them. We can hold them off, but only for a while. There's a boat and oars starboard. Go around and you'll have a chance to get to shore without them seeing you."

The look on Altan's face tells me he has no intention of abandoning the captain or the crew. Neither do I.

But Tang Wei grabs my hand. "Let's go!"

"No," I protest. "We should—"

"Not on your life! And your life is worth more than a ship of pirates. They knew what they were getting into when they offered to help us." She glares at Altan. "*Your* life is worth more, too."

Tang Wei's right, but I can't leave the captain and his crew in the lurch. How many times have I turned my back and ran? No one else should get hurt or die because of me.

I pull out of her grip. "I'm tired of running. You should leave—save yourself."

Her composure breaks. Tears glisten in her eyes as the sky lights up again. I grab her in a fierce hug. "Don't worry, I'll be fine."

I dash off, ignoring Altan's shouts as he tries to catch up with me in the chaos. I'm barely halfway across the ship when the first missile hits.

Flaming arrows detach from the main rocket tube, exploding as they smash against hull. Smoke erupts. I start to cough as a pungent smell reaches my nose and tickles my throat.

"Black powder!" someone yells. "They've got black powder!"

Ten Hells. *Black powder.* I've heard of this material. The Empire has only begun experimenting with it, but rumor has it that our southern neighbors have found a way to harness it for their own weapons. It's said to be a deadly explosive and I can see why.

There's a deafening boom, and something round like a ball sails past our ship. It lands and the sea bursts forth, sending a torrent of cold water onto us. More rockets and flaming arrows rain down. One of the sails goes up in flames.

What chance does one pirate vessel stand against the might of three military-grade naval warships? We're not going to make it if I don't do something.

Slipping and stumbling, I get below deck to the captain's quarters. The door is locked. Quickly, I tap into my magic and blast it open.

The dark sword lies on the table, waiting. Calling.

This time, I don't resist.

My fingers wrap around the hilt, and it molds to the valley of my palm. It starts to glow a smoky sea green. Something seeps out of me, flowing through my hand and into the blade. I feel my magic intertwining with it, bonding with it.

The sword comes alive in my hand.

I come alive.

A vivid sense of purpose seizes me. I sprint back up to the prow, brushing aside anyone standing in my way. The sword guides me as I grip it with both hands and raise it to the sky.

Lightning crackles. Shards of white light split midnight blue into fragments. A blazing splinter shoots down from the Heavens, spiking into the tip of the blade.

The jolt of energy goes *through* me, but there is no shock. Only exhilaration.

I bring the sword down.

And the lightning cleaves an enemy ship in half.

43
ALTAN

Explosions light up the night sky. Bodies and flotsam litter the waters. But everyone on deck stands motionless, our eyes focused on the prow.

On one girl.

The girl who stands ramrod straight, glowing sword in hand, hair dancing wildly like a thousand snakes. The girl who split a naval warship in half with a mere swing of her arm. The girl who brings her arm down again and again as lightning tears apart two other warships.

She raises the sword up to the Heavens again, and the lightning vanishes as suddenly as it came. She looks right at me when she turns around, fiery amber flames glowing in her eyes.

Beside me, Tang Wei shivers. "Looks like your little tigress has finally found her wings."

Dawn breaks over the horizon. Slowed down by damaged sails, we leave last night's destruction behind. The crew gives Ahn a wide berth when she appears on deck and beckons me down to her cabin.

When I enter, Tang Wei looks up and gives me a subdued smile, her usual exuberance gone.

"We're all here; tell us your plan," she says to Ahn.

Ahn takes a deep breath and declares, "I'm going back to my father."

"No, you're not," I say right away. "You can't stop me, Altan. No one can. I'm going to rescue my grandmother."

"Have you lost your mind?"

"I've thought about it, this is the only way." She's too calm and there is something else different about her that I can't put my finger on. "I think I know why my father sent out that decree. He wants to recruit large numbers of men and boys and somehow tether them to the dark sword to form an army. He wants to go to war again."

"An army? What does the sword have to do with it?"

"An army of the *undead*."

Tang Wei's jaw drops. "What are you talking about?"

"That's what Altan's great-grandfather did."

"What?" Tang Wei and I both exclaim.

"Why didn't we know that?" asks Tang Wei

"Historians." Ahn throws a glance at me before pointing at the Obsidian Sword resting on the table. "The Soul Beast showed me a vision and Yuan Long was holding *this* sword. I'm sure of it. He used his life-stealing magic together with the sword's own to command phantoms and spirits—an army of the undead. That's how he conquered those lands. That's how our empire was built. Yuan Long's victories meant that he was free to create his own narrative of what happened all those years ago. That's why we didn't know."

I sink back into my chair, bewildered. Tang Wei sticks her dagger into the table with a grunt, leaving a gash on the wood.

"Did Zhao Yang know the dark sword was in the sea? Were we being played all this while?"

"I don't know," says Ahn. "All I have are faint memories of conversations he had with my mother when I was a child. Leiye tried to warn me back in the bamboo forest. He told me not to get on the ship to find the sword, said he was researching, and something didn't add up."

The sound of my former best friend's name hovers like a storm cloud. "Even if that's true, it doesn't mean that your plan will work," I point out. "You're going back into the lion's den. What makes you think Zhao Yang won't lock you up again?"

"I know him," she says, a small, sad smile on her lips. "He wants the sword badly enough that he'll be glad to have me back. He won't harm me because I'm the only who can use it. I'll tell him I changed my mind because of the Nandah attack. If the south declares war on us, we'll have to protect ourselves and that's where I come in. I know I can convince him."

Tang Wei lets out a low whistle. "I didn't think you were capable of such scheming. I guess you *are* your father's daughter." Ahn winces and Tang Wei says quickly, "I'm sorry, that came out wrong."

"It's fine. Hopefully, Leiye will help. I have another friend in the palace. I hate to drag her into this, but I'm out of options."

Tang Wei and I exchange a look. The time for withholding secrets has passed.

"Her name wouldn't be Linxi, would it?" says Tang Wei, sheepishly.

It takes Ahn a second to figure out the connection. "Are *you* her girlfriend?"

Tang Wei nods.

"She told me she's a farmer's daughter and she grew up in the southeastern plains." Ahn frowns. "That's not true, is it?"

Tang Wei shakes her head. "She grew up in the colonies. Her mother was a Tiensai and her father's a minor official who was loyal to his father." She tilts her head in my direction.

"Did you plant her in the palace?" Ahn asks me.

I try my best to look contrite, deciding that my best course of action is to keep quiet.

"Were you spying on me right from the start?"

Tang Wei raises both hands in protest. "It sounds awful when you put it that way. We were watching out for you, how's that?"

Ahn slumps in her chair, head lolling back. "I'm surrounded by thieves and liars."

"It's good company, seeing that you're one, too." Tang Wei smirks. "Besides, I don't see why I can't need you for your magic and *still* be your friend."

Ahn groans. "Forget about all of that. Let's focus on the important things."

She picks up the dark sword and runs a finger along its slim double-edged blade. There is no design, no carving, nothing unusual on the dull black hilt and metal. It doesn't even look sharp enough to pierce through skin. Hard to believe something so unremarkable is anything special. But I have seen what it can do in the right hands.

I want to destroy it. I want to throw it back into the sea. To break it, to pulverize it, to burn it. But what would its destruction mean for Ahn? What would it mean for me? It isn't the White Jade Sword. But Ahn could use it to achieve the same thing. *How far are you willing to let her go?* I swallow hard. It's her choice. She wants to do this.

"I don't like your plan but—"

Ahn cuts me off. "Neither do I, but I'm going to do it anyway. The question is, are you with me?"

THE ARMY OF THE
UNDEAD

44
AHN

With the help of Linxi and the Lotus Sect, we manage to contact Leiye once we come ashore. Two weeks later, I show up with him at the palace gates, Obsidian Sword in hand. Altan had suggested we make a replica, but I feel more assured if the real one is by my side. There's also a chance my father might be able to tell the difference.

He stands in front of me now in one of the grand halls of the palace, silver mask hiding the scars my mother gave him. I can see the cogs in his mind working as Leiye sells our story: he'd been tracking my movements, cornering me when I got back on land. As agreed, Leiye makes no mention of Altan. He'd already covered up my jailbreak with a story about a Tiensai who tried to assassinate me, and whom I killed in self-defense before I ran off. Leiye had apparently provided a body. I don't want to know how or who.

His story is believable. It also helps that by now reports of the sunk Nandah warships are widespread. The south knows I exist and what my powers can do, which makes me vital to the Empire and my father's plans.

I can't help but admire the way Leiye speaks, his tone the perfect balance of respect and confidence, with enough self-deprecation that my father would never think that his prodigy was deceiving him.

My father approaches me cautiously. His eyes flit to the dark sword in my hand and back to me. "You sold your mother's ring for passage on that ship?"

"Yes," I lie.

"Why did you run? Why did you go after the sword yourself?" he says, his tone precisely neutral.

He hasn't decided what to make of me yet.

"I killed a man—I thought you'd be upset. I was scared. I thought I could find the sword of light myself." I pause for effect before sagging to the ground on my knees, trembling. "I failed, Father. This isn't the White Jade Sword. I . . ." I reach out and clasp his hands in mine, forcing myself to cry, to look right into his dark, dark eyes. "I know I've said horrible things to you. But I didn't mean them. I was confused. I only wanted to make you proud."

His raven eyes soften. He wants to believe me. I know he wants to. Maybe somewhere inside that cold heart, there is a place for his own flesh and blood.

"I don't know what to do, Father," I say, carrying on the charade. "The sword calls out to me. . . . It tells me . . . *things.*"

"What does it say?"

"It—" I gulp and suck in a sharp breath before letting my words tumble out. "It speaks of an army—an army of the undead. When I retrieved it, I saw things, people, souls at the bottom of the sea. Spirits, I think." I hesitate, risking another glance at my father. He's riveted, keen to know more, so I tell him exactly what he wants to hear. "I think *this sword* can create a spirit army."

I drop the weapon and scramble away from it, looking as terrified as I can. It clatters on the marble floor, a dull ring echoing.

"With respect, Your Excellency, I believe Ahn needs some rest," says Leiye. "It has been a tiring journey."

"Yes, yes, of course." I can sense my father trying to contain his excitement. Trying to behave like a normal, caring parent. "Come, my dear." He helps me up. "Leiye is right, you need rest. I will make sure that your old chambers are ready." And because he can't help himself, he continues, "You can tell me more about the sword later."

I sniffle and lower my head. "Yes, Father."

I want to ask about Ama, but I know I need to bide my time and wait until he is no longer suspicious of me. As I follow an attendant out of the hall, I hear my father say, "Have someone watch her at all times."

"Do not worry, Your Excellency. I will guard her myself," replies Leiye.

I hide my smile and walk on.

It's strange to be back in the palace again. Barely three months have passed since I escaped but so much has changed. Much to my relief, Linxi returns as my lady-in-waiting. We spend silent nights in my room, passing a piece of parchment back and forth, scribbling updates to each other before burning the evidence.

I've left the dark sword with my father so that he thinks I trust him. The tug in my chest grows each night, and my sleep remains fitful, full of shadows and sly whispers. But this is a small price to pay to earn my father's confidence.

Every evening, I'm ferried by Leiye to have dinner with my father. Alone. He quizzes me about the dark sword, the spirits, and the Soul Beast under the Emerald Sea. I try to answer as best as I can, pretending to get upset and emotional at points to allay his suspicions that I may be planning something of my own.

It's a game. A performance. Each of us trying to assume the role of the puppet master.

Almost a week passes before I dare to mention Ama. My father has kept her whereabouts secret. Not even Leiye has a clue.

There's the tiniest shift in his expression when I bring her up.

"I never meant any harm when I said I was sending my men to her village," he says as he sips his tea. "Perhaps you thought it was a threat. It must have worried you, but I was only fulfilling a promise I made to you."

He's so convincing that I almost believe him. "When can I see her?" I ask meekly.

"In time," he replies. "You should know there are people out there who wish to hurt you, and that means they may hurt her, too. I can keep her safe, and I have been doing so."

"Thank you, Father," I say earnestly even though I want to scream at him. I have to keep up my act, just like how he is keeping his. "You always know best."

I dip my head respectfully, vowing to outplay him.

Days later, I sit by the plum blossom tree in the eastern garden of the palace, waiting for Tai Shun. He was away on state business and only returned yesterday.

My breaths come out misty in the late autumn air. "Do you think it will snow today?" I ask Leiye. He tails me everywhere, which is equally reassuring and annoying.

"Too early."

"I've never seen snow before, or at least, I don't remember it. My grandmother says it's magical."

"It's white. Then it turns gray and slushy."

"Why do you make snow sound so mundane?" I grumble.

He shrugs. "It is."

"Not to someone who comes from the desert." I chew on my lip, recalling the snowflake that was in my hand when Ama found me in Shahmo. I must've known what snow was like at one point in my life. But that life is long gone, lost memories in a pile of ash.

Leiye glances sideways at the entrance to the garden, expression clouding ever so slightly. "He doesn't know anything and he doesn't *need* to know anything."

"Tai Shun?" I guess. "Do you not trust him?"

Leiye purses his lips. "It isn't a matter of trust."

"Then what is it?"

He stays silent, choosing to straighten his collar. It's obvious he's avoiding my question. I know he isn't an agent of the Tiensai *or* the Diyeh. He has been acting on his own accord all along. But I can't figure out why he'd put his life in such grave danger. Or why he becomes a locked vault of secrets when it comes to Tai Shun.

"Altan said the three of you grew up together in the palace. You were close, weren't you?"

Leiye nods stiffly. "Jin and Tai Shun were better brothers than the ones I had by blood. They were good to me, as was Jin's mother. When she found out about my troubles at home, she sent for me and gave me permission to live here. My father wasn't happy about it, but it was the kindest thing anyone has ever done for me."

"Is that why you're helping Altan?"

"I owe everything to his mother."

"How . . ." I hesitate. "How did you manage to get close to my father? Was it through the priesthood?"

"In a manner."

"What did he make you do?" I whisper, hating myself for asking.

Leiye's expression turns blank. He strides off to stand in the corner, orange priest robes bright against the stone wall. No hint of his father's Qin colors on his person.

I sigh, rolling the pebbles around with my shoe, thinking about how life must've been for Leiye as a child. Illegitimate and unwanted, he somehow found friends among the royal children—a family he didn't have at home. How long did he hide in the shadows, planning and waiting by himself when that family fell apart? What did he sacrifice to get close to my father? What did he have to do to protect his friends?

My duty is also to the prince, he once said to me. Which prince was he referring to?

"Ahn!"

No longer in mourning robes, Tai Shun is dressed in the emperor's color: yellow gold. Crimson embroidery marks his lapels, matching the red gem in the center of the gilded headband around his forehead. A five-clawed dragon stitched in vivid colors coils around the length of his long ivory-and-gold cloak. The emperor's symbol. I smile to myself, remembering the same dragon carved into the amulet Altan wears.

"Your Highness," I say, curtseying.

"I don't remember you being so formal before," Tai Shun jokes, but there's a serious air about him now that wasn't there before. Maybe he's finally coming to terms with his responsibilities. Altan may want the throne back, but it's a family affair I have nothing to do with.

From his corner, Leiye greets Tai Shun with a slight nod before casting his gaze back into the distance. Tai Shun freezes for a moment, staring at the lonely sentinel. Then he turns back to me, forcing a smile that doesn't reach his eyes.

"I was disappointed you didn't say farewell before you left. How was your trip west? I hope your relatives are well."

His manner is open and earnest. He truly doesn't know who I am or what I can do. Did my father hide the news of the sunk Nandah ships from him? Remembering Leiye's words, I weave some random tales of my alleged travels and aunts and cousins who don't exist. In turn, Tai Shun shares updates about the situation with Nandah. His advisors—my father, presumably—are pushing to heighten the Empire's defenses.

"Nandah is attacking us because their king thinks I'm weak," says Tai Shun solemnly. "Our recruitment drive for soldiers continues."

"But winter is coming, surely Nandah can't get their ships here with all that ice?" *And you have me,* I think to myself.

"Our intelligence agents believe they may have a weapon that can break the ice. That narrow strip of water that separates Nandah from us won't hold."

A weapon that can break the ice. It must be the black powder. Judging from the explosion in the sea when that Nandah warship attacked us, the destruction would be devastating if their bombs hit our cities.

"Do we not have any allies we can call on?" I muse. *Or have we made too many enemies?*

Tai Shun leans his elbows on the table, tenting his fingers. "I asked your father the same question. His view of the situation is grim. We just ended a war with Honguodi and there's no reason for them to help us, and it'll take Mengu forever to get across the mountains to be of any aid. Besides, their people's memories are long and their queen was a child when our nations last battled. I see no reason for her to want to help us."

But *I* could stop Nandah with the dark sword. Maybe I could even prevent them from landing on shore in the first place. So why doesn't my father tell Tai Shun that?

An attendant shows up with a tray, cheeks pink and bashful. She's young and looks familiar. I think she's one of the empress dowager's maids-in-waiting.

"Compliments from Her Majesty." The girl lays out the teacups and pours us tea, hand shaking slightly. I try to smile reassuringly at her, wondering if she's nervous because of Tai Shun or me. She bows low again and leaves.

Tai Shun smiles. "Mother is always so thoughtful."

"She is," I agree, sipping my tea.

It isn't long before another attendant shows up. This time, it's a message for me.

After parting with Tai Shun, I make my way to my father's private study, wondering why he has sent for me before dinner. He's seated in his usual rosewood chair, deep in thought. I throw a quick glance around. I haven't been back in here since my return to the palace. Everything looks the same.

He beckons me closer, and I'm struck by how tired he looks. An unexpected pang hits my chest. It must be difficult to carry the weight of one's country on one's shoulders. Then he shifts, and light reflects off his silver mask, reminding me what kind of man he truly is. I harden my heart. He may think he is serving his nation, but that doesn't make his actions right.

"You're here. Good."

"Is something the matter, Father?"

"I was hoping you could *show* me how the sword works."

I expected this request sooner or later, but I pretend to be shocked anyway.

"I don't mean for you to use it on a *person*. If you are not ready, we can wait," he says, a little too hasty. He sighs. "Although I will sleep better if I know for certain we have something that can withstand an assault from Nandah."

He's playing the game. This is a test.

"I can try," I say.

"Are you sure?"

"Yes, I think I'm strong enough. I won't fail you, Father."

He returns my smile and pushes the cabinet back. The wall slides open. I don't feign surprise. He knows I can feel the sword's call. As the wall slides back into place, I notice that there are *six* manuscripts bound in red silk in the cabinet. Leiye must've returned the one he took before my father noticed it was missing.

My father hands me the sword. Immediately, the hilt molds into my palm and a rush of energy shoots through me. My hand trembles. Not because I'm weak, but because I've realized something.

The only living thing in this room apart from me is *him.*

I could kill my father with the sword. I could turn him into a spirit bound to it. All it would take is a flick of my wrist.

You could take his life force. Don't you feel it? It is strong. It will make you more powerful, whispers the other voice that lives in my head.

For a horrifying moment, I am tempted.

Instead, I address my father quietly. "When we were attacked at sea, I pointed this to the sky."

We walk out of his study and into the garden. The days are shorter now and the sun is setting, our surroundings turning a deepening grayish-blue. I feel a little light-headed and it's hard to breathe. I can't tell if it's my nerves or something else. I exhale slowly and clear my mind. Slowly, I raise the sword to the Heavens. Thunder rumbles in the distance.

But I know it isn't because a storm is coming.

I summon my magic, feel it flow through me, mixing with the sword's own energy. The sky fractures, light splintering through clouds. The blade burns with white fire. I hold it down and point at a tree.

The blast catches me by surprise, and I fall over. I stay down, coughing so badly my ribs hurt. There's an ache creeping up my neck and a pounding in my head. Something doesn't feel right. I'd felt exhilarated the last time I used the sword, not like this.

My father is already at what's left of the tree, examining the stump and its ruined bark. When he finally turns to me, it isn't concern that I see in his eyes.

But the wild, feverish gleam of a madman.

45
ALTAN

A day feels like three autumns to a man missing his beloved.

What a lie that old Shi saying is. Each damned minute that passes feels like an entire winter.

It has been a week since Ahn left for the palace and all I have received are ciphered notes from Linxi and nothing from her.

It feels like I'm going mad.

I don't have a word for this feeling inside of me. Whatever it is, I hate it. I want to ram this inexplicable emotion back into the prison it escaped from. Sand may make me weak, but this . . . this unravels me. It keeps me caged in a world where a touch can mean nothing or everything. Where a glance, a smile, a slight shift of the brows— each infinitesimal gesture and movement brings new meaning to my existence.

It is terrifying.

Tang Wei says I have fallen in love. I think she is being ridiculous.

Sighing, I push the window open, just a crack. The sun is almost setting. Tang Wei should be back here at the safe house soon with food. I have laid low, choosing to stay indoors for the most part.

I gaze out onto the capital streets, sniffing the crisp air tinged with an aroma of roast meat layered with a brighter scent of fresh flowers. The familiar sights comfort and sadden me. The water feature with the white stone arch and twin dragons still stands next to the sweet shop I used to visit with my sister. Shīfù's favorite Green Needle Teahouse is along the next street. . . .

This place holds too many memories.

The sound of footsteps on the stairs pulls me out of my thoughts. The shopkeeper from below hands me a letter a messenger dropped off. After she leaves, I rip it open. It looks like Linxi's handwriting, the ink slightly smudged. She must have been in a hurry; the message isn't coded.

Pagoda. Lake. Grandmother.

My pulse races. Reason tells me to wait for Tang Wei, but if Ahn's grandmother is truly there, there is no time to lose. The sooner I can get her out to safety, the less Ahn has to worry about.

And the faster you can have your revenge.

As a boy, I tried many ways of sneaking out of the palace. I never succeeded. Now, I must sneak in. Part of the western wall of the palace compound faces a moat. In Father's time, it was thought the water was defense enough. The guards were stationed at the top of that stretch of wall, not its perimeter at the base where water met stone. If that route doesn't work, I will have to find another.

I hesitate, a nagging voice at the back of my mind telling me to stay. To wait for Tang Wei instead of going in alone.

A sudden crack of thunder sounds, and I look out the window. Strange. There was no indication of a storm coming. Moments later, the sky over the palace grounds lights up in an eerily familiar way.

Ahn.

The drawbridge is up when I arrive. It will make too much noise to form a path over the moat with magic—I'd have to freeze the water. In this silence, the guards would surely hear the ice cracking. Besides, it would take too much energy and magic to do so. I shrug off my cloak and plunge in before I can overthink it. The shock of the frigid water cuts through my bones as I swim. Once I haul myself up, my teeth chatter incessantly.

In the light of the flaming torches above, I count the guards. Six. I'm about to scale the wall when the gong signaling the changing of the guard sounds. I will have to wait until the old guards leave and the new guards get into position before I can take any action. Otherwise there will be too many of them.

I can't risk conjuring up a flame and I don't want to waste my energy drying my clothes, so I change my breathing to increase the circulation of qì inside me, building warmth as I press myself against the wall and melt into the shadows. Turning into an icicle isn't the way I wish to depart this world.

I give the new guards some time to get comfortable in their positions. Comfortable and complacent. Then, I scale the wall easily and swiftly, surprising them with a few choice jabs to their meridian points. They fall to the ground, unconscious. I peel off my cold wet clothes, don the uniform of one of the guards, and pull on his boots. Much better. Grabbing his helmet and armor, I nod a silent apology to the half-naked man on the ground.

After all these years, I still know the palace grounds like the back of my hand. I march along, pretending to be one of the guards, occasionally traveling stealthily by rooftop. Memories charge back as I pass landmarks I recognize. The royal stables where I learned to ride, the study hall where I attended endlessly dreary lessons, the koi pond my sister threw up in. . . .

I spot a pagoda next to the lake. It's new. The old Diyeh temple used to be there before my father had it torn down. Coincidence? A tug-of-war battles in my head. My heart wants to find Ahn first, but my head tells me that saving her grandmother is more important.

Cursing silently, I head to the pagoda. The multitiered tower is well lit, lanterns flickering away under its curved eaves, casting faint reflections upon the dark waters of the lake. Several guards stand at the base, wearing similar uniforms to the one I commandeered. They pay me no heed as I march up, probably thinking I'm one of them.

It is laughable how easily I disarm all of them. Either I'm that good or this tower is so unimportant the most useless guards protect it. Ahn's grandmother can't be held captive here, could she? But Linxi's note was specific. I skirt around, a tiny flame on my fingertip for light, searching for a telltale mark. My pulse throbs when I see that curved line with two dots faintly scorched into one of the rectangular stone blocks at the base of the tower.

The mark of the Diyeh priesthood.

I tap on each stone slab surrounding the sign until one of them gives. A push and it slides inward. Something creaks. A hidden door with stairs going underground. I go down the first steps and close the door behind me. A torch hangs on the wall at the foot of the stairs and in its light, a stone corridor leading to darkness emerges.

Torch in hand, I pad forward silently. Several locked rooms appear on my left and right. Rooms for what purpose? Torture chambers? Some of them are cells with metal grates as doors. All empty.

Curious.

A soft moan comes from farther down the corridor, and I find a heap of rags huddled in one of the cells. It looks to be an old woman. Her head is lowered, shadows obscuring her face, but I see white hair.

Ahn's grandmother.

As I approach, she shrinks back. She must be frightened. That terrible, *terrible* thought surfaces in my mind again, and I work to drown it. The chess piece the priests hold is right in front of me. No one would know any better if I killed the old woman and left this place. No one would know any better if I spirited her away and imprisoned her somewhere else. I'd be able to get the Life Stealer to do whatever I want. Some demon inside me tempts me.

But she's not just the Life Stealer. She is Ahn.

I grip the cold metal bars. *You are not your great-grandfather,* Shīfù's voice whispers in my head. I make up my mind, once and for all.

"Don't be afraid. It's me, Altan. I'm here to rescue you," I say. "Stay back."

I draw a saber and put all my strength into my blow, hacking down at the lock. It breaks easily and clanks onto the ground. I pull the door open and walk in.

"Come with me," I say.

The figure moves. Shadows melt away.

She lifts her head. *"You."*

46
AHN

I wake with a start, choking as my heart thunders in my chest. I felt unwell after striking the tree with lightning and returned to my room to rest. Everything else is hazy. I try to sit up, but something holds me down.

Nightmare.

A scream rises in my throat, wrestling its way out. But all I manage is a muffled cry through the thick cloth gagging me.

"Shhh," whispers a voice.

Goose bumps spring up as the hairs on my arms stand. I hear the scratch of a match. The fizzle of a wick being lit. I squint as a flame blooms and grows, outlining the silhouette of a woman. The shadow's hand brings a lamp to a face, and a pair of exquisitely shaped eyes framed with dark lashes stares back at me. As I adjust to the light, a masterfully sculpted face that is all cheekbones and pillowy lips materializes.

The empress.

A manicured finger reaches out and lifts my chin. In an instant, flames engulf me. An inferno of needles, ants, creatures with teeth nipping, biting, tearing at my skin from the inside. My mind is on fire, pushing against my skull, clawing for escape. I struggle, but my body betrays me. It's a cage keeping me in the fiery abyss.

I hear the strangled cries of an animal taken to slaughter. It takes me a while to realize they come from me. Zhenxi removes her finger from my skin, and everything vanishes.

An illusion.

Shaken, I struggle to breathe as my eyes water. What kind of magic, what kind of sorcery was that? Is she a Tiensai? Or *something else*?

She sighs indulgently. "I can see why he likes you. Pretty, broken thing. When Tai Shun was a child, he found a beautiful kingfisher with a bent wing, half-dead from starvation. He mended it and nursed it back to health. But he would have done the same even if it had been a dull sparrow. You see, like many others, my son loves beautiful things. But what he loves most are *broken* things—things that need fixing. People who need saving."

I barely register her words. All I can think about is her blistering touch.

Her blood-red lips curl into a perfect smile of distaste. Gone is the warm, motherly woman I thought I knew. "Pity. I don't think *you* need him to save you, do you?"

Her delicate nose wrinkles for a moment as she laughs. If you can call it a laugh. It is an intoxicating opera beckoning me into the depths of intimacy. I want to slap the smile off that beautiful face. But I choke on my gag instead. She eyes me lazily like a hungry cat pretending to nap in front of a mouse.

"Poor thing," she coos. "That must be so uncomfortable. I will take it off if you promise not to scream."

I blink and nod. The gag comes off in a flash. My tongue is

cottony, my mouth dry. I struggle, but my limbs are still pinned down, body heavy.

"What have you done to me?"

"I hope you enjoyed the special tea I prepared for you. The effects of the poison will wear off soon. After all, I am not trying to kill you."

The attendant who served Tai Shun and me. She must've known what was in my tea. That was why she was so nervous. "What do you want?"

"I have a proposition."

"You could have asked me nicely over over some fruit and dessert instead of poisoning me."

"True," she agrees. "But this feels more . . . *intimate*." She leans close. "You and I are not so different. I was not created to grovel at a man's feet. I worked for power, snatched it from undeserving hands. You, on the other hand, you were born with power many lesser men covet. *We* should be the ones to rule, the strong prey on the weak. It is life's natural order, the divine hierarchy the gods themselves created."

"I'm nothing like you."

Her nostrils flair. "Do not look at me as if I'm some kind of monster. I am a mother doing what is best for her child. And that is more than what *your* father is doing."

I spit out a curse.

"Let me get straight to the point. My son is weak." She pauses. I can see how difficult it is for her to admit that. "Once he ascends the Dragon Throne, he will be betrayed by politicking ministers, eaten alive by the priests. My son is the one who needs saving. I have done my part, but there are limits to what I can do. I need someone to help him. Someone others will fear. Someone like *you*."

"Whatever you're planning, I won't help you."

A single, elegant finger extends toward me. I shudder involuntarily at her threat.

"Hear me out," she says. "The priests helped to get rid of Ren Long, but I was a fool to think they wouldn't put my pathetic husband under their thumb. Everything Gao Long did—every command, every decree—it was the priests who told him what to do. Someone murdered the previous head priest for me, but I can't count on luck to strike twice. And I will *never* leave my son in the same position as Gao Long was in. A puppet and nothing more. You see, my dear, we are on the same side. We both want the Diyeh destroyed."

"We are *not* on the same side. I don't care about what they do to your son." My words are brash but inside, I worry about Tai Shun's fate. Zhenxi is right. He would never survive my father's machinations. Already my father is hiding things from him in order to manipulate him. And in his attempt to protect Tai Shun, Leiye has also kept him in the dark.

"We both know your father will ask you to raise an army of the undead once the soldiers have been amassed. The threat of Nandah hangs over our heads. Don't be surprised if his command comes sooner rather than later. If you raise that army, your grandmother will live. But for how long? The priests will always have a hold over you as long as she's alive, and the blood of thousands will be on your hands. *I* don't care about conquering new lands. All I want is my son on the throne, safe from the priests and free of puppet strings."

"What exactly are you saying?"

She smiles. "Kill your father and release the priests' hold over the throne. Marry my son and rule with him. You can have anything you want—treasure, power, the *world*."

"Kill him yourself," I spit out.

"Don't you think I would have killed that man a long time ago if I could? The priests will retaliate if they trace it back to me. They are too entrenched in the palace, too many allies and not enough enemies. I want to tear it all down. Start something new—something better."

"Then you shouldn't have murdered Ren Long," I say, loathing every inch of her. Hating myself for ever thinking she was a good person.

"Ren Long was a special kind of fool. You are the Life Stealer; the priests will comply if *you* remove your father. Then, you can get rid of them."

I recall the reverence in the tone of the priest I killed back in the bamboo forest. The man who gazed upon me like I was a god. That thought I had when my father and I were alone in his study and the dark sword was in my hand returns. Even if it were to save the world, I couldn't kill my own father, could I?

"How about I kill everyone? You included?" I say.

"If only you had it in you, my darling girl." The genuine regret in her tone is unnerving. "Oh, another thing. I did say the side effects of the poison will wear off, but the poison itself will stay in your veins, slowing attacking your nerves. You will feel fine, but one day—" She snaps her fingers and I recoil. "I'm the only person with the antidote, and I will gladly give it to you *if* we come to an agreement."

The empress was more than prepared. A step ahead of me, ahead of the priests. I can't let her win. I grin, taunting her. "I won't be *your* puppet. You mistake how much I value my own life."

"How about your grandmother's? Or someone else's? Someone who showed up in the palace not too long ago. Someone who is supposed to be *dead*."

I fail to control my shock.

She stares at me, stripping away my steel layer by layer. Her lips curve into a triumphant smile. "I'm one of the few souls who knows he did not die in the desert all those years ago. Imagine my surprise when I got wind of him stepping foot on the mainland. Imagine my delight when he was spotted in the capital a few days ago. I wonder what made that foolish boy return to the palace tonight? Surely, it can't be for your grandmother?"

"He wouldn't come here . . . unless . . ." An invisible hand crushes my heart. "You *tricked* him."

"Took me a while to figure out that Linxi was his spy. I had to pretend I didn't know. That wench will pay, but it worked out for me in the end."

"What did you do to Linxi?"

"Don't worry, she's alive. For now."

"Don't kill her—don't kill *him*. *Please*." A sob catches in my throat. I hate that I'm pleading, hate that I'm begging, but she has found my weakness. Broken my spine.

"I am not the one who will decide if he lives or dies." The pleasure in her voice sends a rash of shivers crawling up my body. Every word gliding out of that lovely mouth is a gossamer-veiled warning of terrible things to come. "You know, dear girl, it is interesting what you can find in those dusty old scrolls written in dead languages in the Forbidden Library. Fortunately, I had time on my hands, and I needed a . . . hobby. Seems like Yuan Long failed to destroy everything. Stories of a past long forgotten remain. History, I suppose."

She trails a finger down my jaw. There are no flames, no illusions, but I tremble at her touch.

"Men are often blinded by their own hubris. When you become fixated on your own truth, you fail to see the whole. Tiensai history is Diyeh history; one is incomplete without the other. To only be versed in one lore means you only know half of the story, half of the truth. They are, after all, the same people." Her breath is warm on my cheek. "Here is the truth, Life Stealer. The sword of light does not exist."

"But the dark—"

"Yes, *a* sword exists," she cuts in impatiently. "You found it, didn't you? There is no dark sword or light sword: they are one and the same. The dark sword was never meant to be what it has become now. A sword is merely a tool. It is the user who decides its purpose. Yuan Long corrupted it, defiled it with his aberrant use of magic. He shifted the balance in this world and cursed us all. The sins of his blood continue in his descendants. Equilibrium is needed, and a sacrifice must be made so that the land can be healed."

A sickening thought slithers its way into my mind. I stay silent, trying to blink away the world.

"As the Life Stealer, you can restore the dark sword to its natural state and bring balance back," she continues. "Restore it with the blood of Yuan Long's descendant and the last traces of his magic

will disappear from the land." She smiles. "My husband Gao Long
is dead—"

"No," I breathe out.

"—Tai Shun is my son, but royal blood does not run in him. Gao
Long—"

"Shut up!"

"—is not his true father. This means there is only *one* person
alive who still carries the blood of Yuan Long in his veins. There is
only one descendant and one true heir."

Altan.

Every fiber of my body screams, writhing, looking for a way to
unhear her words, to reverse the truth.

"It's not true! You're lying!"

"Am I?" The empress leans back, giving me one last lingering
look. "What will it be? Will you save your grandmother and kill
thousands? Will you kill your father and marry my son? Will you
kill Jin and save the land and our people? Or will you die a lonely
death after everyone you love is gone?"

The flame disappears, and I'm plunged into darkness once
again. I don't know if I'm alone or if she is somewhere in the
room watching me like a snake ready to strike. As the seconds
tick by, despair clutches my mind in its deformed hands, fusing
itself into me.

I blink a few times, struggling to adjust my vision. But the darkness is complete. My head is leaden, spinning. Traces of something floral remain in my nostrils. Stiff and sore, my limbs ache as if they have been in disuse. I rise unsteadily to my feet, hands blindly reaching out.

Cold metal. Stone. Four walls. Narrow—the length and width of my reach.

A cell.

My fist strikes the metal door. If only I wasn't so eager. If only I paid more attention. It was too easy. How I disarmed all the guards, how I found the Diyeh's mark, how all the cells were empty except for one. A perfect trap for an impulsive and arrogant blockhead.

You.

A single triumphant word spoken when that beautiful face showed itself. A face too young to have been Ahn's grandmother's.

Then, that floral scent. And afterward, darkness.

I sink down. My ears pick up the sudden whispery, whistling

"Never mind." I try to brush past her, but she doesn't budge. "Get out of my way."

In response, she jabs two points on my left shoulder with her fingers. There's a sharp, tingling feeling in my spine. I struggle to move, but it feels like there are weights tied to my feet.

"I'm sorry, but I have orders to take you to the premier." She doesn't sound sorry at all.

She must be a henchman of my father's passing as a lady-in-waiting. Maybe she's a priest. And if she's allowed to manhandle me this way, something must be very wrong.

"How do you expect me to get to him if you've paralyzed me?"

She sidesteps and twists my arm behind my back with a swing. I yelp in pain. Her grip tightens, and she twists harder. Something cold and sharp presses up on my throat.

"This is my favorite blade. I keep it sharp and your flesh is so tender," she drawls, her breath wispy against my neck. "I'll release your meridian points, but know that any false move, any *thought* of escape, and I'll slice you up faster than your damned magic can work. Do we have an understanding?"

She doesn't know that Zhenxi's tea has disabled my magic. At the back of her mind, she must be afraid of what my life-stealing affinity can do.

"Sure," I say, nonchalantly flexing my fingers. Her blade tenses against my neck. "Don't worry, I won't waste my energy on you. Now, release me. I don't want to keep my father waiting."

The girl lowers her weapon and taps the base of my spine three times. I stagger as the feeling in my legs returns. She escorts me through the darkened corridors, weapon in one hand, lamp in the other. We pass guards and other attendants, but no one gives us notice. Or at least, they pretend not to. I catch a wayward glance or two and pray that word will spread to Tai Shun. But would he even know what to do? My heart twists as I think of Linxi. What has the empress done with her?

I notice that we're turning too many corners. This isn't the way to my father's chambers or study. "Where are we going?"

The girl doesn't respond. We walk on in silence past the northern wing into an open field. Ahead, a huge stone wall rises.

It's dawn. Light arches over the horizon, silhouetting a figure strung up high between two tall poles on top of the wall. The young man is shirtless, his rust-orange pants bloodied. His head hangs, dark hair flowing in the wind.

A white streak gleaming in the sun.

49
ALTAN

How long have I been screaming? Hours, days . . . seconds?

Time holds no weight in darkness.

All I know is I'm hoarse, my fists wet, blood dripping from flesh skinned and pulpy from hitting the walls. All I feel is that suffocating pressure. All I hear is my mother's endless screaming.

Sand has stopped pouring in.

I'm chest-deep in it, but it is enough to break me. Memories of my father, my sister, Shīfù, that young boy stolen from his mother's arms, countless other faces—they blend into the toxic brew fermenting in my head.

Everyone I have lost.

Everyone I failed.

The stitches holding me together have begun to loosen. To fray. What will they reveal when I finally fall apart?

Ahn's voice sheens through the pall. *Forgive yourself.* How?

Darkness has no answer. And I can't find the light.

Metal grates sharply. I wince as light bounces in from a small rectangular opening in the door.

A face veiled in shadow peers in.

Keys jangle. Bolts screech back. The door cranks open and sand rushes out. I pin myself against the wall, trying not to fall with the sand. Or into it.

Disoriented, I'm defenseless, vulnerable. But the figure doesn't attack.

"Cousin, it's me."

The last person I thought I'd see here.

I stagger out on floundering legs, ignoring Tai Shun's outstretched hand. Hunched over, I fight down the urge to scream. Some part of me is still lost in that dark cell. I need to gather myself. To find myself again.

As my lungs fill, my mind starts to clear. Barely.

"It's true—you, you're *alive*." Tai Shun looks on the verge of tears. He shakes his head in disbelief, the shadow of guilt and pain in his eyes. "All this time, you were alive."

Instinct and habit urge me to comfort him, but I don't move. "Does your mother know you're here?" I rasp.

"No, she doesn't. And I wouldn't have let her do this to you if I'd known."

"Then I should thank you both for your generosity."

He hangs his head. "I don't understand why she did this. Why the sand?"

I wheeze an insincere laugh as I scan the stone passageway. We are not at the pagoda, but some area of the palace dungeons. Guards are passed out on the ground. Or dead. Is this Tai Shun's doing? Is this a *rescue*?

"Why did you let me out?" I take a step back, unsure if I can trust him or if I should just hit him and get out of this place.

"Remember that hidden passage in the rafters we stumbled upon as kids?"

"How is this the right time to reminisce about our childhood?'

"I couldn't sleep tonight. I was headed toward the lake with my flute when I saw Mother going into Ahn's room, so I went up to the rafters. I didn't know you and Ahn were," he pauses briefly, "acquainted."

"We are more than *acquainted.*"

He swallows. "Many years ago, I heard a conversation and I did nothing until it was too late. I have had to live with that mistake every day. *You* have to live with my mistake. . . . I never had a chance to apologize—"

"It's too late," I cut in, tearing off a chunk of sleeve to wrap my bleeding hands.

"Your hands—let me help."

I shove him away, staining his robes with my blood.

"Get away from me," I seethe. "What else did you hear? What else do you know?"

"An army of the undead. It doesn't make any sense—"

"We're dealing with ancient magic, something beyond this world."

"I know the priests take things too far sometimes, but I thought with new leadership things would change. I didn't think Zhao Yang would be worse. He always seemed so well-tempered, his advice so sound. I am a fool to—"

"What did you say?" I interrupt. "What does Zhao Yang have to do with the priests?"

"He is their leader."

"His *face*," I hiss, grabbing Tai Shun by the collar. "Tell me about his face."

Tai Shun gulps, bewildered by my reaction, but he answers me. "Half his face is scarred, like he was burned. He wears a silver mask most of the time."

My heart dives. Feels like I'm back in the cell of sand again.

I release Tai Shun. *She knew.* That night at the soldier's camp, Ahn knew that it was her father I wanted to kill. That *he* had killed my mother.

And she stopped me.

"Jin, I don't see how this is relevant."

"Quiet. I need to think."

Seconds later, my mind remains hollow and cold. If Ahn chose to save her father then, will Ahn choose her father over the fate of our people?

"Jin," Tai Shun urges. "I don't know what's happening, but we should get out of here."

"Do you know where they are keeping Ahn's grandmother?" I say finally.

"She isn't here in the dungeons—I checked."

"Where is Ahn?"

"She was in her room in the eastern wing. She's been poisoned."

I slam the wall next to him. "Why didn't you tell me that from the start?"

"She'll be fine. I *promise*, I can fix it. I've some knowledge of herblore."

"I'm going to get her." It sounds like a question. I'm asking if he will stop me.

As an answer, Tai Shun pulls a small vial out of his sleeve. "Take this. Mother might have poisoned you like she did to Ahn. I extracted this myself from língcǎo. In its purest form, it should counteract most of the effects of whatever Mother may have done. We'll get another for Ahn."

Do I trust him? He didn't have to save me, but he did. And he isn't stopping me now. I down the whole vial without a second thought.

"Thank you," I say stiffly.

Tai Shun's face is grim, his eyes hard. "And don't worry, I'll handle my mother."

"You don't have to do anything."

"I *want* to. For once, let me have some control over my life," he almost shouts. "I never coveted the throne, Jin. I never wanted any of this. Whatever happens, do what you will with me, but promise me this: my mother lives. I know she has done terrible things, but she is still my mother."

That woman helped to kill my father. She gave me the scars on my back. She locked me up in my own hell. But what would her death achieve? More hatred? Another lifelong feud between cousins?

Forgiveness is not weakness.

I look at the boy I once loved like a brother. His gaze is uncertain. Hopeful.

I nod. "You have my word."

Tai Shun grips my arm. At first, I think it is out of gratitude, but then he speaks with a tremor in his voice. "There is one more thing you should know."

"Quickly."

"Gao Long isn't my biological father. I am not of royal blood, which means you're the only one left."

The strange look on his face catches me by surprise. "What are you saying?"

I watch as his lips form sounds that travel to my ears. I hear his words. But somehow, I can't understand. I don't understand.

I'm saying that you, Jin, are the one true heir of Yuan Long. Only you can undo the dark magic in our land.

I was right, after all. *I* am the only way to right all those wrongs. In the end, it is my blood that will atone for the sins of my ancestors.

50
AHN

Soldiers line the fortress walls, swords unsheathed, faces nervous. Tension fills the air. Are they merely following orders? Do they think what my father is doing is wrong? He stares at me, a hand gripping the hilt of the Obsidian Sword. While Zhenxi's poison was working, I couldn't feel its pull. Even now, it's fainter than usual. The toxin lingers in my veins, but I can feel my magic returning.

My father nods and the girl who escorted me here shoves me forward. She kicks the back of my knees and I fall in front of him.

"Father," I beseech, tugging at his robes. "Why have you brought me here? What is happening?"

He pushes me aside. "There is no need for pretense."

"I'm not pretending," I lie. Something must have happened. He must've discovered our ruse. I spare Leiye a glance. He's unconscious, and from the growing puddle of blood on the ground below him, I can only pray that he is still alive. "Father, *please*—"

My father crouches down, squeezing my chin, fingers digging into my skin. "Do you truly take me for a fool? What were you planning to do?"

"I don't know what you're—"

"I caught him with my sacred book. He thought he was clever, replacing it with a replica. But I could tell the difference. So, I bided my time and waited, waited until the thief came back for the missing pages. Never did I expect it to be *him*, the ingrate!"

Disappointment, true and frightening, pools in his eyes. My father believed in Leiye. He cared for him. He won't let this betrayal go unpunished.

"But I don't understand, Father. This has nothing to do with me."

His gaze is sad for a brief moment before fury takes over. "Nothing to do with you? Do you honestly expect me to believe that?"

The first slap catches me by surprise. A real sob hitches in my throat. The next blow only angers me. I keep my head hanging down, face hidden by my hair. I have to get us out of this mess. I focus on my breath. Testing. Searching for an elusive tendril of magic to latch onto. A quiet hum starts to build. My magic must be coming back. My eyes dart across my surroundings again, etching everyone's positions into memory. How many guards and priests can I kill at one time?

"Let me ask you again, what were you planning with that traitor?" my father says coldly.

I refuse to utter a sound, concentrating on my breath and the threads of energy all around me. It's not enough. I need more time.

"Wake him," my father commands.

The priests on either side of the poles work the pulley ropes, bringing an unconscious Leiye down. Fresh bruises bloom on his face and whip marks lacerate his torso. A trail of blood seeps through his trousers, dripping down, adding to the dark crimson on the ground.

They throw a bucket of water at him. He gasps. Coughs. Looks up feebly. The first thing he does when he sees me is to grin, mouth all bloody and raw. *I'm fine*, I can almost hear him say. He shakes his head slightly. *Don't tell him anything.*

A fiery plume blazes from my father's hand. The look on Leiye's face tells me he's willing to be sacrificed. I steel my heart.

My father takes a step closer to Leiye. Still, I say nothing.

"Very well." My father extends his hand, flames growing larger, searing into bare skin.

Leiye starts to shriek.

"Stop!" I scream. I can't bear to watch. Can't stand to hear his pain. "Please, stop!"

The flames vanish and the priests douse him. He looks faint, the flesh on his right arm red and blistering. Once, he marked me with his fire, a healing fire, but fire nonetheless. Now, because of me, he has a mark of his own.

My father glares. "Answer my question and he lives."

I wrench my eyes away from Leiye and tell my father of my plan to rescue Ama, making sure to leave out Altan and Tang Wei.

When I'm done, he sneers. "Not much of a plan, is it?"

Anger roils inside me like a ball of energy. At this point, it feels like I've nothing to lose.

"You're right, but I can still do this!"

I throw out a hand in his direction, but my eyes catch his face at the last second. Memories flood my mind. Of a time when my mother was alive. When my father didn't wear a mask. When they were happy and whole.

A faint splutter of something comes out of my fingers. All that happens in a slight shift in the air. I freeze. Stunned. I thought I was ready. I thought I could stand up to my father.

But I was wrong.

"*Weak.*" My father shoves me to the ground. "Just like your mother."

What happened to him to make him such a monster? What made him put this terrible ambition for his country ahead of his family? Ahead of the people he claims to care about?

"Did you ever love her?" I choke out. Even now, I hear the faint glimmer of hope in my own voice. Even now, my heart wants to forgive him for his choices.

"Yes." It's the barest whisper. But it murders any feeling I could have for this man.

A gong sounds.

"It is time. Chin up, daughter. This is the destiny the gods have chosen for you."

"I am *not* your daughter!"

My head flings back from the force of my father's hand, and I taste blood in my mouth.

"You will raise the army."

"Never," I spit.

"I see you need a better incentive." He gestures at a priest. "Bring her out."

Something in me breaks when I see Ama. They have her

shackled and on her knees. Her white hair is unkempt, her robes torn. A priest holds a flame near her. Ama flinches but she catches my eye and nods at me calmly. Even in death's shadow, she chooses to reassure me.

My father hands me the dark sword.

"Raise the army."

51
ALTAN

"I'm sorry, Your Highness, but the premier gave strict orders that Lady Ahn is not to be disturbed," stammers the attendant outside Ahn's chambers.

Tai Shun glares. "Am *I* not your emperor?"

The girl squeals and throws the door open. I barge in, yelling Ahn's name. The room is empty.

"Where is she?" I shout.

"I don't know," says the attendant, flailing. "I thought she was in there. I was told to come stand outside. I—I know nothing." The girl flings herself to the ground in front of Tai Shun. "Please, Your Highness, I was only following orders. I'm sorry, Your Highness."

"Get out." She scurries away at his order. "What do we do now?" he says, turning to me.

Think, Altan. Think. It feels like all sense and logic have left me. My mind is blank, panic clawing at my chest. All I can think about is Ahn.

"My mother might know something." Tai Shun unsheathes one of my sabers before I can stop him and sticks it in my bandaged hand. "Take me hostage."

"*What?*"

"Just do it, Jin. Bring me to my mother."

His plan clicks in my head. "Don't regret this," I say, twisting his arm behind him. I put him in a headlock, my blade against his neck.

"You were always a good actor. Make it convincing." He nudges me with his elbow. "Come on, let's go."

We make it as far as the entrance to the empress's expansive quarters before we are surrounded by Imperial guards. Zhenxi comes running out, attendants trailing her.

She stops a few paces in front of us, a look of utter loathing directed at me. "How did you escape? Get your filthy hands off my son."

Tai Shun whimpers softly.

"Shun-er," says Zhenxi, her panic becoming obvious. "Are you hurt?"

"He's fine." I push the blade harder against Tai Shun's neck, angling it so that it won't draw blood. He whimpers again. "For now."

Zhenxi struggles to maintain her composure. But if there is one thing I know for certain, it is that her son is her world.

"Tell your guards to leave. I want to have a private conversation."

She narrows her eyes. I shift my grip and Tai Shun hisses as if he is in pain.

She waves a hand immediately. "Leave us."

"But Your Majesty—" one guard hedges.

"I said, leave us!" she bellows.

The guards and attendants file out, some sneaking more than

a curious glance at me. I know they will be somewhere around the compound, arrows positioned to take me out at any time. But it is a risk I must take.

I gesture toward Zhenxi's private parlor. She backs into it, eyes never leaving my blade. Tai Shun and I move as one and, finally, the three of us are alone.

"Sit," I say to my aunt.

She makes an undignified sound and plants herself down. "I have done what you want, now let my son go."

"I haven't told you what I want," I say with a smirk.

"Insolent boy—"

"Maybe you should keep the insults to yourself, seeing that I have your son hostage."

Zhenxi glares. "When this is over, I'll have your head on a platter."

Tai Shun fakes a sob as I pull my arm around his throat back—just a tad. "*Mother.*"

Her lips tremble and I see a shimmer of tears. Splendid.

"First," I say, "tell me where you're hiding Ahn."

Zhenxi blinks hard. "I don't have her. She was in her bedroom the last we spoke. I don't know where—"

"Stop lying."

"I am not," Zhenxi protests. "I . . . I did drug her, but I left her there in bed about two hours ago. I swear."

"I said, stop lying. Where is she?"

"I think she's telling the truth," Tai Shun interjects.

Zhenxi's eyes flash at his tone, scrutinizing her son. I groan to myself. He was never a good actor.

"Shun-er, what is going on?" she says sharply.

I knee Tai Shun in the thigh. "She knows, you fool."

He sighs. But I can tell he is relieved. He never liked deception. Grudgingly, I release my hold and he goes to Zhenxi. We decided on a backup plan if the acting failed, banking on a mother's love for her son.

Kneeling, Tai Shun clasps her hands in his. "Mother, I heard everything you told Ahn. *Everything.*"

Zhenxi flinches visibly, unable to look at her own son.

"I was the one who told Jin about what you and father did all those years back. I overheard you talking about it," Tai Shun continues. "You've made some mistakes."

"Mistakes?" I scoff, the urge to punch him returning. "Killing my father was a mere *mistake*?"

He shoots me a look and I grit my teeth, holding in my frustration.

Zhenxi raises a trembling hand to his cheek. "All these years . . . you knew what I did?"

"Yes," he replies softly. "And I overheard your conversation with Ahn tonight. All of it."

"You know that you're—" She looks away.

"It doesn't matter that Gao Long wasn't my birth father. I never wanted to be emperor, Mother. That is *your* dream for me, not mine," Tai Shun says gently. "Give me the antidote for Ahn and tell me what you've done. Tell me everything you know about what Zhao Yang has planned. Jin has promised to spare your life when he takes the throne back. Rightfully."

Zhenxi brings a silk handkerchief to her eyes, but she doesn't say a word.

"Don't make it harder than it is, Mother." Tai Shun sighs. "I know you were only trying to protect me. But love shouldn't be like this. You shouldn't hurt my friends or family or people I care about just because you're afraid that *I* may get hurt. I'm not a child; let me do what's right for myself and for our people. Let *me* be proud of myself." He lifts her chin. "Look at me, Mother. Know that I mean every word: if anything happens to Ahn, I will never forgive you. *Never.*"

The fight goes out of Zhenxi.

I listen as she confesses to discovering that Linxi was a spy and what she put her through to get answers. Then she shares her grand scheme to use me as leverage to have Ahn kill her own father. She is hesitant, but thorough.

Tai Shun stays kneeling, his face an open book. Horror dawns in his eyes as his mother continues to speak. It cannot be easy for him to accept that the monster in front of him is his mother. In this moment, I realize that while I may not be able to ever forgive Zhenxi, my vengeance doesn't have to cause anyone else harm. *Tai Shun* doesn't have to suffer for her sins.

He is already suffering enough.

"There is one other thing." Zhenxi squeezes her handkerchief so hard that her knuckles go white. Whatever it is she is about to say, in her mind at least, it must be the worst of her misdeeds. "Zhao Yang took Leiye."

Tai Shun pales. He works his mouth, but not a sound comes out. He has always loved Leiye, right from when we were children. The three of us were best friends, but Leiye meant something more to Tai Shun. Whether it was reciprocated, I never knew.

"Why?" I ask, a weight in the pit of my stomach. This can't be good.

"He knows Leiye is a traitor," she whispers. "I found out and I ... I planted some evidence that would lead Zhao Yang to him."

This means Zhao Yang knows everything. Leiye is in danger. *Ahn* is in danger.

"Do you know where he took Leiye?" I say.

"The northern wall." Zhenxi places a hand on Tai Shun's cheek. He is still frozen in place. "Shun-er, I *am* sorry. I know how much he means to you."

"Tai Shun," I urge. "Find Linxi and set her free. I will get Leiye."

He rises to his feet unsteadily. "I must go to him."

"You're in no state to face this, and you can't fight." I grip his arm firmly, forcing him to look at me. "Can I count on you?"

He glances at his mother, then back to me. He nods.

"I trust you," I say, meaning every word. "And I promise I'll bring him back. Alive."

52
AHN

It began with a girl and a sword, and it will end with a girl and her sword.

Once again, the gods have shown no mercy in their humor.

I stand by the wall overlooking the valley where the newly recruited soldiers have assembled, the morning sun reflecting off their armor. Even from a distance, I can tell some of them are only boys. Thousands of them. Idling. Unaware. Like cattle to slaughter, with me as their executioner.

My father holds the Obsidian Sword in front of me. I shudder as that pull returns.

That *want*.

Will you save your grandmother and kill thousands? Or will you die a lonely death after everyone you love is gone?

My hands reach for the dark sword, even as I try to hold back.

But before I can take it, silvery glints scatter across the morning sky.

Blades.

Soldiers around me collapse. Chains shoot out from everywhere, and a flurry of women clad in rainbow robes storm the wall. They twirl in a dance of metal, striking back at the priests.

The Lotus Sect.

Tang Wei slashes the shackles binding Ama with a sword. She pulls her up and takes her away from the frenzy. A priest sends a spray of fire in Tang Wei's direction and she barely dodges it. Ama cries out, moving away from the flames, taking half a step back.

Half a step too many.

Sunlight flashes. A dagger flies through the air.

No! roars my blood. Time slows as I watch helplessly. The dagger is moving too fast. I can't get there in time. Can't push Ama out of the way.

An arrow cuts into my vision, hitting the dagger off its course.

Time rushes forward. I'm screaming, hurtling toward Ama. Vicious arms haul me back.

"Let me go!"

My father drags me away as I kick out desperately. I crane my neck in time to see Tang Wei helping Ama up. *She's alive*, my heart sings. That gives me the strength to fight. Thrashing, I try to wrest the sword from my father. His fingers fan out. Flames torch my hands and I howl. It feels like the empress's illusions, but as I gape at my bubbling skin, I know that this time it's real.

"Ahn!"

Bow in hand, Altan is sprinting toward us in a blur of crimson and gold, deflecting and dodging missiles and flames from the priests.

"Altan!" I scream, struggling against my father's grip.

Altan releases a trio of arrows. A priest falls. He pulls another three arrows across his bow.

"Let her go!" His shout is hoarser than usual.

My father wrenches my head back. Hair tears from my scalp. The blade of the dark sword slices into my neck. I try to summon my magic, but the pain from my blistering hands is too overwhelming.

"If you kill me, there will be no one to raise that army for you," I say.

"I have lost my leverage. I know you won't do it," snarls my father.

He uses me as a human shield, pulling me toward the edge of the wall. The fall is fifty feet. Fifty feet onto jagged, unyielding rock. And then down to the valley below. My father might survive if he uses his magic, but I'm not sure about myself.

Altan draws close. But he's not going to get a clear shot.

"Let me go, *Father*."

"I would rather kill you myself," he growls with a ferocity that hollows me.

"Ahn!"

I turn my head.

Altan notches three arrows in his bow.

I hold my breath as he releases the bowstring. I follow the impossible arc of his arrows as I'm yanked over the wall. I feel the force of their blows behind me. The loosening of my father's grip. Instinct takes over and I grab the sword.

But I am falling.

Tipping over the wall as my father's arm stays wrapped around my waist despite the arrow that strikes it. Something pushes me upward, and my father's arm falls away as he plunges down. I don't know if it is Altan's magic or my father's regret.

Thrown back over the wall, I hit the stone hard. Everything

hurts. I heave a breath and try to stand. The sword shimmers smoky green in my hands. Hands that shriek as the blisters burst and blood drips. Still, I hold on to it. The sword that has caused such misery. The sword that can make everything right again.

I clutch the hilt. Desperate. Determined. No one should have it. I must destroy it. My mind's eye shows me the vision of Yuan Long. An old man, full of regret, kneeling by the sword that he coveted. The sword that brought his own downfall. His words, whispered to the gods, echo in my ears.

Free me.

He tried to free himself of the lure of power. Tried to atone for his sins in the end. But little did he know that his act of killing himself bound his dark magic to the sword and tainted the land. If the blood of one Life Stealer disrupted the balance of the world, surely it means the blood of another will restore that balance. And without the Life Stealer, the sword will be rendered useless.

You can choose to protect.

The sword isn't the elixir that everyone is fighting for.

I am.

"Ahn!" Altan wraps me in his arms.

I allow myself to feel for a moment before gently pushing him back.

"This needs to end." My voice sounds like someone else's.

He releases me, looking like he's desperate to commit my face to memory. Does he know I'm doing the same thing?

"End this," he says. "I know it has to be me. Do it before my courage fails."

I see in his eyes that he's prepared to die. I smile. "Don't you understand? It has to be *me*."

"What—what are you talking about?"

My fingers graze his cheek and he shivers at my touch. "*You* are immune to the life-stealing magic. The sword can't harm you."

"Gods . . . what have I done?" he whispers. Horror spreads across his face. "*What have I done?*"

I raise the sword.

"Stop—no! We can find another way—"

"This is the only way." I point the dark sword to the Heavens.

Thunder rumbles. A flash lights up my world.

Altan's face is the last thing I see.

And then, darkness.

53
ALTAN

I die the moment she plunges the sword into her own chest.

My heart splits. A new chasm opens.

I catch her as she falls. Hold her as the pale green light drifts from her and out of the sword. Hold her as she stops breathing. Hold her as my stitches unravel and I fall apart.

Before my eyes, the dark sword transforms into an iridescent white jade.

It was here all this time, hidden in plain sight.

The cruelest joke.

I bury my head in her chest, listening for something.

Anything.

But there is only silence.

54
AHN

I open my eyes to a sky teeming with purples and blues, warming to a vibrant orange on the far horizon. I stare at my hands. They look normal, the flesh unburned. I *feel* fine. There's no ache where my father struck me. There's no pain or wound in my chest.

Am I . . . *dead*?

There's a soft chirp. A giant bird is in front of me, its emerald and violet feathers shimmering softly. Tilting its brilliant head side to side, its large intelligent eyes observe me.

I did not expect you.

"Who are you? Where is this place?" I look around. All I see is this strange, vivid dreamscape of nothing. It's just me and the giant bird. A phoenix, I think.

This is my realm. Some find it by passing a trial. Others find it through other means. It seems you have made a big sacrifice.

"Realm? Are you a Soul Beast?"

The creature nods. *What is your request?*

"I—I get a *wish*?" I say, dumbfounded.

The Phoenix makes a sound like a laugh. *Call it what you will. What is your wish?*

My mind goes blank. "I don't . . . I don't know."

You may forfeit your wish if—

"No!" I exclaim. "I wish, I wish that . . ." I look up when I find my thought. "I want everyone I care about to be safe."

As you wish.

The Phoenix spreads its wings. Teardrops roll from its eyes and burst, the faint sprinkle touching my face. I smell grass and honey and I'm suddenly sleepy. So, so sleepy.

55
ALTAN

Warning shouts pierce through my haze. The nothingness fades as my senses return. Sounds of metal clashing, the smell of fire and smoke. . . . I see Tang Wei shielding Ahn's grandmother, fending off attacks from the priests. Her comrades from the Lotus Sect are thick in the fray, but they have suffered casualties. Tai Shun and his reinforcements are nowhere to be found.

"Jin."

I look up. Leiye's face is beaten and bruised, one eye swollen. Blood trails down his side. His arm. Fury ignites in my chest. They *burned* him.

"You look a mess," I say.

"Still prettier than you." He grimaces as he leans on his sword. "Get up, Jin. We have to fight."

"You're in no shape to fight."

"I bet I could beat you up right now." He rests a hand on my shoulder. "Mourn her later. She would want us to finish this."

Something raw breaks free from that broken place inside me. Not anger, not rage, but a precise understanding of who I am and what I am not. Leiye is right.

I have to end this.

I lay Ahn down gently and turn to him. He can barely stand, but his eyes tell me everything I need to know. Leiye will always be beside me. He always has been.

"Like that day at the stables?"

He nods. "We only have one shot at this."

My lips curl. "Then we better get it right this time."

I release my magic. The air around me moves, and the wind picks up speed. Leiye extends his good arm. Flames blaze out in plumes. Magnificent, terrifying, glorious. On his cue, I rotate my wrists, and the wind funnels his fire.

Tang Wei yells a warning to the Lotus Sect. I direct the blaze, wrapping each priest in a fiery lasso, drowning out their screams, their cries. As the priests burn, the Lotus Sect disciples throw their daggers, striking a deathblow on each and every one of them.

Leiye drops to the ground, breathing heavily. I sink to my knees, spent.

It is done. But what does it matter?

She is dead.

I return to her, lifting her in my arms, holding her close.

The nothingness returns. As my tears fall, I whisper a prayer to gods I once spurned.

I don't know how long I kneel for. Holding her, desperately praying her into existence. An eternity seems to pass. Then, an impossible gasp.

So soft, so fragile.

I don't dare to hope, but what else is left if not hope?

I bend over and listen to the most beautiful music in the world: a faint, but steady beat of her heart.

ONE MONTH LATER

56
ALTAN

A hushed layer of white blankets the palace grounds, snow crystals softly glistening in the weak rays of winter's sun. I watch the flurry of activity below me. Attendants and officials scurry around, preparing for the coronation. *My* coronation. It will be held during the Spring Festival, just before my nineteenth birthday. An auspicious time, according to the soothsayers of my court. Still several weeks away, but apparently it takes a lot of time and a staff of hundreds to muster the pomp and circumstance required.

Nandah has abandoned their attack for now. In return, I have opened diplomatic channels to settle the dispute over the Southern Colonies. The lieges of other nations will attend the festivities as a show of faith that cordial relations with the Shi Empire have been renewed. Even the reclusive Queen of Mengu is coming, though I wonder what her true motivations are.

With Tai Shun's support, I have reclaimed the throne and started to dismantle the Diyeh priesthood, flushing out their loyalists from the courts. But we both know spies still lurk in our midst.

Reports are coming in that the desert is slowly retreating to its original confines, that spring buds are appearing in forests despite the season. Captain Yan sent word of a massive storm that swirled near the Dragon's Triangle, causing green smoke to rise from its waters. All the spirits—those lost souls my great-grandfather tethered to the sword—finally set free.

I have avenged the deaths of my family and regained my birthright. I have wanted all of this for more than half my life. But I'm not sure if it is peace I have found.

I brush the snow dust from my shoulders before leaping down from the roof, unintentionally scaring an attendant out of her wits. It must be strange to see one's soon-to-be emperor scaling down buildings. Everyone knows what I did that day on the northern wall; it is futile to pretend to be someone I am not. More important, I don't want the Tiensai to live in the shadows anymore.

The attendant is stunned that I know her name and that I'm retrieving her basket of fruits with my own two hands. She scuttles off after a series of bows and frightened apologies. A warm silvery puff of air blows from my lips. All this formality takes getting used to.

I search for Tai Shun in the Imperial medicinal hall. He has been studying with the royal physicians lately, using his natural inclination for herblore and healing for good. Part of me believes he is trying to atone for what his mother did in the past. I wish Shīfù were still here, he would have loved to nurture Tai Shun's talent.

"Your Majesty," stammers one of the physicians when he notices me lurking by the entrance.

Everyone starts to greet me with bows and murmurs. Even Tai Shun. At least no one is prostrating. I jerk my head toward the courtyard. Tai Shun sets his jar down and follows me out.

"You wish to speak with me, Your Majesty?"

"I told you," I say, exasperated. "There's no need to speak to me that way and, by gods, stop walking *behind* me. How are we supposed to have a proper conversation like that?"

He laughs and steps up. "Since we're dropping all formalities, what do you want, Jin? Make it quick, I've better things to do than to amble with you in the blasted cold, it's bad for my old injury."

"I didn't give you permission to be rude," I retort. I notice his slight limp, and the faded memory of his fall from the roof drives a pang through my chest. "I'm sorry, I'll be quick, and we can go back into warmth. I didn't want to talk to you inside with all the guards and attendants."

Tai Shun laughs amiably. He seems happier now, a burden lifted off his shoulders. Some of that weight has landed on mine. It wasn't easy, but I found it in myself to forgive him. I wish I could say the same about his mother. I pardoned Zhenxi for her role in the murder of my father, but she will be imprisoned in the dungeons for the rest of her life.

"How are your studies? What strange balm or concoction are you creating in your lab?" I ask, realizing it has been a while since I have spoken to him one-on-one.

"I've been studying some texts I found in the library—in the forbidden section you gave me access to," Tai Shun says. In my attempt to discover the true history of the Tiensai and our people, I have allowed the ancient texts to be examined by scholars. "Did you know that music can have healing powers?"

"I'm not surprised."

"Yes, but what I'm investigating is whether I can use the principles of Tiensai magic and meld it with the healing aspect of music," he says excitedly. "My flute, for example. I'm using it to compose new melodies based on—"

"You can tell me more another time," I cut in before he gets carried away. "There's something more pressing I want to discuss with you. I was thinking, maybe you shouldn't abdicate."

He recoils visibly. "Jin—"

"Forget I asked."

"Cold feet?"

I shrug.

"I believe in you." He stops walking, expression downcast. "I have taken much from you; I will not take anymore. Besides, I'm not of royal blood."

"Nonsense." I clap him on the back. "You're my family."

"And you are my emperor."

His eyes crinkle, and the smile returns to his face, earnest and sincere. I see the boy who once followed me everywhere when we were children, who looked up to me, who thought the best of me.

I force my shoulders straight. I can't let him down.

"There you are!" shouts a familiar voice.

"Oh, not now," I sigh, fingers pressing the bridge of my nose.

Tang Wei waves at us from a distance. The Lotus Sect suffered losses and I owe them a debt. Which in Tang Wei's mind somehow translates to her having access to a set of rooms in the palace. I wonder how long she intends to stay.

She saunters over, arm tightly linked with Linxi's. Leiye trails behind them, smirking. He must have told them where to find me.

I eye the three of them sourly. "What do you want?"

"You seem to be in a foul mood on this lovely morning, Your

Majesty," Linxi says. I'm relieved to see that the bruises on her face have faded, and she has no problems walking by herself now. The effects of the torture she went through will not be permanent.

"I was in a perfectly fine mood until someone interrupted my stroll," I say.

Tang Wei grins slyly. "It's the Winter Solstice today, Golden Boy."

"I order you to address me as Your Majesty."

She laughs. "How petty. You're not emperor yet."

"Annoy me some more and I'll banish you."

"Abusing your power already?"

"Did I tell you about the time he broke his mother's precious vase and blamed *me* for it?" Leiye pipes up.

I shoot him a dirty look. "You should tell them about all the times I covered for your accidents when you were still figuring out how to use your magic."

"It's the *Winter Solstice*," repeats Tang Wei impatiently. She looks ready to give me one of her tongue-lashings.

"So?" My days have been so occupied I have lost track of time.

Leiye raises his eyebrows meaningfully at me. Linxi shakes her head like I have done something terrible.

"What?" I snap.

Tai Shun shrugs, looking as lost as I am. No one else responds.

"What's so special about the Winter Solstice?" I mutter to myself.

The Winter Solstice . . . What am I missing?

Oh.

The palace staff barely conceal their astonishment and amusement as I sprint wildly across the hallways and courtyards, demanding if they saw the girl with the burned hands. The girl the world once called the Life Stealer.

"It's your birthday!" I yell when I spot Ahn from afar.

I skid to a stop when I notice her grandmother standing right there. Bowing awkwardly, I try to collect my dignity. Grandma Jia gives me a knowing smile and whispers something to Ahn who makes a face back at her.

"I was just about to leave," Grandma Jia says to me kindly.

I bow low and she shuffles away.

Ahn and I are alone. She ignores me, staring up at the bare branches of a tree. I'm nervous for some reason. I don't have my daggers or sabers with me, nothing to keep my hands occupied. I decide to lean against the trunk, only to yelp in surprise when my fingers touch the ice-cold bark.

I clear my throat, feeling like an utter fool. "Well . . . happy birthday. We should celebrate."

Ahn shrugs, looking disappointed. "They haven't bloomed yet. I guess it's too early?"

"What?"

"The plum blossoms. I was hoping to see them. At least I got to see snow."

She catches a falling snowflake on her tongue, tastes it, and laughs. But her laugh is different now. Less bright, less carefree. Her hands are still wrapped in bandages, and from the stiff way she's moving, I can tell she hasn't healed completely from her self-inflicted wound. All that will heal in time. But I know there is a different kind of pain, a different kind of scar somewhere deeper.

Our exchanges in the past month have been brief and tense. The chasm between us feels like it is growing each day, a dark void filled with things unsaid. I don't even know if she has forgiven me for killing Zhao Yang. I've been too scared to ask.

She turns to me abruptly. "I'm leaving tomorrow."

I must have misheard her. "What did you say?"

"I'm leaving the palace tomorrow," she repeats, slower.

"Absolutely not. You're in no condition to travel." She glares at me and I stand straighter, trying to look important. "As your *emperor*, I command you to remain here."

"You don't even know where I'm going, and you can't stop me, *Your Majesty*," she says in a reasonable tone.

She's right. I can't. I won't stop her. Her freedom is not mine to possess. I rake a hand through my hair, forgetting that I'll ruin my royal hairdo. "Tell me then, where are you going?"

"I got a message from Li Guo. He's in Cuihai Port. I want to see him, to thank him."

"He can come *here* to see you," I say, agitated. The sense of loss I already feel is almost too much to bear. "I'll even let him stay in the palace. There's plenty of room."

"Altan." Her voice trembles. "I'm going to take a ship to Xinzhu. My mother lived there for a while. Maybe someone will remember her. I need to know if Zhao Yang was telling the truth about her."

"I'm coming with you."

"No, you're not. You have a country to run," she scolds. "I shouldn't have told you."

"I'd have tracked you down even if you hadn't told me."

"And just how would you have done that?"

"Gold follows you. Apparently, there's a red thread somewhere out there tying us together. A nomad seer told me so." Ahn's eyebrows lift in disbelief and I cringe at my own words. They sound so silly, but I can't think of anything else to say.

Tell her, Tang Wei's voice nags in my head. *She's leaving tomorrow, maybe forever. Just tell her. Don't be a coward.*

"There's something you need to know before you leave," I blurt out.

"Go on."

Why does she look so bored? Does she not want to be here with me? A thousand chattering thoughts enter my mind. I shove them aside and inhale.

"I'm in love with you."

"I know."

I stagger back like I've been slapped. "You—you knew, and you said nothing?"

Ahn's eyes widen. "I wasn't aware that there was anything I needed to say."

I scrub a hand across my face, taking in a long breath and letting it out slowly. I can't decide if it's anger or anguish I feel.

"I just carved my heart out for you and the best you can come up with is *I know*?" I say hoarsely, feeling sick and weak.

She laughs. "Don't be dramatic, Altan. If you'd carved out your heart, you'd be dead."

57
AHN

His hair is growing out and he looks so handsome in his Imperial robes, every inch the emperor he was destined to be. But all I see is the boy from the desert. The boy in black who caught me stealing a mangosteen. Except now, any evidence of that coiled-up energy and predatorial fierceness, that *fire*, is gone.

Altan looks like he's about to faint.

"It's because I killed your father, isn't it?" His voice is quiet, pained.

My smile fades and the ache in my chest blooms.

I would rather kill you myself.

I turn my back to Altan. "That monster was *not* my father. He killed your mother. I tried to protect him once, and you saved my life in turn. We're even."

The brisk chill of silence deepens. Too much has happened between us and too little of it is good. My father's words gnaw at my being, making me question everything.

Under the bandages, my ruined hands itch, damaged skin crusted over. I haven't tried to use my magic. I know it is in me somewhere. I feel it, but I have chosen to reject it. The sword of light or whatever it's called is locked up in the palace vaults, never to be seen again. Never to be used again to reign terror on the world.

The snow flurry has passed and the sky above me is now cloudless, reminding me of the desert. Closer, sunlight gleams off small mounds of fresh snow resting on the plum blossom tree, and its branches dance in the breeze. As I stare, wondering if I will ever find that girl from the desert again, I notice a tiny pink-and-white petal peeking out from a nascent bud on the highest branch. Fragile, but alive.

It is time to forgive yourself for whatever has happened in the past. Move on and live well.

Ama's words ring in my head. Maybe, just maybe, what little good I found is worth salvaging. It's pointless to spend my life looking backward, missing out on living for elusive what-ifs, obsessing over questions that will never bring the right answers.

When I finally turn back, Altan is crouched down on the ground in an undignified manner, face in his hands.

"Are you crying?" I exclaim. He looks up. Thank gods, he's not. But he looks like he may.

He stands and takes my hand gently, careful not to hurt me. "Then what is it? What's going on between us? Is there . . . an *us*?"

My eyes trace the familiar sharp planes of his face, the double crease between his brows that forms every time he looks at me with this intensity. The scars that make him who he is.

"I need time. But I think we're going to be fine." Warmth spreads in my chest when I realize how true my words are.

"We *will* be fine," he says, determined.

I smirk. "Remember how a long time ago you said that some girl should try and see if she could toy around with your heart for no reason other than her own amusement?"

He blanches, and I regret my ill-timed joke.

"I'm not saying that's what I did," I groan, wanting to slap myself for being so foolish. "I mean, I might have *thought* about it as a joke then, but that's not what I did. I wouldn't do that to you—or to anyone."

Altan doesn't look like he understands anything I'm saying. The horrified look on his face remains. Frustrated, I grab his collar and pull him close.

He doesn't react when our lips meet. Not even a little. I step back, unsure of how to feel. He just stands there, confused.

I wrinkle my nose. "*That* was disappointing."

He blinks, and the truth sinks in. He starts laughing. A hearty laugh, whole and full of joy. Drawing me close, he wraps an arm around my waist, his hand lifting my chin.

"I can fix that," he murmurs, voice husky in my ear.

Someone claps. Loudly.

"*There they are.*"

"*About time, Golden Boy!*"

Altan groans. "Not again."

He waves his long sleeve. Snow rises from the ground in an opaque sheet, cocooning us in a curtain of solid white. The voices fade and all I see is Altan. And when he pulls me close, his kiss fills me with light.

EPILOGUE

The girl looks up at the cloudless sky, eyes following a moving spot in the otherwise empty azure. Her posture is relaxed, confident. But her mind is far from calm.

For want of something to do as she waits, she grabs the thick braid trailing down her back and coils it into a bun at the nape of her neck, securing it with a rib bone of a small animal, sharpened to a fine tip. She pulls her furs close, shivering in the chilly wind. Living in the far north for a decade has not acclimatized her to the frigid winters here.

Soon, she hears someone climbing up the slopes behind her. A messenger.

He bows curtly and unfurls a small piece of parchment. "My lady, you have a message from the queen."

"Read it," the girl commands.

"It has come to pass. Return to the palace immediately and travel south with me to Beishou."

The girl's golden-brown eyes gleam. "Is that all she has to say? Is she certain of the new emperor's identity?"

The messenger nods once. The girl dismisses him. He pivots on his heel and makes his way down the slopes.

Alone again, she glances back up at the dark spot in the sky. Her whistle rings loud and piercing, and the spot grows bigger. As it nears, its feathers glint in the sun. The girl raises her right arm, steadies it. A large golden eagle swoops down and lands, talons gripping the leather sheath around her forearm.

"How are the thermal winds today, Gerel, my love?" she says to the bird, stroking its downy feathers. It chirps, head quirking this way and that. The girl laughs softly. "Yes, it's cold. But don't worry, we're going south."

She smiles, crooked and mischievous, the right side of her lips lifting higher than the left, a single dimple appearing near her chin. An old memory floats in her mind.

Of a girl. Of a boy.

We will find Father's murderer. We will take back what's ours. We will go home.

"It's time for me to go home. It is time for me to take back what is rightfully mine," she murmurs, remembering the boy she once loved.

The brother who had become emperor.

ACKNOWLEDGMENTS

Firstly, I want to thank *you* for sticking with this tale until the end, and for flipping to the acknowledgments section. Maybe you were curious, maybe you flipped the previous page by accident, or maybe you're like me—for whatever reason, I stay in the theater until the end of movie credits and I always read the acknowledgments at the back of a book.

Debut books are special. Many are books of the heart. Some are penned in a rushed, fevered state, while others are written through many long years filled with anxiety and uncertainty. I wasn't sure what story this would turn out to be when I first had the image of a girl standing in an ever-expanding desert, alone and weary. And of the boy she meets, who was equally lonely from shouldering the weight of legacy. In the end, it became a story about family, about grief, about trauma, and mostly, about hope.

Books are not created from a single person's imagination. The book you're holding right now would not have existed without the encouragement, support, and labor of so many people. To everyone who had a hand in transforming *Jade Fire Gold* from a nascent idea in my head to an actual book in a reader's hand—thank you, thank you, thank you.

To Elana Roth Parker, thank you for seeing something special in my story and for believing in me. To the LDLA team, your support through the years has been invaluable.

To my editor extraordinaire, Alice Jerman, I've learned so much from you. Thank you for helping me take this story to the next level, for patiently answering all my questions, introducing me to really delicious tea, and most importantly, thank you for your kindness. It has been a privilege to have you as my editor.

To Clare Vaughn, I'm so grateful for your tireless work behind the scenes and your cheerful emails always bring a smile to my face. To Vanessa Nuttry, Nicole Moreno, Gwen Morton, Jill Freshney, Veronica Ambrose, and Megan Gendall, thank you for the beautiful interior of this book, and for catching all my typos, rogue commas, and random capitalizations or lack of. Most of all, thank you for letting me keep my em dashes.

Catherine Lee and Jenna Stempel-Lobell, you literally designed the cover of my dreams! To Zheng Wei Gu (GUWEIZ), thank you for bringing that vision to life with your immense talent.

To marketing mavens Lisa Calcasola, Audrey Diestelkamp, Kadeen Griffiths, and Emily Zhu, to publicity powerhouse Lena Reilly and the rest of the publicity team, and of course, to the wonderfully talented Epic Reads crew, thank you for your creativity and enthusiasm. To Andrea Pappenheimer and the entire sales team, and to Patty Rosati and the School and Library team, thank you for all the work you've put into getting my book out there.

A special shout-out to Hannah VanVels. It was you who gave this book a chance to come alive. To Laura Rennert and the team at Andrea Brown Literary Agency, thank you for picking up the reins and guiding me forward.

To everyone at Hodder & Stoughton, I couldn't ask for a better team in the UK and beyond. To editorial wizard Molly Powell, publicity genius Kate Keehan, marketing stars Maddy Marshall and Callie Robertson, Claudette Morris and Matthew Everett in production, and special editions logistical mastermind Sarah Clay, thank you so very much. To Aaron Munday, thank you for designing such a beautiful cover for the UK edition, and for fulfilling my secret dream of having multiple covers for my book. To Paul Kenny, Cindy Kan, Emmanuel Wong, and the Hachette UK/Asia team, thank you for all your hard work and energy.

To Daphne Tonge and the amazing team at Illumicrate, a huge thank you for supporting *Jade Fire Gold* from the beginning. To Anissa de Gomery and the lovely book fairies at FairyLoot, thank you for granting my wishes. And another massive thank you to Korrina and the incredible OwlCrate team!

To the generous and talented authors who took the time to read and blurb my book: Joan He, Elizabeth Lim, Hafsah Faizal, Chloe Gong, Roseanne A. Brown, and Swati Teerdhala.

Thank you to the wonderful book community. To booksellers and librarians, thank you for doing what you do best. To readers, book bloggers, bookstagrammers, booktokkers, including Sherna @bookworm.swiftie, Abi @boohoo.books, Cossette @cossettereads, Rogier @roro_suri, Deidre @inabookdaze, CW and Skye from The Quiet Pond, Shealea @shutupshealea, Fadwa @wordwoonders, Jo @thebookrising and so many more . . . thank you for your support. I don't know your last names or even your real first names, but I do recognize your Instagram handles and your Twitter avatars (even though you keep changing them lol). Every interaction brings such joy, and I'm so honored to have you in my corner (T_T).

A special shout-out to Mike Lasagna—the book community is so lucky to have you. Another shout-out to Prissi @prissanthemum, I'm so amazed by your dedication to your cosplay of Ahn and I'm floored by your talent.

Writing is often a solitary process, and one that's full of self-doubt. So naturally, I've to thank everyone who was there from the start. Thank you for sticking with me through this wild ride.

To Cindy Pon, my utmost gratitude for taking those difficult, early steps so that authors like me have a path to follow. To Thao Le, the first publishing professional who made me realize that maybe I *could* write a publishable book after all. To my Pitch Wars mentor, Akemi Dawn Bowman, for giving me the opportunity to learn how to tear apart a draft to find its true heart and create a better, fuller story from the process.

Thank you to #the21ders, you're an incredibly talented and kind group, and I'm so lucky to be debuting with you. To Anna Bright, Shannon Price, Leigh Mar, Lily Meade, thank you for being so supportive through the years. A special thank you to Alexa Donne, for your insight. And to Rachel Griffin, for your constant encouragement.

To *Jade Fire Gold*'s early readers, back when it was unimaginatively titled *The Life Stealer* (lol), or when it was *A NOUN of NOUN and NOUN* (I know, I know), or when I titled it *Orange Juice and Fries* out of equal parts despair and terrible humor—thank you for your feedback and encouragement. Judy I. Lin, Roselle Lim,

Gabriela Martins, Victoria Lee, Grace Li, Hannah Whitten, Nafiza Azad, and Meredith Ireland: I love that you're all thriving and can't wait to hold your current and future books in my hands. To Lori M. Lee, Amparo Ortiz, Emma Theriault, Rosiee Thor, Sarena Nanua, Sasha Nanua, Rebecça Coffindaffer, Ciannon Smart, and Kristin Dwyer: Thank you for sharing your time and knowledge with me. Meredith, Roselle, Axie Oh, Akshaya Raman, thank you for letting me whine about *debutitis* and for all your sound advice.

To Carrie Gao, for sending me the best art, for listening, and for being a solid human being. To Eunice Kim, for all the memes and laughs. Hopefully, we got to have dessert together again by the time this book is out. To Anissa, I'm so blessed to have you as a friend. You're one of the sweetest and most badass people I know. I hope we get to hang out in person someday soon!

To Andrea Tang and Allison Senecal, thanks for all the late night (early morning?) screaming and crying, and for brightening up my life during this freaking panorama-panini-pandemonium thingie. Please stay hydrated -wink-. To Han (*hold han best friend*), Haley, and Zeba, my anchors in the turbulent sea of publishing. To Gina Chen, since you're reading this in October, are you still in love with *bacon* hmm??? (I told you I was going to do this ha! Thanks for the shenanigans.)

To Deeba joon, my voice of reason in trying times, a deep, heartfelt thank you to you. To Rosie, your friendship, invaluable advice, and incredible humor has kept me afloat. To Swati, you showed me what determination and grit means and you never fail to lift me up. To Julie Abe—instead of making a bad taekook joke, I'm just going to say, borahae.

To Bangtan Sonyeondan, because why not? Your music got me through my darkest times and continues to be my writing background soundtrack. Namjoon, thank you for the genius that is *mono.*; your lyrics will stay in my heart. Strong power, thank you. Everyone, stream "Epiphany" for good skin.

Thank you to Joan, the wisest of them all. You're an inspiration.

Em, you said I had to include your name so here it is ‾_(ツ)_/‾. But seriously, *thank you*. Thank you for randomly barging into my DMs yelling about *Hamlet*. Thank you for listening to my rants, for putting up with my incessant angst and whining, for reading all my awful (and sometimes good?) words. Thank you for happily jumping into the BTS hole with me without a second thought and thank you for your honesty. Most of all, thank you for being you.

Shen-Ru, Bettina, Claire, Karen, and Fiona: I can't believe we've known each other for half our lives. OMG lǎo le!

Darian, my brother from another mother, you finally get to read this. You better like it. To Fi, I'm so glad we get to grow old together (^_^).

Hsing, Mimi, Kevin, and Chey: thank you for welcoming and supporting me. To Mama and Gong Gong, I was able to write this story because of you. I hope you're proud of me. To my mother, for making sacrifices so that I didn't have to.

To Z, for your morning cuddles and annoying meows, and for being excellent company whenever I write. Even though you're a little brat, you're the cutest thing in the world.

To C, (&).